Praise for MR. NOBODY



"[A] tricky psychological puzzle . . . It's a joy to encounter a suspenseful book whose turns lurk, rather than lumber, around the corner. The story in *Mr. Nobody* corkscrews and somersaults. . . . Past mysteries haunt the present in ways that are both startling and claustrophobic. . . . [Catherine Steadman] is even better at writing than acting. If her first book, *Something in the Water,* was the Steadman gateway drug, then *Mr. Nobody* . . . will get you hooked. Let's hope, for purposes of withdrawal mitigation, there's a third."

—*The New York Times Book Review*

"Twisty . . . a highly imaginative tale tinged with Hitchcockian tension and kinetic pacing . . . Steadman's deliciously provocative novel dishes up enough questions to fill the entire space devoted to this review. She cleverly cloaks them in more mysteries, turns, and shocking revelations. Much like *Something in the Water, Mr. Nobody* pits fascinating characters against each other and allows them to act on their worst impulses. . . . There's a good chance [Steadman's] intelligently descriptive, written-for-TV-and-film writing style grew out of her experiences in front of a camera. Her literary instincts are spot-on, and the protagonists she creates feel as alive as some of the characters she's inhabited on film. . . . This talent for inhabiting characters carries over into her writing: Mr. Nobody and Emma Lewis, though invented, seem so real. Mr. Nobody turns out to be somebody, and his unmasking makes for a delightfully compelling story."

—*The Washington Post*

"[*Mr. Nobody*] somberly explores trauma and its aftermath, but ample twists and a rollicking pace make it a perfectly thrilling read."

—*Vanity Fair*

"Riveting."

—*Entertainment Weekly*

"The alarming questions keep piling up, even as the puzzle starts to take shape."

—*Newsweek*

"Once again, Catherine Steadman is adding a dash of eeriness to her mystery novel."

—*PopSugar*

"A mesmerizing psychological thriller . . . In a series of exciting twists and shocking turns, Emma and Mr. Nobody come to discover they are connected in ways neither could have imagined. Steadman's story is wholly unique and exceedingly well executed. Suspense is peppered in all the right places, and every bread crumb dropped throughout the story returns in wildly imaginative ways."

—Associated Press

"Even better than *Something in the Water*—Catherine Steadman's new novel, *Mr. Nobody*, is original, ingenious, and utterly gripping, with characters you'll really care about as they race toward the brilliantly unexpected ending."

—JP Delaney, *New York Times* bestselling author of *The Girl Before*

"Very clever, brilliantly compelling, another amazing read from Catherine Steadman."

—B. A. Paris, *New York Times* bestselling author of *Behind Closed Doors*

"Steadman once again brilliantly paces the action from the very first scene. . . . As in all good thrillers, lights unexpectedly snap out, a creepy house is hidden down a tree-woven lane, and long-buried secrets emerge. . . . A spellbinding thriller perfect for those dark and stormy nights."

—*Kirkus Reviews*

"The elaborate plot, filled with seemingly impossible twists, drives to a suspenseful conclusion."

—*Publishers Weekly*

## Praise for **Something in the Water**

Named One of the Best Books of the Year
by *Glamour* and *Newsweek*

Finalist for the ITW Thriller Award
for Best Debut Novel

"A psychological thriller that captivated me from page one. What unfolds makes for a wild, page-turning ride! It's the perfect beach read!"
—Reese Witherspoon
(Reese's Book Club x Hello Sunshine book pick)

"Arresting . . . deftly paced, elegantly chilly . . . Steadman brings . . . wit, timing, and intelligence to this novel. . . . *Something in the Water* is a proper page-turner."
—*The New York Times*

"Deliciously dramatic."
—*Entertainment Weekly*

"Thrilling . . . the perfect beach read."
—*PopSugar*

"With unreliable characters, wry voices, exquisite pacing, and a twisting plot, Steadman potently draws upon her acting chops. . . . A darkly glittering gem of a thriller from a new writer to watch."
—*Kirkus Reviews* (starred review)

"Captivating . . . daring . . . The threats and increasingly bad decisions accelerate with Bourne-like velocity. . . . Steadman [is] a newcomer worth watching."

—*Publishers Weekly*

"An unbearably tense debut with a knockout premise, *Something in the Water* had me hooked from the very first sentence. Thrilling and thought-provoking, it's the perfect beach read. I devoured it!"

—Riley Sager, *New York Times* bestselling author of *Final Girls*

**By Catherine Steadman**

*Something in the Water*

*Mr. Nobody*

*The Disappearing Act*

# MR. NOBODY

A NOVEL

Catherine Steadman

BALLANTINE BOOKS
NEW YORK

*Mr. Nobody* is a work of fiction. Names, characters, places, and incidents are the products of the author's imagination or are used fictitiously. Any resemblance to actual events, locales, or persons, living or dead, is entirely coincidental.

2021 Ballantine Books Mass Market Edition



Published in the United States by Ballantine Books, an imprint of Random House, a division of Penguin Random House LLC, New York.

BALLANTINE and the HOUSE colophon are registered trademarks of Penguin Random House LLC.

Originally published in hardcover in the United States by Ballantine Books, an imprint of Random House, a division of Penguin Random House LLC, in 2020.

This book contains an excerpt from the forthcoming book *The Disappearing Act* by Catherine Steadman. This excerpt has been set for this edition only and may not reflect the final content of the forthcoming edition.

ISBN 978-0-593-15948-4
Ebook ISBN 978-1-5247-9769-0

Cover design: Carlos Beltrán
Cover images: Getty images; Shutterstock

Printed in the United States of America

randomhousebooks.com

2 4 6 8 9 7 5 3 1

Ballantine Books mass market edition: July 2021

FOR ALL THOSE CHASING GHOSTS

*Better by far you should forget and smile*
*Than that you should remember and be sad.*

—CHRISTINA ROSSETTI, "REMEMBER"

*Yesterday, upon the stair,*
*I met a man who wasn't there*
*He wasn't there again today*
*I wish, I wish he'd go away . . .*

*When I came home last night at three*
*The man was waiting there for me*
*But when I looked around the hall*
*I couldn't see him there at all!*
*Go away, go away, don't you come back any more!*
*Go away, go away, and please don't slam the door.*

*Last night I saw upon the stair*
*A little man who wasn't there*
*He wasn't there again today*
*Oh, how I wish he'd go away . . .*

—HUGHES MEARNS, "ANTIGONISH"

# MR. NOBODY

If the car crashed at this speed the impact wouldn't be enough to kill us instantly. Which you might think is a good thing.

But it's not.

The one thing worse than dying on impact is not quite dying on impact. Trust me, I know, I'm a doctor. And now that I'm thinking about it—I'd be genuinely surprised if this rental car even has airbags.

Sparkling snow-covered fields hurtle by at speed. White-dusted hedgerows, sheep, ruts, and ditches—the background of my childhood, a winter blur of pastoral England. Crisp sunlight high in a rich cobalt sky.

I flash a look to the driver—face locked in concentration—as the brakes squeal and we change down a gear, grinding into another blind corner. All I can do is will us on and hope we make it in time. Before my patient does something terrible.

We accelerate out of the bend, the drag of it pulling us sideways, perilously close to the narrow lane's now forest-lined edges. I let the imagined consequences of a car crash flash through my mind: I see the fragile sweetmeat of our neocortexes smashing forward at a hundred miles per hour into a quarter of an inch of solid skull bone. I hear the thick packed-meat sound of our heads connecting with the dark matte-gray plastic of the dashboard and then, instantly, whiplashing back into our headrests with blunt force. A double cranial impact. War on two fronts. The reason armies get defeated.

That delicate gray matter that we all take for granted, the part of our bodies that makes us *us*. All that we are, crashing forward and backward at high velocity into our own skulls. Frontal, parietal, and occipital blunt-force trauma. Massive hemorrhaging, internal bleeding, bruising, and atrophy. Dead tissue. The brain damaged beyond repair. Who we were: gone.

And then a new thought tops those terrifying images: Even if we somehow managed to survive all that, I'm probably the only person who would be able to fix us afterward. I'm the only doctor with relevant clinical experience in a hundred-mile radius. The irony smarts.

We swerve tight around another bend, branches jab into the broken window next to me, and I dodge farther into the car.

I need to focus.

I squeeze my bleeding fist, hard, letting the pain thunder through me. Focus. No more mistakes. This is all my fault. Everything that's happened. I could have stopped all of this if I'd only done better, looked harder. If I'd picked up on certain things, if I'd seen the signs.

My eyes flick up to the road ahead of us. I see it fast approaching on the horizon: the lay-by, the path that leads directly down to the sea. That wild expanse of water. That's where he'll be. If we're not too late.

There was another time, long ago, when I wasn't focused either. I missed the signs then too and I let something very bad happen. But not this time. I promise. This time will be different. So different. This time I will stop something awful from happening. I will fix it this time.

And, if I'm brutally honest with myself, perhaps this is exactly what I've always wanted it to come to. A chance to fix things this time around.

I mean, no one becomes a psychiatrist by accident.

# 1

# THE MAN

## DAY 1

The bright glare of light as the soft skin of two eyelids part.

A body sprawled on the sand.

The fast flutter of eyelashes as awareness blossoms within and, just like that, he's awake. Consciousness floods through him; he feels the skin of his cheek pressed against the brittle cold of the beach. Confusion.

Sounds of the sea. Waves crash and pull back, the pop and *shhh*.

It's early morning in January. A British beach in the depths of winter. Miles of golden-white Norfolk shore with the crisp dawn light throwing everything into high definition.

Wind-borne sand grains blow in architectural ripples across the flats straight into the man's unprotected face. He squeezes his eyes tight shut against the sting of it.

A hot throb of pain crests sharply inside his skull, and the papery skin around his eyes creases deeper, his forehead puckering, as he flinches from it. The unanticipated pang lengthens, stretching itself inside his head, almost too much to take. A sharp gasp of breath and the pain stabs back, harder. His hot exhale drifting away in the cold sea wind.

He tries to relax into the pain, letting the wave of agony wash through him, over him. And it seems to work; the feeling begins to still within him. He lies there limp on the sand for what seems like an eternity, letting the restless throb slowly quiet.

He hurts everywhere. The ghost of a thought drifts through his mind.

*Where am I?* It floats gossamer thin in the air, fluttering just beyond his reach.

He takes another cautious breath and tentatively tries to raise his head, careful not to stir the lurking pain nestling in his skull. Damp sand, like candied sugar crystals, sticks to his stubbled cheek as he shifts his weight up onto aching forearms, cautiously testing the limit of their strength as he squints out into the morning light.

*How did I get here?*

Gulls skip along the sand as he searches the landscape for an answer—but nothing here looks familiar.

*What happened?*

He takes in the silent forest that backs the beach, its dark canopy beyond unreadable. No clues. No hook to hang understanding on.

*Okay. Where was I before I was here?*

He looks up at the haunting gray vault of winter sky hanging overhead and wonders if he might be dreaming. If he might be in bed, safe back at home, wherever that might be. But the clouds look back, heavy and full of rain. He shivers.

It is only now that he notices his clothes are wet, their sodden fabric clammy against his skin. He shudders, cold to his bones. He must move, he knows that much, he must get warm, or risk freezing in this weather.

He needs shelter. He looks back toward the trees that skirt the beach. The wind whips sharp needles of sand into his skin, tiny pinpricks against his numbed flesh.

Struggling clumsily to his feet, he begins to process the extent of his injuries as each muscle is asked to move.

Upright, he hesitates. He turns in a small circle, checking the sand around where he lay. A natural instinct telling him to look, nothing more. To look for things he may have lost, belongings left behind, although what those would be he does not know. But then, he must have *some* belongings, mustn't he?

He thinks for a second before jabbing his numb hands into his wet pockets.

*There must be something.*

His pockets are empty. He is momentarily flummoxed into inaction.

*Wait. What the hell is going on?*

He runs a quick hand through his damp hair, trying to grapple back control of the situation, trying to wrangle the logic of it. He must remember something, surely? His hand skims the back of his head, and the throb of agony at the base of his skull washes over him again, pinching tight. He sucks in a sharp breath and whips back his hand to see the dark smear on his fingers.

*Blood.*

He squeezes his eyes shut, breathing through the pain as it slowly subsides. When he opens his eyes, he notices something, on the other side of his hand. He turns his palm over and there on the back in blue ink—writing. A faint ink mark faded by seawater, a word. He stares down at it, perplexed.

*Strange. What does it mean?*

The word dances on the tip of his recollection, the answer so close he could almost reach out and grasp it. But it rolls away, out of reach, evasive, mercurial. Like the bright filaments that play on the inside of his eyelids each time he closes them.

He shudders, the cold snapping him back to the immediate situation. He needs shelter.

*It will come back,* he tells himself. He gives himself a brisk shake and starts to walk inland purposefully.

Wet sand squelches up between his bare toes as he walks, cold and thick like poured concrete. All the while the tendrils of his brain search, delicately, for something to cling onto.

*What is the last thing you remember?*

Silence. The sound of sea-foam bubbling and popping as it dries in the wind.

His thoughts roll on.

*How did I end up here?*

*Did something happen to me?*

Suddenly the realization hits him. He stops abruptly.

*Wait. Who am I? What's my name?*

He stands frozen, his short brown hair tousled by the wind. His mind races.

*Where am I from?*

He can't remember. He looks down quickly at the blood smear across his hand. The word on the other side. The panic rising now with incredible speed.

*Why can't I remember? Why can't I remember my name?*

The weight of what this means bears down on

him with each cold snatched breath he takes. Fear pumping through him, primal and quickening.

*Oh God. It's all gone.*

His world shrinks to a pinhead and then dilates so wide, suddenly terrifyingly borderless. He has no edges anymore. Who is he? He has no self. He feels the panic roaring inside him, escalating, his heart tripping faster. His mind frantically searches for something—anything—to grab hold of, his eyes wildly scanning the landscape around him. But there is no escape from it, the void. He is here and there is no before. There are no answers.

Thoughts thrumming, he fumbles to check his empty pockets again. Nothing. No ID, no phone, no wallet, no keys, nothing with a name on it. No way to find out.

He tries to slow his breathing, to stay calm. He tries to think clearly.

*If something has happened, someone will find me. Someone will find me and take me back to where I was before. I'll remember. Someone will know me. And everything will come back. It will be okay. I just need to find someone.*

He looks up, eyes finding the forest again, and the indent of a path. He sets off, his pace frenetic. He needs to find someone.

*Wait.*

He stops abruptly again. A jolt of self-preservation.

*Maybe you're out here alone for a reason.*

He studies the word written on his hand. It is all he has to go on but it is not enough.

*Is it a reminder? A warning?*

Perhaps something very bad has happened? He thinks of his head wound. If he was attacked, being found wouldn't be the best idea, at least until he knows what happened, or who he is. He could still be in danger. It's impossible to tell yet.

He commits the word on his hand to memory and then he rubs the ink away against his wet trousers until the mark is gone. He'll remember it. Best to cover the evidence in case he's found.

A thought flexes itself deep inside his head, awakening. Something creeping on the edge of recollection, a memory, or the ghost of one. Just out of reach. Someone saying something to him. If he could only remember. Someone telling him something important, so important. Something he needed to remember. Something he had to do. Suddenly it comes to him.

**Don't fuck it up.**

A memory. That's what they had told him, but who exactly he can't recall. He grasps at the memory. Its warning, the threat, so strong and clear.

**Don't fuck it up.**

*Don't fuck what up? Think. Think.*

He chases the thought but it disappears out of sight. He notices his own bare feet beneath him on the sand. A thought surfaces; he remembers reading once that suicides often remove their shoes before killing themselves. Is he a suicide? How he knows the fact about the shoes he does not know. Did he take off his shoes, did he leave them, and his things, and his life, in a tidy pile somewhere? Abandoned? But why would he do that? He doesn't feel sad. He doesn't feel like the kind of person who would kill himself. But then, maybe nobody ever does?

*Don't fuck it up* is all he has to go on. But what if he already has?

Another memory flashes out of the darkness. A burst of something. Someone telling him.

**You need to find her.**

Find her? He straightens. It's a crystal-clear directive. A purpose.

*Is that why I'm here? To find someone? Who is she to me?*

He thinks of the word he removed from the back of his hand, and blinks.

*Why do I need to find her?*

The memory is what it is. There is no more. Whoever she is, he needs to find her.

*They must have said more.*

He tries to force the memory but the throb awakens deep at the base of his skull. He lets the thought go.

All he knows is he was told by someone, instructed by someone . . . he can't remember who told him, or what they sounded like, or their face. But he trusted them, he knows that much.

How can he find her—this woman—if he doesn't know who or what he's looking for?

A sound in the distance breaks the man's concentration. A voice calling out. Instinctively he turns toward the forest, his heart pounding. There is no one there. The wind perhaps, though it sounded more like a person calling—a name. It came from the forest, a voice carrying over the wind. He stares long after the sound has gone. Certain he heard it. Someone.

But there is no one.

He turns back to the water.

The sound comes again. This time from immediately behind him. A voice. He freezes. There is someone standing right behind him.

He turns slowly on the wet sand. Someone *is* there. A young woman. She wasn't there before.

*Where did she come from?*

He blinks, trying desperately to make sense of what is happening. His thoughts racing.

*She wasn't there before, was she? Is this her? Is she the one I need to find?*

But in the same instant he knows.

*It isn't her.*

He studies her as she stares back at him. She is talking to him, her expression confused, concerned, as if she may have been speaking for a while. She's saying something, words he can't quite understand; her language garbled, the sense not apparent.

His head throbs deeply.

But there is a look in her eyes and everything he needs to know is in that look. He's safe for now. That's as clear to him as the sand, and the cold, and the bright high-vis yellow of the woman's coat.

And suddenly, for a heartbeat, he understands *exactly* what is happening to him. That this has happened so many times before, this exact scene, it's a loop he can't ever escape. And he briefly understands a tiny part of what he needs to do next. And with that knowledge panic, in a giant wave, crests over him. The bright pinch of pain inside his skull explodes to life and he crumples onto the sand.

# 2

## DR. EMMA LEWIS

### DAY 6—LONDON

*This is my pager. There are many like it but this one is mine.*

Like a song I can't shake, or an advert jingle, it runs through my head as I jog to Ward 10, the pager vibrating deep in my pocket, in time.

*This is my pager. There are many like it but this one is mine.*

I know, as mantras go, it's not original. But to be fair to all concerned, it only started out as a joke at medical school. And the joke became a habit and, weirdly, these days, it does actually calm me down. That's the thing about habits. They're comforting. They're hard to kick. Like smoking. And I don't do that one these days. I'm not that kind of girl anymore.

I'm not any kind of girl anymore—I'm a thirty-year-old woman. I'm the lead consultant neuropsychiatrist in a busy London hospital. If I ever actually left work, it wouldn't be "Ms." on my restaurant reservation, it would be "Dr." If I ever had time off to go to restaurants, that is.

You have to watch out for habits, when twelve-hour shifts slide effortlessly into twenty-four-hour shifts. But as habits go, there's nothing wrong with mantras.

God, I need a cigarette.

When I get to Ward 10, Mr. Davidson is yelling at the top of his seventy-eight-year-old lungs. Which has the combined effect of being both disturbing and at the same time strangely sweet. But perhaps the main takeaway is the sheer volume. A visiting couple and a porter stand stock-still in the hallway, heads cocked toward the commotion coming from his room.

Their expressions settle when they clock my doctor ID lanyard; it tends to have that effect. Over the years, I've noticed the doctor's lanyard tends to illicit either relief or apprehension.

I flick off my angry pager and plop it back in its pocket. Doctors are some of the only people left in the world you're likely to see carrying pagers. We still use them because they're reliable. Unlike mobile phones, pagers don't have dead zones; they work everywhere, even on the heavily insulated X-ray wards of a hospital. And they don't run out of battery after a few hours; pagers can run for over a week between charges. And they're durable. Throw them as hard as you possibly can against a concrete wall while crying, for example, and they just won't die.

When I enter the room in question I find a junior doctor, two nurses, and Mr. Davidson's forty-year-old son standing impotently by as the bedbound Mr. Davidson continues to shout, his voice quavering at the assembled group, tears rolling softly down his tired, crinkly face. All heads turn to me as I enter. The lanyard does its thing.

The junior doctor throws me an imploring look,

his expression telling me he'd be more than happy for me to take over. I give him a nod. This is, after all, why they paged me.

Mr. Davidson's screaming and the general vibe in the room make it clear that an impasse has been reached. Mr. Davidson doesn't want to be touched or manhandled.

"Good morning, Mr. Davidson," I say brightly, trying to top his energy.

There's a slight break in the rhythm of his yells. He looks at me, surprised, and I continue with his full attention. "My name is Dr. Lewis. Do you remember me, Mr. Davidson? I'm your doctor. Emma Lewis." I give him a reassuring smile as if to say, *Of course you remember me, we're old friends*.

He clings to my smile, seduced from his train of thought, and his yelling finally subsides. He gives me a tentative nod. Not fully invested in the idea that we know each other just yet.

"Can you tell me what's wrong, Mr. Davidson?"

His tearstained face uncrumples as he struggles to unpick my question.

"Are you in pain, Mr. Davidson? Whereabouts do you feel it?" I nudge him on. He looks away from me now, toward the window.

It's hard to tell to what extent Mr. Davidson recognizes me, if he does at all. Howard Davidson has problems accessing and storing memory; I've been treating him for three weeks, ever since he was admitted. Recognition is a complex neurological process and humans are very, very good at masking the absence of it. People adapt around memory losses. They rely on other things—visual cues, social cues—they get good at reading people, situations; they find ways around things until an answer presents itself. But regardless of whether Howard Davidson recognizes me, he trusts me, he's stopped shouting, and that is definitely progress.

I approach his bed cautiously. He turns to look up at me with his big wet eyes, curious, and exhausted. I gently place a hand on his arm as reassurance.

He peers down at my hand, his chest rising and falling as he fights to get his breath back to normal. He doesn't pull away from my touch, he doesn't lash out. Patients with memory disorders can often become uncharacteristically aggressive, physically violent, but when his gaze floats back up to me it isn't hostile, it's entreating.

"Where exactly are you feeling the pain, Mr. Davidson?" I ask again, softly.

He takes in air in great heaves, not a huge surprise—he's been yelling continuously at the top of his voice for quite a while to a confused and frankly deeply concerned audience. As he stares up at me, gulping in snatched breaths, he looks like a man lost in a foreign country.

He taps his chest. His heart. That's my answer. The answer to my question. That's where he feels the pain: in his heart.

I nod and give his arm another gentle squeeze.

*I understand.*

Mr. Davidson nods back solemnly, and promptly bursts into a cataclysm of coughs.

There's nothing wrong with his heart—well, not physically, anyway. What's physically wrong with Howard Davidson is his brain. As far as Howard is concerned he's a thirty-two-year-old man trapped inside the body of a seventy-eight-year-old. He woke up three weeks ago with no memory of the last forty-six years of his life. In his mind he left his house in 1973 and woke up here, an old man. What's wrong with Howard Davidson is visible only on a scan.

Large sections of his neocortex have atrophied, died. All the memories stored in those areas are gone; a huge portion of his life, to his mind, never happened. Three weeks ago, he was fine, pottering around his garden, walking his dog, reading, deep in the flow of his own life, enjoying his retirement, but that old man is gone now.

Howard Davidson was found wandering down the middle of a four-lane highway near Shepherd's Bush, and brought to the emergency room. After we ascertained from his relatives that he had no history of Alzheimer's, that up until that morning he had apparently been quite happily enjoying the life of a retired MP, an MRI scan was taken.

The atrophy present in the brain scan was found to be indicative of vascular dementia, specifically single-infarct dementia. A single stroke had instantly killed off a massive portion of his hippocampus.

Forty-six years of life and memories erased in the blink of an eye. He has no recollection of having had children, or running for office, and he still believes he lives with his young wife, Ginny, near Goldhawk Road. All long-term memories end there.

I pour him a glass of water from the jug beside his bed. He takes it with a shaky hand. Then I turn to face the ragtag lineup behind me, looking for some kind of explanation for Mr. Davidson's current state, although I already have my suspicions.

His son catches my eye. Simon Davidson and I have met before, briefly, on the day Howard was admitted.

I'll let you in on a secret they tell us at medical school: Sometimes things can't be fixed. Sometimes things must be lived with. Adapted to. Simon Davidson didn't want to hear that.

I've been in this profession long enough to trust

my instincts in situations like this, and right now my instincts are telling me that Simon is almost definitely the issue at fault here. Doctors and nurses don't tend to make grown men cry. Well, not in a professional setting at any rate. So I give the medical team a nod and they shuffle, gratefully, out past Simon.

"Simon, would it be possible to talk to you outside briefly?"

Simon's eyes widen slightly at being the only person singled out. "Er, yeah. Yes. Sure." He gives me a pragmatic nod and starts to leave.

"I'll be right with you in one minute." I offer him a reassuring smile as he pushes out the door, but he's frowning, unconvinced. However, I need to settle Mr. Davidson, my actual patient, before I can deal with his son.

I watch the door softly puff closed behind him.

"Who was that horrible young man?" The voice comes shaky from behind me.

I turn and take in Mr. Davidson's frail form, his crumpled features, his kind eyes. I feel an ache of sadness in my chest. He means his son, of course. But the thing that really gets me is the caution with which he asks me the question, the caution for me, in case he offends me, in case the horrible man is a friend of mine.

"It's all right, Howard, it's just me and you now," I reassure him. I move back to the bed and take his delicate wrist in my hand, counting off his pulse. Elevated but fine. "Did the man who was just in here upset you, Howard?"

I know the answer already. This isn't the first time this has happened since Mr. Davidson's been here, not by any means, nor is he the first patient who's reacted in this way.

Howard Davidson shifts to sit a little higher in the bed. "That young man. Not the other doctor, the small man. He told me that Ginny had died. My wife. *Ginny*. And I don't know who he was or why he'd say a thing like that. I mean, why would he say it?" He studies my face, a fallen toddler unsure yet whether to laugh or cry. "And the way he said it, so strange. Just 'She's dead,' plain and simple, when I asked when she'd get here, just like that, like it was nothing. My Ginny dead." He thumps his fingers against his chest; he's agitated again at the memory. "Why would he say that?" He peers up at me, watery eyes panicked. "Ginny's okay, isn't she? She was fine when I left the house. The other doctor wouldn't tell me. She's all right, isn't she? I should never have left the house." His frail hands become fists now on the bedsheets.

Ginny died eleven years ago, at sixty-two, from thyroid cancer. To be fair to Howard's son, he was probably just trying to remind his father, but no doubt would have done so in that slightly weary way people tend to reiterate facts to dementia patients.

"Is Ginny all right?" Muscle tremors flutter under his eyes. He's tired.

I take his hand lightly. "Yes, Ginny's perfect, Howard. She's very good. She sends her love, and she told me to tell you that she can't make it in this afternoon but she'll see you first thing tomorrow." I say it because he is my patient and it will make him feel really good, and he won't remember I said it tomorrow.

He smiles and squeezes my hand as hard as he can, eyes filling. "Thank you. Thank you, I was so worried about her. I don't know what I would do without my Ginny. And if I didn't even get a chance to say goodbye, well . . ." Of course, he did get a chance to say goodbye—eleven years ago, at her bedside, in this very hospital.

Mr. Davidson will not be able to remember the words of this conversation, but he will remember the feelings it brings up.

I'm not lying to him. I'm just not being an asshole.

We can't inform Howard that his wife is dead every time he asks us, it would be beyond cruelty. Why repeat the worst day of this man's life every day of his life?

Outside in the hallway I try to explain this to his defensive son.

"Are you suggesting we're just supposed to lie to him? Every day? Until he dies?" Simon's voice is low but the tone is harsh.

This isn't a discussion for a corridor but I don't think any venue would sweeten what I'm about to say. "You just have to ask yourself, Simon, who exactly would benefit from his remembering your mother's death? Why are you so keen on making your father remember that one event?"

He stares at me, blindsided by my questions. Confused by the subversion of the customer-is-always-right rule he assumed also operated in hospitals. He swallows whatever vitriol he was about to say and replies simply, "I want him to remember it because it's true. It's important he remembers it because it's *true*."

"Yes, it is true, Simon. But lots of things are true. I could theoretically wander up to Oncology right now and tell everyone up there that ninety percent of them definitely aren't going to make it, but what on earth would be the clinical benefit of that? Your father isn't going to get any better. He won't remember these things, no matter how often you tell him. It will only upset him. And if you tell him, he will hate you, Simon. He may well live another fifteen or even twenty years. He may outlive us all. I think we'd both like his remaining years to be happy ones. I'd advise you to let your sister take over as next of kin from now on and to limit your visits if you're not happy with what I'm recommending. And if you do insist on continuing to visit your father, I'm going to have to ask you to stop deliberately agitating and upsetting him. He's a vulnerable adult and what you're doing is bordering on psychological abuse." As harsh as that may sound, Howard is my patient, it's his welfare I'm here to safeguard, not his son's.

Simon glares at me for a second before he replies.

"I see," he says finally. "Um, well, obviously, I hadn't realized I was causing him so much distress. . . ."

People don't want truth from us doctors, not really; they may think they do but they don't. People want doctors to be like priests. They want hope delivered with authority.

I catch sight of an RN waving over to me from the nurses' station: she gestures to a phone receiver at her ear. I suggest family support counseling to Simon and say goodbye.

With a rallying smile, the nurse hands me the phone. On to the next.

"Hi, Emma." The voice on the other end of the line is my secretary, Milly. "Sorry to chase you round the building but there was a phone call earlier from the U.S. I told them you were on call and they said they'd call back at half past. And I haven't seen you since, so I thought I should let you know."

I look down at my wristwatch: 8:27. I can make it back to Neuropsychiatry in that time—at a jog.

"Who was it, Milly?"

"Er, a man named Richard Groves. Dr. Groves."

I frown at her down the line. "Richard *Groves*? That can't be right. Are you sure?"

"That's definitely what he said his name was." She says it with mild disinterest. I can hear her continuing to type as she talks.

"*The* Richard Groves?"

The line goes silent for a second. "Um . . . I don't know, Emma, sorry. He just said his name and I wrote it down. Why? Who is he?"

I momentarily consider explaining who he is to Milly, then think better of it. She wouldn't have nearly the right reaction if I told her who Richard Groves was. If she googled him, which I'm absolutely certain she won't, she'd see a career spanning thirty years at the forefront of neuroscience, she'd see bestsellers, essays, university placements, corporate and political consultancies resulting in new tech, new procedures, new government policies. If she googled my actual job title, which again she wouldn't, but if she did google the word "neuropsychiatrist," Richard Groves's name would come up in the Wikipedia "Notability" section. Mine would not. Well, not yet.

"Okay. Did he at least say what he was calling about, Milly?"

"Um . . ." I hear a rustle of papers. "Um, no. No, he didn't."

I have met Richard Groves twice. The last time briefly at a medical conference networking session in Dubai three years ago. I wrote my thesis on him, and I had—have—disagreed with some of his methods, but that's what medical papers do. That's the scientific method, right there. He was affable when we met, *collegial*, but I wouldn't say we were quite on telephone-chatting terms. Out of the blue doesn't even begin to describe this phone call. Why the hell is he calling me from America at 8 A.M. on a Monday morning?

It's a question I'm pretty sure Milly won't have the answer to. I look at my watch again—two minutes now. I can make it if I run.

# 3

# THE MAN

## DAY 1—PEOPLE ARRIVE

*"This is Bravo Seven for Sierra Four-Three. Sierra Four-Three, proceed immediately to the car park at Holkham Beach. Report of suspicious behavior: IC-One, white, male, thirties-forties, approximately six foot, dark clothing, erratic behavior. Elderly caller has eyes on suspect, has been advised not to approach."*

*Static.*

"Received, Bravo Seven. Sierra Four-Three en route. Go ahead, over."

*Static.*

*"Non-urgent call. But proceed with caution, suspect may be under the influence or possible mental health issues. Appears to be in some distress. No visible weapons but potential suicide risk, over."*

*Static.*

"Received, Bravo Seven. Sierra Four-Three proceeding to location. On our way. Out."

Fifteen minutes later, the patrol car is the only car in the beach car park. The long stretch of ochre shingle usually packed with vehicles during the holidays is now abandoned, deserted for the winter season. The officers—one female, one male—exit their car, the slam of doors the only sound as their breath clings in warm clouds in the early morning air. As they crunch their way out toward the beach path, the female officer slides up the zipper of her fluorescent high-vis coat, a sharp slice of color cutting through the forest.

The path opens, its gravel giving way to the boardwalk over the reed marshes that connect the forest and beach. Ahead, the vast expanse of Holkham Beach rolls out before them. An elderly man stands waiting on the blustery peak of a steep dune and they cross the soft sand to meet him. Their approach catches his eye and he turns, waving his umbrella to draw attention.

He shouts something down to them but his words are lost in the wind.

The female police officer throws a look to the male officer. He drops back almost imperceptibly as she takes the lead. As they reach the dune's crest, the full extent of the beach rises into view, the long flat sweep toward the breaking waves and the North Sea. It's choppy out there today.

The two officers can make out his words now, over the wind, mid-sentence—

"—don't know what's wrong. I asked, but I couldn't seem to get through to him. He just kept going. He's gone on down there now." The old man throws an arm up toward the east and the officers' eyes follow his motion down the beach. "Over there. Do you see?"

In the distance a receding figure, walking away, alone on the empty beach, in no particular hurry.

"I told them on the phone already," the old man continues. "No way I could stop him, you see. Had to come up here just to get a mobile phone signal anyway. Terrible reception. I told him to wait, someone would be here soon, but he just kept going. Not sure if he even heard what I was saying. There's something . . . wrong with him. I don't know, he's not in good shape at all. Soaking wet for a start. And on a day like this."

The female police officer turns away from the figure on the beach, back to the old man. She takes him in: a smartly dressed early riser on his morning walk, paper under arm, umbrella, raincoat, hat, he's prepared for the weather. His cheeks ruddy in the cold. "Did you make the call yourself, sir?" she asks.

"I did. I didn't think anything of him until he got closer. Some mornings there are other walkers out this early, especially on the weekends, but when he got closer I saw something wasn't quite right. And I thought I should say something," he persists, "you know, just in case."

"Just in case?" the female officer asks, her curiosity piqued.

"He needed help," he clarifies.

The female officer looks down at the tracks in the sand below the dune. A line of bare footprints leading all the way back to the west cove, perhaps two miles, certainly as far as the eye can see. She looks east, out toward the walking figure in the distance. He has no shoes. Then, as if on cue, as if he can feel her eyes on his back, the figure stops.

He stands there motionless, letting the wind roar around him. His wet clothes slapping heavily against him.

And then he drops. Half collapsing, half sitting, onto the wet sand.

The male officer turns to the female officer, touches her sleeve. She gives him a nod, then turns to speak to the old man. "Sir, this is Officer Poole and he's going to take a statement from you, about what's happened. Are you okay with that?"

The old man nods.

The male officer retrieves a slim black notebook from his utility pocket, flips it open, and begins.

Officer Poole's questions fade out of hearing in the wind as the female police officer moves off in the direction of the sitting man.

A series of thoughts flicker across her face as she walks out across the sands. She depresses the button on her radio.

"This is Sierra Four-Three. We are at the scene. I have eyes on the suspect, IC-One, approximately six foot, dark clothing. East Holkham Beach. Subject has no shoes. I am approaching with caution." She continues to close the wide gulf between them, the sand twirling in tiny whirlwinds between him and her. There is something surreal about the scene. It makes her think of the past. There is something Gothic about it, she decides, something so expansive. And for some reason the start of *Great Expectations* springs into her mind. A convict washed up in the marshes.

Without a second thought she pulls her radio up again, depressing the button. "Bravo Seven, this is Sierra Four-Three. Can we run a check on HMP Bure? Anyone unaccounted for, let me know. Suspect may be missing person, over." It's just a feeling, nothing more, an instinct, but she knows sometimes instincts are right.

Her radio crackles to life loudly. *"Acknowledged, Sierra Four-Three. Running prison check now. Stand by. Over."*

He doesn't turn at the sound. She's closer now, she can see his clothes, soaking wet, just as the old man said. His body shuddering, struggling to maintain core temperature and failing. The early stages of hypothermia, she thinks.

"Sir?" she shouts, trying to lift her voice over the howling wind, but the wind throws it back in her face.

Still, the figure does not turn. She is close now, close enough to see the rise and fall of the man's shoulders, the shallow pant of his breath in the icy air. She pauses.

The radio on her chest bursts loud with static again. *"Sierra Four-Three, be advised that is a negative, repeat negative on HMP Bure. All accounted for. Advise. Over."*

The figure before her still does not move, he does not appear to hear, as her fingers fumble to silence the radio.

She moistens her lips, makes another assessment.

The suspect is not responding. He has no visible weapons but could possibly have a concealed one, though where he might be hiding it she does not know. His clothes are loose and wet, clinging to his chest and arms. He could already have hypothermia. He could be in shock. His behavior could be erratic.

It would be possible for her to overpower him for the short amount of time necessary for Officer Poole to make up the distance across the beach between them, should she need to, in the unlikely event the suspect becomes violent.

She proceeds, with caution. "Sir?"

A movement. His back muscles tense at the sound of her voice. He can hear her, that much is clear.

"Hello, sir? Can you hear me, sir?"

He does not respond.

"Bit of a cold morning for a swim, isn't it? Why don't we all head in somewhere warm?"

He remains motionless, his back to her.

"Can I ask what exactly you're doing, sir?"

The distance between them fills with the roar of the wind and waves.

She makes a decision and moves in a wide semicircle up the beach until she has an angle on his face.

He's looking out at the sea, his features slack, tension around his eyes, lost in thought.

He could be in shock, she thinks; it certainly looks like it. In which case whatever has happened to him has already happened, this is the aftermath of something. Whether he is the victim or the perpetrator remains uncertain.

"Sir, I'm going to need you to respond to me. Can you do that?"

He doesn't answer.

Tricky, she thinks. They usually run at you or away from you at this point. Either they're being chased by you or rescued by you. She can't tell which she's doing here. The other shoe usually drops at this point.

But then he has no shoes.

"Sir. I'm going to need you to look at me." He briefly glances away in the other direction as if he hears something in the distance.

She tries again.

"Sir, I'm going to need you to turn around—"

He turns, calmly, and looks straight at her.

His features are striking though softened with age. An attractive man in his late thirties or early forties, she guesses. She takes in his thick dark hair, his brown eyes, the shadow of stubble across his jaw sprinkled with the first signs of gray.

Then their eyes lock and the sounds of the beach around them seeming to fade away, a bubble forming around them, a connection.

There is something odd in the way he looks at her.

When questioned afterward she will struggle to accurately articulate how his look made her feel . . . but after some thought she will settle on the adjective "peculiar."

A calm descends over them, like being underwater, like falling through the air, together. Like a dream.

A gull shrieks and the female officer's attention flicks up and away for the fraction of a second, but the spell is broken.

She looks back just in time to see the man's eyes flutter as he slumps softly down onto the wet sand, unconscious.

"Oh shit," she mutters. Her words again lost in the wind.

Her eyes dart up the beach to where Officer Poole and the old man stand, both dumbly staring back.

Officer Poole starts running, sand flying out behind him.

She snaps back into action, diving forward onto the sand, moving the huddled body into a recovery position, gently adjusting his head and freeing his airways. Her hands coming away streaked with slick, wet smears. A head wound.

Officer Poole stumbles to a halt over her. "What happened?" he pants.

She looks up at him, depressing the button on her radio, pulling it toward her mouth, by way of explanation.

"This is Officer Graceford, come in, over." She eyes Officer Poole as she waits. "Check for ID," she prompts Poole.

The radio crackles to life. *"Received, Graceford. Go ahead, over."*

Poole is on his knees now, his hands urgently

searching the man's body, probing pockets for identification.

Graceford speaks quickly and clearly into the radio. "We have a medical emergency on Holkham Beach eastern. Closest access point Holkham car park. Requesting immediate medical assistance. Over."

Poole shakes his head. "No ID. No bag, nothing."

Graceford depresses the button again. "Assistance required for unidentified white male, in his thirties or forties, unconscious, potential head injury, initial assessment indicates early stages of hypothermia and shock. Unclear if drug related. Please advise. Over."

*Static.*

*"Sierra Four-Three. Be advised. Paramedics are en route from King's Lynn, ETA eight to ten. Are you able to administer first aid on-site? Over."*

Poole nods to Graceford and starts to remove his jacket. He throws it to her and immediately sets about unlacing his work boots.

"Yes, yes, we're administering basic first aid on-site," she says into her radio. "ETA acknowledged, Dispatch. We'll try to keep him warm out here. Do not advise moving at this stage."

*"Received, Graceford. Stand by."*

Graceford clips her radio away with numb fingers and shrugs off her own coat. She shifts the unconscious man onto it and places Poole's coat over him.

Officer Poole, having removed both of his boots, begins to remove his socks too, one bare foot dancing on the cold sand to keep his balance. Gingerly, he thrusts each of the unconscious man's feet into his still-warm socks.

Next Graceford tosses Poole his own discarded boots, which he pulls onto the end of each limp leg.

Poole looks down at his watch. "That's five minutes. Another three to five to wait." Now coatless and shoeless, he rubs his hands together briskly to warm them.

Graceford nods. She releases the man's wrist. "Pulse is fine."

Poole scans the horizon. Three hundred and sixty degrees. Nothing. Nothing but the fading form of the old man. On his way home.

"What do you think this is then?" he asks Graceford.

"Hard to say." She looks pensive. "No ID . . . No shoes. He could have wandered off from the hospital, maybe? I checked with Dispatch about Bure Prison, that was my first thought, but the prisoners are all accounted for there. Could be drugs, a mental health problem?"

"What was he saying to you?"

"Nothing. Nothing at all. Which was . . . weird."

"You think he might have attempted suicide?" He studies her blank face.

She looks down at the silent body. "He's soaking wet. So he definitely went into the water—for whatever reason. Either he planned to get out again or he didn't, but I don't see a towel."

Poole looks down at his feet, now turning blue. "Well, it's fucking freezing, I know that much." He gestures toward the dunes leading back to the car park. "Shall I go over, and meet the ambulance crew there? They should be here any minute."

"Yeah, you go. Once they've picked him up we'll sweep the area. See what we can find. ID, shoes, clothes, wallet . . . he must have had a bag or something. It'll be here somewhere. He couldn't have got here without it."

Poole nods and heads off before suddenly turning back. He raises his voice, shouting over the wind.

"Unless he didn't get here by land? He might have got here by sea, if you know what I mean." Without waiting for an answer, he shrugs and sets off at a jog back in the direction of the car park.

Graceford looks down at the wet man, his ribs rising and falling. Maybe Poole is right, she thinks; maybe he came off a boat.

Another figure rises into view over the top of the dunes, unseen at first.

This figure is not a paramedic; he is not wearing a high-vis vest; he carries a camera in one hand, its neck strap dangling loosely above the wispy dune grass.

Graceford sees him first.

"Oh shit," Graceford whispers to herself.

She rises quickly to her feet, takes a deep breath, and shouts as loudly as she can, her chest aching against the noise of the wind. She shouts in the hope that Poole will hear her.

"GET HIM OFF THE FUCKING BEACH, CHRIS!"

At the top of the mound Mike Redman doesn't catch Graceford's words but he catches her tone. He pauses.

He takes in the tableau stretched out before him. Graceford bent over a crumpled form, surrounded by miles of empty rolling sand. Beautiful.

A barefooted Poole, sprinting tragicomically toward him, mouth wide, mid-shout. Perfect.

Redman raises his camera. And starts to shoot.

Over the clacking of the shutter the wail of a siren whispers through the wind into audibility.

# 4

# DR. EMMA LEWIS

## DAY 6—THE PHONE CALL

I burst into my empty office, fumble on the lights, and grab the receiver halfway through the third ring.

"Hello?" It comes out louder and more flustered than I had anticipated. I feel a hot blush flash through my cheeks even though I'm the only person in the room. I've essentially just shouted at the world's most preeminent neuroscientist. *Happy Monday, Emma, you're doing a sterling job.*

There's a brief pause on the other end of the line before the caller regroups.

"Um, hello, sorry. Am I speaking to Dr. Lewis?" The voice has the warm hum of an American accent. "This is Richard Groves calling for Dr. Lewis. May I speak with her?"

"Yes, sorry, Dr. Groves. Yes, it is, yes, Dr. Lewis speaking." Complete gibberish. I take a second, cover the receiver, and try to catch my breath from three flights of stairs and too many busy corridors. "Sorry, Richard, that I missed your first call, I wasn't available earlier. It's a bit crazy here at the moment . . . well, always, actually . . . but you know what it's like . . . I suppose." I bury a groan in my free hand. Oh God, I should have thought about what I might actually say when I answered the phone. Bugger.

But rich laughter greets me from the other end of the line. "That I do, Emma. That I do. Not to worry. I've got you now and that's all that matters." I raise my head from my hand. The voice is kind, there's a calm authority to it. And it's a voice I recognize very well, from the brief times we've met and of course from his TED Talks and audiobooks; there's something instantly reassuring about it.

I realize he's stopped talking.

"Er, so, how can I help, Richard?" I move a box of case notes from my office chair and sit down, hard, into its puffed leather.

He clears his throat, suddenly businesslike. "Well, here's the thing, Emma—is it okay if I call you Emma? Or do you prefer Dr. Lewis?"

"No, no, Emma is fine." Now I realize that I've already called him Richard and I didn't even ask. Ugh.

"That's great, Emma. Okay, so, I'll cut to the chase. The last time we met was—"

"In Dubai?" I cringe at the thought of our last meeting.

"Yes, that conference on advances in neuropsychiatry, I think. We spoke about retrograde amnesia, and fugue. Misdiagnosis and testing methods."

"Um, yes, yes we did." We spoke about memory loss and psychological trauma. We spoke about *misdiagnosis*. I feel the back of my neck flush hot because I know what's coming. I push on, regardless. "Yes, that's right. I think it was in regards to my paper. . . ."

"Yes. Yes, it was," he agrees, and I hear a smile in

his voice. His recollection of events obviously amusing him. Thank bloody God for that.

Our conversation in Dubai was the second time we had met and it had gone pretty well, in comparison to the first time we met.

The first time we met he was giving a lecture on the neurobiology of amnesia at Stanford. I'd received a research grant and I'd used the opportunity to travel to the U.S. to hear the talk and try to arrange to meet him in person to clarify some points about the cases he'd worked on. Now, to be fair to me, I was young. I still had the idea that confrontational debate in an educational setting was a productive method of getting anything at all done. Which it turns out is not, in fact, true. And on top of that it turned out that I had also sort of misunderstood the tone of the evening. So when the Q&A finally opened out to the audience, it would be fair to say that, as I lowered my shaky hand and started to ask the first of my three questions, I was not greeted with quite the professional curiosity that I had naively expected from Groves's eight-hundred-seater auditorium of paying guests.

I feel the cringe twang again deep inside me.

"Listen, Richard, can I just say again, I am so sorry for what happened at Stanford. I just, I can even . . ."

He's chuckling now, oh God, somehow that makes it worse. What a lovely man.

"Emma, I told you the last time we met. It's fine. I mean, I wish we'd discussed your questions in a more *private* setting but, heck, that's the nature of medicine, right? You've got to be able to question things. Anyway, put it out of your mind for now."

I hear the receiver pull away slightly at his end of the line and a muffled yawn.

"Sorry, Emma," Groves continues. "It's not you. You'll have to excuse me but I'm on Eastern Time, it's, er, 3:32 in the morning here in Massachusetts. Long past my bedtime." He gives a tired chuckle, warm and throaty. "We're pulling an all-nighter in the lab. So I thought, why not call you in England at a decent hour while I'm up anyway." I realize it's still Sunday night where he is. He's pulling an all-nighter on a Sunday; Jesus, the Americans work hard. Monday morning in London suddenly feels infinitely more manageable.

"Well, I'm glad you called! So . . . what is it I can do for you, Richard?" Even as I say it I wonder if there genuinely is anything I could help him with. It seems unlikely. Unless, of course, he needs someone to embarrass him publicly at another upcoming function.

I hear him sigh heavily. "Ugh, okay, Emma, I really hate all this. You see, I'm usually a planning-ahead man, not a fan of changes to my schedule, snap decisions, that sort of thing. I suppose it's a pretty old-fashioned way of working but it's what I'm used to. So, I apologize if you're the same, but I'm afraid the reason I'm calling is all quite seat-of-the-pants. Anyway, to cut to the chase, I got a call this morning, *my* morning, from the UK about a patient over there and it made me think of you. Sorry, just one moment—" He breaks off; there's the scratch of something being pressed against the receiver mouthpiece on his end. I notice I'm standing up; I'm not sure when that happened.

I wait. I look at my gray office door, the gray slat blinds, the neat piles of green patient folders on my desk. Then his voice comes back like warm honey on the line.

"My apologies. The natives are restless here. Where was I?"

"You got a call and thought of me," I prompt, sitting back down.

"Ah, yes. So, I got a call from Peter Chorley, at Cambridge. Do you know Chorley?"

I rack my brains, but I feel like I would remember a Peter Chorley if I'd ever met one. "No. I don't think I do. No."

"He's got tenure, head of Neurolinguistics at Cambridge. No background in our field but he does a lot of advisory stuff, freelance, over there in the UK, government consultancy, initiatives, boards—that sort of thing. Jack of all trades, to some extent. Anyway, he called to gauge my interest on working with a patient over there in England. He thought it would be exactly my kind of thing—but as you can tell, I'm pretty swamped up here. So, long story short, I suggested you."

I clutch the phone hard as if it might suddenly and inexplicably be yanked from me, my breath catching in my throat.

*Oh my God.*

Richard continues. "You're there already, you know your stuff, it's a small field and this is exactly what you've been after, am I right?" He asks it triumphantly, a man doing someone a solid favor.

I genuinely cannot believe this is happening. "Er . . ." is all I manage.

"It's an intriguing case. I promise you, you'll love it," he adds encouragingly.

And I'm absolutely certain I will love it, but that's not the problem. The problem is I'm pretty sure Richard Groves has made a mistake and dialed the wrong number.

I try to think if there are any other neuropsychiatrists who (a) look like me, or (b) have names similar to mine.

He must be trying to get hold of someone else, surely? Things like this don't happen. Or at least they don't happen to me.

But then, neuropsychiatry isn't a *huge* field, especially in the UK, especially when it comes to specialists in memory. And now that I really think about it I might be one of the few British specialists who's actually had the balls to introduce themselves to Groves and spoken to him in person—we don't tend to get out much, neuropsychiatrists; social time does tend to eat into precious work time. So perhaps I am pretty high on his list of options after all. And who am I kidding? I *pushed* for this, didn't I? I pushed so hard for this chance. Every time I've met Richard I've pushed. I talked, I listened, I hung on his every word. I basically low-level stalked him for this opportunity. I've foisted my diagnostic theories down his throat at every juncture. And I sure as hell never saw anyone else pushing through the crowds to get to him to debate diagnostic methodology. God knows no one's pushed to be at the forefront of his mind more than I have. So maybe it isn't so strange? Perhaps in a way I chose *him*.

"I know it might seem like a shot out of the blue, Emma. But you've been on my radar for a while now. You know how rare these cases are. And you're over there. I could've called Tom Lister at John Radcliffe; he's . . . well, he's not as—shall we say—invested as you are in new research. Let's be straight. You've got ideas, theories—I've read your research material—but you haven't had a real stab at a fugue case yet. And you were right, about brain imaging, we should have used it, every case should, it should have been used to rule out or verify fugue. If I'd had the tech twenty years ago, I'd have been shouting at doctors in lecture halls too. It's what I'd use now myself, and I know for damn sure it's what you'll use." He gives a youthful laugh. "Listen, I know you're busy over there, you've got your own thing going on in London, it'd mean traveling north, uprooting for a while, but I really think this could be the opportunity you've been after. I wouldn't be where I am today if someone hadn't taken a shot on me, and this is me giving you yours. What do you say?" He leaves the question hanging in the air, an ocean between us.

Richard Groves has read my work. Of course he has. He's a fucking genius, I bet he reads everything. But he liked it. He agrees with it. It's right. I'm right.

I peer up at the anemic gray of the ceiling tiles above me: huh, somehow there's a coffee stain up there. I have no idea what he's suggested me for yet, but whatever it is I should definitely do it, I'd be crazy not to.

"What's the case, Richard?" I ask, grabbing a pen and a stack of Post-its from the desk.

His tone is enthusiastic. "Mr. Nobody," he says. My pen hovers over the Post-it paper expecting more but nothing comes.

"Sorry? What was that, Richard? Mr. . . . ?"

"I know, it's ridiculous—as usual. The press are calling him Mr. Nobody. He's the guy they found on the beach the other week. The one in the news." He pauses expectantly once more, waiting for some kind of acknowledgment from me but I am still in the dark. I suppose now might be a good time to tell him that I don't really watch the news. I mean, I hardly have time to do my own laundry and the last thing I want to do with the little free time I do have is fill it with problems I can't solve. The most I read is the free paper on the underground on the way to work and I only skim that. Perhaps in this case, though, a little TV could have gone a long way.

I depress the computer's power button as stealthily as I can and swivel my chair and the phone away from its burst of startup noises. Google will be able to fill me in.

"Er, yes, I think I saw something. . . ." I fudge as the home screen settles.

But he clearly sees through my delay tactics. "Ah, okay. I'm guessing you haven't seen it. Let me give you the potted history. I'll get the exact location details to you but he's in England, it's a coastal town, outside London. But diagnosis-wise, at this stage, it's looking like retrograde amnesia or dissociative fugue." He pauses to let that information sink in.

Retrograde amnesia or fugue. The loss of all stored biographical memory, through trauma—physical or psychological. Patients with either would retain all skill- and knowledge-based memory, as these types of memories are stored in different areas of the brain, but lose personal memory. A patient would know, for example, what the idea of *home* is, but he won't remember his. He'd remember how to drive a car but not where he usually parked it. His past would be a blank slate, he'd remember nothing of his life before the physical or psychological trauma that caused the amnesia. Like walking into a room and forgetting why—except you also don't know where the room is, or where you were before you walked into it.

Retrograde amnesia is caused by physical damage to the brain and it's very, very rare. But fugue is even rarer and, unlike retrograde amnesia, fugue is caused solely by psychological trauma. I suddenly understand why Richard Groves is calling me in particular. In my thesis I argued Groves may have misdiagnosed certain fugue cases. I stuck my head out over the parapet of recent graduation and criticized the received wisdom, challenging the established method and arguing publicly that historically most fugue cases were likely misdiagnosed. He's offering me a chance. A chance to prove it.

I take a deep breath. "I see." There's silence on the other end of the line. I realize he wants me to ask the most important question of all, the nub of the matter.

"Which do you think it is Richard? Retrograde or fugue?" I ask carefully. We both know how important the distinction is. If this is a genuine fugue case, it could give invaluable insight into an extremely rare condition. We've only really been able to test for it since the 1990s, which means study cases are few and far between.

"I haven't seen any scans yet," Richard answers cautiously, "but what they're telling me sounds intriguing. It isn't presenting as malingering, and it wouldn't have got this far if it was, especially in light of the oversights on the Piano Man case. People are very keen to spot that kind of thing early. I have it on very *cynical* authority from Chorley that we're dealing with something much more complex here. The powers that be over there seem pretty eager not to fuck the situation up. Yes, it's definitely fair to say they don't want another Piano Man situation."

It suddenly occurs to me how big a deal this case could be. If I take it, I won't just be treating an extremely rare RA/fugue patient, I'll be responsible for averting another NHS diagnostic shit show. Because that's exactly what the Piano Man case was.

Ten years ago, another man was found, this time in Sheppey—the Isle of Sheppey in Kent—in a seaside town during the off-season. He was soaking wet and wandering along a coastal road, in an evening suit. He had no identification on him; the labels had been cut from his shirt and suit. Admitted to the local hospital, he seemed unable to speak to the doctors and after neurological testing and psychiatric evaluation he was diagnosed as fugue.

Given a sketchpad, the man drew a detailed picture of a grand piano on a spot-lit stage. When the staff took him to the piano in the hospital's chapel, he played the whole of Beethoven's Moonlight Sonata from memory. And he was dubbed the Piano Man.

The Piano Man's procedural memory was perfect, he remembered how to play, in spite of the fact that he'd lost all personal memory.

The hospital staff encouraged him to play daily, in the hopes that it would help his recovery and trigger memory recall. Staff and patients would gather at the back of the chapel to listen, enthralled as the music flowed out of him from who knew where. Inevitably, the press got hold of the story. A photo circulated of the lost-looking man, in the hospital's garden, in his formal evening suit, a stack of chapel musical scores tucked under his arm, supplied by well-wishers. He looked every inch the lost musical genius that he swiftly became in the eyes of the world. The media went crazy for him, the public went crazy for him. And, overnight the world found out about the Piano Man. The name was almost too perfect, considering the other meaning of "fugue": a piece of music made up of many voices repeating the same melody.

And the media storm that brewed became a fugue in itself. So many voices. People demanding to know who he was. Where he came from. But, most importantly, what had happened to him.

It played out loud and brash across the tabloids

and for one summer the Piano Man caught the imagination of the world. The public wrote their own stories, projecting their hopes and fears on his blank expression.

Meanwhile, British neurologists, psychiatric nurses, and a host of other medical professionals fumbled and fudged different treatment plans and the police tried to track his family down. None of which came to anything. Until finally one day the Piano Man decided to speak. And what he said wasn't what anyone had expected.

He wasn't the man the world had been hoping for; he was simply an ordinary man, an imperfect broken person just trying to disappear. He'd been misdiagnosed. He wasn't in a fugue state; and he didn't have retrograde amnesia.

The National Health Service, police force, and government came under scrutiny for their complete and utter mismanagement of the whole case. The Piano Man was thrown out with the rubbish, a sad malingerer, a fraud who fooled everyone.

But I wouldn't call what he did malingering, that seems too harsh a term. Malingerers tend to fake for financial gain or to avoid incarceration or military drafting. But the Piano Man just wanted to escape his everyday life for a while.

When Richard next speaks his tone is soft, parental. "I'd take the case myself if I wasn't already neck-deep here at MIT. You know, I haven't had a potential fugue for years now. There's a lot I'd do different, a lot I know you'd do different."

He's right. I've never had a fugue patient. There aren't that many around and men like Richard with years of clinical experience tend to scoop them up. Groves has treated cases similar to this one, although he had nothing to do with the Piano Man case—

though he did work on a similar case, "Unknown Young Male" in 1999. It was the case where a twenty-year-old patient wandered into the Buffalo General Medical Center in upstate New York, soaking wet, with a shaved head, asking if anyone could help him find his way home, as he couldn't remember where he lived or who he was.

In fact there aren't many fugue patients Richard hasn't worked with. He led on the Lost Man case in 2007, where a businessman came to on a bus in Denver with no memory of his life up until that moment.

And the case of patient H.G. (Heather Goodman), who found herself in a Starbucks queue in Portland with no wallet or idea of who she was or how she'd got there. It turned out her amnesia was epilepsy-led and she regained her full memory after only ten days.

Richard has consulted on almost all the recorded fugue cases over the last thirty years, which is why he's the go-to specialist for cases like this, but that might change, that could change, if this goes well. And it could go well, couldn't it?

"I'll do it," I say before I can think of the million reasons it's a terrible idea and talk myself out of it.

"Great! That is excellent news, Emma!" Richard crows, and I feel a warmth spread right through me. "Good. I had a feeling you would. Now, listen, I hope you don't mind but—"

There's a sharp bang on the door and Milly pops her head around.

Richard continues, "—there should be someone turning up there soon. I didn't want to be presump—"

Milly waves for me to listen, her face uncharacteristically animated.

"Sorry, Richard, one second," I say, lowering the phone. "What is it?" I ask.

"There's someone here to see you. He doesn't have an appointment that I can see, but Greg from Caroline Miller's office just called and said the appointment has already been okayed with them! With Caroline Miller!" Milly's voice is hushed but her pitch is high. Caroline Miller is the chief executive of the whole hospital. We only ever see her at events and general meetings. "Did you know about this?"

"What's the person waiting's name?"

Milly blinks at me blankly. "Oh, sorry, his name is Peter Chorley."

I nod. Ah, okay. Well, that makes sense.

"Thanks, Milly. Tell him I'll be out in a second." I don't know whether to be pleased or annoyed that Richard was so certain I'd say yes, but then I suppose he is a neuropsychiatrist and human nature isn't exactly brain surgery, is it? Oh, wait, it kind of is.

I lift the receiver back to my ear as Milly slips out of the room.

"I think whoever was on their way is here, Richard."

"Ah! Perfect timing. I'll leave you to it then. Listen—let me know how it goes, I'm interested. Your secretary has my number. If you need anything at all, you know where I am, Emma. Don't be a stranger."

# 5

# THE MAN

## DAY 1—BACK ON THE BEACH

"I understand that, Mike, I do." Officer Poole and the photographer for the *Brancaster Times* have reached an impasse in the car park. Mike Redman's camera hangs from the thick Nikon strap around his neck between them. "I appreciate that you have a job to do, but let us do our job first and then . . . fire away. Does that sound fair? The most important thing is we get this guy taken care of. Could you just put the camera away, please, mate?"

Mike scowls, obviously not considering Poole to be his mate.

Officer Poole shifts his six-foot, four-inch frame into Mike Redman's personal space and gives him his most reasonable look. "Come on, mate, just put it away." Mike is unmoved.

"Look, Mike, the last thing we need is for this guy's family to find out the state he's in in the bloody local news. There's a procedure. So can you please delete those and just . . . just get back in your car. Now."

In the distance an ambulance siren wails closer.

"Can't do that, *mate*." Mike smirks, with clearly no intention of deleting anything.

Officer Poole exhales loudly and rubs a hand over his face. "Ah, come on. Look, we both know how you got here so quick. Play the game, Mike. You've been warned already. I don't know why you keep testing the system, 'cause we're gonna have to charge you at some point, Mike. You know you're not supposed to be listening in on Airwave. It's an arrestable offense to listen in on police radio and you know it, mate. I don't know what equipment you're using but it's not legal, the frequency's supposed to be secure. We will search the office, Mike, I'm serious. We will come down there and search it."

"You seriously think *The Times* is going to let you search their office? On what grounds? You've got absolutely no cause. Personally, I'd check for a leak on your end, *mate*. Wouldn't be the first time."

"Okay, first of all, Mike, you don't work for *THE Times*, okay? You write for the fucking *Brancaster Times,* so don't get uppity with me. Secondly, if you did work for *The Times,* you wouldn't be out here arguing with me in a rural car park, would you? So, do everyone a favor and put the camera away."

Behind Mike, at the edge of the car park, an attractive woman rises from a bench, finishing a phone call. Poole has been deliberately ignoring her. Now she pushes her long red hair off her shoulder and makes her way toward the driver's side of the only other car in the car park. Chris Poole's face falls. Things are going to get much more complicated now.

She's in her early thirties, relaxed, confident as she rests one arm against the open car door and reaches in languidly to pull out a full take-out coffee from the cup holder. She holds Poole's gaze as she sips.

"Is there a problem, Officer?" she purrs. This is Zara Poole. Officer Poole's wife.

Zara is the only person that can suck the wind right out of his sails and fill them up again. And after all these years, he still feels like the teenage boy Zara flirted with at school whenever he's around her. She still makes him nervous because, if he's honest with himself, she's the only woman he's ever really wanted to impregnate but she hasn't let him, yet. They've practiced, obviously, but Zara isn't quite ready to step back from work. Meaning power-play situations never tend to end in his favor.

"Zee. Honey, can you get Mike to stop, please? No pictures. No anything. Just . . . let's just call it a day now, shall we?" Officer Poole holds his wife's gaze, his weary face imploring. "Zara?"

She grins. "Out of my hands, sweetheart. Photography is not my department. I just do the words! And, um, Chris honey, quick question? Where are your shoes?" All eyes travel to Officer Poole's naked feet.

Poole gives Zara a look. This is the kind of thing they've talked about before. Undermining him at work. They'll talk about this later. Again.

He changes tack. Letting his uniform do the talking.

"All right, that's enough now. I'm going to have to ask you both to get back in your vehicle, please." He ushers Mike over toward the car, his arms wide like a shepherd's.

"Okay, Chris. Okay," Zara reluctantly acquiesces.

"I'm going to have to ask that you both remain within your vehicle until the medical crew arrives."

Zara slips into the car's leather interior shaking her head. "Unbelievable . . ."

An ambulance flashes into sight through the hedgerows.

"Sir." Officer Poole gestures again to Mike Redman. "Sir, if you could also get in the vehicle." The photographer looks through the windshield to Zara. She nods. A police caution wouldn't sit well at the paper.

Mike strolls toward the car as the ambulance roars into the lot, flashing and whirring like a fairground ride. Officer Poole depresses his radio button. "Graceford, this is Poole. Ambulance has arrived at access point. Stand by. Over." Poole sets off at a jog to meet the first paramedic as he dismounts from the passenger side. The female driver cuts the siren.

*"This is Graceford. Received. Pulse still stable. No change here. Over."*

"Hypothermia? And shock, yes?" the paramedic asks Poole. He grabs his kit bag and slams the passenger door in one fluid motion.

"Yes, both. He could have other injuries; we didn't want to move him. He's currently stable but unconscious. It's this way." Poole and the male paramedic set off back toward the beach. The female paramedic follows with a stretcher under her arm.

Zara leans back into the warm leather of her car seat and sips her hazelnut latte. She slips her mobile phone out of her bag and scrolls through her contacts. She taps out a message and presses send. Mike, still standing outside the car, leans in through the open passenger window.

"You know him, Zara, is it worth popping over and grabbing a few more photos, or will he kick off?"

Zara thinks for a second. "Best not. He's a bit crabby at the mo. Just grab some iPhone wobble-cam footage. We can pass it off as a member of the public's footage if we use it. Don't be too obvious, though, Mike, okay?" She smiles. "I don't want a divorce. It's not even a year yet."

She watches Mike wander back toward the beach, making his way through the tall grasses on the dunes. Apparently, Mike used to work freelance for the *News of the World*. When it existed. He only moved back to Norfolk because his mum got sick. She watches his receding back and thinks, *There's always been something slightly off about Mike, but at least he gets the job done.*

Her phone starts to vibrate in her hand. She checks the number and answers.

"Yeah, so, what we've got so far is an unidentified male washed up on the beach. No ID. Witness confirmed. An old guy, we caught him before he left, got a statement. Yeah, I've got some story ideas. I'm thinking a Brexit angle. Illegal immigrant washes up, or broken-Britain Middle Englander failed suicide? Either way . . ." She stops and listens.

"No. No. We don't know yet. That's the point, if he speaks English we'll go, you know, no job, la la la. If he's foreign we'll do the immigration angle. It's fine whichever. . . . Okay, great, that's great. Listen, I'll get more and put something together, get it over to you by five. See how you feel, if you want it it's yours." She takes another slurp of coffee. "Yeah, sure, but don't contact me through the office, I'm going to go freelance on this one. Mobile. Great. Okay, Len, I appreciate it." She presses end call and looks out at the swaying grasses of the dune. Mike is nowhere to be seen.

The wind slicing through the open window sends a shiver down her spine. She clicks on her heated seat and the stereo, letting the soothing sound of music drift out from the walnut dash. She closes her eyes.

And drifts, suspended for a moment, lost in her thoughts.

A scream rips long and horrifying through the wind and the low mumble of the radio.

Zara sits bolt upright in her leather seat. Out of her field of vision, on a grassy dune that slopes down to the beach, Mike Redman rises slowly from his crouch to stand, his camera phone raised and still filming.

On the beach the fallen man's screams fly up into the sky. He has regained consciousness with strange hands on him. All over him.

Midair, his legs gripped firmly by the paramedics, he twists, spine arching, writhing with every ounce of strength he has left, his legs kicking out, arms lashing, scratching. He screams. As if he's trapped. As if he's being tortured.

Officers Poole and Graceford stand lost for words for a microsecond before diving in to assist.

Graceford, dropping to her knees in the wet sand, restrains the man's arms, pinning them to his chest, securing the upper body. Poole places his hands down firmly on the man's flailing shins.

"Sedative," the male paramedic directs to the other.

"Got it," she replies as Poole nods to her: he has the legs secured. She nods back. Retrieving a small pre-prepped syringe from a Velcroed drug roll, she rips at the paper and plastic.

"Vein," she calls out.

The male paramedic has already rolled up the left sleeve of the man's wet black top, securing the elbow crease in place. "Ready," he replies.

As the female paramedic leans in, the man screams louder.

In the distance Zara's head, then shoulders, then

body rise into view. She stops in her tracks as another scream rips through the air.

She pulls her coat tight around her as she stares out across the open expanse of sand to the huddled figures in the distance.

"Sweet Jesus," she whispers to herself.

And suddenly the screaming stops.

# 6

## DR. EMMA LEWIS

### DAY 6—PETER CHORLEY

Peter Chorley looks exactly as I'd imagined. A reassuring mixture of tweed, butter, and library dust. A kind but sharply intelligent face. Peter is a comfortably dressed Cambridge professor in his sixties. He greets me with a smile, his eyebrows raised mock-conspiratorially at the unusual nature of our first meeting; his handshake is firm and surprisingly warm considering the bitter January cold he's come in from. I notice his cheeks are flushed and he's slightly out of breath from his brisk walk from King's Cross station to the hospital.

Thankfully, Peter Chorley doesn't fancy the hospital canteen, so we head back out into the bitter chill of the London streets. I suggest the Wellcome Collection Café, just next door, to get us out of the cold quickly. It's a medical museum that boasts the tagline "a museum for the incurably curious," but they also do great coffee and a nice line in homemade pastries, which hits all my major sweet spots. I've been coming in here since I moved to London to start medical school. These days I tend to pop in and do admin on my laptop, when I get one of my increasingly rare breaks.

We order our coffees and choose a table overlooking the museum bookshop.

Peter stirs a brown sugar into his espresso. "Richard was very keen on you from the get-go," he says judiciously. "His first choice. I'll be honest, we had to look you up; we weren't that familiar with your previous work, case studies, patients, what have you. But it's impressive. Your work. And regardless of your relative lack of clinical hours in this exact field, Richard's opinion is trusted. It carries a lot of weight. As you know, he's the go-to on this sort of thing. Has been for years."

A warm feeling spreads through me. I was Richard Groves's first choice. But then, I already knew that, didn't I? Still, nice to hear it out loud. I take a sip of my coffee to try to cover the wave of childlike pride I feel sweeping over me, reminding myself that this is still a job interview, even if it doesn't feel like one.

Then I snap myself out of it. After all, I don't even know who exactly it is who is interviewing me just yet. "I really appreciate you coming all the way down here to meet with me, Peter," I reply. "But I have to ask: what exactly is your role in all of this? Richard mentioned you specialize in neurolinguistics, is that right? You don't have a background in neuroscience yourself? Are you connected to the patient's hospital?" I ask, because although very exciting, none of this quite seems to make sense to me yet. The call out of the blue from Groves, the sudden arrival of Peter. I'm not really sure who is asking me to do what. What does Peter Chorley have to do with all this?

He takes a sip of his espresso and gazes out across the bustling café before looking back at me.

"Ah, yes, sorry, neurolinguistics as charged." He gives a pinched smile. "No, no background in your chosen field. But I like to keep up with most areas, or at least I try to." His laugh is self-deprecating. "For my sins, I've been asked to coordinate on this, to source a specialist. I'm here in a purely advisory role."

"I see."

"Yes, it may not look it but I do have a fair few years of clinical experience under my belt, as they say, but now I just tend to advise on the occasional initiative. And teach, of course. No money in any of it, of course." He chuckles. "But I doubt any of us got into it for that!" His eyes twinkle at me knowingly and I smile back.

He got that right. NHS pay isn't great. For perspective, I earn about as much as the average recruitment consultant in London and less than the average mortgage adviser. Of course, I could be earning a packet as a Harley Street psychiatrist—I just don't want to. I don't just want a job, I want a vocation. A life.

"So, you're working for the government on this? The NHS? The civil service?"

Peter smiles back at me, amused. "Yes. Yes, I am." There's that twinkle again.

*Wait, which one? The National Health Service or the civil service?*

He holds my gaze, inscrutable. He's not going to tell me who he works for.

*He's not going to tell me? What the hell is going on?*

I suddenly get the paranoid feeling I might be taken for a ride here. I understand the need for patient confidentiality and the point has been drummed home that this case is going to be tricky in terms of press intrusion, but this is ridiculous. It's obviously

Whitehall. Boarding school children playing at politics. "Riiight. Sorry. I'm sorry, Peter, but you are going to have to tell me who exactly you work for or I'm afraid I'm going to have to pass on this."

Peter leans forward quickly in his seat, eager to dispel any worries. "Emma, look, I can't stress enough how keen we are to have you on board. They've requested you as a substitute for Richard because they are—and I am—confident you can diagnose and treat this patient in the correct manner. But there are certain things . . . There is certain information that . . . well, due to the nature of this case, we'd, or rather they'd, prefer to hold back—at least for now. Until we have some sort of idea what kind of situation we're dealing with here. There is a concern about the identity of this man. Information around it may prove to be sensitive, but we don't know yet." He lets that sit with me for a moment before continuing. "I am the last person in the world for revelling in the dramatic, Dr. Lewis, but if you accept this temporary post, then there will be a substantial amount of, well, of nondisclosure paperwork."

His words throw me for a second. I wasn't expecting that.

He continues. "Which I personally may or may not have *already* signed. . . . Do you see?" He taps out a little tune with the flats of his hands on the café table.

"Right," I say carefully. "I see." Peter has signed a nondisclosure agreement. There are certain things he can't tell me about this case.

Why on earth would they have him sign nondisclosure forms? Concern about the patient's identity? *Who the hell do they think the guy is?*

"Then you understand my predicament. Good." Peter smiles. "We're on the same page." He tips back the last of his espresso and dabs his mouth with a paper napkin. "Thank you for your patience with this, Emma. I know it all seems very strange. And very sudden. Well, it certainly does to me." He frowns slightly, eyes drifting over the concourse once more.

If there are certain things I can't know, then I think it's about time I heard the things I can know. I straighten up in my seat. "So . . . what exactly *can* you tell me, Peter? About the patient. About the case. Could you give me an overview? Richard suggested retrograde amnesia or fugue. But of course there's the possibility of malingering, which no one has mentioned?"

"He's not faking, Dr. Lewis. If he's a fake then he's the best malingerer I've seen in my forty years of medical practice. I examined him yesterday at the hospital. He's not speaking, hasn't said a word since he turned up. I ran some structural scans on the language processing areas of his brain. But there's no atrophy—I have no idea why he's not talking." He holds my gaze now, all softness gone. The air in the café changes and the hairs on the back of my arms rise slightly. This is exciting.

Peter delves into the rucksack on the floor next to him and retrieves a slim silver laptop. "Have a look," he says. I feel another shiver of excitement fizzle through me as he opens it up and slides it across the table.

"These are the initial scans—for your eyes only. I mean that." He holds my gaze pointedly until I nod an assurance.

I study the screen. A secure medical results site. I scroll down and click on the only file visible, labeled *Patient M. Scans*. "Has Groves seen these?" I ask.

"We sent a link through to him yesterday. I don't

know if he had a chance to look them over before he passed on the case. But the file portal is password protected."

I click on the attachment and the gray and bright white of a CT scan fills the screen. The delicate crenulations of the patient's brain. Peter's right, there is no atrophy, no areas of brain have died. I look to the hippocampus, the tiny seahorse-shaped mass of tissue nestled under the cerebral cortex, the area of the brain responsible for the creation and storage of our episodic memory. It's the unassumingly small piece of brain tissue responsible for holding a whole human life together.

The hippocampus in this scan is intact—no physical damage, just the light gray that represents living tissue. Not the dark mass of dead cells you'd expect to see on an Alzheimer's or dementia scan. There are signs of a wound and slight contusion at the base of the skull, probably from a fall or a blow. The injury might have been enough to cause a mild concussion perhaps, but not major damage; it's unlikely to have caused memory loss, but there are no other immediately observable causes on the CT scan. I let my thoughts run with the idea of the concussion—there's the outside chance that if the patient is epileptic, a seizure could have caused his memory loss. But after six days it would have returned, he would be remembering by now. So if the problem isn't physical or electrical, it must be psychological.

Which means—this could be a fugue.

A real live fugue patient. His memory loss in all probability has been caused by mental trauma. Meaning: something very bad happened to this man.

But then it catches my eye, I see it, a tiny dark speck buried in the pituitary gland. I missed it initially, but there it is, faint on the scan.

My eyes shoot up to Peter.

I know for a fact this type of pituitary growth has been present on other fugue patients. In previous cases it's never been given much credence, as pituitary tumors are usually inert. But could the pituitary be linked to fugue?

"Oh my God."

His eyes meet mine and he raises an eyebrow. "Yes. You've seen it? Took me a bit longer. I only noticed it on the train earlier. I had to get my glasses. Tiny." He fishes them out now and swivels the screen around so we can both study the minuscule fleck of darkness on the scan. "Yes, obviously a CT is not the ideal imaging to pick this kind of thing up on. An MRI will help us more," he mutters. But then, I'm guessing whoever ordered these CT scans wasn't looking for what we've both found. They would have been looking for large-scale brain trauma or atrophy. What we've found appears to be a tiny growth. So easy to miss nestled in there.

Peter looks up from the computer screen. "Listen, we can get fresh scans done once you're up there. At the hospital. If you're happy to go up there?" he asks. It's a straight-out question. Will I go? He's striking while the iron is hot, while I'm intrigued by the material.

I study the scan again. That dark speck. What on earth could that have to do with his memory loss? The pituitary gland has pretty much nothing to do with the hippocampus, nothing to do with memory, as far as we know. As far as we know *yet*—I'm hooked.

I look back to Peter. "Where do I sign?" I grin.

But Peter doesn't smile back. In fact he frowns. Looking more concerned than ever. This was not really the reaction I was expecting.

"And you're sure you're okay with the location? You don't want to ask me any more questions?"

"What? Why would I?"

I now wish more than ever that I'd had a chance to google the news stories before Peter showed up. I don't even know what hospital the patient's in. Is there something wrong with the location?

"I don't mean to put you on the spot, Emma, but you don't know what I'm talking about, do you?"

"You're right, I have no idea what you're talking about, Peter. Sorry. Why would the location be an issue?"

"I see. Right, my mistake, I just thought you might . . . Well, I thought you might have changed your mind about the job. Or had stipulations, when you saw more of the details."

"What details? I haven't seen any details."

He studies my face. I stare blankly back.

"Ah, well then," he continues tentatively. "I suppose I had better fill you in. They found him on Holkham Beach, Dr. Lewis—near where you grew up, not too far from where your family home was, it would seem, in Norfolk."

I feel my stomach flip and the room around me spins. Because there is no way Peter could know that: where I came from, where I grew up, who my family was. Nobody knows that. I had a different name back then. Before everything happened, before we moved away. How could Peter know where I used to live?

*Does he know what happened there?*

"Obviously, Emma, we had to do a background check prior to contacting you. Surprises aren't exactly ideal when the media are already swarming over this case. But, needless to say, what happened back then, it isn't an issue for us if it isn't an issue for you. I wouldn't be here if it was. I just wasn't sure if you'd want to, to be perfectly honest, considering what happened there."

I feel my face flush.

*He knows what happened there.*

I try not to let my breathing change. I try not to let my body betray what I'm feeling.

What kind of background check did they do to find that out? That information isn't just available on the Internet. But I suppose they have access to old police records. Yes, I guess he would need to do that, especially if they're worried about the media; it makes sense.

I look down at the table and try to get a hold on myself, my heart thudding in my chest.

"That's why I came down in person, you see, Emma. I thought you might need a bit of extra persuading. Considering . . ."

I turn back to Chorley now. His eyes are flickering across my face, assessing; God knows what he sees there. I'm too busy trying to keep my breathing normal to worry about that. Too busy trying not to think about what exactly his background check threw up. The photos of that night. The aftermath.

"I see." I say it slowly and clearly. "I hadn't realized. I didn't know the case would be up there." To my credit my voice doesn't crack.

His eyes soften. "I'll totally understand if going back is not something you'd be comfortable with. We could keep looking. I'm happy to tell Richard you aren't available after all. I'm certain he'd understand. And I wouldn't divulge your reasons, obviously. . . ." He trails off.

"Richard doesn't know, does he?" I blurt. I don't know why this is so important but it is.

Peter gives a concise shake of the head. "We don't pass along background check information."

I let out a breath I hadn't realized I was holding. Thank God. I would hate for Richard of all people to know.

My brain is whirring. What does this mean? So many good things have happened today. This perfect offer out of the blue, this opportunity, the chance I've been waiting for. But I'd have to go there? Why does it have to be *there* of all the places in the world?

I've spent fourteen years of my life trying to get away from that place, what happened there, and now . . . now I find out that the only way forward, the only way out, is back.

But could I go back? Is it worth it?

I look out at London bustling by the café windows, and across the street, outside Euston Station, I see a man and a woman waving as they rush to greet each other. The crowd swirls around them as they hug, then there's a cheek kiss, she rumples his hair, he pulls her bobble hat down over her eyes, and she laughs. I look back at Peter.

"I'd need to check with someone else before I say yes. Does that work for you?"

"Yes. Of course," Peter agrees. "Of course."

# 7

# THE MAN

## DAY 1—HOSPITAL

At the nurses' station, Rhoda, a Trinidadian triage nurse with warm eyes, looks down at the intake notes she's just been handed and carefully squeaks the words UNKNOWN MALE out onto the large Triage whiteboard. She adds his priority status next—P2—seriously ill or injured but not in immediate danger. He needs a CT scan for his head injury.

In cubicle 7 he lies silently curtained off as the ward bustles around him. The unconscious man is hooked up to an IV drip, an oxygen mask cupping his blueing mouth and nose. It mists and clears and mists with each breath.

His wet clothes have been removed and replaced with a crisp medical gown. Metal foil blankets help to slowly raise his core temperature.

Rhoda erases the name from the cubicle 4 box; her last patient, discharged. She checks the other priorities on the board. There are three P2s on the board. It's a tough call. She checks her watch—she's technically finished her shift. She should call it a day, or rather a morning, but she looks up at the words she's just scrawled out.

Cubical 7: UNKNOWN MALE.

The words snag her interest. Time for one more before she clocks off. It must be fate, she thinks, and nods, scrawling her own name onto the whiteboard next to his.

As Rhoda turns, the duty nurse catches her eye and raises a comic eyebrow. "Last patient, right? No more," she warns, mock-stern.

Rhoda smiles. "Last patient, I promise, Maeve. Got to go pick Coco up after the shift." Rhoda thinks of Coco's fluffy little face. *Ha, such a good doggie.* "Can you call ahead to Radiology, Maeve?" Rhoda asks. "Book the CT, we'll get that done first and hopefully ICU will have space by then. And Maeve, could you page up another doctor? That junior doctor is still up to his eyeballs with that missing-finger situation. He isn't going anywhere soon."

Maeve lets out an unexpected burst of laughter and sets about calling Radiology.

Rhoda grabs the unknown man's medical notes again and breaks into a gentle jog back toward cubical 7, her white nursing shoes squeaking across the linoleum.

"Oh, and porter, please!" she calls behind her as she disappears out of Maeve's sight.

In cubical 7, Rhoda works fast. A series of actions she has gone through multiple times over the last thirty years. Pulse, blood pressure, fluids, ready for transfer.

She looks through his entry notes again. She reads the notes on his behavior in more depth: "disorientated, aggressive, highly agitated, and nonresponsive." Excellent, what a wonderful combination to end the shift with, she thinks.

*Well, we'll just have to see what we can do with you.*

The patient's breathing changes infinitesimally in depth. Rhoda looks up from the clipboard.

*Oh God.*

The man begins to stir under the blankets. The notes say, "Patient has been slipping in and out of consciousness for approximately 35–40 minutes." There might not be long to get him transferred before he wakes up again and this all gets slightly more complicated.

She pokes her head out through the cubicle curtains. "Porter, *now,* please," she calls, louder this time.

Behind her the man shifts in his bed. Rhoda sighs. He's waking, looks like it's happening regardless. She moves around to the man's bedside and steels herself.

He stirs again and suddenly his eyelids flick open.

He looks directly at her.

She smiles down at him. "Hello, you." Her tone is gentle, maternal. "How are you feeling?"

The man stares up at her warm face floating above him. He takes it in, studying it. He was on the beach and now he is here.

His brow slowly knits as he looks at her, her kind eyes, the small scar hidden in her hairline. *Does he know her? No. He doesn't know her.* Rhoda watches the realization flash across his face.

"My name is Rhoda. I'm a nurse. You're in a hospital now. But there's no need to worry, you're fine, everything is all right. I'm just here to help you. Okay? That's all I'm here for. Now, you've had a little knock to the head but we're going to get it all sorted out. Everything is going to be just fine."

*A knock to the head?* His eyelids flicker in concern.

"Nothing too serious," Rhoda counters. "Nothing for you to worry about just now. All you need to do is lie there all cozy and let me do everything. Have a nice relax and let me do it all. Do you understand? You're in safe hands with me."

His muscles slacken back into the bed as he stills himself. He blinks up at her and lets out a sigh that clouds his oxygen mask.

"Trust me?" Rhoda asks.

He looks up at her and she looks straight back down, solid and safe.

His eyes fill and when he blinks, tears run in two rivulets down either side of his face. He exhales deeply again and tries to raise his arm. Rhoda rests a hand on it lightly, she feels the quivering of his muscles beneath the sheet.

"Okay, then. That's a deal. You trust me and I'll get you all fixed up. Shall I?"

He blinks at her slowly, consenting.

*What the hell happened to you?* she wonders, and moves her warm hand to his shoulder.

"Do you remember banging your head? Do you remember that?"

The man closes his eyes to concentrate, breath momentarily held. When he looks back at Rhoda, there is only thinly masked confusion. *He can't remember.*

"It's okay," she soothes. "It's okay if you don't remember that. That's perfectly normal after a bang to the head. It doesn't mean a thing. We're going to get you nice and warm and do a quick scan of your head to see what's what. How does that sound? Does that sound like a good idea?"

He grimaces.

"Yeah, maybe no nodding!" Rhoda soothes. "That's where the knock is, on the back of your head there. It's not a big one but it'll be a bit sore for a while. So, no more nodding, okay? You just relax."

He blinks in acknowledgment. *No more nodding.*

She throws her gaze out toward the ward and seems to reach a decision.

"Right, you know what, let's just get going without them." She releases the footbrake on the gurney and smiles. "If there's no porters, then I'm just going to take you over for the scan myself. If you want a job done right—"

She pulls back the curtains.

# 8

## DR. EMMA LEWIS

### DAY 6—JOE

Isn't it funny how you can successfully not think about something for months or even years, you can almost forget, almost, and then one simple sentence or word can bring it all back with a sudden sickening immediacy?

Peter and I say our goodbyes outside the café and I head back to the hospital, my mind whirring. I need to center myself; it's just that I wasn't expecting that, to be confronted with the worst moments of my life. Not today, not when things seemed to be going so well.

I scan the hospital lobby as I enter—faces, so many faces, all with their lives and their own stories. I try to shake off the feeling that everyone who sees me knows, knows exactly what happened fourteen years ago. I try to shake off the sharp shame of it, the dread. The feeling I've managed to avoid for so long. Even if sometimes memories of it stop me in my tracks on Oxford Street, my Christmas shopping bags trembling in hand, as strangers swirl around me. Or make me fall silent mid-sentence in restaurants with countless prospective boyfriends. Even if they make me question my instincts in every aspect of my personal life, and mean my only freedom, my only escape, is through work. Even if they are the reason I have chosen to live alone, in case, just in case, somehow, I make it all happen again.

Like anyone in recovery, I try to be wary of certain people, places, and things.

And somehow, over the years, I've managed not to reveal it, to keep it all inside, the sadness and the regret, like a gaping hole inside me.

I take the glass elevator up to the third floor, watching the heads of patients and visitors recede beneath me and feeling my familiar stomach-flip of vertigo. My primal fear of heights snapping me back to reality. A decision needs to be made. Peter will be waiting for my phone call this evening. I'm going to need an answer by then. Do I stay and keep pretending none of it ever happened? Or do I go and face the past and perhaps make something good of it?

The elevator doors open and I head down the corridor to my office. Milly isn't at her desk when I round the corner. I check my watch. Lunchtime. She won't be back for a good half hour yet. I need to speak to Joe. Joe's who I need.

I flick on my office lights, lock the door, and sink into my chair. On the desktop I bring up FaceTime, wiping the dust and various marks from the screen and camera with my sleeve. I guess it's been a while since I needed to make a video call.

Joe is my brother, and whenever I make a big decision in life, it's Joe I tend to run it by. Don't get me wrong, though. I'm not saying I ever actually follow his advice, but I at least know that whatever advice Joe gives, he'll give it to me straight. And that's what I need right now. I need another person's gut reaction. Plus, Joe is the only one who knows about Norfolk. Well, Joe and Mum and Dad. I've never told another person what happened. I don't think I'm even allowed to. Which has made relationships hard, to say the least.

My last proper relationship was with an orthopedic surgeon. Harry. It lasted three years. He was easy to spend time with but I didn't want to marry him, so, yeah. I don't have someone like that just now.

Joe has a family; he's a husband and a dad. Which is great. I'm an auntie.

Joe's got ties, responsibilities, connections. I do not. So, I've sort of come to value his opinion more as the years go by. He seems, for want of a better word, happy.

I pull his name up on Contacts and shrug off my coat. I take a stab at fixing my hair in the dark reflection of the screen and press call.

Joe lives in Hertfordshire, about twenty-five minutes from our mother's house. I couldn't do that but I suppose it must be handy for babysitting. I know he'll be in; he works from home. He's an architect who has the good fortune to be able to pick and choose which projects he works on, which is convenient now that they have little Chloe to look after.

The electronic bounce of the FaceTime call tone cuts out sharply and Joe's face replaces mine on the screen. He's in. He's always in. He's reliable that way.

"There you are!" Joe's one of those people who always answers their phones no matter how busy they are. I admire that level of accessibility, because I am not one of those people. He beams at me. I expand the pixelating window until his smiling face fills my screen. His glasses are at a crazy angle on the top of his head, his hair disheveled—I needn't have worried about mine.

"Here I am!" I call in response. Our greeting.

He catches sight of himself in his own window and sets about mushing his hair. He's always been a hair musher. He's only thirty-one, and yet he's somehow managed to look like a harassed thirty-year-old since his second year at uni.

"So, where exactly have you been for the last week, missy? Thought you'd at least call us when you got back to London after Christmas." He continues typing as he talks, as if I'm right there in the room with him.

"Sorry. Work." I shrug a what-can-you-do and Joe glances up, frowning.

We spent Christmas together at Mum's, the whole family. And I didn't call when I got back because . . . well, life, I suppose. Actually, probably, work. Things get surprisingly busy in hospitals around the festive season.

Joe isn't impressed. "Hmph. Right, well, just so you know, Mum started checking the traffic news for crashes, so . . . make of that what you will."

"Listen, Joe, I need your advice. Something has come up. But you've got to promise me you won't tell Mum, all right?"

"What are we—seven?" he chuckles.

"I need you not to tell her, Joe, please?" There's urgency in my voice and his smile fades slightly.

"What is it, Em?" he asks, instantly serious.

"I've been offered a new job and I don't know if I should do it, or even if I want to do it yet, so I don't want you mentioning it to her. I don't want her to worry about it. I don't want her going through anything she doesn't have to. . . . But—I might have to go back to Norfolk."

His gaze hardens at the word.

"Why?" he asks bluntly.

It's a good question.

If I didn't have his full attention before, I have it now. He stares at me grimly, as if he's seen a ghost. And in a way he has. We don't talk about the past; all of that got left behind with the house.

"It's a job opportunity, Joe. A big one. Have you seen the news?"

He's silent for a moment before he speaks.

"Er, yes, I have. Why? Which story? This isn't to do with the dead girl on Hampstead Heath, is it?" He looks away, rubs his eyes, suddenly tired.

What dead girl on Hampstead Heath? God, another thing I haven't even heard about. And Hampstead Heath isn't too far from my apartment either. I really need to start watching the news.

"No, it's nothing to do with a girl on Hampstead Heath. Joe, they found a man on a beach near Holkham. They have no idea who he is, or where he's come from, and neither does he apparently. Like the Piano Man, in Kent. You remember him, right?"

"The guy on the news? You mean Matthew, right? Yeah! That's happening in Holkham, is it? Jesus! I thought this one was in Kent too. Shit. Must have got those two stories mixed up in my head. Yeah, I've seen the story. Yeah, Matthew's such a weird story."

*Wait! Matthew?*

"Hang on, Joe. What do you mean *Matthew*? Are you saying the guy on the beach is someone named Matthew? How do you know that?"

Joe scowls, baffled by my flurry of questions.

"Joe, nobody knows what his name is, or who he is, that's the point of them hiring me! I mean, they're calling him Mr. Nobody, so how the hell do you know what his real name is?" Literally everyone seems to know more about my potential patient than I do.

"What are you talking about, Em? Matthew's not his *actual* name, that's what they're calling him at the hospital. I guess they can't call him Mr. Nobody in a hospital, can they? Apparently, this nurse just started calling him Matthew and it stuck. I suppose they've got to call him something, but it's all a bit, well, a bit stupid, to be honest." Joe rumples his hair. "They called him Matthew because apparently something *odd* happened in the hospital," he says skeptically. "I dunno." He studies my face and puts two and two together. "You're seriously thinking about taking this job and you haven't even researched it yet, have you?"

My brother can read me like a book. "No. No, I have not," I admit tentatively.

"Let me guess, because of *work*?"

"Yes. Work. That is correct."

He sighs. "Well, Emmy, you're in for a treat when you finally do get around to it; it's an absolute shit show up there. Get googling. The press are already camped out all over Kings Lynn. It's a media circus. That Piano Man case on crack. Oh, and *Matthew* means 'gift from God,' by the way, just so you know the level of crazy we're working on here." He studies me, disapproval written large across his lovely face. He sighs again, loudly. "I'd say run a nautical mile from this crap, but something tells me you've already made your mind up and you just want me to agree with you. Don't you?"

I smile penitently. "Yeah, I think you're right, Joe. I think I do." There's no use lying to him. I've never been able to anyway.

"Can you handle going back, though, Em? Seriously. I mean, really, can you handle it? I know you'll say you can and you'll make it work somehow, but could you?"

"If I'm honest? I don't know, Joe. I won't know until I get there, I suppose. But I have to give it a try, don't I?"

"*No*. No, you don't have to give it a try, Em. Sometimes you can just let things go. Let an opportunity go, if it's not right for you. Sometimes it's not a test, or a challenge or whatever. . . . Sometimes it's just you, pushing yourself too far."

I know deep down he'd want me to do everything differently. From the start. That if he'd had his say, I wouldn't even have gone into medicine. I'd have been an artist, a painter; I was good at art when we were young. But things happened. Life happened and here we are. We're so different, he and I. It's funny how different two people with the same genes can be.

"Well, I *do* have to do it, Joe."

"You don't, but okay. That's your answer then. Do it. And I'll be here if you need me." Then his brow creases. "But what will you do if they find out what happened? There's a lot of press up there, Em."

"They changed our names, Joe. No one will know who I was or that I was ever there before. That was why we moved, right? The police, the social workers—that was the point, wasn't it, that no one would find out? Unless the police themselves decide to tell the media, there's no way anyone will be able to find out. The system is in place for a reason."

He frowns, unconvinced. "But you'll be there, physically, in person, with people who knew us back then. People who went to school with us. What if someone recognizes you?"

I hadn't thought of that. I stare at him now, silenced. But, I was so different back then. It was such a long time ago. I looked different. A different person. A different name. I lost my puppy fat at seventeen, right after we left. My once open, soft face lost its plump rosy cheeks and matured. Cheekbones, collarbone, breasts. I grew into myself, boys started noticing me. I'm certain nobody there will recognize me now.

"They won't, Joe. They'll remember an awkward sixteen-year-old. I mean, I'd like to think I might have changed slightly over the last fourteen years!"

He studies my face trying to judge whether I'm right, then nods back tentatively. I do look different. I often wonder if he misses the old me. The me from before. But that girl's gone.

I plow on. "And even if they do recognize me, Joe . . . so what? We'd be all over the news for, what, like maybe a week, tops. No longer than we were before. And then it just goes away and the world moves on and we go back to our lives. I can handle that, we handled it before. All of us."

"We did but I don't know if Mum can do all that again. She's happy where she is. I don't think she could just go back to her life if who she was got out." I think of Mum in her cozy cottage. I think of her coffee mornings with her friends, her Pilates group, the quiet happy life she's built around herself in her small village. No one there knows. And I remember too how, like me, at the end of every day, she goes home to an empty house. Her friends are all she has. If the truth came out, things would change for her. Could she handle that again?

If I do this I could ruin all of that for Mum. But then what? Never take a job in the spotlight for fear that our secret comes out, our dirty secret? Agree to stay quiet, stay hidden until when? I feel the burn of injustice in my chest.

"Wait, Em. Does whoever offered you the post know who you are?"

*Who I am?* I take a breath before answering. "Yeah."

"Em, why would they choose you for this job if they knew what happened in Norfolk? I thought they *didn't* want a media circus—"

I cut him off. "They don't, Joe. And for the record, they chose me because I'm bloody good at my job. Okay? And they were concerned it might be a problem for me."

"I know you're good at your job. But who are these people?" He holds my gaze, questioningly, insistently. He's not going to let this go. "You don't know their motives on this. They must have chosen you for a reason—plenty of other people are good at their jobs."

I take a breath. "I was recommended. Look, Joe, are you asking me not to do this?" I say it with a calm I don't feel. My heart hammering. "Because it's not just this job that you're asking me not to do, is it, Joe? I'd have to turn down *any* job that puts me in the spotlight. I'd have to turn down anything high profile, wouldn't I, because if I wander out into the light then the spotlight shines onto all of us, doesn't it?" I hear myself saying it. Oh God, I didn't mean to turn this conversation into *that* conversation. I feel a rush of remorse. "Sorry, Joe, I don't know why I'm taking this out on you. It's ridiculous, sorry. I just—I want this. I can't *know* that I'm good enough and then just walk away. What happened was *not* our fault. Why should we have to spend the rest of our lives paying for it?"

He takes a moment before replying. "Look, Em. You shouldn't ever hold yourself back because of it. But—" He stops himself and shakes his head.

"But what, Joe? Say it."

"But"—he continues very carefully—"and I say

this because I love you, Em, and you know I do—you need to ask yourself *why* you need this so much. Why you *need* the spotlight. Just ask yourself what you're so desperately looking for. If it's even out there. If you go back to Norfolk, I'll deal with Mum, don't worry about that. I'll explain it to her and she'll be okay with it, I promise. But you really need to try to understand why you're going back at all. What you're looking for there."

"None of this is about Norfolk, Joe, I'd go wherever the job was. I wish it wasn't there, obviously, but I'm not going to let that stop me. And it's not like I have a lot of reasons to stay here in London. I want more than all this. For myself. For my career. I'm really good at what I do, Joe, and I'm going to help this man. That's why I'm going."

He studies me, concern in his warm eyes. "First be very sure you know who exactly it is you're helping, Em."

# 9

## THE MAN

### DAY 1—THE SEARCH BEGINS

Back at the beach a silence falls between police officers Poole and Graceford.

It's Graceford who speaks first. "Don't worry, I'll talk to them." She nods back toward Mike and Zara, who have now made their way from the dunes to meet them. Graceford gives Poole a rallying clap on the arm as she passes. She'll take over.

Poole hears their voices behind him but thankfully their words are just out of his earshot. He turns to see how Zara's taking it. Her usually beautiful face is pulled into a tight pinch as Graceford speaks. Poole turns away. Zara has always had a problem with Graceford.

A car door slams; he turns to look and Mike is in the car now, Zara still leaning on her car door, half in, half out, nodding reasonably. She smiles sweetly at Graceford before swiveling into the driver's seat and slamming the door closed.

Zara's car rolls with pointed slowness out of the car park past them.

Gone. No goodbye then, Poole thinks.

"So?" he asks as Graceford rejoins him.

"So," she answers flatly, and changes the subject. "What do you think about the man on the beach?" She avoids Poole's gaze, casting her own back toward the sea path.

At best she's trying to keep things professional, at worst sparing his feelings.

He tries again. "What did she say?" He gestures out in the direction of the long-gone car.

Graceford clears her throat, looks away again. If she's honest with herself, the nuances of other people's relationships have never really been her strong suit. But she understands that she is expected, in this type of situation, to give some kind of response to Chris's question. She's supposed to have some kind of opinion. Reluctantly, she obliges.

"She said, 'Sure, no problem, Officer.' I mean, what else is she going to say to me? I'm a police officer. And she's breaking the law."

Officer Poole looks down at the loose gravel of the car park and sees his pale feet blueing in the January air. Shit.

"They've been warned, Chris," Graceford continues. "No one at the station cares if she's your wife, and I don't either. She can't keep doing it, Chris, she's wasting police time." Graceford shifts uncomfortably. She can't tell if she's said too much; Poole's still staring down at the ground. "They're breaking the law and they keep doing it."

Poole raises his head. "I know, Beth! I know. Believe me, I know that. But I've said to her, you've heard me say to her! Haven't you?"

Beth Graceford nods and looks away.

Poole knows that means the conversation is over.

He clears his throat and pulls himself together.

"Okay. Okay! Right," he says, changing his tone,

"let's get going, shall we? That beach isn't going to search itself. Is that spare uniform still in the boot of the patrol car?"

Graceford nods. "Neil's spare uniform? Yeah, course it is."

A mischievous smile plays across Chris's face. "Remind me why he kept it there?" he asks as, barefoot, he follows Graceford gingerly across the gravel.

"You know this, Chris. In case someone vomited on him." She intones knowing full well where this line of inquiry is heading. She pops open the hatchback.

Graceford had previously been partnered with Sergeant Neil Jarvis for the first five months of her posting on the Norfolk coast.

Chris's grin broadens. "In case someone vomited on him! That happen a lot, did it? Enough to warrant the extra uniform?"

"Yeah, it did actually, Chris. It happened to Neil an above-average amount of times. So, yeah, it did warrant the extra uniform," Graceford says with the weary authority of a recurrent eyewitness.

"Okay, then." Poole nods mock-sagely. "Fair enough in that case, I suppose."

She rummages around in the back of the car. "Not sure why he left it, though. Maybe 'cause of all the vomit that's been on it? Size nine boot okay?"

"Hmph, guess they'll have to be." Chris takes the boots and, leaning against the patrol car to brush the gravel from his feet, he slides his sockless feet into their cold leather. "I suppose we should go look for this guy's stuff then. What do you reckon his story is? Homeless? Attempted suicide?"

"Nah, neither, I don't think. He didn't look homeless."

Chris nods. "No, he didn't." Chris wouldn't ever

say it out loud, but he'd been surprised, the guy had been good-looking—well, all-right-looking, for a bloke. Not that good-looking guys didn't try to commit suicide too, he supposed.

Graceford locks the car. "It all had a bit of a weird vibe, don't you think? I don't know. Anyway, let's see what we can find." She sighs. It's a big stretch of beach. "I'll call it in and you make a start, Chris."

Chris climbs to the crest of the dune and the wide flat expanse of Holkham Beach spreads into view. It's even windier up here. Still, he can hear the sound of his own heartbeat in his ears from the exertion. Inside his new boots his toes are reluctantly coming back to life.

He can see right out to the offshore wind farm a mile out to sea, the monolithic forest of turbine arms rotating with the weight of the North Sea wind. He closes his eyes and sucks in a deep breath, then lets it out.

Best make a start, he decides. He opens his eyes and scans the landscape, looking for anything the man might have left behind. A pile of warm clothes, a bag.

But there isn't anything. Nothing but outcrops of seaweed littering the beach, dark clumps of debris washed to shore. It's hard to pick out details from this distance; it's possible any one of them could be clothes, perhaps, shoes, a rucksack containing a wallet or a phone or keys.

He turns back to Graceford, still on the edge of the forest path, radio in hand. He can't hear what she's saying but he watches her mouth move. She's probably talking about Zara, about Zara and Mike. About how the local press always seem to arrive suspiciously early these days, just after a police call goes out, in fact.

Chris wishes he'd never mentioned the whole thing to Zara in the first place.

They'd been at home watching a Netflix true crime; he'd been trying to impress her and he'd stupidly mentioned that it was, in fact, possible to hack into the UK police radio system too. It was just a stupid passing comment, he'd been showing off. That had been about a month ago now, but after they'd binge-watched that show, Zara had started showing up places right after Chris got there. And it hadn't been only Chris's callouts either. Other people had started to notice too.

He hadn't asked outright how she was doing it, because he didn't want her to tell him, because then he would definitely have to arrest her. Which wouldn't be great after only a year of marriage. God knows how she got hold of the illegal radio equipment she must be using.

He watches Graceford in the distance.

But what can he do? It's hard not to speak to the press when you wake up next to it, he thinks. When it crawls all over you in its expensive underwear. When you do your morning pee while it brushes its teeth. It's hard not to talk to the press when it looks like Zara and you're married to it.

Best to focus on the job at hand. Finding out who this guy is. Graceford looks up from the walkie-talkie and sees him staring. She raises her hand. A thumbs-up.

It's okay for now, Chris decides. Maybe he'll try another chat with Zara tonight.

He looks at the beach, at the dark clumps scattered along its two-mile stretch, and makes his way down the steep dune to the first one.

# 10

## DR. EMMA LEWIS

### DAY 7—INTO THE WOODS

It's a long drive to Norfolk, but the morning traffic loosens after London and cool January sunlight streams across the miles of empty English countryside as they roll past my car window. As I get closer, motorways turn into A-roads, then B-roads, and soon I'm winding right out onto the coastal way flanked on one side by ancient oak forest and on the other side by the vast planes of salty beach marshes that stretch out into the North Sea.

I collected the rental car early this morning; someone from Peter Chorley's office arranged it, it's all been made very easy for me. I just have to follow the reassuring voice of the satellite navigation toward the accommodation someone else has booked for me in Norfolk.

Above the glittering wet marshes, flocks of birds soar as I drive past, thousands of black pixels continually reconfiguring against the crisp blue winter sky, always almost on the verge of making sense. I crack my window and let the scent of the countryside roll in. Salt sea air, mixed with warm earthy forest mulch, and on its edges, the rich scent of bonfire. It hits me before I can anticipate it, the memory. The smell of burning leaves in the cold air, the crackle and spark. I try not to think of it and the sharp sad ache that always comes with the memory. I close the window and blast the heater on.

When I get to the postcode Peter emailed me all I can do is pull up on the verge of the B-road and stare at it, engine burring along, indicator clicking out time—it's not what I expected, but the GPS reassures me I have reached my destination. I don't know what I was expecting exactly, perhaps sterile student digs or a room in the hospital's on-site student-nurse accommodation.

In front of the car sits a little wooden sign. The sign points off of the main road and down a thin graveled track leading into the heart of the woods. The sign, at a slight angle, reads CUCKOO LODGE.

*Hmph. Okay.*

No one mentioned that name in the email, which is slightly strange. But then, everything about this situation has been strange so far, so why break with tradition?

Luckily, there's no other traffic on the main road, so I have a moment alone to reassess. I turn off the engine and scroll through Peter's texts to check the postcode again. Did he mention a Cuckoo Lodge in his text message? His email gives only the satnav coordinates and the address: 1 Market Lane. I look up at the gravel lane through the windshield. Is that Market Lane? It definitely doesn't look like it leads to market. Unless it's a market in the woods. Did I type the postcode in wrong? I check the satnav postcode against the text info. No, it's all correct.

I look down the bumpy little lane again. Dark

woods rise high on both sides. It's literally in the middle of nowhere.

*This can't be right, can it?*

Why would Peter put me here? I mean, it's not exactly near the hospital, or accessible in terms of local amenities, is it? I'd better make sure I stock up food if this is it because the nearest village, Wells-next-the-Sea, is a good twenty minutes' drive from here.

*But there's only one way to find out if this is it, I suppose.*

I restart the car, check my rearview mirror, and bump down off of the tarmac and onto the crunchy gravel of the lane. *One Market Lane, here I come.*

I'm sure there's a reason Peter's put me in the middle of nowhere. I guess he wants me as far from the media, and therefore the hospital, as possible. It makes sense. I'll certainly be safely tucked away from the Princess Margaret Hospital. And I'd be lying if I said I hadn't been slightly worried about ending up near Holt, near our old family home.

It's impossible to say what effect seeing the old house would have. I haven't been back there since it happened. We didn't even go back for our things at the time; they wouldn't let us.

I won't go back now either, if I can avoid it.

I decide Peter must have partly chosen this location on my behalf. He'll have put me here so I don't even have to drive past my old home every day. Good old Peter.

I let down the window again; I need to wake up. The breeze flows in, bringing the scent of wet earth and dead leaves with it; no more bonfircs for now.

The lane is longer than I had expected. The tall trees flank my car on both sides. The forest beyond on either side is dense. I'm right in the heart of the

Norfolk National Nature Reserve; these woods go on for miles in either direction.

I catch a rustling motion in the undergrowth beside the car as it crackles along the gravel. At least no one can sneak up on you out here, which is reassuring—you'd definitely hear them coming.

A bird bursts from the woods to my right, soaring high across the track ahead, and then I see it. Cuckoo Lodge. The lane ahead opens out into a small clearing where the house looms, majestic, framed by forest.

It's unexpectedly beautiful, placed right in the center of the dark clearing at the end of the long lane, an intricate little red-brick house hidden in the woods. A neo-Gothic Victorian dream with a wood gable over its front door, chocolate-box chimney stacks, and an engraved York stone plaque between its two uppermost windows, commemorating the date it was built. I squint up through the windshield but it's too far away to read yet. I shiver and close the car window. There's a chill in the air now.

The building might be the most perfectly symmetrical thing I've ever seen, a gingerbread house made real, its dark windows reflecting the sky. There's a low wooden fence encircling the house at waist height, a small hinged gate at its center.

I pull the car up to the left of the clearing, as close to the grass verge as I can. It feels rude parking here but I don't know where else to go, the road simply stops outside the house. I turn off the engine.

Silence floods the car; I let it soak in for a moment before popping the door and stepping out. Now that I'm closer I see the stone plaque reads CUCKOO LODGE, 1837.

*Eighteen thirty-seven, that's weird.* I don't know many historical dates but I do know that this was the year the young Queen Victoria succeeded to the throne. Which is bizarre because off the top of my head the only other historical dates I know are 1066 and 1492! And it suddenly occurs to me how strange it is that someone who specializes in other people's histories knows so very little about actual history.

I look up at the house that is nearly two centuries old. It's impressive. I definitely wouldn't be able to afford this in London.

But then, I'm not entirely sure I would want to. I try not to think it, but standing there in front of it, it's hard not to feel that there is something slightly peculiar about it, some strange quality.

If I had to describe it, I would say it feels like the house is watching me.

I know, it's a ridiculous thing to say, obviously, I know that. In fact, I probably know that better than most people would, because I know the exact neurological reasons my brain is thinking that.

I know it's just a trick of the mind.

You know that feeling you get sometimes of being watched, of somehow knowing before you know, that someone is watching you? Well, it's a neurological phenomenon called blindsight. It's a completely normal feeling, a simple evolutionary process, perfectly explicable.

Blindsight describes the process of seeing things that you weren't consciously aware you were even noticing. It's just the subconscious processing of visual stimuli. A lot of the things we process day-to-day bypass our conscious minds; they get processed subconsciously, but, to us, it seems as if we are just getting a funny feeling.

I know the reason I feel like the house is watching me is because as I drove up to it steadily in the car my subconscious brain was tricked into thinking the house was slowly looming toward me. My brain decided the house was getting closer to me rather than me getting closer to it. It's why tracking shots in horror movies work so well on audiences.

I know it's the silence, the darkness of the woods, and the unusual surroundings all compounding, on a subconscious level, to leave me with a feeling of unease. It's just my instincts doing their job. Sometimes they're right, sometimes they're wrong, but where would we be without them?

I know *why* the hairs on the backs of my arms are raised, but a part of me still can't help but wonder if the house in front of me *is* actually watching me.

I find the key exactly where Peter's email tells me to look, under the leg of the bench by the door. I slide it into the lock and the door creaks open in front of me.

Inside is just as beautiful as outside. Deep plush sofas. Persian rugs and polished wood. I could definitely get used to this.

I wander from room to artfully curated room and wonder who on earth is funding all this. This is a nice house. This is an expensive house.

But then I remember that the first choice for this assignment was Richard Groves. And Richard Groves doesn't exactly work pro bono. My employers were probably expecting to plow a fair amount into this anyway and I'm definitely the cheaper option. Maybe me staying here has nothing to do with Peter Chorley protecting me. Maybe whoever organized the accommodation arrangements just couldn't be bothered to rebook.

The house is fully stocked. There are flowers in vases in every room. In the white-tiled Victorian kitchen, the fridge is full of supplies.

There's a printout from Peter on the kitchen counter next to a neat stack of the patient's medical files and press cuttings. Whoever opened the house up earlier today and did all this must have dropped this off too.

I read.

*Dearest Emma,*

*I hope the accommodation is acceptable and to your liking. I apologize for the remote location and distance from the hospital but I'm sure you will appreciate the need. Thus far the case has attracted quite a bit of media interest and we've found them to be both persistent and invasive.*

*We have, however, supplied you with most basic amenities—food, household necessities, Wi-Fi, and some other bits and pieces to help you settle in. Let me know should you require anything else.*

*I've instructed the hospital staff to supply copies of all medical files pertaining to the patient. I know you've been sent the scans already, but if you're anything like me I'm sure you'd much rather have something solid to study at this stage.*

*We've also left you cuttings of all the major news articles that have come out surrounding his story, as you expressed concerns around the effect they may have on the patient himself. And of course, as you mentioned, as hard as we all try, a hospital is not a closed system.*

*There are a few eyewitness stories prior to admission that may be of interest, in terms of narrowing down this man's prior movements, but I'll leave all that to you. We can also arrange for you to meet with any of the patient's current caregivers or anyone else close to the case you may think it helpful to speak to.*

*As I stressed in our last phone call, budget is not an issue. Please don't see it as an impediment to expediting a diagnosis.*

*And, again, if you need any assistance from the local authorities in terms of relevant information, then please come through me and I can oil the cogs, as it were. The last thing we want is local red tape clogging up the process.*

*And, whilst of course this case is time-sensitive, with taxpayers' money/patience being a notably finite resource (!), we don't want you yourself to feel rushed. Our primary concern is a* solid *diagnosis—there is no room for error here. Avoiding a situation in Norfolk similar to the publicity disaster in Kent is paramount; we have no desire for this to escalate.*

*So, that being said, whatever you need and whatever we can do to facilitate a quick, clear, and watertight diagnosis and corresponding treatment plan for this particular patient will be entirely at your disposal.*

*You have my direct number. Feel free to contact me any time, night or day—I'll be available. I am your first port of call should you need outside assistance.*

*Best of luck,*
*Peter M. Chorley*

Excellent. No pressure then.

# 11

# THE MAN

## DAY 1—CHOSEN

Rhoda looks down at her patient on the gurney as they roll out into the ward. "Right, you," she says with a smile. "Apologies in advance for my driving skills. It's going to be touch-and-go for the paintwork but you should be just fine. Hold on tight."

A muted smile plays across the man's face and he gently closes his eyes. He's tired—he hadn't realized how tired until now.

Around them, he hears the ebb and flow of the emergency department. He opens his eyes and catches brief snapshots of other people's lives as he's wheeled past cubicles. Half glimpsed through curtains he sees an elderly woman sobbing; he turns his head away. An Indian man is gasping into a handheld mask, then it's on to a plump little girl laughing and bouncing on her father's bed as he lies watching her, smiling. The next curtain is closed; only a rasped groan emanating from within. He squeezes his eyes shut and pulls down his oxygen mask, breathing in his first breath of disinfected hospital air, with its hint of something earthier at the edges.

Rhoda glides them smoothly and skillfully down the corridor and into the elevator. The white noise of the hospital muffled as the elevator doors close. Rhoda allows herself a moment; she rests her eyes too, letting the night and morning that was slide off her. When she opens her eyes, the man on the gurney is staring up at her, as beatific as a grazing cow. She smiles. *You caught me.*

The elevator pings and its bulky doors open; the sounds of life flood back in.

At the Radiology nurses' station Rhoda has a soft conversation with the ward sister. It's quieter up here, calmer.

They look over at the man. The ward sister nods and calls over two nurses' aides in forest-green tunics. There is a brief exchange, then Rhoda wanders back to her patient on the gurney. "Right, handsome." She smiles. "I am going to have to leave you now with these two very charming gentlemen." She points to the aides. "They are going to help get you all scanned and sorted out, okay?"

But it's not okay.

The patient's eyes swivel to take in the aides; they look bored, tired, gray. They do not look like they care. The man's breath quickens, panic rises. They do not look like Rhoda. They do not have the same look in their eyes.

The man's hand shoots out and grasps Rhoda's wrist, not roughly but firmly.

*Do not leave me. Please.*

Rhoda jumps slightly, ever so slightly, at the suddenness of the motion. But manages to let out a quick laugh to cover her surprise.

"Oh, okay? Not a big fan of that idea then?" she chuckles. She looks around at the aides.

When she looks back, the patient is shaking his

head forcibly against the pillow, wincing at the pain of it.

"No, no. Stop that. Look, it's fine," she reassures him. "These nice men are going to look after you just as good as me. I promise. Look at those lovely faces, how could you not trust those faces?"

The man blinks obediently at the two faces, placid and ghoulish in the hospital strip lighting.

Rhoda leans in closer. "I got to get gone. I shouldn't have come up here with you in the first place, but if I get back now I can let everyone know where I am. I might even avoid a talking-to. Would you let me do that? Would you help me out?"

He looks at her beseechingly. She loosens his hand from her wrist, gently, and he lets her. She places his hand deftly back down under the blankets, pats it once, and smiles. "Okay then, I will see you later," she promises.

As she turns to go a lot of things happen at once. The man struggles to sit up, reaching out after Rhoda, but seeing the sudden movement, the aides break into a sprint. They grab the man, pushing him roughly back down onto the gurney, restraining him.

Rhoda turns back and a doctor rounds the corner just as the man's shouts begin. Rhoda stands there, frozen, helpless as her patient thrashes against the restraint of the two men. He arches his back away from the bed, part held, part scrambling to get away. The doctor joins the melee, carefully trying to disconnect the patient's IV, which is dangerously close to being ripped from the man's arm in the struggle.

"Nurse!" he barks at Rhoda.

She gasps and she begins to step forward, then remembers that her shift is over. Technically, she shouldn't even be here. She holds back a moment, watching the doctor's hopeless attempts to pacify her patient. "Sir?" he says. "Sir, I'm going to need you to calm down please. Sir!"

Rhoda takes a breath and makes a decision. She pushes her way back to the gurney, leans over to look down at the struggling man's face. Then, carefully, she places both hands on either side of his head, a hand on each cheek. Seeing her, he stops struggling.

"Easy now. Easy now," she croons. She slips his oxygen mask back over his mouth and nose.

It's just the two of them. The rest of the scene disappears. The whoosh of air in his oxygen mask. His heartbeat thundering in his ears.

The patient lets his body relax back into the thin mattress beneath him. He breathes. He looks up into Rhoda's warm brown eyes and blinks.

"Look," the doctor says, "I know it's not your department and I know your shift's over, but this will all be so much easier with you here. It just will. I don't know how we're going to get him in the scanner otherwise. We'd need another two members of staff just to hold him down. If I ring down to Triage and let them know what's happening, will you stay for the scan?"

Rhoda peers over the doctor's shoulder. The clock on the wall behind him reads 8:37. She's missed the handover in Triage anyway. And Annie will figure out what's happened if she's a couple of hours late to pick up Coco. It should be fine.

Rhoda stays.

The man lies quietly in the creamy bulk of the CT scanner as it swirls around him. He breathes as Rhoda told him to. He tries to remain calm. He thinks of Rhoda's face looking down at him earlier. He knows she's not the one, not the one he's looking for, but she's all he has right now. He lies motionless as the machine accelerates around him, the sound of an airplane pounding down the runway seconds from catching the air and taking flight. A sound memory that seems to have no source as he interrogates it further. He squeezes his eyes shut tighter and tries not to think about everything else he can't remember. He tries to clear his mind.

The man is retracted from the machine by a whir of mechanisms. Rhoda lifts his head from the plastic frame and gently removes his earplugs. With the help of a female radiology nurse they transfer him back to his trolley.

Behind the glass of the suite the radiologist stares down at the images loading up onto his screen. The shadowy slopes and ridges of the patient's brain tissue mapping out digitally before him. His eyes trip quickly, darting over the images as he looks for diffusion, patches of nebulous white, which could be signs of a stroke. Or a cranial bleed. Either could explain the patient's erratic behavior after a head wound.

No diffusion, no bleeds.

But there. A tiny flare of white. Something. Maybe.

A neurologist is summoned. This man is older, his movements slower as he leans in and studies the scan.

"Ah, interesting," he says. But he does not sound interested. "I think we should call Dr. Carver, actually," he says, removing his glasses. "This is more his sort of thing. Carver will have a better idea. Best page him." He smiles a placatory smile and leaves.

The man on the gurney is moved onto a temporary open ward with five other patients. Rhoda makes him as comfortable as she can. He looks across at her sitting next to his bed, the ward bustling around them, patients in various stages of illness and recovery going about their bedbound days.

Rhoda gives her patient a quiet smile; he smiles back. And that is when the man three beds down starts to shout.

And what happens next happens very quickly.

# 12

## DR. EMMA LEWIS

### DAY 7—IN THE DARK

The winter light starts to fade outside Cuckoo Lodge.

I perch on the front garden bench watching as the sun dips beneath the densely packed treetops. Smears of pinks and peaches streak the sky and the forest is full of evening birdsong. I check my watch: four-thirty, much earlier than I would have expected sunset to be, but then, it's been a while since I've seen an actual sunset. At this time of day, I'm usually stuck deep within the bleached white bowels of an overlit hospital. The cold from the flagstones underfoot is beginning to seep up through the wool of my fisherman socks. A shiver runs through me. I wrap the cashmere blanket I brought out tighter around me. I suppose I'd better go inside. I gather my things and start to head in. I throw a glance out into the close-packed forest, the tangle of branches just visible between trees, the murk beyond. A Rorschach test in the woods.

It got dark so quick. And no one wants to be alone in the forest, in the dark, that's for damn sure.

---

Time to turn on some lights. I lock the door and flit from one room to the next, flicking on lights, their warm glow creating company of sorts.

Next I set about getting a fire going. The woodstove in the living room is beautifully stacked and ready to be lit, the handiwork of some poor assistant, no doubt, along with the fully stocked fridge. I needn't have worried about running short of supplies out here. I'm basically a bear ready to settle in for winter.

And for some reason I've also been supplied with my own brand-new wellies. I found them box-fresh waiting by the back door. God knows how they knew my size. Actually, now that I come to think of it, they probably got that information from the hospital, which has my scrub sizes. Someone has really thought of everything. Peter and whoever. I suppose, as far as Peter's concerned, the less reason I have to leave the house, the better.

The fire crackles to life, leaping from paper to lighter brick to kindling. I close the woodstove's door, then go in search of Peter's "Welcome" half-bottle of wine in the kitchen. Just to warm me. Just to settle those first-night nerves and send me off to sleep at a sensible hour. Because, God knows, tomorrow is going to be one hell of a first day at work.

I curl up on the Persian rug in front of the flames, glass in hand, and sip my wine, the patient's medical records spread out all around me.

There's a lot to go through, yet as I sit there surrounded by the sea of papers, the case feels more manageable somehow, like a puzzle that I might actually be able to solve, piece by piece, a thousand-piece jigsaw that just needs time and focus. My patient a tangled knot to be gently loosened. Peter was right, I do prefer working with hard copies. I like being able to see what I have.

I pore over the test results again, eyes flicking from the patient's CT scans and the newer MRI scans on my laptop, to printouts of blood tests, cerebrospinal fluid analysis, virology reports, and hormone levels.

A clearer medical picture is starting to form of my patient. Just the edges at the moment, but the tests and scans he's already undergone show me the faintest outline of something already.

Here's what I know. His brain is not physically damaged—that much is evident. The concussion he arrived with a week ago has left no lasting damage. There are other potential physiological causes that could be in some way responsible, which I can and will start testing for tomorrow. He may suffer from epilepsy or a nutritional deficiency; he may suffer from a non-related condition that requires medication, the side effects of which could somehow be responsible for his memory loss. Testing for outlying conditions would certainly be worthwhile. I jot down a quick list of possible tests in my notepad. Some screenings we'll have to send away for results. Princess Margaret Hospital, where I'm heading tomorrow, isn't big; its resources are acceptable, but they're nowhere near London standards.

The tiny fleck I noticed when Peter first showed me the CT scan is clearer on these new MRI scans. Pituitary cysts aren't uncommon. Most people can live and die without ever even knowing they have a cyst on their pituitary gland; these cysts only tend to get found accidentally when doctors are scanning for other things, and are rarely a cause for concern. However, if this cyst had recently fluctuated in size and exerted pressure on a neighboring area of the brain, it could be in some way responsible. But it's unlikely. The area of the brain responsible for memory retrieval, the hippocampus, is nowhere near the pituitary, so I'm not sure exactly how the cyst could directly affect it. But it's certainly strange that other fugue cases have had similar growths. Something to look into further. I note it down. The speck is something to monitor but, at this stage, I'm happy to put it on the reserve bench in terms of possible causes and instead consider it a potential symptom, or anomaly.

If I'm totally honest I'm already erring on the side of this not being a physiological condition. The scans show the patient's hardware is intact. If he were a computer and you took him to the Apple Genius Bar, they'd tell you it's a software problem.

So, assuming the patient's hardware isn't broken, then we're looking at a software problem. Psychological trauma.

And mental trauma isn't that unusual a cause of memory loss. Post-traumatic stress disorder being the prime example; whether it's soldiers back from war or children in the care system, PTSD is a lot more common than people think.

Up until fairly recently, in medical terms at least, the general wisdom was that psychosomatic illnesses were controlled by the sufferers. As if somehow the patient could just "pull themselves together" and then they'd miraculously recover and return to their normal lives. These days we know better. Psychosomatic illnesses are software errors, not *user* errors. If a patient's memory loss is due to psychological trauma, he would have about as much control over his illness as you would have over a system failure on your laptop. No matter how much you wanted those wiped family photos back, they are locked in that old hard drive and you're going to need a lot of patience and a pretty pricey specialist to help you get them out of it.

I take another sip of wine. The good news is that memory loss caused by psychological trauma is often only temporary. It tends to return over time once the real or perceived threat is removed. Patients slowly begin to regain memories—the trick is making sure the patient is in a safe and therapeutic environment when those memories, good and bad, do resurface. Or the consequences can be troubling.

A week ago, something very bad may have happened to this man. If he's been through intense trauma, then hopefully, now that he has some distance from it, we should be in a position to help him remember what happened. Or, at the very least, help him move on from it.

I start to draw up my plan of action for tomorrow. I need to be prepared. This is important, for me and for him. We can't afford to mess this up, not with the whole country watching. My pen glides fast in wide loops and curls across my yellow legal pad as I pour out my ideas.

The low lights in the living room flicker.

I glance up at the lamp nearest me. It glows steadily. But there was a flicker before, I'm sure of it. A break in the electric current. I stare at the bulb. It flickers again, like a moth against glass, then all the lights in the room and through the hallway flicker back in response. *Oh no. No, no, no. Not the lights . . .*

And as if the thought were a wish, the whole house plunges into darkness.

*It's just the fuse box,* I tell myself. *Houses aren't haunted, people are.*

The edges of the room are no longer visible; armchairs, bookcases, and cushions have been swallowed up into the darkness. The kitchen is nothing more than a black void beyond the archway. Only the firelight remains, carving deep shadows into the space.

My pulse is racing high and fast in my chest. Jesus. There is only darkness all around me.

These things happen all the time in the countryside, I tell myself. These things happen all the time in remote cottages deep in the woods.

It takes my eyes a fraction of a second to adjust to the light of the fire.

I hear a noise outside, low and animalistic, a creature, a fox perhaps. I look to the patio doors, suddenly keenly aware of all the life outside this cottage. I realize that up until this moment I've been lit up like a Christmas tree in here, exposed for all to see. But in the dark glass I see only myself. My own ghostly face looking back at me, reflected, flickering in firelight. I quiet my breath and listen again for noises outside; I listen so hard the room buzzes with silence and the popping fire.

It's just a power failure. *Grow up, Em.*

I'd better find a flashlight and the fuse box and hope it's just that. If it's not, then it looks like I'll be heading to bed. I know from experience that you can't do anything useful after dark during a power outage.

I find a flashlight under the sink in the kitchen and head for the basement.

My mind creeps back to Holt again, to our old house. The staircase downstairs into the dark, the glow of a light from the study, the sound of dripping. I shake the memory away, shuddering.

It's colder in the basement, the air damper. Shadows leap and dance at the corners of my vision. I remember the thick pooling of dark arterial blood, from long ago, the sound of breath rasping behind me.

*Stop it, Em. Stop it.*

I throw the switch on the electric panel and the house leaps back to life. The darkness vanishes and I'm standing in a basement laundry room. No spiderwebs and rot here, just appliances and laundry detergent.

I guess I overloaded the circuit turning on all those lights. Lesson learned.

# 13

# THE MAN

## DAY 1—MR. GARRETT

Rhoda watches as the situation unfolds.

There was nothing out of the ordinary about him at first, just another patient sleeping three beds down from Rhoda and her patient. He woke and shuffled awkwardly up to sitting, under the covers, his bleary eyes taking in the ward around him, perplexed.

A young nurse along the ward noticed him waking too; her eyes flicked out toward the corridor, apprehensive, before she made her way over to the waking man.

Rhoda watches as the young nurse places a gentle hand on her patient. He frowns. "Where is she?" Rhoda hears him ask the nurse, his eyes scanning the beds around them. "Where's Claire?"

Rhoda doesn't hear the young nurse's reply but she recognizes the expression on her face as she quietly speaks to the older man.

Rhoda knows that bereavement notice needs to take place in a private consultation suite, with a doctor or with a member of the bereavement care team.

You can't give it on the ward. The young nurse will be asking her patient to wait for the doctor to arrive.

"I don't need the doctor." His voice is tight and hoarse, a trill of panic running through it. "I just need to know where my daughter is."

Rhoda remembers his details from the Triage board last night. A car accident. A drunk-driving collision. The drunk driver had walked away with only bruises, but this man and his teenage daughter had sustained severe injuries. Rhoda's eyes float up to the name on the whiteboard above his bed. Mike Garrett.

Although she can't hear the nurse's words, it's clear to Rhoda from the nurse's body language that the daughter didn't make it. Rhoda feels a deep ache in her chest. The worst news to give, the worst news to get.

"I don't need a doctor to tell me where she is, *you* can tell me. For God's sake, just look on your system or something. You can tell me that, can't you?" A few more eyes swivel onto the scene. "I want to know where my daughter is! Do you understand? I DON'T CARE IF THE DOCTOR'S ON HIS WAY!"

Hearing a raised voice, the duty nurse pops her head around the ward doorway and quickly makes sense of the scene. She makes a decision and calmly heads over to join the young nurse at the red-faced Mr. Garrett's bedside.

"Can I help, Mr. Garrett?" she asks, her tone kind, delicate.

"Yes, I want to know where my daughter is."

The duty nurse takes a breath and looks down, and when she looks up at him again his breath catches in his throat. Finally, he sees in front of him what Rhoda sees, two impotent nurses trying not to tell him that his daughter died from her injuries.

"Oh God. Oh God." He tries to choke back the sobs, wild eyes unseeing. "She's gone, isn't she? My God."

The duty nurse gives the younger nurse a look and starts to curtain off the bed. "I'm sorry, Mr. Garrett. I'm so sorry. If you can just wait until the doctor gets here, we can—"

But Mr. Garrett is already pulling back his sheets. He staggers up out of bed onto unsteady feet.

"No, no, no. I wanna know where the bastard is. Tell me where the guy is who did this to her. Where is he? Is he here?" Mr. Garrett turns around, taking in all the patient-filled beds on the ward. "You wouldn't be stupid enough to put him here, would you?"

Everyone on the ward is watching now.

"Mr. Garrett! I'm going to ask you to return to your bed, or I'll have to call security." The duty nurse throws a look to the young nurse behind her, who turns to leave.

"Don't you dare! If you do, God help me!"

A sharp burst of fear shoots through Rhoda. Her eyes widen, pupils dilate, her breath catches and holds, her posture stiffens. This is the thing that the quiet man lying next to her in his hospital bed notices. He turns his eyes away from the scene and back to her.

But Rhoda does not notice. Rhoda is transfixed by the scene playing out as the hospital-gowned man strides farther into the ward toward their end, his wild eyes gliding over patients.

Rhoda's gaze flicks back to the young nurse's face. She's biting her bottom lip, eyes furiously calculating her options. Rhoda can see it coming before the young nurse knows herself. She's going to make a break for it. She's going to run for security.

Her body tenses and then she bolts. She flies out into the corridor, around the corner and out of sight.

The man spins at the movement and yells out after her but she's gone. Suddenly vulnerable and feeling the exposure of his situation, he looks around him for the closest thing he can use to protect himself when security arrives. He lunges toward the nearest patient bedside cabinet and grabs a ribbon-festooned gift bottle of whisky. He grasps it tight, knuckles whitening as he raises it like a club, its warm caramel liquid gleaming as it sloshes inside.

The duty nurse takes a step back. "Please, try to stay calm, Mr. Garrett. . . . If we could just—"

But Mr. Garrett turns from her, disinterested. He steps farther into the ward, squinting intently to read the small whiteboards above the beds. Looking for a specific name. Rhoda shifts forward ever so slightly in her chair. Somebody should call out. Shout for help. Perhaps she should, but that could just escalate things. She darts a glance out into the hall, for someone, anyone.

She needs to act, she thinks. She takes a breath and starts to rise from her chair—but a movement comes from the bed next to her. Her patient is sitting up; he looks at her not panicked, not concerned, and shakes his head. *No. Not you.*

She frowns. He is telling her not to intervene.

Mr. Garrett has reached their end of the ward. He scans the names, the faces below them. Rhoda and her patient look to each other as his gaze falls on them. Rhoda's patient looks her serenely in the eyes and she doesn't move. She heeds his advice and Mr. Garrett turns away. He turns and starts to walk away.

Suddenly someone breaks through the small crowd of people by the door, a young male nurse, making a run at the armed man. Other bystanders move back to clear his path. Mr. Garrett's eyes flare and unthinkingly he reaches out, snatching at the nearest body, a man in his seventies, frail, wearing a Fair Isle sweater many sizes too large for him. The whisky bottle crashes to the floor, shattering, splashing glass and richly scented alcohol across the ward. The old man drops his shiny new magazine with the shock of it and it lands with a loud slap on the wet hospital linoleum. Mr. Garrett holds him roughly in front of him as a kind of shield, and the approaching male nurse stutters to a halt.

"This isn't what I wanted, you know," Mr. Garrett tells the ward. It comes out shakily, off-key. "I just, I just want—argh!" He squeezes his eyes shut hard to think. "He killed my little girl. She was fifteen," he tells no one in particular. He's crying now, fat wet streaks down his anguished face. The old man trapped in his arms scans the surrounding faces searching for a clue to his fate, still held tight in the hold.

"He killed her. And what? He gets to survive? No, he doesn't get to go home! I have to bury her! No, he doesn't get to survive, and go home and live his life! You tell me where he is. Or I'll find him myself. SHE WAS FIFTEEN, FOR CHRIST'S SAKE."

The duty nurse looks across to the male nurse. She shakes her head.

The male nurse swallows, straightening his shoulders before speaking carefully. He's new and young and totally out of his depth. "It looks like the man you might be talking about has already been discharged, sir. Earlier this morning, so . . ." He doesn't know what else to say but it doesn't matter. Mr. Garrett seems to crumple inside.

He releases the old man, who falls forward onto the wet glassy floor, shaking. Mr. Garrett sinks back onto the edge of an empty hospital bed as the male nurse cautiously bobs forward to help the terrified old man from the floor, pulling him back to safety.

Mr. Garrett slowly reaches down to the floor and picks up a long thin sliver of broken whisky bottle glass. He studies its razor-sharp edges thoughtfully before raising it up to his throat. His face gleams with tears.

A gasp from somewhere in the ward. Rhoda realizes she's holding her breath. Next to her, her patient pulls back his bedsheet. He has quietly removed his own IV and mask and now he gently gets out of bed.

Rhoda's gaze flashes swiftly to him, her eyes wild with concern. He gives her a soft smile. *I know what I'm doing.*

Mr. Garrett looks up at the movement. A patient, out of bed, making his way toward him. He presses the sliver more firmly against his throat, his quivering hand breaking the skin enough to release a thin line of red. But the patient keeps moving toward him, undeterred. His eyes locked on the quaking man, his gaze placid and steady. Confusion suddenly furrows Mr. Garrett's brow. "Was it you?" he splutters. "Did you do it?" He stands now, turning the glass blade on Rhoda's patient.

But Rhoda's patient shakes his head. He is not the man Mike Garrett is looking for. Mike lowers the glass ever so slightly, perplexed by the advancing man. This isn't what's supposed to happen, he thinks, this man doesn't look scared, he looks kind. A fresh sadness seems to burst over Mike and he slowly sits back down.

Rhoda's patient is feet away now. The room watches mesmerized. There's an assurance to the way Rhoda's patient moves, a calmness. He seems to know what he's doing as he approaches the increasingly confused man. Close enough, Rhoda's patient stretches out a hand, palm up. Mike studies him, then lets out a deep ragged breath, something inside him breaking under the strain—he begins to sob, in wretched gasps.

The patient takes another step toward him. Then, gently, almost tenderly, he takes the shard of glass from Mike's unresisting hand. He places it on the bedside cabinet and sits down next to him. The patient reaches out and Mike lets himself be taken into a strong masculine hug, his body loosening limply into that of his new friend. His eyes squeeze tight shut, and remembering all that he has lost, he lets himself fully surrender.

After Mike has been led away to another room, Rhoda makes her way over to her patient. "That was very brave but you should have let me help, you know. I could have helped."

The patient shakes his head mildly.

*No,* his eyes say.

He brings a hand up to her head now by way of explanation. Careful not to touch her skin and the angry comma of scar tissue near her hairline.

*No, not you, not again,* his eyes seem to say. *Not this time.*

Rhoda's eyes widen and her breath catches.

*He knows,* she realizes. *He knows.*

What happened to her. How she got her scar. The scar that hasn't fully healed yet. Inside and out. Her eyes fill. *He knows and he was protecting me. He protected us all.*

She smiles up at him. He gives her a smile straight back.

"Well," she finally says, "aren't you just a gift from God."

# 14

## DR. EMMA LEWIS

### DAY 8—FIRST DAY

I grab the keys to the lodge, pull on my running shoes, and let the door bang shut behind me. I need to get my run in before work, as it'll be pitch black by the time I get back. It's drizzling slightly, which I actually like, the scent of rain fresh and pure in the early-morning air.

I decide to take a route out through the back gate of the garden that looks like it heads deeper into the woods. I want to see the forest in the daylight. I need to get used to it somehow, this dark tangle encircling me. I unhook the gate and set off at a brisk pace. The uneven ground is more interesting to negotiate than the well-kept footpaths of Regent's Park. It's only when my watch starts beeping that I become aware I'm soaked, my hands are numb, and my buzzing mind is finally clear. Time to turn and head back the way I came.

Back at the lodge, I cook a quick breakfast and hop in the shower, letting the warmth seep back into my bones. I'm not entirely sure what the traffic is like between here and the hospital, so I decide it's best to set off early; they're expecting me at nine o'clock. Once I'm dressed, blow-dried, and made up, I dash out through the rain again to the rental car, my new friend, my connection to the outside world. I think about turning on the radio but decide that I don't want to break the soft bubble of silence surrounding me just yet.

The comforting aortic pump of the windshield wipers is my only company for the rest of the drive. The quiet beauty of the countryside thins as I near the bland gray of King's Lynn, and finally I see Princess Margaret's rise like a concrete lighthouse from the drab sea of the suburban town. I feel my pulse quicken; the last time I was here things were not good. I try not to think of that night . . . the coughing, the blood. But my cortisol spikes regardless.

I park and look up at the hospital, my view blurring as rain splatters the windshield.

I'm here for a reason, I tell myself. Somewhere inside is my patient. Waiting. The knot to be loosened.

Near the hospital entrance the news vans are setting up for the day. Crews milling, bustling with umbrellas, coffee orders, production runners with anorak hoods up, darting between the gaps in a recently erected press cordon, huddled together texting and laughing.

It won't be like last time, I tell myself. They won't know who I am as I slip past them, at least not today. This afternoon they'll find out I'm the new doctor on the Mr. Nobody case but nothing more. They won't know who I really am; that information would take a lot more than an Internet search.

But then, I suppose, time has a way of releasing the truth from its bedrock and floating it up into the sunlight.

I might get mobbed with questions as I leave tonight. But it won't be like last time. And for now, I am no one.

I grab my bag, filled with my notes and my laptop, and dash from the dry heat of the car through the wet of the car park.

I pull my coat collar up high over my head as I run, partly to protect my first-day hair, partly as a barrier as I near the press area.

But no one even glances up as I pass by.

I'm early. The clock above reception reads 8:39. I let my eyes drift over the lobby: The two security guards standing by the entrance of the main corridor to the wards, are they there to stop the press getting in? I wonder. Or to stop someone getting out?

Normal hospital life flows about me, nurses arriving for shifts, visitors buying morning papers in the small shop. The layout is different from what I remember, it's been refurbished recently. A fledgling queue is forming already at the coffee concession opposite the reception desk, which I make my way over to. I sign in with the elder of the two receptionists and she peers down suspiciously at my name on her list. "Dr. Lewis?" she says, looking back up at me, frowning. "Oh, right. Well, that's a surprise, we assumed you'd be a man." She sounds annoyed. I attempt a smile but she remains unimpressed. "It's the 'Lewis,' I suppose," she posits. "Sounds masculine."

*Okay.*

I give her a supportive smile. I'm pretty sure it wasn't "Lewis" that tipped the gender balance in her mind. But I'll give her the benefit of the doubt—first day, isn't it?

She holds a small camera aloft to take my picture, prints out the photo ID, then wordlessly assembles my day visitor lanyard and hands it to me. I stare down at it, unsure exactly what's supposed to happen next. The younger receptionist finishes giving directions to another visitor and smiles over at me. "Dr. Lewis, isn't it?" she asks. I give her a grateful nod. "Someone from HR will be up in a minute. You can have a wander if you like." She indicates the lobby newsagent and coffee bar. I thank her but head over to the metal seating near the windows. More coffee would probably not be a great idea.

I look down at my lanyard, a grainy digital image of me caught off guard, below it the name Dr. Emma Lewis. That's me. That's who I am.

Visitor ID lanyards aren't usually hospital practice, nor are the security guards on the ward entrance. At least not in any hospital I've ever worked in. But this situation is slightly different, I remind myself. This is a different political climate. And given the media outside and the government's interest in who this patient is, or could be, a little added caution can only be a good thing, right? ID verification stops outside threats.

After all, I could be anyone, couldn't I? I could be a journalist. I could be paparazzo. I could have a hidden camera embedded in my bag filming everything. I could be making a BBC *Horizon* documentary on poor healthcare.

I bet those press photos spread all over my bedroom floor back at Cuckoo Lodge made someone a hefty amount. There's definitely a market for information. People want to know.

I feel eyes on me. But when I look up, everyone in the reception area is going about their own business.

No one is looking. I let out a sigh. I need to relax. I'm not on display yet, nothing has happened yet.

I swivel in my seat and look out at the rain-soaked car park. Watching the weather is grounding, relaxing—there's neuroscience behind that but I won't bore you with the details and take away the magic. I watch the rain collect and twist in rivulets as it glides and judders down the glass panels.

I notice his hair first. Across the car park, a man stands talking to an older woman. I recognize that close crop of blond curls, at least I think I do. Neither is carrying an umbrella. His back is to me, so I can't quite tell yet, for sure, but I feel the queasy tingle of nerves in the pit of my stomach regardless. It's funny how just recognizing someone in a crowd can cause such a strong physical reaction. He's tall too, just like I remember. I brace myself for him to turn, to see me staring back at him through the smear of rain, for the spark of recognition to flare in his eyes. I steel myself for the inevitable look of disappointment on his face. The woman he's talking to gets into her car and he turns. It's not him. Relief flashes through me so powerfully that I shudder. He's nothing like him really; it was silly to think it was him. Good. The last thing I needed was a school reunion on my first day in a car park full of press.

I count the press vans out there. Five, by the looks of it: BBC East, BBC News, ITV, Channel 4, and Sky. I wonder where all the print journalists are.

I look back at the people in the lobby. The man in a Barbour jacket propped in the corner, his black scarf balled into a pillow as he naps. The teenager by the security guards, head bowed, texting. The middle-aged woman in a beige-colored suit sipping coffee in the café as she jots notes in a pad. A gaunt sharp-featured man whispering to a smartly dressed redhead in the coffee queue. Her eyes catch mine for a microsecond and she looks away, absorbed in what the man is telling her.

And I suddenly wonder if *everyone* here is press.

# 15

# THE MAN

## DAY 1—NOT A WORD

Poole and Graceford arrive at the hospital nineteen minutes after the incident call goes out. They aren't the responding officers, that's the job of the King's Lynn station. Poole and Graceford are here because, in some capacity, their unidentified suspect from the beach was involved in this new incident.

Their search on the beach was unsuccessful. No handy pile of clothes, no car keys or wallet, no shoes or coat. The identity of the man is still unknown. Trevor Kwasi, Princess Margaret Hospital's head of security, makes his way over to meet them as soon as they enter.

"He's gone down to the King's Lynn station already," Trevor informs them, hitching the waistband of his trousers, which is clearly in a losing battle with his comfortable girth. "His name was Mike Garrett. Adams and Rhys from King's Lynn just took him. You just missed them." He checks his watch, to clarify. "There's still a King's Lynn officer up on the ward, Mel Wheatly, she's taking witness statements, if you guys want to make your way up."

Graceford gives him a nod.

"I asked all the witnesses to hang about in case you lot need to talk to them too."

From the initial radio call, Graceford and Poole had assumed the suspect was their unidentified man, but now they realize they were wrong.

Leading them up to Level 2, the security chief explains what he knows, which isn't yet much.

"Mike Garrett was looking for a discharged patient, a guy called Martins. Apparently, Martins drove the car that hit Garrett's car late last night. Drunk-driving incident. Garrett's daughter died—she died en route here. Martins came away with only bruises. He was discharged into police custody shortly after admission. To be fair to him, he was broken up about it, called 999 himself from the scene. Anyway, Mike Garrett couldn't handle the news. God knows what he would have actually done if he'd found Martins. And your guy, he somehow managed to sweet-talk Garrett into handing over his weapon. No struggle, nothing."

"How? What exactly did he say to him?" Poole asks, frowning.

"Couldn't tell you," Trevor puffs, pausing on the half-flight landing to catch his breath. "I've been hearing some pretty mixed things from witnesses. I think your best bet witness-wise is a nurse called Rhoda, I'll point her out to you once we're up there. She was with your guy when it happened, so if anyone should know . . ." He shrugs and sets off again, leading them up.

"We'll need to talk to the patient too, the man from the beach. Is he still on the ward or has he been moved?" Graceford asks.

"Er, well . . . here's the thing. You can't really *talk*

to him." Trevor gives a wry chuckle as he opens the Level 2 doors. "See, he's not saying anything."

"What do you mean, he's not saying anything?" Poole asks sharply. "You mean he's still not talking?"

"No. The officers from King's Lynn tried. The nurses tried. Nothing."

"Wait, Trevor, he's not talking about the incident, or he's not talking at all?" Graceford persists, her brow furrowed. "Like, he's mute? You've got to be kidding me, Trev. You seriously think he's mute?"

"Or maybe he's not all there," Trevor says. "I don't know, I'm not a doctor. Maybe he's done something and he's just keeping schtum. How would I know? Or he's foreign, he might not even speak the language. Might not understand what we're saying. Immigrant or something."

"Okay, well. Let's not jump to any conclusions. The last thing we want is an immigration officer down here. We all know how much everyone loves those guys." Graceford looks back to Poole. "Where's the nearest detention center, Chris? Could he have come from there?"

"There's Yarl's Wood Immigration Removal Center in Bedford. Or maybe Fulton Hall Removal Center in Lincoln— but that's too far. You think it's likely, that he's illegal?"

Graceford shrugs. "I hope not, for everyone's sake. And I don't know why he'd be on a beach up here. Unless there's some new North Sea crossing route we don't know about yet? I suppose he could have just paid for passage on a fishing boat. The Norwegians get pretty close to the coast here."

"Surely we'd have found a life vest or something on the beach. There's no way he could have made it in without one."

Graceford nods in agreement; neither of them are

convinced. Besides, the man they found didn't look like a refugee, at least not like their ideas of one. But why would he be silent? Perhaps he has a reason to stay quiet.

A nurse looks up as they enter the ward, scanning their uniforms and expressions with weary eyes. She rises to greet them with a tentative smile. "How can I be of help, Officers?"

Rhoda leads them to one of the ward's single-occupancy rooms, where the patient is lying in bed, his head turned away toward the window.

"Hello, stranger," Rhoda says, tapping at the open door.

The patient pulls his gaze away from the overcast sky and seems unfazed as the two uniformed officers fill the small room.

"I've brought some nice people to talk to you." Rhoda's tone is soothing. "Nothing too stressful, I promise. This is Beth," she says, indicating Officer Graceford, "and Chris. They'd like to ask you a few questions. They are the police officers who found you this morning. You feeling up to that now?"

The man in the bed regards them placidly. He gives Rhoda the smallest of nods, then shifts himself carefully up onto his elbows, resting back against the pillows.

The officers pull up chairs and take a seat. When Graceford speaks her tone is kind. "How are you feeling now? You're looking much better." It's true he's almost unrecognizable from earlier that morning. There's color in his cheeks, an air of self-possession about him. Graceford wonders if they've given him something, a sedative perhaps. She'll need to ask about that later.

The man gives a restrained smile in answer, eyes shifting back to Rhoda. Graceford throws a quick glance to Poole. "They mentioned to us you weren't speaking," she says. "Is there any particular reason for that, sir? Can you understand what I'm saying?"

The patient's brows knit slightly but otherwise his expression remains serene. He stays silent.

Either this man genuinely doesn't understand what she's saying or he's a bloody good actor, she thinks. Poole and Graceford get lied to every day and people aren't usually this good at it.

"Do you understand any of what I'm saying to you, sir?" Graceford asks, louder now. The man looks back to Rhoda again, who nods him on encouragingly. He holds her gaze and shakes his head slowly; he doesn't want to do this anymore.

Poole tries now. "Sir, can you tell us what your name is?"

The man moves his head to look at Poole. Poole points a finger at his own chest. "Officer Poole," he says in a labored and heavily accented voice. Graceford has to look down into her lap to stop herself from exploding with laughter. Poole is now pointing toward the patient, who watches him with intelligent eyes. "You?" Poole asks.

The patient nods. He understands. He's been asked his name. He looks away from the police and the nurse and out at the murky sky. When he turns back he shakes his head, but this shake is different.

He can't answer their question because he doesn't know the answer.

# 16

# DR. EMMA LEWIS

## DAY 8—TEAMWORK

When I enter the empty conference room, Nick Dunning, the chief executive officer of the Princess Margaret Hospital and until recently its chief of strategic management, is dumping packets of sugar into a steaming coffee, spilling most of it on the table as he, distracted, taps away at his phone. According to Peter, it's Nick I'll be liaising with at the hospital. But at the moment he's mid-email, head bobbed down over his phone. He looks up briefly as I round the conference table and take a seat, and flashes me a friendly harassed smile before plunging back into whatever crisis is playing out in the palm of his hand.

I pull my laptop and notes from my bag. And busy myself with them, fishing out my proposed action plan of tests and diagnostic methods. I study his face as he scrolls.

He's a lot younger than I thought he'd be, dressed casually, a brushed-cotton collar peeking out from under a chic gray sweater. Stubble, fashionable horn-rimmed glasses that perfectly match the golden brown of his eyes. He's very attractive.

After a moment he looks up again. "Sorry. Sorry, Emma. Nick." He stretches his hand across the table and shakes mine warmly. "Rushed off my feet. It's been a bit crazy around here the last couple of days." He tips his phone by way of explanation. "I've been putting out a lot of fires, as you can imagine."

"I can." I smile back blithely. Rushed off his feet is an understatement if ever I heard one. The amount of patient complaints and follow-ups over what happened on the ward last week alone would be work enough. Never mind having to field the level of intense public interest in one particular patient. "It's no problem at all, take all the time you need, Nick, if you want to finish up." But he puts his phone away briskly and picks up his coffee cup. I put my notes down and give him my full attention.

"Right," he says.

"Right!" I say.

We share a moment.

"God," he adds.

"Yep," I say with a little nod. "Can I just say straight up front," I gush, "that the last thing I want is for you to feel like you are crisis-managing this alone, Nick. Or that I am in any way here to take over. I want to work with you, I need to. I don't know the hospital and I don't know the case yet. I'm just hoping that we can get this situation sorted out together, quickly, as a team?"

"Yes, exactly." He tastes a gulp of coffee and grimaces. "That's exactly what we want here too. I can't say how relieved I was when they sent over your details. I liked the tone of that misdiagnosis paper. The previous cases you reexamined. It's reassuring." He flashes a relieved smile.

He's definitely not what I was expecting and I bet I'm not what he expected either. I suppose I was expecting the CEO of an NHS Foundation Trust hospital to be, well, older, a bit soft around the center, a middle-aged man in a cheap suit. Not my age and . . . well, attractive.

But I suppose the next generation of healthcare needs the next generation of management.

He taps a pen gently on the table in front of him. "Are there any questions you've got straight off the bat, Emma?"

"Well, I've looked through the notes and at this stage it's looking like a psychiatric condition. I'm thinking post-psychological trauma, but I'm going to need more information, which means more tests. An EEG to check for seizure disorders. I need to be sure we haven't missed anything physical that could be causing this. But I think our key diagnostic tool is going to be an fMRI. I'll need to do that as soon as I can."

His brows furrow slightly. Like most NHS Trust CEOs, he has no specialist medical training. The job of hospital administrator is a nonmedical posting. He'll have sat in on meetings about the patient, for sure, and he'll have a degree of knowledge but it will only be lay knowledge.

I explain. "The fMRI will tell me if the patient is lying, faking his symptoms. As I know you know fugue has a bit of a history of that. He could be malingering for some reason or he could be Munchausen's, meaning he's doing all this for attention. Don't get me wrong, it doesn't sound like it, but the only real way to be sure is to do an fMRI. That should tell us whether the hippocampus is being activated to access memory. You can't fake memory loss in a scan."

"And what about this mystery speck on his CT scans? The pituitary . . . ?"

"Oh, the cyst, yes. Probably not related at all, but

I will be looking into it, one hundred percent, you can take my word for that."

His face relaxes slightly. "Great."

"Can I ask what's been happening regarding the patient's lack of communication?" I ask.

"Sure." He dives in, eager to update me. "We've been trying to organize a multilingual translator to come in. As you know, the media have been chomping at the bit with this whole foreign national thing, so I've been apprehensive about arranging anything that might confirm or strengthen those rumors without you having met him first. I'd rather hear your thoughts. I don't want to add petrol to the flames here, obviously."

My breath snags.

*Petrol to the flames? What does he mean by that?*

*It's a saying, Em, relax, it's just a saying,* I tell myself.

Nick catches my discomfort but misconstrues it. "Of course, I can arrange the translator straightaway, if you need me to?"

"No, no. I think you're exactly right. No need for that just yet. His silence could be a number of things at this stage. Something may be affecting the language-processing areas of his brain; I'll need to run some tests. Or he may not be talking because he's scared. Any form of memory loss can be deeply disorientating. I'd like to do an initial assessment this morning, Nick, if it's possible? And—has he communicated in any other way with anyone here at the hospital? Made any connections with other patients or staff?"

"Yes, I think so."

"Well, I'd love to pull anyone else he's communicated with in for a quick chat, if that's possible. It'd be useful to know in what ways and to what degree he's been making himself understood over the last . . . what? Eight days?"

"Yes. Yes, of course I can find out who he's been communicating with. We'll make sure you get the opportunity to speak to those people, no problem."

The idea suddenly occurs to me. "Of course, there is always the possibility that the patient is deaf or has preexisting speech problems. Do you know if anyone attempted to communicate with him via sign language?"

Nick squeezes his eyes shut tightly for a second. "Shit."

I'm guessing that's a no.

He rubs a hand across his forehead. "No, not to my knowledge, no."

"Don't worry, this is why I'm here," I reassure him. "It's just another avenue we'll cover. There's also the possibility that he might have sustained damage to his vocal cords if he did almost drown the morning he was found. Either way, best to cover our bases on those points before moving on any question of language."

"Yes, that's for damn sure." He wets his lips now before continuing. "Can we just talk about the press? I know it's not your remit but there are a lot of crazy ideas floating around out *there*. Do any of them sound . . . I don't know, do any sound like possibilities to you?"

Having dredged through hours of media coverage online the night I agreed to take the case, and again last night in bed, I'm aware of what those floating ideas are. "Well, um, the idea that he may be military and have returned from deployment in Syria is theoretically a possibility. Dissociative amnesia is a form of PTSD. He could have had trouble reacclimatizing to civilian life. It's a possibility. The refugee idea is equally plausible; refugees are just as likely as a soldier to suffer from PTSD, they're in the same war zones. Failed suicide, yes, possible. A fisherman falling off a fishing boat, sure, it's a possibility, but as far as I'm aware, there's no evidence of that, no one missing. Um . . . and second coming of Jesus, slash, he's an angel, medically speaking not my remit—"

Nick lets out a loud laugh and I smile.

"—oh, um, and in terms of the Russian idea along the lines of the nerve agent released in Salisbury. Chemicals are definitely worth testing for, although, to my knowledge, he's not showing any related symptoms." I pause for a moment to see if there's anything I've missed. "I mean, it is very strange, given the amount of press coverage, that nobody has come forward in eight days to identify him. That should be telling us something. Although I'm just not sure exactly what it's telling us."

"Yes, quite."

"Have the police made any progress?"

"In a word, no. They've been keeping us in the loop, but they haven't been able to trace his journey before the beach. No abandoned cars found in the area. They've checked CCTV at King's Lynn train station and the local shops, but he hasn't shown up on anything yet. Plus, no ID on him, as you know, and his fingerprints aren't on the national database, so no luck there."

"Have the police run DNA?"

Nick raises his eyebrows. "No. No, I don't think they have yet," he says hopefully. "Definitely worth asking them for an update as of today." He taps a note into his phone briskly, then looks at me with a smile of gratitude. "Can I just say, Emma, I've never been so glad to have the troops called in on me. Something tells me before long we'll have something solid to show for our efforts." He rises, signaling that our meeting is officially over. "Right, I hope you don't mind me springing this on you, but I've asked all nonessential staff to gather up in the canteen—I thought you could do a quick intro and get your face out there so they all know who you are. How does that sound?"

*Not good, Nick. Not good.*

# 17

## THE MAN

### DAY 2—HOW COULD HE KNOW A THING LIKE THAT?

Rhoda arrives for her shift forty-five minutes early, her rucksack heavy on her back. After what happened yesterday they've asked her to stay on the patient's ward again today. They told her she'd be staying on with him at least for today, considering what he'd been through on the ward and given his unusual situation.

If Rhoda were a cynical person, she'd say the hospital might be trying to cover their backsides over what happened there yesterday. How had that situation been able to occur on an active ward? Why had a confused and recently bereaved man been placed on an open ward and left unattended? It was a valid question that a lot of people were already asking.

There had been reporters hanging around the hospital entrance last night after her shift ended, a woman and a man. They asked her what she thought about hospital security. What she thought about immigration. What she thought about the patient found on the beach that morning. Did she think he was a hero? they asked. Did she know his name? She hadn't wanted her picture taken, though they'd asked her politely if she would, but it had been a long day and she had worried it wouldn't come out well. Finally, she had told them she needed to go and she'd thought no more about it.

Since the scuffle on the ward she'd replayed the incident with Mr. Garrett over and over in her mind.

Should she have done something? What if her patient hadn't stepped in? What if it hadn't gone the way it did, if something very bad had happened? People could have been hurt because of her failure to act.

She'd tried to remember her counselor's words while she made a cold-plate supper for herself that night, her cream cockapoo Coco bouncing around her heels. Her counselor has been telling her for the past five weeks, since the incident in the park, that it wasn't Rhoda's fault. But it's hard not to blame yourself when something bad happens to you. Because she knows if she'd just fought back, then maybe things would have been different. The fact is, in actuality she did nothing and she let something terrible happen to her. She knows she can't blame herself, she shouldn't blame herself, but she does.

Her thoughts had circled back around to her new patient, the odd feeling she'd had that he'd *known* about what happened to her. It was the way he'd looked at her, the way he'd pointed out the scar running jagged down her temple, her dark skin puckered and still tender where the stitches had been. She'd been styling her hair differently to cover it; people at work had only noticed her new hairstyle. But Rhoda noticed the scar every time she looked in the mirror. And—somehow—he'd noticed it too.

How had he known? She hadn't told anybody what happened to her in the park. She'd only called the police, grudgingly, after realizing that she wouldn't want the same thing to happen to someone else next time, someone younger or older, someone frailer.

She'd reported it but she hadn't told anyone else, not her friends and certainly not her family. She didn't want them to see her that way, to think of her like that. She'd lied in those days after it happened and told anyone who asked that she had slipped on the stairs in her building, rainwater on the steps, and people had grimaced and sympathized but thought no more about it.

The police had filed a report but they told her that they couldn't do any more without eyewitnesses. And there had been no one else there that day. Just her and Coco and the skinny old man with his walking cane, sitting on a park bench. She'd noticed his dog, a Staffie, nosing around a bin for scraps, off the leash.

It had all happened so quickly.

Usually Rhoda would unleash Coco as soon as they got to the park, letting her run free in her dizzying circles as happy as can be. But that day, seeing the Staffie there, running loose, she'd kept Coco close.

Her intuitions had been right because as soon as the Staffie had looked up from its search and seen Coco, the dog had bolted full-pelt straight for her. Rhoda had fleetingly thought to pick Coco up, but she hadn't had time and it hadn't mattered anyway because just before making contact with Coco the big dog had swerved and knocked Rhoda down onto the muddy grass. A flash of pain had ripped up her leg and into her hip. A shout came from across the park, the old man's voice calling angrily to his dog, making his way to help her as fast as his cane would allow. At least that was what she'd thought, but as he got closer and she'd raised a hand so he could help her up to her feet, that's when the first blow came. His thick wooden cane struck her so hard across the cheek, the blow knocked the air straight out of her. She'd gasped a breath in to shout out, but the next blow came down before she could make a sound. And all the while he was shouting at her. Poor Coco, dancing around her on the grass yapping furiously.

None of it made any sense as he glared down at her while swinging his cane a third and final time, his hate-filled voice saying terrible things, a storm of ugly words she would only begin to process afterward. He told her she was stupid, a stupid bitch, why had she got in the way of the dog, she was a stupid fucking n*****, and suddenly she knew why this was all happening.

Disbelief in burning hot waves had flushed through her. She hadn't thought things like this happened anymore, not here in this country, not now, and yet, somehow, here she was.

After the third blow the old man had pulled back, spittle hanging grotesquely from his chin as he scowled down at her. Then he'd lowered his cane, looked around the park purposefully, and called to his dog before turning and stalking away. Just like that.

The way he'd walked off, in such an ordinary, everyday way, her ears ringing and blood stinging her eyes as he'd left her to bleed in the mud. That was the thing that made the tears come as Coco whined and nosed around her.

Rhoda lay almost motionless, stunned, crying hot tears of confusion, scalding tears of rage. What had been a nice afternoon walk was now a nightmare. He'd walked away and she couldn't think of what to say or what to do, so dizzy and disoriented she'd screamed at the top of her lungs after him.

"HEY! HEY!"

And at that, he'd turned back briefly to look at her, his eyes scanning the still-empty park beyond her. But seeing no one else, no one but the two of them, he'd turned and stumped away, his stupid oblivious dog following obediently at his heels.

Rhoda stayed in the park long after he'd left. The last thing she wanted was to see him again farther down the street back toward her home. She needed to fix herself, wash her face, check the throbbing wound on her forehead, but she had no pocket mirror in her bag. Rhoda knew she was a brave woman, she'd been a nurse for nearly three decades, but for some reason she'd not fought back. When the moment came, she did nothing. Why? She'd asked herself then, and every day since.

She'd talked it all through with the police counselor of course. It was shock, he'd told her. Simple as that. The old man had caught her by surprise; no one expects to be attacked in a public place in broad daylight walking their dog. No one expects frail old men with canes to be a threat. She had been blindsided, plain and simple.

Just as she'd been blindsided again on the ward. But this time someone else had been there to help. He'd looked into her eyes, and he'd understood her fear. He'd stepped in for her. He was her lucky charm. Her gift from God.

So, when she gets to work, she heads straight to his ward and shakes out the contents of her bulging rucksack on his bed. He sits motionless under the blankets, watching, as six thick books tumble out, alongside pens, pencils, and a brand-new sketchpad, with their discount stickers still attached.

Rhoda smiles at him. The library books are foreign dictionaries, the library maximum was six, and the sketchpad was the idea of one of the police officers yesterday.

If he couldn't talk, then perhaps he could draw? the policeman had suggested. Perhaps he could communicate where he was from or anything he could remember?

He looks down at his gifts now, arrayed on his blankets, and he smiles a knowing smile to Rhoda. *Thanks,* his eyes say. Her gifts promise that today they will get to the bottom of this, together.

"I've been thinking," Rhoda says, laying the books out so that the patient can see the titles and covers. "I know you can't remember your real name just yet, but how do you feel about a temporary one? Just for now?" Her fingertips absentmindedly touch the scar by her hairline. "I know it's not ideal but it would be nice to call you something, what do you say?"

He looks down at her pile of books, eyes flitting from one to the next, then back up to her. He nods.

# 18

## DR. EMMA LEWIS

### DAY 8—PUBLIC SPEAKING

Nick leads me up to the hospital canteen on the top floor. I follow, my mind whirring.

He chatters on as we take the stairs up two at a time. "Sorry for the stairs, the elevators take forever and I told everyone to be ready up there at half past." He glances at his watch and then back over his shoulder at me. Catching my expression, he smiles. "Listen, seriously, there's no big speech required, don't worry about that. Nothing too stressful, just a quick mission statement so everyone knows who they're working with and who to speak to if they have questions. Okay?"

It's hard to tell how pale my face has got but I suddenly feel intensely light-headed. I pause on the stairs for a second, pretending to be out of breath. A speech in front of most of the hospital staff. I feel sick. This is *not* keeping a low profile. I suddenly wonder: How much has Peter actually told Nick about me and my history? I'm guessing nothing, otherwise Nick would appreciate the implications of me "getting my face out there." But what can I do?

Just pray that no one I was at school with went into medicine and works here, I suppose.

Nick pauses. "Sorry! I'm rushing you, aren't I? Sorry, take your time. They can wait a few more minutes. It's just all a little fraught at the moment, morale up and down—things like this help. Makes sure everyone feels like they're part of the team, in it together."

"Of course, it's fine. I just—I haven't had much exercise over the Christmas break, ha," I lie.

It's fine, I tell myself; even if someone does recognize me, they aren't going to blurt it out in the middle of a speech, are they? People don't do things like that in real life. They'd come and talk to me after. Right? *Right?*

*Stop it! No one here is going to remember you. You have a different name. And you look completely different. So stop it.*

I smile up at Nick.

At the top of the stairwell, he turns to me again.

"So, it's just through here. Shouldn't be more than forty, fifty people. I'll do a quick intro and then you can introduce yourself, a bit about your background and maybe a basic outline of the diagnostic plan. I'll open up a quick Q&A and then we're done."

I take a fortifying breath in and nod. "Great."

Nick's hand goes to the door and I suddenly realize I have no idea what we are calling the patient. "Wait, Nick. What are we calling him? The patient?"

"Oh, bloody hell, sorry, Emma. We're using Matthew for now. I know—but he seems to like it and we can't call him Mr. Nobody, obviously. So we're stuck with it for now. I should have mentioned before." He suddenly looks as vulnerable as I feel, which, thankfully, takes my focus off of myself for a second.

"No, it's fine," I reassure him. "Let's get through this bit and then you can take me to meet Matthew."

He nods happily, back on safe ground, and with that he pulls open the doors.

My hands are slick with sweat, my chest fluttering. I take in the faces as we enter the canteen. Nurses, junior doctors, paramedics, porters, canteen staff, groundskeepers. I try to scan each face for any sign of recognition. The crowd has hushed with our entrance and all eyes are on us as we make our way to the front.

Nick clears his throat and starts to speak. I notice a woman, standing by the hatch of the kitchen, turn toward us and I realize with sudden dread I know her. I rack my mind for who she might be, how I know her. She's looking back toward the doors now, frowning. She's waiting for someone. I struggle to focus on Nick's words.

"—enormously lucky to have her with us. So, if you could all give a big hand to Dr. Emma Lewis, I'll turn this over to her."

I find myself stepping forward to join Nick, my eyes still locked on the woman. Then her eyes find mine, she gives me a tight smile before her gaze is pulled away by a younger woman sidling up beside her and I suddenly realize how I know her. It's the receptionist from the lobby downstairs. Jesus. That's how I know her.

I need to calm down. I need to stop being paranoid. Everything is fine. The relief I feel is overwhelming and I can't hold back a smile. I let my body relax ever so slightly, take in my expectant audience, and begin.

# 19

# THE MAN

## DAYS 3-6—PATIENT

Rhoda sits patiently by while Matthew undergoes further scans on day three. He is assessed by multiple doctors, none of whom fully understand his problem, and none of whom manage to pry a single word from him.

He is moved to the psychiatric ward.

Rhoda moves with him. She plumps his pillows, she changes the dressings on his head wound, she brings in more library books and together they sift through the dry pages, hoping to find a glimmer of recognition in the darkness.

There is a small piece in the local paper that evening, an article about the man found on the beach. The patient doesn't see it but Rhoda does. She particularly likes the photograph they used. The picture shows Matthew in the distance, a blurred dot, Officer Graceford with him and Officer Poole running toward the camera, caught in the moment, Poole's mouth half open, shouting something at the photographer. The picture has an otherworldliness to it, like a painting.

She takes the evening paper home and carefully cuts the article out with her kitchen scissors. When this is all over, she decides, when he's better, she'll give Matthew all his cuttings, if he wants them. The picture is beautiful, she thinks. The great sweep of Holkham Beach, dunes she recognizes even without the caption under the photo.

The article beneath is about Mr. Garrett, how Matthew saved the day, right after being admitted to Princess Margaret's. The article mentions how Matthew hasn't spoken a single word since they found him. Portrayed as a mysterious hero, and easy on the eye, Rhoda can see how that would make a good story. Like a fairy tale, there is a magic to it, as delicate as filigree, and she feels that magic around him too.

Whoever wrote the article got it right, she decides.

Another day passes. It's day four and Rhoda administers Matthew's meds. He takes the pills from her trustingly, as if knowing in his heart she wouldn't drug him. He doesn't trust the doctors, he doesn't know why exactly. He goes along with their tests, he tries to listen to their words, to what they say, but he is really only waiting. Waiting for everything to come flooding back in, like it should, soon. And he is waiting for her to appear. He knows she will come. It is just a matter of time.

To Matthew's mind the psychiatric ward isn't that much different from the ward he was on before. He knows there is something wrong with his brain, with his memory, and he's picked up enough from his interactions to see the move coming. But the doors aren't locked here, and his room isn't padded, it's just another blank hospital room.

There's a courtyard garden on this ward, which Rhoda takes him out to if it's not raining. She brings him in a puffer jacket from home. It smells of talcum powder and geraniums and it's not new, but it keeps him warm, for which he is grateful.

He's felt the cold more since the beach. He wonders if that might be because he's not used to the weather here. Perhaps he comes from somewhere warm. There's no way to be sure, it's just a thought that occurs to him. He's had so many fleeting notions of what his life was, is, but they float away as they come to him with nothing substantial to anchor onto.

He looks at the books Rhoda brings, the words in them, and he waits for the moment when they fall into place, as he knows they must.

That afternoon Rhoda finds another story in the papers. The tone suddenly different from before. They use her name. She realizes that the questions she was asked in the lobby by the reporters on that first night have been threaded into this article. She knows now she shouldn't have spoken to those reporters. Her words sound foolish at this remove.

Thankfully, she sees it first, before the rest of the hospital staff. She's set a Google alert, to know when to get the paper; her niece had shown her how to over Christmas.

Somehow they'd managed to get a picture of Matthew walking in the garden. He's not wearing his puffer jacket in the picture, so it must have been taken the day before, the day he moved to the psychiatric ward. She has no idea how they took the photo; no one noticed a photographer on the closed ward. You'd think someone might have seen them, she thinks, but then that wasn't usually something they had to worry about at Princess Margaret's. That would have to change from now on.

The article accompanying the picture was wrong, Rhoda thought. This time they hadn't got it right.

The picture was misleading. It showed Matthew, his dark hair tousled, his jaw stubbled, standing in the ward's garden, his face contented, calm, his good looks somehow more pronounced against the rich greens of the bushes. And in his hand, its text clearly visible, one of her books from the library, a book she knows he only happened to be holding, just one of many language books he'd tried to look through that day. In the picture Matthew is holding a Ukrainian language book.

On the fifth day the story hits the national headlines. More details about Rhoda herself, about Matthew's new name, make their way into and across the tabloids and broadsheets. The story of a wandering man with no name found on a beach, a man who did not speak but could disarm a man and defuse an incident. Theories. Appeals to anyone who might recognize him. Questions about how the patient was being dealt with in the hospital.

A video of Rhoda talking to the reporters appears online.

When Rhoda is called into Nick Dunning's office on the patient's sixth day and ushered into a seat next to someone from HR, she realizes what the full impact of her words may have been, that she might be part of something much bigger than she had anticipated. The hospital isn't angry with her, how could they be, she hadn't been aware that the reporters she'd spoken to had been filming her, on a phone, as she spoke to them. That much was clear from the footage, but as Nick explained firmly, "This can't happen again."

Nick calls a general staff meeting. The hospital is crawling with press, and while he understands it isn't a doctor's or nurse's job to act as a bodyguard, he informs them that there will be security on all wards going forward, in light of the current situation and in light of the recent incident on a ward. Protecting patient safety and privacy must be a priority moving forward.

Nick mentions one last thing before the staff mill out: There will be a new doctor coming. A specialist from a London hospital. Someone for Matthew, someone who specializes in his exact condition, an expert.

And to her surprise a little shiver of dread passes through Rhoda as she joins the others shuffling out. The idea of Matthew remembering his real name makes her frightened, because in her heart Rhoda knows that as soon as he remembers who he is he'll leave.

# 20

# THE MAN

## DAY 8—FIRST SIGHT

It's *her*.

He sees her as soon as she rounds the corner of the ward, and his skin starts to thrum.

He knew something would be happening today. They brought him to the dayroom earlier than usual this morning. There were less staff on the ward. He'd felt instantly that something was coming.

And now he sees her, striding down the corridor, flesh and bone as real and solid as the building around her. Walking confidently toward the dayroom, toward him. He watches her from his safe position as she stops to talk to someone; she's too far away yet to notice him. He studies the gentle swish of her chestnut hair, her face in motion, pale and strong. The clean lines of her jaw, her cheekbones. But it is her eyes he can't stop looking at as they brush over the ward, over nurses, doctors, other patients. Her intelligent eyes, picking up everything, missing nothing. She's stopped at the nurses' desk just outside the dayroom. Surreptitiously, he scans the other patients around him. To see if anyone else sees what he sees. Do they too recognize her?

But the other patients are oblivious, they haven't noticed. His eyes glide back to her, he watches her talking, listening, that open, beautiful face. It's her. She's come. For him. He doesn't remember who she is yet but he knows she is the one he's been waiting for.

His head wound prickles along his scalp, still not fully healed. With a shudder he remembers the word written on his hand in ink, the word he'd rubbed away.

A warm burst of laughter flutters and snaps him back to the here and now. She's laughing at something one of the nurses is saying. It's a generous laugh. He can tell from her body language that it's not a great joke but she's invested in them liking her. She wants them to know she's not a threat, they are safe, all is well. The group she's talking to relaxes, he watches it happen, they open to her, softening instantly.

And then a realization creeps over him: he can't remember what it is he has to do. The panic he felt on the beach begins to flex inside him. She's coming and he can't remember who she is. All he knows is time is running out, he has to do something. Fear, cold and clinging, grips him as he struggles to remember what it is he's supposed to do now that he has found her. He knows with crystal clarity this first meeting is crucial. It's the most important thing he'll ever do.

His eyes dart around the room again, searching for something to trigger a memory.

*Remember! Remember something.*

He looks back out to the hallway. She's holding a file now, some notes, she's nodding as she flicks through the sheets of paper. She's a doctor. Okay. Is that good? She'll be coming any second and he can't remember who she is or why this is all so incredibly important.

*Is she dangerous? Should I run?*

He flicks his eyes across to the only other exit in the room. The large floor-to-ceiling windows, rain-spattered. He is on the second floor. Outside the insistent glow of the hospital the pale sky hangs listless. In the distance, the blur of dark treetops, a forest.

His breath catches in his throat. A forest.

And then it comes. A memory.

. . . the cold of a forest.

The tiniest flash of memory; he squeezes his eyes shut, chasing it. He's running through a wood, at night, running fast over the slippery mulch of the forest floor, his chest heaving, his throat burning as he struggles to catch his breath. Underfoot twigs snapping, his clothes snagging on branches, the echo of his footfalls resounding through the deep chill of the night. His heart is pounding. And then he hears something else. Another person's breath, right next to him, the soft gasp of it. A girl's breathing. Labored, scared.

His eyes flash open.

*Oh God. That doesn't seem right. That doesn't seem good. What does it mean? Why am I running?*

Dread fills him. Something is very wrong with what he just saw. He looks up now at the hallway. Someone is pointing over in his direction, saying something he can't quite make out, and suddenly she is looking straight at him. Her eyes locking with his. All her focus on him.

Her expression flickers, she seems to sense his fear, he can read it on her face, her concern, her empathy. But who is she? Her face shows the briefest flash of confusion.

---

Emma looks back at the patient sitting at the far end of the dayroom, silhouetted against the pale glass of the windows. Behind him the rain-soaked landscape rolls all the way to the North Sea. He is watching her. But it's the way he is watching her. His expression. He recognizes her. She feels a flutter in her chest. Does she know him?

The look in his eyes, it reminds her of someone a long time ago—but it can't be, it can't be him. That would be impossible. She knows it's not him. He's gone. Long gone, one way or another. The patient doesn't even look like him, he's too young to be him, his features too dark, too chiseled. The man she knew was softer. But the eyes, the eyes have the same quality. She tries not to let herself think it but . . . but there's definitely something about him. An understanding of what went before.

She then does something without even thinking: while the nurse beside her talks on, she nods back directly at the man. It's almost imperceptible, but he sees it.

His breath catches in his throat.

He remembers the warning he was given. *Don't fuck it up.*

Easier said than done.

*You need to speak to her. So you have to remember.*

She says something to the nurse, smiling, and she starts to make her way toward him.

*She's coming.*

His heart is racing now, adrenaline sizzling through him. He rises from his seat as the prickle of pain in his skull spikes. A fresh throb of it rips through his head; the room spins out beneath him and suddenly he's falling. His palms and knees smacking down hard onto the plastic flooring. The dayroom swirls around him, in and out of focus. His eyes find her somehow, her shoes nearing as she runs to him, then her hands touch his shoulder and finally her face comes into view, inches from his, the unexpected warmth of her breath on his cheek.

"Can you hear me, Matthew?" she says.

And just like that *her* name comes back to him.

Emma can't quite make out what he says, it's mumbled. The patient's breath coming in loud snatches as he tries desperately to stay conscious. She leans in closer to catch it, her ear close to his lips.

He says it again.

"Marn?"

She pulls away sharply to look at his face, her eyes wide in shock; she needs to see the look in his eyes as he says that, to see who he is, to see what he means. But she is too late. As she pulls back, he crumples down in front of her, unconscious.

Emma orders the junior doctor to monitor the patient; blood pressure and vitals are taken. According to the patient's notes he's blacked out three times since he was admitted eight days ago. Emma reassures the ward staff that the patient's losses of consciousness are most likely the result of stress response. But she instructs them to test for the usual physical causes—cardiac, neurological, orthostatic, metabolic, or drug-related—to be safe.

She doesn't mention the look the patient gave her just before he collapsed. And she certainly does not mention what he said to her, or that he spoke at all.

As people had rushed to assist them it became

clear that no one else had seen, or heard it. She had barely heard it herself.

If she heard it at all, she thinks. Because he couldn't have really said that, could he?

He couldn't know that name. They've never met; she'd remember meeting someone who looked like him. Besides, he would have been too old to have been at school with her back then, he's about ten years older than her. The first time she saw him was online two days ago, when she googled his case after speaking to Joe. All her knowledge of her patient comes from her research, the grainy YouTube footage from the beach, the photos in the newspapers, and his medical records.

But then, why would he say "Marn"? She blinks back the emotion. She hasn't heard that name for years.

She casts her eyes quickly around the busy ward; other patients are filing into the dayroom from breakfast. Is it a joke? she wonders. A prank? But that would be in pretty poor taste. And patients don't tend to lose consciousness as a joke.

She'd been doing so well. She hadn't recognized a single face in the crowd gathered upstairs in the canteen. No telltale eyes boring into her. She'd been starting to think everything might just be okay.

*Marn*. The name burns in her brain. He knows her. He knows who she is. She tries to push it from her mind as she heads back toward the nurses' station.

Perhaps he didn't say "Marn," she thinks. Surely she misheard. He could have mumbled anything. But the look of recognition in his eyes . . . well, patients with memory loss often pretend to recognize new people. Why should this patient be any different?

The duty nurse pulls up the patient's notes on the

system. "I'd be interested to find out exactly what happened just prior to his previous losses of consciousness," Emma prompts the nurse, her voice steady. "What exactly the context was."

The nurse nods and taps away at the keyboard.

As Emma waits, her phone vibrates. She turns away and fishes it out of her pocket. It's a text message.

Any miracles yet? Lol

She stares at the message, her pulse racing. She reads it again. Her thoughts whir as she tries to process the words. Who sent this? She reads the message again, slowly; she checks the number, it takes her another second to register that it's just Joe. Joe's new number. She represses a sigh. *Miracles,* of course. It's just her brother trying to be funny. She lets out a dry chuckle at her own paranoia and the nurse looks up at her in inquiry.

"Sorry," Emma blusters, smiling. "Just got a text."

"Ah, I see. Good news, I hope." The nurse smiles and turns back to her screen.

Emma looks down at Joe's text, her thumb poised over the keys, unsure if she should tell him what just happened. How could her patient have known that name? She wants to share the burden of it with every fiber of her being.

But what if she misheard? Joe will think she's gone completely nuts if she tells him what she thinks she just heard, she knows it. How would she even explain it to him? That somehow her new patient, who has no memory of who he is himself, or where he comes from, somehow seems to know her name? Her *real* name.

*Marn. Marni.* Her name. Her old name, before it

happened, before they changed it, before their whole family had to move.

Or perhaps the patient had thought she was someone else called Marn?

*Oh, come on, that's ridiculous, it's hardly a common name.*

She used to spend half her time before the name change explaining that she wasn't named after Hitchcock's Marnie, she'd been named after the actress Marni Nixon. Nixon, "the hidden voice of cinema," the woman who sang the role of Eliza Doolittle in *My Fair Lady,* Maria in *West Side Story,* Anna in *The King and I,* and countless other roles when starlets didn't have the voice for them. A ghost singer. A Marni with an "i."

Now, her thumb suspended over the phone, she hesitates. She can't tell Joe what just happened. He'll think she's cracking up, cracking up again, now that she's back here. She can't tell Joe what she thinks her patient said, and she absolutely cannot tell him who her patient reminded her of, because that really would sound crazy. That person died, a long time ago. Best not to say anything yet, not until things start making more sense.

She exits the messages app and slips her phone back into her pocket.

She can't tell anyone, she realizes, because the first thing anybody will try to find out is who, or what, "Marn" means. She needs to work this out herself.

She thinks of Joe's text, she thinks of miracles. Of what happened eight days ago on the ward. But that wasn't a miracle, she reminds herself, because there are no miracles—there are only people and their actions.

# 21

# DR. EMMA LEWIS

## DAY 8—ABOUT MATTHEW

"Has he spoken?" I ask carefully. "At all? To you? Has he said anything?" I'm sitting across from Rhoda Madiza in the hospital canteen. I want to keep the conversation as informal as possible, since I'm sure she's wary of talking to anyone after the media mauling she's been through over the last week.

As far as I can tell from the medical notes, Rhoda has been the patient's primary caregiver for the duration of his stay here, which is highly unusual in an NHS hospital. Nurses tend to stick to departments, seeing whoever whenever; they do not move around with a particular patient. But Rhoda is the only person who's been able to communicate with the patient since his arrival. And I need to know if I'm the only one he's spoken to yet. If anyone could tell me, it would be her.

"No, nothing. He hasn't spoken to me. Not a peep, from day one."

My face must register a degree of disbelief, as she's quick to add "I tried, trust me. If he'd said anything to me, I'd have been on the phone before he'd even finished his sentence. We've been trying language books and YouTube videos. But no. No talking yet, just pictures. He's got a sketchpad like the police suggested."

*Oh God, just like the Piano Man. I bet the press lapped that up.*

"He draws pictures of things, the forest mainly, the views from the windows. And it's useful if he needs something—you know, he'll just draw a picture of it, fold it up, and hand it to me. A hot drink. A snack. Something to keep him occupied. He enjoys jigsaws. But that's as far as we've got." Rhoda smiles warmly, but there's a hint of disappointment there. I can see she wishes she'd gotten further by now. There's a strength of character, a zeal to her—I can understand why the patient took to her so strongly. She blows on her tea before sipping.

I nod. "I see. So, no verbal communication."

In that case he's spoken only to me. Interesting.

Unless, of course, I imagined it. The last time I was here so many things happened. I wasn't thinking clearly before we left. Could coming back here be subtly weeviling its way into my mind? Has it made me paranoid? I am definitely experiencing stress being back here, but can I realistically be suffering from full-on delusions so quickly? No. He definitely spoke, but there's surely a strong chance I might be wrong about what he said to me.

Rhoda puts her cup down.

"And how does he seem to you?" I ask next. "Aside from the silence, has he shown any signs of mental illness? Any suicidal tendencies?" She blinks at the question, not what she was expecting.

Rhoda takes a thoughtful breath before replying. "Sorry, you just threw me a bit. Doctors don't tend to ask my medical opinion very often." She smiles. "It's nice." She clears her throat and considers her answer. "Well, at first when he checked in I thought maybe he could be suffering from schizophrenia or a personality disorder. But I've cared for patients with both and he's—I don't know—much more *switched on,* if you know what I mean. He isn't listless and he hasn't let himself go." She gives a little frown, suddenly embarrassed that I might think she was referring to the way he looks. How handsome he is. Strange how no one is mentioning the way he looks. How good he looks. But then, that wouldn't be appropriate, would it? We all know that wouldn't be appropriate.

"The doctors are saying maybe depression or manic depression. But it's not. He seems fine most of the time, you know, happy, in spite of everything that's happening. More levelheaded than some people who actually work here." She gives me a quick smile.

She's not a doctor but her insights are important. They're based on clinical observation, and are even more important in this instance, when the patient himself can't describe his own symptoms.

"So, would you say he's presenting quite normally except for the lack of communication and the panic attacks he's been having?" I stop myself, I shouldn't have mentioned panic attacks. I don't want to lead her answers; I need to choose my words more carefully. "Sorry, is that how you would describe them? Panic attacks?"

"No. Not attacks, exactly." She shakes her head thoughtfully. "It's more like . . . well, this will sound strange, but more like he suddenly *remembers* something. Like he sees it in his mind's eye. It's not panic so much as he shifts up a gear into a . . . like a heightened state, I suppose."

Okay, now we're talking.

What she's describing is PTSD. But, of course, I don't want to be the one to say it. As it's my primary hypothesis I need to be certain I'm not the one seeding it in Rhoda's head. She needs to tell me herself in her own words.

"Heightened in what way, Rhoda?"

She gazes out into the canteen concourse, frowning.

"Like a dog in a fight, I suppose. Like he sees something and he suddenly doesn't know whether to run or to fight. Every time I see it happen to him, that's what it reminds me of. But then, I'm not a doctor," she concludes self-deprecatingly.

PTSD patients relive their traumatic event; they replay it every time something triggers the memory. The same event over and over in their heads. Anything can trigger it, a face, a tone of voice, a sound. It's called hyperarousal and it's one of the key symptoms of PTSD.

"How is his sleeping?" I ask.

Rhoda gives a throaty laugh. "No problems in that department." She shakes her head merrily. "He loves an afternoon nap." But she catches herself. "But, come to think of it, he does do most of his sleeping in the day, to be honest. I hadn't thought of that until now. I couldn't say if he sleeps at night, I'm not here for the night shift and no one's mentioned anything."

"That's interesting." Insomnia doesn't work like that. What this sounds like is that his circadian rhythm is out of sync, his sleep hormones firing at all the wrong times.

"Rhoda." I lean forward. "The incident with Mr. Garrett . . . Would you say the patient displayed any skills or knowledge that the average person on the street might not?"

She looks suddenly suspicious, like I'm trying to trick her into saying something foolish. "I'm not really sure what you're asking exactly," she says carefully.

"Did he look, to you, like he might have any police or military training?"

"Oh!" she exclaims, surprised, and raises her eyebrows as she considers the idea. "Well, he seemed to be very sure of himself, of what he was doing, yes. Like he'd done that sort of thing before maybe, that he could handle the situation. And you know, I think *that's* the reason Mr. Garrett let Matthew end it—it just seemed like the right thing in the situation." She looks at me hopefully; she clearly likes this line of reasoning. I smile at her.

"Rhoda, it would be really helpful if you could try and get down on paper anything else you may have noticed about the patient. In particular, the context surrounding any losses of consciousness he's had. I've already asked for the ward notes but I'd really like your version of events. You've had more time with him than anyone else, and that way we can try to build up a picture of what might be triggering him."

Why did seeing me trigger him? I think of his face across the dayroom looking back at me, his expression. How did he know my name and why would that trigger him?

"Yes, of course. Not a problem." Rhoda smiles, clearly delighted at being asked to be so heavily involved in his diagnostic plan. But why shouldn't she be? She's been the one looking after him, she's the only continuity he has here.

"Rhoda, can I also ask you—" I stop myself, this is tricky territory.

Rhoda studies me, alert to my sudden change of tone. "Of course, you can ask me anything."

I choose my words carefully. "Rhoda. You named the patient Matthew, didn't you? Why did you do that?"

Her face falls. Then after a moment she lets out a soft sigh. "Oh God, not that again. I wish I'd never said a word about it." She softly shakes her head, contrite. "People always take things the way they want to hear them, don't they? That interview, I didn't know they'd twist it up like that. All blown out of proportion. Mr. Dunning's already had a word with me about not speaking with the press—"

"No, no, it's fine." I try to reassure her; she's misunderstood my intention. "I just wanted to know if there was a reason you chose that name in particular?"

Her embarrassment turns instantly to wariness. "You mean the 'gift from God' thing? I'm not religious, if that's what you want to know. My family was, but not me. I just had this feeling—oh no, I can't. This is . . . it's all just silliness."

"No, Rhoda, it's fine. Please, just tell me. I'm not going to judge you." Who am I to judge, anyway? For all I know, I'm hearing imaginary voices.

She doesn't relax, but she replies, "Well, I can't explain it, so I won't try to, but he knew something about me." She shifts up straighter in her chair. "He knew something he couldn't have known. He just couldn't." I feel the hairs at the back of my neck rise.

She's had an experience similar to the one I've had with him. He knew something about her he couldn't have known.

"What do you mean, he knew things? Do you mean personal things, things about you?"

Rhoda looks out at the canteen before letting her

eyes drift back to me. She nods. "Yes. He knew something, something extremely personal, and he wanted me to know that he knew and that he understood. Or at least that's what it seemed like to me, at the time. I know it sounds crazy, and I'm not a spiritual person, Doctor, usually, but—this was strange. You know?" She rubs a tired hand over her left eye and I catch sight of a small scar along her temple that I hadn't noticed before. "I'd rather not say what exactly he knew . . . if that's okay?"

"Of course."

"And there was the way he was with that other patient. . . . I've never seen anything like it, not in real life, anyway. Only on TV. He was so . . . calm. So sure of the situation. And to answer your original question, I guess I just thought the name Matthew was nice." She shrugs. "Better than calling him 'the patient' all the time. Matthew may mean 'gift from God' but I obviously don't believe that's what he is. I mean, come on—I'm a full-grown woman with twenty-seven years' nursing experience. I don't believe in angels. He's just been a breath of fresh air, you know, a stroke of luck when I needed it the most."

"But you do believe he knew things? About you?"

She chuckles. "Perhaps not. Who knows? Perhaps he's just very good at reading people? He certainly read me like a book. Whatever it is, he deserves to have a name, right?"

I smile in agreement. "Right."

Rhoda stiffens and it's only then that I realize someone is standing directly behind me.

"Sorry to interrupt, ladies. I was hoping to have a quick chat with you, Dr. Lewis, if that's all right. Or is now a bad time?" It's a voice I recognize. Shit. I swivel in my seat and look up as my heart leaps into my throat.

*Oh my God.*

"Could we have a quick chat, Dr. Lewis?" Chris Poole asks again. This is who I thought I saw in the car park this morning, but now that he's standing here right in front of me I realize how wrong I was then. Chris got really tall, and very good looking. I take in his uniform now too. Chris is a policeman. Chris Poole, from school, is a policeman. And as he looks down at me expectantly I realize that he one hundred percent recognizes me. This is not good.

"Um. Talk? Right, yes, yes, of course. Er, Rhoda, would you excuse me?"

"Of course." She rises and smiles at me in a knowing way, one that I don't fully understand, before leaving.

I turn back to Chris, who is grinning broadly.

*Oh shit.* Seriously? I mean, don't I look completely different? I guess there must still be something left of the old me in here somewhere.

He opens his mouth but I cut him off. "No, Chris. Stop. Before you say anything, just shush. Let's go to my office." I throw a quick look around the canteen: people are just going about their day, thankfully showing no interest in us.

Chris drops his smile as instructed. But the crinkles at the corners of his eyes remain.

*Jesus. He really is pleased to see me.*

"Can we, please?" I gesture out of the canteen.

"Oh, yeah, sure, lead the way," he says cheerfully.

# 22

## DR. EMMA LEWIS

### DAY 8—CHRIS POOLE

As soon as the door closes, he pulls me into a bear hug. His strong arms close around me, smushing my face against the expanse of his uniform jacket.

"What the hell are you doing here?" I hear his voice rumbling through his chest and it's oddly soothing. Irritated, I force myself to pull away.

"That's a very good question," I say evasively.

"I was not expecting to see you today. At all." He pulls back to take me in. My adult face, my late-bloomer features. "God, look at you. You look . . ." He pauses. "Different. And you're a doctor now!" His eyes scan me as if he'll somehow locate the doctor part of me if he looks hard enough. Or perhaps he's looking for the teenager part of me he used to know? "Not just a doctor. *The* doctor, I hear? Congratulations . . . mate."

"Thanks, Chris. And you . . ." I reciprocate, gesturing to his uniform. I step back and walk behind my desk, putting it safely between us. He stands there studying me, a smile in his eyes. He always was sunshine, Chris, warm sunshine. I can't help but smile back at him, in spite of everything. In spite of the fact that him recognizing me might screw up everything. I've only been here a few hours and bloody everyone seems to recognize me.

Chris and I were in the same year at school, we were all in the same big group of friends: boys, girls, it didn't seem to matter so much back then. Where are they all now? Do they have kids? Are they all still alive?

"How long's it been?" he asks, then answers his own question. "It must be, what, fifteen years. What have you . . . how have you been? How's Jim?"

"Fourteen years actually . . . and it's *Joe* now. Yeah, he's good; he's married, has a kid." Chris's eyes widen in mock horror at the mention of a kid, I guess it's safe to say he definitely doesn't have any just yet. "And I'm good . . . I'm . . . God, I don't know where to start really, Chris, sorry, it's been such a long time," I gush. "Um, but it's great to see you!"

He pulls out the chair opposite me and negotiates his bulky uniform down into it. This is not going to be over anytime soon, I realize with a sinking heart. This is the police liaison Nick told me to expect this afternoon. Chris is the one who's come here to give me an update on the police investigation. I'm going to have to get through this reunion before we get to the meat of the case. I sit down, still smiling, keeping the desk between us. I hope he doesn't see the panic in my eyes.

"It's great to see you too," he says earnestly. "Really good. Honestly." Then his expression changes. "I, er, I looked you up a few years ago, Marn." He uses my old name, and he's doing it deliberately. He's broaching the elephant in the room. "To see what happened to you after . . . well, after you left. Looked you up on the station system; I only had the name

Marni Beaufort, though. Probably shouldn't be telling you this, should I?" he says with a raw honesty I find strangely intoxicating. I shrug mutely. Oddly enough, it feels good to know somebody noticed us dropping off the face of the planet.

He nods understandingly. "I saw they'd changed your name on the police database." There's a question in there somewhere. And we both know the question is, *After everything that happened, are you okay?*

"Yeah," I reply as simply as I can, but it comes out breathier than I had intended. Yeah, they changed my name and yeah, I'm okay. Most of the time.

There's a silence filled with more questions, unasked ones.

"I just didn't realize you were a bloody doctor, though!" He beams at me again.

I laugh, grateful for the change of subject. "And you're a policeman?"

"I know. Like father, like son." He grimaces, but then his face turns ashen as he realizes what he's just said. *Like father, like son.* "Oh Christ, sorry. I didn't mean because of . . . Just 'cause—"

"Yes, I know, Chris, it's fine. Your dad was a policeman and now you're a policeman. It's fine. Seriously." I smile. "Yeah, I remember your dad. He was a lovely, lovely man."

Chris relaxes. "Dad? Let's not get carried away here. He's all right—well, on occasion. Christmas was a little fraught if you ask me, but yeah, he's all right, all told."

We stare at each other as another silence falls between us. I take in his features, his softly tousled blond hair, his strong stubbly jaw. "Chris," I say finally. "You can't tell anyone. Who I am. You can't mention anything about before."

His half-smile vanishes. "I know, *Emma*." He uses my proper name, my new name, and I like the way he says it, the fullness of it. "No, of course, I know. This Mr. Nobody case is already all over the place, I don't think bringing Marni Beaufort into it would be at all helpful. No need to worry on my account. I just came to tell you that we're here to help in any way with your investigation. And likewise, if and when he does start talking, keep us in the loop, okay? We're eager to get him back to his family or whoever is missing him. But for now, we can supply you with all our background on the case so far, if that would be any help?"

"Yes. That would be great."

"Just to warn you, though"—he frowns—"there's not a lot to go on. We checked his clothes for labels but they'd all been removed. No distinguishing marks, no tattoos. No fingerprint or dental matches. DNA hasn't thrown anything up but if he's not from here he wouldn't be on the UK system anyway. We've put him on the British missing persons database now and as of four days ago there's a hotline that's been set up by the *Daily Mail*. You can imagine how useful some of the caller tip-offs are! But we've got to field everything they pass on to us, so it's . . . well, let's just say we're wading through a lot of . . . stuff right now. Which I should probably be getting back to."

He rises now with a sigh, all six feet four inches of him, and slides his notepad out of his uniform pocket. He scribbles something down on it, then, his eyes flicking up to mine, he leans over the desk and holds it out to me. A note. Like in school. I glance down at the scrap of paper. It's a phone number. When I raise my gaze, he's watching me. "My mobile," he says. And for a second, he's right there, so close, towering over me, in my personal space. I can smell him, the scent of rain and fresh fabric softener. Our fingers brush as I take the paper from him and I feel a jolt of longing surge right through me. Something I haven't felt in a long time.

*Oh, please, no.*

His eyes hold mine. The piercing awareness that anything is possible. The awareness that if either of us made a move, something could happen. Something very exciting could happen.

He breaks the moment nodding toward the note in my hand. "Just in case you need me to check anything out for you or if he starts talking," he says, holding my gaze again. "Just call me, Emma. If I can I'll help out."

And then out of the corner of my eye I see it. The soft glint of a wedding ring.

Oh.

"Great. Thanks, Chris." I rise, businesslike now, trying not to let the bizarre mix of arousal and disappointment I'm currently experiencing show. "I really appreciate you not mentioning . . . you know, about my name and everything. Oh, and thanks for this." I raise the scrap of paper he's just handed me, for clearly only professional reasons.

He nods a quick goodbye and turns to leave. But to my surprise, he stops by the door and turns back. "You live in London now, right?"

I nod.

"Um, so whereabouts are you staying while you're up here?"

Something in my chest flutters ever so slightly. Even though it shouldn't, and even though that makes me a terrible person.

"They've put me in a house in the middle of the woods," I say jokingly. "Near Wells."

"But nowhere near Holt?" he asks. He's being protective. My chest flutters again. He's watching me honestly, openly, like nobody has for such a long time. He's worried I'm near Holt, close to where it happened.

And then another feeling I haven't felt in years floods through me. Sadness. Deep, thick, suffocating sadness. For the first time since I've returned to my hometown, I feel the warning prickle of tears behind my eyes. I swallow awkwardly. "No, nowhere near Holt," I reply, by way of thanks. *Thank you for caring*. But I don't think I can bear it.

Unsatisfied, he studies my face for a moment longer before nodding. "Good then."

He turns to leave once more but swings back again, frowning. "Sod it, listen, Emma, it'd be nice to catch up, you know, if you get any time. I know you'll be busy but"—he points to the note I now realize I'm still gripping tightly in my hand—"you've got my number. Lots of nice pubs in Wells. So . . ."

*Oh God. He's asking me out for a drink.*

"Right." I stall, unsure what to say. But then I say what I want to say . . . because life is short. And I am so lonely. "That'd be lovely."

After he leaves I study the creased note. The solid scrawl and curl of his hand. Then I crumple it up and throw it in the trash can beside the desk. After a few seconds I bend down to retrieve it, hastily smooth out its creases, and tuck it safely away in my bag.

*Seeing him is fine,* I tell myself. *You're not a bad person, Emma. Just one drink—as old friends. It can't hurt, can it?*

# 23

## DR. EMMA LEWIS

### DAY 8—FACEBOOK

Back at Cuckoo Lodge, I pour myself a deep glass of red wine and kick off my shoes. On the drive back from the hospital I called Peter Chorley on the car speakerphone, told him about Chris. How Officer Poole was aware of my history here, who I was, but that it shouldn't be a problem in terms of the case.

"But will it be a problem for you, Emma?" I'd registered the sliver of concern in his voice and found myself pausing slightly longer than I would have liked before replying.

"No. It won't be a problem, Peter." Because Chris is the least of my problems right now. I thought it but I didn't say it. I didn't mention who else knew my name today either.

"And how did your initial assessment go?" Peter had asked. I told him we'd had to postpone due to the patient's condition. A half-truth but not a lie. He'd seemed disappointed but circumspect, ending the call with a rallying "Ah, well, tomorrow is another day."

I collapse into one of the deep-cushioned sofas

and sip my wine, letting its heat warm me from inside. Alcohol-induced vasodilation. That's its medical term. Sexy, like sinking into a hot bath. A lot has happened in a day, but aren't first days always like that? Well, maybe not always like *this*.

Peter had promised me he'd be following up with the local police and ensuring they were all aware of the situation, of why my name was originally changed and the legal ramifications, and potential consequences, of disclosing that information.

It was bound to happen. I was bound to run into somebody. I grew up here. I went to school here. I knew I'd run into old faces. People I used to know, people from the past I've tried to forget, because it's not healthy living in the past. It robs you of a future. But for the next few weeks I'm going to have to do just that—live in the past.

So, I guess I had better prepare myself.

I lean across the sofa and pull my laptop over, flipping its lid open. If I'm really going to do this, be here, for the next few weeks, then I had better arm myself for battle. Knowledge is power, after all.

I type the word "Facebook" into the empty search bar and it springs onto my screen. I don't have a Facebook account, I never look at Facebook. Even at medical school when everyone was berating me for being either a Luddite or a hipster, I continued to abstain because, if I'm honest, it scares me. My face out there connected and connected and connected until it all leads back to that one night. The night when my whole world was shattered and it was easier to just throw the whole thing in the trash than try to fix it.

But now I need to know what I'm up against. Who there is here that I might run into, what might await me tomorrow. It can't be a surprise if I see it coming. The screen in front of me asks if I would like to join

Facebook. I would not like to join Facebook; but needs must, so I take a gulp of wine, set down my glass, and start to type in my personal information. "Emma Lewis."

It's funny how people can become living ghosts. A few years ago, I saw one of my old teachers on the underground. She didn't recognize me, of course; she hadn't seen me for over a decade. I wouldn't have looked like the messy freckled girl she remembered. But the instant I saw her I was back there, I could feel her firm hand on my shoulder as she led me silently down the empty school corridors toward the headmistress's office. She'd pulled me out of class; everyone else was still in theirs, and the usually noisy hallways were eerily hushed. That hand on my shoulder. That was the last time I saw her. The last time I would see any of them.

It's hard when other people know all about the worst moments of your life. The headlines made sure of that.

I stare at my empty Facebook page and I think of the gold band on Chris's finger today, of how I could have just asked about it but I hadn't. I type "Chris Poole" into the search box and hit return.

His page fills the screen, his handsome, grown-up face; he's looking at someone slightly off-camera mid-laugh, and he looks so happy I feel a stab of loneliness.

He's thirty, same as me—well, three months older to be exact. He's married. He's been in the police force since he graduated from East Anglia Uni with a 2:1 in geography nine years ago. There's something about the course of Chris's life that I find so reassuring in its clarity. If I was to make a real page of my own, it would not be quite so straightforward as his.

Impulsively, I open a tab and google his station.

There are two other men and one woman listed on the local police website. The men are both sergeants and the woman a PC—police constable—just like Chris. She has a warm, kind face, shiny brown hair pulled back securely in a low ponytail; she looks nice. I bet she and Chris like each other. I don't recognize her from school at all. I type her name into Facebook—Beth Graceford. Divorced, born in Falmouth, studied English at Falmouth University and worked for a publishing company in Falmouth. Interesting. I guess she needed a change. A big one. Good for her; I know from experience how hard that can be, upending your whole life and starting again somewhere new. And it explains why I don't recognize her, she only transferred to Norfolk last year. I type in the two sergeants' names: likewise both are not originally from the area. So far, so good.

I take another sip of my wine and think.

There's something I've wanted to check, very badly, since I first logged on, but I've been trying with every ounce of my willpower to ignore the impulse.

I type in Chris's name again. His page springs up again and this time I click on photos. I know she'll be there.

I find her instantly, tall and pale and feline, her long red hair loose over one shoulder, striking against the white of her wedding gown, her green eyes ablaze with happiness, and next to her, so close, his arm entwined with hers, stands Chris. He doesn't look at the camera; his eyes are on her. I realize I've been holding my breath for a while. I let it out and tap on her photo tag. Zara Poole, Chris's wife. I click on the link.

I recognize her from the hospital lobby that morning—she was talking to someone in the coffee shop queue—but I don't recognize her from school, so it comes as a shock to see she did actually go to Waltham House too. I try to remember redheads from back then, any girls who were that stunning. Surely that would have stuck in my head. Her bio tells me her maiden name was Zara Thompson. But then I see her school dates. She's younger than us, by three years. She would have been thirteen when I left. That's why I don't remember her and it's highly unlikely she'll remember me. I click on her profile picture. Zara looks back at the photographer teasingly, invitingly, her lips parted ever so slightly, and I wonder if Chris took the photo. I catch myself wondering if they're happy.

*Shit. This is not why I am on here.*

I feel a tight gnaw of shame in my stomach. I definitely shouldn't go for that drink with Chris.

I click out of Zara's profile back to Chris's, and then a strange thought strikes me. Is there a chance I could know my patient? Perhaps he did recognize me, and in the same way I couldn't place Zara perhaps I can't recall him because he's older than me. He wouldn't have been a student at the school then, but he could have been a teacher. Perfectly plausible. Although odd that no one else would recognize him from this area. I realize what I really need to do is get my hands on a list of everyone who was working at Waltham House in the years I was there. That would be a start. I could ask Chris. But then I might have to explain why I needed it. Or maybe, knowing Chris, I wouldn't have to tell him, maybe he'd just trust me enough not to have to explain, if I said it was for the case. Which of course it would be. I grab my phone and tap out an impulsive message to him.

For the next two hours I keep searching, recalling, and tapping in the names of everyone I can remember from those years, all those almost-forgotten children of my childhood.

Chris's dad was chief inspector at the Burnham and Hunstanton station. Local police. I should have known Chris would still be here; his family have been and always will be local.

Our family, on the other hand, had no choice but to leave.

Then the thought occurs to me again: If my patient does know me, he knows about what happened. Could he be faking his symptoms to get me to come back here? The lure of intrigue. After all, a patient like this is the only reason I'd ever come back here. It's a paranoid thought and I shut it down. A shiver runs through me and I pull the cashmere throw tighter around me as my thoughts continue to slip and slide over the idea. It would be hard for anyone to pull off what he's doing alone if they were faking, but perhaps he's not doing this alone. I think I hear something in the darkness beyond the patio doors, but when I stand up to peer out I see only my own reflection in its black mirror.

I need to know if my patient is lying. I need to make sure I do my fMRI test as soon as possible. I need to know if this case is really fugue, if he really can't remember who he is. Or if he's doing something else entirely.

# 24

# ZARA AND CHRIS

## DAY 8—SECRETS AND LIES

Zara is on her laptop, fingers clacking over keys, her legs curled gracefully underneath her on the sofa, when Chris finally returns from the hospital. The winter sun is setting outside their Georgian windows, and she's bathed in a soft peach-and-lilac glow.

They bought the house for its period features, the fireplaces, coving, big sash windows—if they couldn't move to London, Zara had argued, then they'd get the best money could buy in Norfolk.

She looks up briefly from her screen as he wanders in. He watches her working, her eyes momentarily masked by a stray curtain of glossy red hair.

"You're back early," she says wryly. He's not. Sarcasm plays across her screen-lit face. "So? How did it go?

"Yeah. Long day," he says, shrugging off his jacket and perching on the edge of an armchair, lost in thought.

Today was supposed to be Chris's day off. He'd been called in to pay a site visit to the hospital and have a conversation with the new doctor about the case. He hadn't been too surprised to be called in, not since the hotline went up. Everyone had been working extra shifts since that had started. When he'd gotten to the station to change into his uniform, he'd been roped into following up on a whole tsunami of hotline leads, none of which had amounted to anything.

Overnight, the well-intentioned hotline had turned into a complete free-for-all. People from all over the country calling in, with all kinds of bizarre sightings and tip-offs, and they, the Burnham and Hunstanton station, had to follow up on nearly everything. Assess the information, grade it in order of relevance or urgency, and flag it up if the lead looked promising. That's a lot of paperwork.

When he'd finally headed over to the hospital it'd taken him a good half an hour to track down the new doctor. And she'd turned out to be *Marni Beaufort*.

He'd found her. Found her in the hospital canteen. After fourteen years.

Seeing her had been very confusing. And now he felt . . . weird. But kind of good weird. He couldn't stop thinking about her. How she used to look playing lacrosse at school, her cheeks flushed in the cold, her mischievous grin, her freckles. The Beauforts had been rich back then, crazy rich. Before it all happened, obviously. And all that wealth had somehow lent them this air, this healthy seductive glow. That calm, the ease, like nothing was ever a struggle, even winning, which the Beauforts seemed to do a lot.

Zara looks up from her article and frowns. She's pretty sure Chris didn't hear what she just said.

She asks again. "How was it with the new doctor, honey?"

Chris's attention snaps back to her, he gives a

quick smile. "Yeah. Yeah, it was good," he says, getting up and heading into the kitchen.

"And . . . ?" Zara probes further, following him into the kitchen, leaning against the doorframe and watching as he stares unseeingly into the fridge.

"And . . . er, and yeah, she was nice." Chris realizes this line of questioning will not go away unaddressed. "Her name is Emma Lewis. Dr. Lewis. She seemed nice. She's from London. Seemed good at her job. The hospital says they're lucky to get her. I told her I'd send her everything we have that could help. And that was it." He closes the fridge door empty-handed. He's not exactly sure what he was looking for in there—but he didn't find it.

"Did she say what she thought it was?" she presses. "What's wrong with him?"

"No. I didn't ask. First day, isn't it?"

"And what's the general mood at the station? Any leads? Is that why you've been so long?"

"Just got dragged into all that hotline stuff as soon as I got there."

"But there must be some interesting stuff in all that, right?"

"Yeah, interesting is definitely the word for it."

Zara frowns. "If it's that pointless, can't they get someone else working on it other than you guys?"

"Not really, Zee. There's never enough of us, even when nothing's happening. We can outsource to other stations but that still means transferring information and making a bunch of outgoing calls for every incoming call we receive."

"Uh-huh." She nods and slides onto the kitchen table bench. Chris can tell she's desperate for information. She must have had a slow day. She leans forward on her hands in a parody of an attentive schoolgirl.

"You know I can't actually tell you any details, Zee. You know that."

"I'll make it worth your while." She pouts provocatively.

"Stop it."

"Can't help it," she says, and changes tack. "Look, honeybun, I am trying really hard, you know how hard I work, I'm trying to pip a lot of people to the post here. And this story is an absolute gift to me. *Nothing* happens here and then suddenly this happens right on our doorstep. I hate to bring it up again but we stayed here, Chris, we didn't move to London, we stayed here and that's all great, honey, but if this story can raise my profile then I can get a better job. A national paper. I wouldn't have to move, we wouldn't have to, I could write from here and just go in to the city once or twice a week. Writing for real, not just this local piecemeal shit I'm doing right now. So, please, Chrissy, throw me a fucking bone, okay? I'll be good, I promise."

Chris shakes his head slowly. "Unbelievable."

"I know, okay. Before you say it, I've heard it before, Chris, you'll lose your job, blah, blah, blah, loss of trust. You won't, Chris. You won't lose your job. Police talk to press all the time. That's life. It's not like I'm asking you for the nuclear codes or anything, I just want a vague update on what's going on with this case. Something that I can package up nicely and sell to editors. I'm doing as much research and tracking on this as you are, honey, I'm on message boards all day, Twitter feeds, you name it. If we share information then surely everybody wins, right? What do you think?"

Chris sits down slowly opposite her, palms on the table, weighing up all she's said. He does worry he's held her back. That someday she'll hate him for it.

"Okay." He pauses, then lets out a low groan. "Something. Oh God, okay. This is what I can tell you. But don't go crazy with this, okay? You promise?"

He knows with absolute certainty that he can't ever mention Marni. But he can give his wife something.

"I promise." Zara purses her lips, trying to mask her moment of pure triumph.

"Okay." Chris pauses, thinking it through one last time. It should be okay to tell her this. "The doctor they sent up today, Dr. Lewis, she's a specialist from London. She was hired by . . . well, let's put it this way, our orders at the station are now coming in from slightly higher up the food chain than before." Zara's brows knit together. "It looks like the government has stepped in on this in some way," Chris clarifies. "They're trying to keep everything locked down up here around this guy for some reason. And before you ask, I don't know what the reason for that is. I have no idea."

Zara nods thoughtfully.

Chris continues. "And this fucking hotline has completely swamped us, Zee, there's too many calls to process. Too many leads. Ever since the story broke. We've got people calling saying he's an illegal immigrant, people saying he's their missing husband or missing son, people saying he looks like an actor they recognize from TV, people saying they saw him in Scotland the day before—you name it, people are saying it." He stops, noticing Zara reach for her mobile phone. "So don't write anything about the station, Zee. You can write about other stuff but not the station. We're handling it."

"Sure, no problem. I'll leave you guys out of it." She rises, leans over the table, and kisses his forehead in one quick motion. "Thank you, thank you, thank you. I love you," she singsongs as she dances back to her laptop.

Chris sighs. He lets his forehead rest flat on the table in front of him for a second. As she wanders back in he raises his head to look up at her.

"And, Chris hon, you can't say any more about this government thing, can you?" she asks. Chris lets out another groan.

"No, okay, don't worry," she adds hastily. "But this doctor. Who is she? I mean, has she done anything like this before? Has she worked for the government on anything else?"

Oh shit. Not Marni. He raises his head now. He thought if he gave Zara something to go on, she'd be happy. "I don't know," he replies. "I don't know if she has. But I doubt it."

Zara looks up sharply at this. "Why do you doubt it?"

"I don't know," Chris flounders. "I guess, she's young, ish. Well, about my age." *Shit,* he thinks. "And, I don't know, she just seems . . . well, as in the dark about this as everyone else. From what I sensed . . . meeting her today."

Chris is a bad liar, he knows this. Better to just avoid questions in the future, he thinks. Thankfully, Zara seems satisfied by his awful answer and wanders out of the kitchen. He lets the tension in his shoulders release and gently rests his head back down on the tabletop.

He wonders if Emma has worked for the government before. Because it's incredibly strange that they chose her for this job, considering her history up here. Whoever assigned her must have known what happened, and surely they'd realize how much the press finding out would harm the investigation, wouldn't they?

But the press won't find out, he tells himself. He'll make sure of that. But if someone else recognizes her, he wouldn't be able to control that. Hell, *he* recognized her right away. But then, he would, wouldn't he, he'd spent the formative years of his life staring at her and her brother across classrooms and playing fields. Other people might not have looked so hard, they might not see Marni's features hidden in Emma's adult face. There's no way Zara will see it. Emma Lewis doesn't look anything like Marni Beaufort, that's for sure, not anymore.

Later that night, while Chris is brushing his teeth in the bathroom, his mobile phone receives a text message. Zara leans across the bed and checks it. There's no name for this contact on his phone, just a number she doesn't recognize.

> Sorry to text so late. Would it be possible to get a list of past employees at Waltham House? I can't say why just yet but I think it might be helpful. Also, might have to rain check that drink. Snowed under.
>
> Emma x

Zara stares at the words intently, as all the possible permutations of what they could mean blow like a forest fire through her mind. Leaving sadness in their wake.

The sounds of Chris pottering in the bathroom drift in to her, she opens her mouth to call to him, so he can explain, tell her it's all a misunderstanding, she's got the wrong end of the stick, but she stops herself. Better to wait and see, she reasons. After all, if she asks him now, he might lie and she's not sure she could handle that. And after a moment that seems to stretch back through their entire lives together, Zara places Chris's phone back down where she found it. She wriggles quietly down into the soft comforting cotton of their bed and reaches up to turn out her bedside light.

# 25

## DR. EMMA LEWIS

### DAY 9—THE NIGHT IT HAPPENED

Chris didn't text me back, but that doesn't mean anything, does it? He was probably already asleep. Lucky sod. I look down at my mobile on the bench next to me. The clock reads 02:00 A.M.

I can't sleep. Guilt, too many thoughts, too many feelings, flowing through me. And I've only been back one day.

I sip my tea and look up at the stars. I've come out for fresh air. I thought about jumping in the car and driving all the way to a petrol garage to buy a pack of cigarettes, but I made a steamy mug of tea instead and came out here to clear my head. It's not as scary out here as it was before. The darkness is somehow comforting.

Looking up past the trees, I can see the glittering arch of the Milky Way carving across the night sky.

It's beautiful, but everything here reminds me of the past, of what happened, especially this sky. I'm so tired of trying not to think about it.

—

It was Bonfire Night. Fourteen years ago. Most years we'd spend it at home; we'd help Dad light our own bonfire in the top field, piling dried leaves and fallen branches, cardboard and old papers. Dad would set up elaborate firework displays while we fetched him coffee to keep warm. Sometimes a school friend would come over, one of Joe's or mine. Sometimes some of Mum and Dad's friends came over. They'd drink Glühwein and chat with our parents as they perched, blankets on knees. The garden would be rigged with Catherine wheels, thin Roman candles, and tightly packed rockets dotted around the lawn, ready to be lit. Joe and I would have hot chocolate with tiny little marshmallows melting into gloop on its surface and chase each other around with sparklers, carving our names in light into the air. But we didn't do that this year, we went somewhere new, which should have raised some red flags at the time but didn't. That night we went to the county fireworks display at Holkham Park.

We all piled into the Range Rover and Dad drove us out there, the red taillights ahead of us building as we headed toward Holkham. When we got to the gravel car park, we joined the bustling throngs of families carrying rugs and hampers as they poured into the parkland, walking the chalkstone track toward the distant lights of the event.

It was freezing that November. We'd wrapped up warm, hats, scarves, shakable pocket warmers; Mum covered every eventuality. The green was skirted by a temporary village of stalls offering refreshments and early Christmas gifts. Mum trekked off across the half-light of the field and brought us back a steaming jacket potato each, filled with beans and butter and melting cheese, which we scooped greedily into our mouths with plastic spoons, the foil hot in our gloved hands as we made our way on to the main event.

In the distance we could see its peaks burning, past the stalls and over the treetops, the spires of it roaring into the night sky, the bonfire. The biggest I'd ever seen, constructed in the center of flat parkland, towering over the surrounding landscape. The crowd was more thickly packed here, a looping semicircle around the enormous flaming pyre. The low hum of happy chat as everyone stood and watched, bursts of laughter, cheers as a log or some other structure within the flames crumbled in a sudden burst of sparks, the occasional whistle and wave to straggling family members.

We stood pressed close to one another, the four of us. The smell of Mum's perfume, Dad's jacket. The orange glow of the burning mound playing across faces, its warmth bathing us.

Dad broke out the sparklers, other families around us shrieking and laughing as they used theirs. I remember him fumbling through his pockets to find the clear blue lighter Mum usually used for the kitchen candle. But after a while he decided he must have left it on the counter at home. Little things like that stick in my mind, the clues he left me sprinkled throughout the night.

Dad asked another man if we could borrow matches and he lit our sparklers with them. I remember looking down at the sparkler in my hand, its sharp white petals flashing in and out between my fingers. Shapes drawn in the air. Afterglow on the eyes. The scents of chestnuts and fire. I burned my fingers holding the stick too long and Joe told me I was stupid not to have dropped it sooner. Mum brought us four bright red toffee apples, the coating thin enough to crack straight through in a bite, the apple beneath dense with sugar.

A full orchestra accompanied that night, playing gargantuan Gothic symphonies and soft dreamscape concertos as we watched crates, logs, leaves, old furniture, and other detritus burst into flames, becoming beautiful again.

We stood and watched it all burn, from the red ember at its center, up into the crisscross maze at its heart, to the pale cream of the cresting flames lapping the black night. And in the sky above, flecks of bright burning gold breaking free and floating. And, higher still above that, the stars, the whole glittering firmament. So many stars.

The music swelled and then the fireworks display began.

The first crack and flash of pure white light shot straight up into the chilly winter air; an explosion of diamond dust.

And then color after color, faster and brighter and louder until the whole sky was lit with pulsing, flashing, magic. And then, as swiftly as it started, it was gone.

The night sky empty but for the afterimage on our eyes and the ghost of smoke in the wind.

I stare into the starlit sky above Cuckoo Lodge and I close my eyes. Such a beautiful night. I try not to feel guilt for what happened next. It wasn't my fault. Not really. But that was the last night any of us saw him. When I open my eyes, I brush the warm roll of tears away.

My phone bursts to life next to me, the ringtone loud and alien in the dark. I fumble for it. Why would someone be calling me at 2:09 A.M.? I wonder if it's

Chris, calling about Waltham House. Or if it's Peter and the story of who I am has leaked already.

"Hello there, is that Dr. Lewis?" It's a man's voice, businesslike, professional.

"Yes. Who's calling?"

"I'm calling from Princess Margaret's. I'm one of the night nurses on the psych ward. Listen, I'm really sorry to call at this hour but it says in the patient notes to call you immediately if there is any change—"

I sit forward on the bench. "What's happened?"

"Well, er, I thought you'd want to know that the patient has started talking."

I freeze. *He knows who I am and he's started talking.* "What did he say?" I ask.

"Okay, so, it doesn't make a lot of sense to me, to be honest. But when I went in to do checks about half an hour ago the patient was sitting up in bed reading and I said, 'How are we doing tonight' or something like that, you know, just to be polite, I knew he wasn't talking, but then he did. He said, 'I'm fine, thank you.' Just like that. And then I asked if he needed anything and he said he'd like to speak to Dr. Lewis. And then he said to tell you that he's sorry you burnt your fingers that night."

My heart leaps into my throat. My mind races until I suddenly decide that I just must have heard him wrong.

"Sorry. What did you say?" I hear the wobble in my voice.

"I know, sorry, I have no idea what that means either—"

"No, say it again. What he said," I bark.

"Er, okay," he continues, cowed. "His exact words were 'Tell Dr. Lewis I'm ready to talk to her. Tell her I'm sorry she burnt her fingers that night,' and that was it really." He tails off, fearful of further admonishment.

I stare out into the shadows beyond the garden, the suffocating darkness of the wood, my breath shallow.

*He knows things about me.* Just like Rhoda said.

But he couldn't have been there that night. *He's sorry I burnt my fingers.* How could he know something so intimate, something so slight, unless he had been there? And if he knows that, what else does he know? And more important, what else is he saying at the hospital right now? He's calling me Dr. Lewis now but he knows my name was Marni.

"Hello? Doctor?" The voice on the line drags me back.

"Yes, sorry. I'll be there in . . ." I shoot up from the bench and look over the low fence to the frosted windshield of my car and then down at my sleepwear and socks. "I'll be there as soon as I can—just tell him I'm on my way."

# 26

## DR. EMMA LEWIS

### DAY 9—WHAT'S MY NAME?

When I enter the room he's talking, a few nurses and aides clustered around him. His voice is low and calm but I can already make out a British accent. Not Ukrainian, not Syrian, not any of the other heavily accented dialects that the papers had been so eager to hear him speak. He's just plain old English.

He falls silent when he sees me enter and heads turn in my direction. Their expressions are inscrutable. It's impossible to know what he's told them, what he's already said, if he's mentioned me, and yet I search their faces for clues.

The way he's looking at me, as if I'm an old friend he hasn't seen in years, as if we knew each other so well.

"Marni?" he asks simply. It's unmistakable in his tone. He knows me.

My glare rakes across the group and their stares scatter like pigeons. I need to say something, I know, and I need to say the right thing.

"My name is Dr. Lewis. I'm the specialist handling your case, we saw each other very briefly yesterday. Do you remember?"

I feel bad disregarding his clear recognition of who I am, but we will get to that in good time, preferably alone.

"What should I call you? Is Matthew all right?"

I've confused him. He blinks. "Matthew's not my real name. You know that, don't you?" he asks.

"Yes, I know. Do you remember your real name?"

He looks hurt for a second and I wonder if I'm being too cold, too distant to this person who so very clearly knows me.

"I can't remember my name, no." He shakes his head.

"Would you like us to stop using the name Matthew? Is there another you'd prefer?" I ask, my tone gentler now.

"No."

"Okay." I make a decision. "Would everyone mind stepping out and giving us the room, please? I'm sure you've all got other patients to see to." There are looks of disappointment but the room quickly clears.

"Marni?" he says again. He's studying my face intently; he seems less sure this time, this time it really is a question.

"Why do you keep using that name, Matthew?"

"Because it's your name. I can't remember mine but I can remember yours."

*No shit.*

"How do you know that name, Matthew?" I hold his gaze. If this is some kind of game of chicken, I want him to know I'm up for the challenge.

"I don't know. I just do." He sounds confused. Peter was right. If this guy is faking, he's the best I've ever seen.

"What else do you know? Do you remember anything else?" I make my way over to his bed and sit beside him.

"Only glimmers. Running through a wood at night." The memory seems to cause him concern; his face darkens. "I don't know if I'm chasing or being chased." He looks at me for some kind of reassurance but I have none to give him.

"Are you scared in the memory?" I ask.

"No, not *in* the memory itself, but when I recall it, it scares me."

"Do you think this memory explains how you ended up on the beach nine days ago?"

"Er, I don't think so." He hesitates. "This memory is old. Maybe years ago. It was at night. There was someone there with me. Something went wrong." He closes his eyes sharply as if to block a thought. I notice his fingers start to tremble in his lap.

"It's okay, Matthew." I move to him and place a gentle hand on his shoulder. He lets me, and I feel the warmth of his skin through his cotton T-shirt. "We don't need to go back over it right now. Why don't you tell me about something else? What other things do you remember?"

He looks up reluctantly; there are dark circles under his eyes. "Little things," he answers. "About people, the people here. I seem to remember these strange things about them. Or rather I know them. What makes them tick, things that have happened to them, things I shouldn't know, but somehow I do. How could that be?" He asks in such a reasonable way I almost try to answer, but I stop myself. I shake my head instead.

"What kind of things do you know about people, Matthew?" I ask calmly, trying to keep my desperate need to know at bay.

"About you, you mean? What do I know about you?"

It's like he can see right through me. He's smart and yet there doesn't seem to be any edge to what he says. How does he know my name? How does he know what happened that night? My heartbeat is so loud it's hard to think. Was he there? Could this be him, somehow?

"If you like." I manage to keep my voice steady, professional.

He raises a hand tentatively toward mine, his touch light and warm. He turns my palm and studies my fingertips. I realize what he's looking for and my breath catches in my throat. He finds it. The tiny dashes of white. The almost invisible scars on the sides of my two fingers and thumb. The little burn marks I've had since that last Bonfire Night. His thumb gently brushes the mark and his gaze finds mine.

*Yes, he knows what happened that night.*

It's a crazy thought but it hits me so hard a wave of emotion rolls up from inside me. He looks sorry. Sorry for what happened. I break his gaze and gently pull back my hand.

"I asked your name earlier," he says. "It's not Marni anymore? They told me it was Emma Lewis. Why did you change it? Was it because of me?"

I inhale deeply to mask the shudder I feel run through me. But I can't escape the fact that he really does remind me of someone. There's just something about him, I can't quite place my finger on it yet. I know it can't be him—he died fourteen years ago. "Why would that be because of you? Who is it that you think you are, Matthew?"

"I don't know yet. I just have this awful feeling

that I did something. To you. Did I do something terrible to you?"

I suddenly feel sick. I look at his face, it's ridiculous to think it. This isn't him. He looks nothing like him, and besides, I saw the body. This must be some kind of sick joke. But Matthew doesn't look like he's joking—his eyes are earnest, a frown is forming between his brows. He's worried by my silence.

But I'm genuinely lost for words. This is not a normal situation. I have no framework for this. A sudden instinct flares inside me: he could be dangerous, he could be here to hurt me. This can't be the person I think he is, but he could be someone who knew him. Someone with a reason to come back. I remember what happened the last time I was here—before we left and tried to reinvent our lives—the very real death threats, the vile letters in the post, the terrifying phone calls. Anger and poisonous hate after what happened. People wanted revenge. Perhaps someone still does?

Matthew watches me from the bed, his handsome face concerned. He certainly doesn't look angry, he looks sad.

*In a way, isn't that exactly what he would look like, if he came back?*

*Don't be ridiculous, Emma, people don't* come back. *Of course it's not him, he's gone. He's dead.*

No, I do not know this man, he's a stranger. He's obviously overheard some things about me in the hospital and internalized the story. Memory-loss patients will cling to anything that fills the gaps; often they don't even know where they've picked things up from.

It happens all the time. There was a famous psychological experiment done in the nineties, the "lost in the mall" experiment, where members of a family were reminded about four episodes that happened in their childhoods. Unbeknownst to them, one of the stories, about being lost in a mall, was entirely fabricated. They were then each asked to recall the details of what had happened to them in each of their four stories. The subjects of the test all ended up clearly recalling being lost in a mall. Each remembered something that never happened—and each had no idea he or she was doing it. We plant our own false memories. And we don't even know we're responsible for it.

Matthew must have heard someone say my old name here, heard the story, and subconsciously processed it. That would explain it.

However, that does mean that someone here in the hospital knows that I am Marni Beaufort. And the only way they could have known that I was coming back here was if they'd been keeping an eye on me. I study Matthew's features. Could he have been the one keeping an eye on me? There's one clear way to find out if he's lying.

"Matthew, would you agree to undergo an fMRI test tomorrow? It's relatively straightforward. It would involve us scanning your brain while I go over some of your memories with you. Do you think you'd be okay to try that with me?"

He scowls and adjusts his blankets. "What is it for?"

I think about equivocating but decide instead to show him my cards. "The test will tell us if you're lying. What you're suffering from—dissociative fugue—is extremely rare, but very easy to prove, or disprove, and I'd like to do that. It will show us if you can remember, or not, and to what extent." Now it's his turn to show me his cards.

He doesn't hesitate. "I think that would be a very good idea, Dr. Lewis."

I pause for a second before nodding. That wasn't exactly how I thought that would go. He one hundred percent believes everything he's saying.

He honestly thinks he knows me. The itch to know more is no longer bearable. "Matthew, what did you mean when you asked me if I had changed my name because of you?"

Panic flares in his eyes, then fades. "I don't know what I did exactly, but I know it was bad. I have these feelings, these awful feelings, they keep bubbling up inside me." He looks down at his hands clasped tight in his lap, as if he were praying. "I wish I could remember what happened, but I can't, and—and maybe that's for the best, you know?" He looks up at me. "I didn't mean to hurt you. Any of you. But I knew I had to find you."

"You had to *find* me? Have you been looking for me, Matthew?"

"I must have been looking for you. I think that's why I ended up on that beach. I know it seems strange but I knew you'd come and find me if I waited. How could I know that?"

"I don't know," I answer honestly.

"Do you recognize me, Emma? Honestly?"

I feel a tug in my chest and I hesitate, unsure of how to answer. I don't recognize him and yet he does remind me of someone so strongly. "Why do you think you were trying to find me?" I ask instead.

He shakes his head. "Because . . ." He sighs heavily and takes a ragged breath. "Because I put the flame out, honey."

His words slam into me, a full-body hit, knocking the air right out of me. *Oh God, it is him.* I feel a rush of nausea—I'm going to be sick.

"And I want you to know that I'm sorry, Marn. I'm so sorry."

I don't stop to think, I stand and leave the room. It's only as I start to run, shoes squeaking down the empty hospital corridor, body shaking, that the vomit comes.

# 27

# DR. EMMA LEWIS

## DAY 9—fMRI

It starts to snow on my morning run. Great soft clumps drifting down through the gaps in the forest canopy as I follow the track that leads away from the lodge.

I only got back from the hospital at around 4 A.M. this morning so I decided to give myself at least five hours' sleep. I'll go in later. Matthew needs time to rest before we do his fMRI scan anyway. I'll head in after my run but right now I need time to process exactly what happened earlier.

After bolting from his room, I managed to pull myself together in the staff locker room, thankfully before anyone saw me. Back in my office I shot off an email to Nick Dunning, asking him to move around some appointments and fit us into radiology for an fMRI today. When I woke, Nick had replied, telling me he'd booked the fMRI in for this afternoon, which is ideal. It gives me enough time to source some prompt images and questions for the test.

I let ideas flash through my brain as I run, my sneakers crunching over frozen leaves and hardened mud while the snow floats sleepily down around me and settles. Today I need to distance myself from the patient, I need to put my messy life to one side to diagnose him. While he may remind me of someone long gone, I do not know this man. And I must remember that no matter what he says, he does not know me. I need to keep that foremost in my mind, whatever happens today. God knows how he knows the things he's been saying, but there will be a logical explanation, and I need to stay far enough away from the subject matter to find that reason.

Back at the lodge, I knock the snow off my shoes and plonk them down by the still-glowing fire. I slept on the living room sofa when I got back this morning, rumpled blankets and pillows evidence of my stay. Order slowly breaking down.

When I get to the hospital I tell the nursing team to prep Matthew and have him sent up to Radiology. I head to my office and email the questions and photos I'll need for the test over to the Radiology Department as well. Only then do I pick up the phone and call Peter.

"He's talking, Peter."

"Emma." There's a pause on his end before he speaks again. "Well, that's fantastic. And what's he saying exactly? Anything helpful?"

I think carefully before I speak; how much should I tell Peter? "He doesn't know his name or who he is. At least that seems to be the impression. You were right, the symptoms seem real. I've ordered an fMRI scan to verify the amnesia and the extent if there is any."

"Good. And he consented to that?"

"Yes, instantly. It was . . . unusual."

"Humph, interesting." He hesitates. "Look, Emma, I think in this particular case it might be worth conducting the scan on your own. Just in case anything sensitive should come up . . . that we aren't expecting. Perhaps once you're set up, best to have anyone else leave the room." He lets the idea hang there for a moment.

My stomach tightens. Is he worried Matthew might reveal who I am?

"Sorry, in case *what* comes up, Peter?"

He chooses his words carefully. "I know you've signed an NDA, but, of course, we can't have everyone at Princess Margaret's signing one. I mentioned before, there are . . . *concerns* relating to the patient's identity."

His evasiveness annoys me. "Tell me what the concerns are, Peter. If I'm going to lock myself in a room with him, I think I deserve to know."

"Uh, well . . . yes, I suppose if you put it like that. There is a concern from the Ministry of Defense that the patient may be military, a missing person. Obviously, it's not ideal that this is only coming to light now—but there we go. There are some conversations going on re jurisdiction—nothing to be concerned about just yet."

What the hell does the Ministry of Defense know about Matthew? "Peter, what makes them think he's military? What's informed that conclusion?" I hear the sharpness of my tone.

"I'm afraid I'm not privy to that just yet, Emma. If it becomes . . . relevant then I'm sure we'll be informed."

"Peter, come on, am I at any risk here? From my patient? I need to know. Do the MOD think he's dangerous?"

There's a silence on the line. Which isn't comforting at all. I suddenly feel so far outside my comfort zone that I almost consider hanging up. But Peter's voice cuts in just in time. "No. No, I don't think it's that sort of situation, Emma. I certainly don't believe so, that hasn't been mentioned by anyone at this stage. I'm confident we would have been forewarned if it was anything like that. But of course, I would say use your own best judgment on this, Dr. Lewis."

*Wow. Thanks, Peter.*

When I reach radiology, Matthew is already safely in position on the MRI tray bed, his head strapped inside the plastic head frame, his face hidden from sight. Rhoda is leaning over him explaining the procedure. She looks up when I enter and rests Matthew's hand back down onto the bed.

"Rhoda, I'm going to need the room to myself once we get started. No other staff members present. Are you okay with that?"

She looks surprised but eager to assist. "If that's what you need, then I can definitely do that, yes, doctor."

"Great. I've already spoken with the radiologist so it will just be Matthew and me. I think the more straightforward we keep this for him, the better."

"Of course." She nods and turns back toward the man on the bed. "I'll get him in and ready and then just let me know and I'll slip out."

Once Matthew is safely inside the machine Rhoda makes her way out of the room with a smile. I seal the ward doors behind her and slip into the control room, engaging the magnetic shield door behind me, sealing Matthew in the MRI room. I find my seat at the control-room console and, through the thick glass that separates me from Matthew, I watch the

MRI bed's smooth motion into the machine. I lean forward and turn on the mic in front of me.

"Matthew, it's Dr. Lewis. Can you hear me?"

I watch his face spring to life on the video screen next to me as my voice comes through his headphones. He opens his mouth to answer.

"I won't be able to hear you, Matthew, so try not to speak, just use the keyboard Rhoda gave you to answer. Press either yes or no. You'll see the questions on the screen above you and you just need to answer yes or no. Rhoda should have given you an emergency squeeze ball as well. I want you to squeeze that as hard as you can if you start to feel concerned in any way or if you need us to stop, okay?"

I watch the screen. He taps *Yes*.

"Good, that's great, Matthew. Now basically, this is how it works. The fMRI will show me the areas of your brain that receive the most oxygenated blood when you perform a task or when you respond to any stimuli. Those will be the areas you're using to perform whatever function we're testing. We're going to start by taking a basic structural scan, so just relax and try not to move. The banging noises are the pictures being taken, so don't worry when you hear them. Now, it's very important you don't move during the scan or the image will be blurry."

He taps *Yes*.

"Excellent. You won't hear my voice for about eight minutes while the scan is under way, okay?"

He squeezes his eyes shut briefly. *Yes*.

"Okay, here we go." I turn off my mic and initiate the structural scan. I watch his face on the screen as the fMRI pounds noisily to life and the first images of his brain begin to take shape on the next monitor.

He looks calm in spite of the overwhelming intensity of the machine thundering around him and I wonder if what Peter hinted at could be true, if he has some kind of military training. I've known the sounds and confinement inside those fMRI units to make the manliest of men uneasy, but not Matthew, he looks perfectly at ease. I lean forward and quickly jot down a final question for the scan. It can't hurt.

The screen flashes. I turn on the mic again.

"That was great, Matthew. Nice clear images. Now we're going to dive right into the next couple of tests, if that's okay?"

I watch his face on the screen. He smiles and taps *Yes*.

"I need you to perform an action in this test. I want you to tap each finger in turn on your thumb of your right hand and just keep doing that until the screen above you says stop."

*Yes*.

We steam through the basic brain activation tests: motor function, sound processing, visual processing, and then we get to the meat of the scan.

"Okay, Matthew. Now I'm going to show you some images on the screen. I just want you to think about what you see, how the images make you feel and what they remind you of. You don't need to direct your thoughts in any particular way. It will all just happen naturally, so just relax."

*Yes*.

"Then if you're okay with that, we'll go straight into the question portion of the scan. A question will show on your screen. All you will need to do is choose a simple yes or no answer."

He pauses a second before tapping *Yes*.

"You're doing great, Matthew. Don't worry about a thing."

He smiles and I click off the mic.

---

I set up the photo sequence and press start.

A photograph of an empty beach.

His eyes flick fast over the image, pupils dilating fractionally, he inhales sharply.

I watch the fMRI light up. His cortex now aglow, pulsing, as it processes the image. Then his amygdala, the fight-or-flight center, blazes, processing his emotional response to the stimuli. Immediately followed by a flare in his hippocampus—relevant memories are being sourced. Memory Retrieval 101.

Matthew remembers being on the beach. But then, we knew that, didn't we?

I check the video link; he's very pale. I check his vital signs: his pulse is slightly raised. To be expected; the last time he was on a beach must have been absolutely terrifying.

Now to test whether his memories go any further back than that day on the beach.

I flick to the next photo in the sequence.

A stock family photo—a young couple, each holding a child in their arms.

I watch the fMRI images as they register. Cortex firing, only a dim glow from the amygdala, and nothing from the hippocampus. Interesting. Either Matthew can't remember having a wife and child or he's never had either.

I flick to the next picture.

Another family photo this time from the 1980s—a couple in their forties with a seven-year-old son; it's more formal in style.

I've chosen a stock image from the eighties so it will resonate more with Matthew's memories of being a boy, and potential memories of his own parents, if he can access them.

I watch the fMRI screen. Visual cortex glows, and then the amygdala leaps to life, a burst of brain activity blazing on the screen. An extremely strong emotional reaction to the idea of parents or childhood. But as I study the dark mass of the hippocampus, there is nothing. *Nothing.* He has no memories of a family. I realize I'm holding my breath. I double-check the screen. No, there is no activation.

He really can't remember.

A fizz of excitement thrills through me. Matthew might be the first fully verifiable case of fugue.

In spite of everything that's happened over the last two days, I feel a bright burst of joy inside. I can't help but smile to myself. Buoyed, I flick to the final image.

A thick green forest fills the screen.

I watch his face on the screen, his pupils widening as he makes sense of it. Last night Matthew mentioned having one clear memory, of being in a wood.

I look to the fMRI screen. His visual cortex activates, but his amygdala is strangely subdued, given how he spoke about the memory. I study the screen and then a sudden flash, an intense burst of activation in the hippocampus. A flash of memory. I jolt forward, leaning into the screen, and a constellation of areas in the cerebral cortex glow in answer to the initial flash. I've never seen anything like it, such a localized and specific reaction. I glance at his amygdala again. There's hardly any emotional engagement. No emotional connection to these memories. My focus is pulled by a sudden low beeping below the screen.

The lower screen is flashing—Matthew's heart rate has soared well above the recommended level. I hover my hand above the fMRI's emergency stop button and turn to check on his face on the video screen. Then I pull back my hand in surprise. Matthew's face is utterly calm. His breathing is normal. I check the readouts again. His heart is pounding. He should be hyperventilating, but none of it is visible. The bright areas of his brain's center for self-control, the dorsolateral prefrontal cortex, are glowing with vivid intensity. Somehow he's masking it, suppressing it, he's using self-control.

*Incredible self-control.*

I click off the last photo and reset the system, taking a second to shake off the oddness of what just occurred. I let his heart rate settle.

We need clear readings for the next portion of the test. The most important portion.

After a moment I turn on my mic again. "Matthew, are you okay to continue?"

*Yes.*

I check his vitals and everything has made its way back to the appropriate levels. I guess we're safe to move on.

I bring up the Q&A intro screen, explaining that I will not speak but he should respond to the text on the screen by pushing either *Yes* or *No* on his keypad.

*Yes.*

I start the sequence.

**Were you found on a beach?**

*Yes.* His hippocampus activates briefly, the same as before.

**Do you know your name?**

Matthew pauses for a microsecond, then taps *No*. His hippocampus does not activate although his amygdala flares and his heart rate spikes.

**Do you know what happened to you before you found yourself on the beach?**

Matthew closes his eyes. *No*. No activation in the hippocampus, only amygdala and dorsolateral. That's fascinating—self-control again.

I pause, finger poised over the final question in the sequence. His pulse is high but not above recommended levels. I click the next question. There's no simpler way to find out if we're dealing with a dangerous man, someone who the military might be concerned about misplacing.

**Have you killed?**

He looks directly up at the screen, his pupils constricting as if he can see right through the camera to me. He seems to hold my gaze, unflinching and steady. On the fMRI his dorsolateral glows white-hot, overshadowing everything else. There's that self-control again. The beeping starts once more on the screen below, and I tear my eyes away from his.

His heart rate is way too high: tachycardic.

I hit the emergency stop button on the fMRI machine and jump up to release the control room shield door. I heave the door open and race into the scanning room, slamming my palm into the bed release mechanism on the side of the machine. The hydraulic system kicks in and the bed glides out achingly slowly from the bulk of the fMRI. I see him now, he's gasping for breath, head still lodged in the head brace, hands fumbling at its clasps. I run to him and swiftly unhook the fastenings.

"Matthew, are you all right? Can you hear me?"

He clutches at his chest now, desperate, deep in the throes of a panic attack. He can't breathe. My eyes swing to the readout next to him, his blood oxygen is lethally low at fifty. I look around the room but there is no one here to assist me. Damn it. I smash my hand on the emergency call buzzer and grab an fMRI safe oxygen tank, wheeling it quickly to the bed. I push the head brace away, and twisting the tank valve I slide the mask safely over his face, before I kick off my shoes and scramble up behind Matthew on the bed. I pull him back toward me, cradling him, his head and shoulders resting against my chest. It's not flattering but I've got him. I slide one arm under his shoulder and brace him. I need to calm him, to get him to slow his breathing. I need to lower his ludicrously high heart rate. He needs to breathe.

I hold him tight. "Shh, shh, Matthew. It's okay," I soothe, but he struggles against me, wheezing and fighting for breath. "It's okay, Matthew, you just need to calm down, breathe slow. Everything is fine. Just breathe." He loosens back into me, his breath still snatching noisily in his throat. But at least he's listening to my voice. "That's it, Matthew. Good. Now nice and slow. In through your nose, out through your mouth. Good. That's perfect. Everything is going to be okay, Matthew." He takes a noisy breath in through his nose, and lets it out audibly through his mouth.

"Good. That's good. I'm right here. Everything is fine. I promise you." I feel the weight of him against me, his fear, his trust, his vulnerability.

There wasn't time to get an fMRI reading on that final question, *Have you killed?* But, in a way, what just happened might be answer enough.

# 28

## DR. EMMA LEWIS

### DAY 10—A VISIT FROM JOE

Matthew is recovering on the ward. It's Friday and I'm taking the day off, to the extent that a doctor on call can ever really have a day off.

When I open the front door of the lodge, I find that everything is smothered in thick white. There must have been another flurry of snow overnight. The forest branches bend low with sparkling weight, while the garden, bench, and long lane all the way to the road glitter brilliantly in the winter sunlight.

I zip up my down jacket to my chin, pat my pocket to feel for the lump of my hospital pager, and scrunch briskly out across the snow to my car. I'm heading to pick up Joe from the train station.

I texted him late last night and, like the hero that he is, he texted back that he'd drop everything and come first thing. I need someone to talk to, some perspective, just for a day. He can't stay the night, as Rachel's working tonight and can't watch Chloe, but at least I'll have a few hours' company.

I drive through a fresh winter wonderland, the radio playing in my car the only sound in the muffled white. After everything bad that happened to me here it's still impossibly beautiful, this place.

Thankfully, it turns out they do salt the roads, even this far out of town, but as I turn off onto the rural station lane I see the council budget obviously doesn't stretch this far. When I reach the station entrance Joe's waiting, ankle-deep in snow, beaming from ear to ear, the only one on the platform. He pulls me into a hug as soon as he jumps into the car. He holds me tight for a long time, my left leg jamming hard against the hand brake, but I don't pull away, I need his love.

"There you are," he says.

"Here I am," I agree, head buried in his jacket, safe for a second.

I suggest we head back to Cuckoo Lodge and have some hot chocolate before we head out for a cold walk along the beach. Joe's already wrapped up warm in a Barbour and wellies but I need to grab some boots.

Joe keeps the conversation ticking over on the short drive, diplomatically sensing I'm not quite ready to talk about anything more serious just yet. He tells me Mum's fine with me being here, whatever I need to do for myself I should do, she says. He tells me about his little Chloe and her new obsession with his briefcase. I'm glad of the distraction. I need to clear my head and reset my bearings before I can talk to someone else about what's happening here. I knew I needed Joe.

I sense him tense slightly when we pass a sign for Burnham Market, at least twenty miles from Holt and our old house. No one else but me would notice, but the story he's telling me about Chloe gets a little louder, a little funnier.

He hasn't been back here either since it happened.

I've forced him back. He's here for me. I glance across at his face as he talks, and I wonder how he stayed so well adjusted, so sane. So lovely. With his job and his wife and his gorgeous baby girl. I'm not jealous, I'm amazed, and incredibly grateful to have someone like him in my life.

As I pull down the drive leading up to Cuckoo Lodge, Joe gives a low whistle of appreciation. I feel an odd sense of pride. The house is beautiful, especially in the snow, and because Joe's an architect, its beauty isn't wasted on him.

"Oh sweet Jesus," he murmurs. "This is where they put you? This is part of the Holkham estate, right?"

"I don't know, is it? It's definitely Victorian."

"Yeah, no shit, Sherlock."

I laugh and he leans forward to study the chimneys, the cornicing, through the windshield.

"You like?" I tease.

I make us our hot chocolates and we carry them out into the back garden with some blankets so we can enjoy the winter sun on our faces.

And almost immediately Joe broaches the subject we've both been evading. "So, shouldn't you be at work? Isn't that what they're paying you for?" He smiles and sips his chocolate.

"I thought you were supposed to be encouraging me to work less!" I say with a surprised laugh, but inside I feel a sharp pang of guilt. My patient is still ill, I could be doing something, but instead of working I am here. I know I can't work seven days a week, but time off always make me uneasy. "There's not really much I can do at this stage, Joe. My patient's talking now, but his memory is limited. And yesterday was pretty intense. I told him to take it easy today. I've got a big day planned tomorrow and he needs to rest. I'm going to take him on a trip, visit some places that might trigger some memories. He must have got to that beach somehow; we'll try the roads nearby, local stations, anywhere he might have been just prior to being found. He's making me a list today of anywhere he can think of that might help. But aside from that there's really nothing I can do. And I'm on call, if anything comes up. I can be there in thirty minutes."

"Em, are you going to tell me what's going on?" he asks when I've finished. He's no longer smiling. "Or have you just invited me down here for my sparkling conversation?"

"Oh God, Joe! Okay, here it is. It's so—well, it's beyond weird," I blurt out. "The patient, he knows who I am. My patient."

"Isn't that a good sign?" He hasn't grasped what I just said. He's grinning.

"No. No, it's not, Joe. He knows my real name." I feel a selfish relief when I see his smile freeze. Because now I know it's not just me going through this anymore. Misery loves company. "He called me Marni. He knows what happened. He knows all about Dad."

"What do you mean?"

"Exactly that. Yesterday morning he just started talking, out of the blue. He said he needed to talk to me and when he did *he said he was sorry, Joe*. About what he did, to us, to everyone. He said he was sorry I burnt my fingers." I let that fact hang in the air between us.

Joe grimaces and empties his drink into the snow. After a moment he asks, "Who does he think he is? Dad?" He's deadly serious now.

"I think so, yes."

"Christ! And you do too, don't you?"

"Don't be ridiculous, Joe, of course I don't. He's about twenty years younger and he looks nothing like him. I just, I don't know what the fuck is going on here. What the fuck is going on here?" I want to weep.

"Do you recognize him at all?"

"No."

"He's not one of Dad's old work friends or something?"

"Too young."

"You think he's still alive, don't you?" The bluntness of it shocks me. I pause too long. "He's gone, Emma, remember? You saw, we all saw. We buried him. He is not somewhere out there. This isn't him, it isn't someone he's sent. I don't know what this is but it's not that." I break from his gaze and stare out at the sparkling forest. "It's some kind of misunderstanding. Or it's a trick, Em."

"It's not a trick, Joe." If there's one thing I know for certain it's that my patient isn't lying. "He really can't remember. He wouldn't be able to fake the scans I put him through yesterday."

"Then he must have picked these ideas up somewhere else, right? Overheard things? Someone might be putting him up to it."

"That's what I thought. But that still means someone at the hospital *knows*. That they knew I was coming even before I got there. Which is weird, Joe. My patient said my name the first time we met."

"But you said he only started talking yesterday!"

"Officially yes. I didn't mention it to anyone at the time, but he said my name on my first day. I heard him. He whispered it."

"He what?" Joe frowns. "Whispered it? Are you sure?"

"He mumbled it. It wasn't threatening or anything."

"Why the hell didn't you tell anyone? Why didn't you say anything?" He stares at me, incredulous.

I look away, down at the hot chocolate in my hand. My fingers are freezing. "You know why, Joe. And . . . because I thought maybe . . . maybe I'd imagined it."

"Bloody hell, Em! You really shouldn't be back here, should you?"

"I know, Joe, I know. Please, just help me out. I need you to help me out here."

"Okay. Okay. So." He shakes his head with disbelief and refocuses on the facts. "Someone at that hospital knew you were coming here before you arrived, because your patient was there days before you even agreed to treat him. And this someone knew that Emma Lewis was Marni Beaufort? How would they know that, Emma? The police are the only people who know we changed our names. And that was years ago. It's protected information. How could anyone find out?"

I think of Chris. Chris the policeman, with his database and his searches. *Shit.*

I can't tell Joe about Chris. "But that's not all of it. I—oh God, this is going to sound so insane—but I think he might be dangerous."

"What, who? Your patient?"

"Yeah, I'm not supposed to talk about him, I signed an NDA, but the government seems to think he could possibly have some kind of a military background. They won't tell me. It's classified."

Joe slams his empty mug down hard onto the snow-covered table. "What the hell is going on up here? You shouldn't be being asked to do things like this. It's—you don't have training in that—"

Suddenly my pager buzzes to life in my pocket.

The hospital.

I throw a look to Joe as I fish it out and check the display. "Shit. One second. I need to call them."

He eyeballs me as I rise and head deeper into the garden.

"Hi, it's Dr. Lewis," I answer. "Oh, okay, really? I see . . . I see. Um, okay, well, is there someone in particular I should be speaking to? Right, okay, right, and can I speak to DC Barker now?" I lock eyes with Joe as I say this new name; his eyebrows rise.

"Okay," I continue into the receiver. "Wait! No! No, sorry . . . No. I do *not* give my consent to that, at all. No. I'd have to discuss . . . Well. I understand that, of course. Right, well, I'll be there as soon as I can. Right. Thank you for letting me know." I hang up and turn to Joe.

"The Metropolitan Police are at the hospital, they've taken over from the local police force. Apparently, now they think he's some boy that went missing—abducted—in the early nineties. The police have got a social worker with them and they're trying to get access to the ward right now. Apparently, they want to question him about it before he meets the parents."

"Jesus Christ," Joe exclaims. "First they think he's a soldier and now he's some missing kid?"

"God knows what evidence they think they have, Joe, but he is not ready for this kind of shit. Even the most basic questioning is triggering panic attacks. If they wade in, with no proper medical training, and start questioning him about being held in captivity for almost thirty years—God knows what kind of trauma that'll cause. Especially if they're right about it!"

I dash into the house and grab my car keys, Joe following after, incredulous. "Stop, Em! Just stop! Stop what you're doing!" he barks, bringing me instantly to a standstill. Joe never raises his voice. "Em, listen to me. This situation is insane." I read the concern on his face. "You should not be putting yourself through this, there's no need for it, let someone else do this job. You shouldn't have come back here. I know we talked it through before you agreed, but I didn't realize it would be like this—with the police and press and what's been going on with this particular patient—plus, I thought you were in a better place yourself, Em. I *thought*—no, you *made me think*—you would be able to handle all of this, coming back here."

"I *can* handle it, Joe," I protest fiercely, but I know I'm lying. Because Joe wouldn't be here if I could handle it, would he? *Shit.*

"Em, we can just go home, you know. Right now. You can just call the hospital and tell whoever you tell that you're resigning. The world won't collapse. We can just go. I mean, the Met showing up unannounced sounds like a pretty good reason to step back anyway, doesn't it?"

I feel my resolve falter—he's right, there's something so incredibly off about all of this—but then I remember Matthew's words that first night. How could he know those things unless he'd been there that night, or known someone who was? I need to know who he is. I think of his trust in me yesterday as he struggled for breath. I push the feeling away.

"No. I said I'd do it, Joe. I told my patient that I'd help him. I promised him that everything would be okay."

Joe's tone softens. "That's not your call, Emma. You don't get to control whether everything is okay or not. You're not omnipotent. You can only do your best. This, all of this, is too much. For someone so intelligent you can be so stupid! Let someone else handle it. This guy—whoever he turns out to be—is not your responsibility."

"No, Joe, he is. He actually is because that is my job. I wish I could leave it to someone else but no one else here has my expertise. I'm the only person here, medically, who *can* help him." I'm saying it but I don't know if it's true. I'm sure there are other doctors Peter could call. Maybe Richard Groves could take over remotely. Perhaps it might be better, for Matthew, for me, if I did step aside, given his strange connection to me. I take in Joe's exasperated face. "All right," I say, finally. "I'll stop. I'll just do the rest of today, okay? Then I'll stop. I'll tell them I need to hand over."

Joe holds my gaze. "Promise? You'll sort this Met thing out and then you'll let them know you're done? You'll resign from this case?"

"Yes," I say, fingering the car keys in my hand. If Matthew is the missing Benjamin Taylor, then all my questions about how he knows me are redundant anyway, aren't they? The sooner I find out if he's Benjamin, the sooner I'll know this is all in my head. "But right now, I really need to go in, Joe."

He sighs, then nods. "I'll come to the hospital with you and get the train back home from King's Lynn. You can call me later, let me know how it goes."

I turn back to him. "Wait, Joe, I don't think you should come." He looks confused, so I explain. "The press found out Matthew was talking yesterday, they're all over the hospital. I don't want you to have to go through that. It's like before."

The color drains from his cheeks and he swallows before rallying. "Well, they better watch out, hadn't they, 'cause I don't know about you, but I've certainly learned a few tricks since then." He gives a winning smile just as my phone explodes into life again.

# 29

## DR. EMMA LEWIS

### DAY 10—TINKER, TAYLOR, SOLDIER, SPY

Media tents line the back of the car park like festival booths. There are television trucks, presenters getting makeup touch-ups while they scan scripts, production runners dashing back and forth. Someone's even set up a food truck to feed them all. And I thought it was bad when I left last night after the news broke that Matthew was talking. It seems I'm the last to hear about the Met's involvement in the case. I feel Joe shift in the car seat next to me. *Oh God, I shouldn't have brought him here. Why did I let him come?*

They recognize my car as soon as I pull up to the staff bay, and start shouting and running toward the car—they know I'm Mr. Nobody's doctor. And they know that if I'm back at the hospital, then something is definitely happening. I look to Joe. He nods and pops his car door. Thankfully, I catch sight of the security chief, Trevor, ahead of the throng rushing toward us. When he gets close enough he eyes Joe quickly before launching into an update.

"The Met just gave a press statement out front.

The parents are on their way, apparently." He curses. "These lot are all here to see the Taylors."

I catch Joe's eye. *Jesus.*

A barrage of questions rolls toward me. "Dr. Lewis, can you confirm that Matthew is the missing Taylor child?"

"Benjamin Taylor disappeared in September of 1992. Do you have any knowledge of his whereabouts over the twenty-seven years he's been missing?"

"Have you spoken with the parents yet, Dr. Lewis?" I become aware that a camera crew is now filming us as we walk, the cameraman walking backward in front of us as our strange parade rushes on.

"Is the patient making a speedy recovery, Dr. Lewis?"

"Does he have any memory yet of the trauma he's been through?"

"Was he held against his will for the duration?"

"Can we expect to see Benjamin out of hospital soon, Doctor?"

Trevor fends them off, holding the crowd back as we head inside. As we break through into the lobby I gasp in a breath and three security guards block the way of the press after us. The doors slide shut, muffling their shouted questions. I try to keep my expression neutral, even though every pore wants to scream *Leave us alone*. I'm keenly aware that we're still on camera. Joe's expression is unreadable, except for his eyes. In them I see that haunted look I remember so well. We've been through walks like this before, Joe and I. And they don't get easier.

As I leave Joe with Trevor to head back to the train station via the back entrance, he hugs me, tight. "Call me after you've done it," he whispers.

---

Matthew is waiting for me on the ward.

He's standing with his back to me, staring out the window at the crisp winter blue of the open sky, not a cloud in sight. "They told me I might be called Benjamin. I don't feel like a Benjamin." He speaks with a lightness that almost breaks my heart.

"I'm sorry this is all happening to you, Matthew. I don't really understand yet on what basis they're making this connection."

He turns to face me. "Do you think they could be right? Is this who I am? Benjamin Taylor?"

"I don't know," I say, sitting down on his bed to work through it properly for the first time. "Let's look at the facts." Joe managed to find an old news story from the nineties on his phone on the drive here. "Here's what the authorities know. . . . Twelve-year-old Benjamin Taylor left his house in Tottenham on the twenty-seventh of September, 1992, to walk to school—but he never made it there. At the time, there was a national search for him; they did a reconstruction of his last movements and they questioned a number of suspects. But Benjamin was never seen again." I'm careful now. "His parents didn't stop looking, though. They were very vocal during the campaign and they've kept up Benjamin's website all this time. Ben's father has been checking the missing persons database every week since. That's how they saw your photo."

Matthew looks at me. "That's a sad story."

"Yes, it is," I say solemnly as he sits down next to me.

"But . . . what would I have been doing for the past twenty-seven years?"

God, what a question. "I'm not sure, Matthew. But if I had to make this fit, in any plausible way—which we really don't have to do—but if I had to? I'd say the fact that your circadian rhythm is completely screwed up could, potentially, be down to a lack of natural light. If you'd been kept somewhere. Your head wound, your memory loss, all of it could point toward trauma received during some kind of escape. The police must have a reason for suspecting you're Benjamin. Plus, the Taylors seem to recognize you. And you are the right age."

"You think I've been in a basement for almost thirty years? That's your theory?"

I can't help but smile slightly. "No, I don't think you've been in a basement for twenty-seven years—but that could be what they're thinking."

"How would I have escaped from this hypothetical basement?"

"I don't know, but I'm guessing it would definitely be possible for a man of your height and build to overpower a man in his, by now, say his . . . sixties?" I can't help it but I giggle slightly at this. "Oh God, this is awful."

"This is a horrible story, Emma," he says, with that lightness of tone again. Thankfully, right now he has no connection to this story.

I mean, even if he is Benjamin Taylor, let's not make him remember being Benjamin Taylor—nobody wants to be the person who was potentially locked in a basement for decades.

"They want to meet you. The parents," I say carefully, watching his reaction. I'll pull the plug on this in a heartbeat if he needs me to.

"Why do they want to do that?"

"Because they want to know if you're their son, I'd imagine."

He rises and walks over to the window. "But even if I am," he says, looking down at the media swarming below, "I'm not really, am I? I don't remember being anyone's son yet."

"No, you certainly can't be expected to be something you don't even remember."

Silence fills the room and when he speaks again I jump slightly at the sound.

"Who do *you* think I am?" he demands. I can't read his expression against the stark light of the window.

"I don't know, Matthew. That's what we're all trying to find out, isn't it?"

"I know, but *you*—who do you really think I am? Not as my doctor, not as my psychiatrist, but as a person."

I stifle a shudder. I can't tell him who I think he is. The man I think he is died fourteen years ago. Matthew moves away from the light and his face comes into sight, his intelligent eyes studying me.

I push the thought away, taking a moment before answering. "I think there's a possibility you may have been in the military. I think you could be suffering from PTSD. Of course, there is the possibility that the PTSD could be from any kind of trauma, but I think it's unlikely that you have been held against your will for the last twenty-seven years. That much seems clear to me, both professionally and . . . as a person."

He studies me, then nods. "Okay. That makes sense." He sits down in the visitor's chair and rubs his face. "I'll meet them," he says decisively. "If it helps them. But I have no interest in being Benjamin Taylor."

For a moment I think I've misheard him. It's such a strange way to put it, but I understand what he means. He doesn't believe it's true but he wants to see if any of it triggers something; he needs to know. And he wants to help these people. Perhaps he is Benjamin. At this stage he could be anyone.

"Are you sure you want to do this?" I ask.

"As long as you're there. Yes."

# 30

## DR. EMMA LEWIS

### DAY 10—FACES IN A CROWD

We hear them arriving outside, the distant rumble of the press coming to life by the hospital entrance, questions, endless greedy questions. The scrum and jostle outside sounds like no more than a polite murmur from here, now that we have moved to the quiet of the visitors' room.

There's a tap on the door and I rise from my seat as Nick Dunning pops his head around it. "They're just making their way up. Should be with you shortly. The Met have asked that the social worker be present to take notes. Is that okay?"

"That's not a problem, thank you, Nick. We're ready whenever they are."

He nods efficiently, his eyes gliding to Matthew to double-check. Satisfied with what he sees, he gives another nod and leaves.

I look to Matthew: he offers me a wan smile. I give him one back, then as I watch him bring a plastic cup of water to his lips I notice the slight tremor in his hand and suddenly for the first time the idea that Matthew might actually *be* Benjamin Taylor seems a reality. I remind myself of his extraordinary levels of self-control. It occurs to me that Matthew might not be telling me everything he remembers. The scan was only yesterday but a lot can come back in a day. He might be starting to remember things. This could be who he is. He catches my eye and I start to speak, but as I do the visitors' room door opens.

Mrs. Taylor is dignified and calm, a beautifully dressed woman in her sixties. She holds Mr. Taylor's hand tight in hers. Eyes flutter wordlessly over faces. Introductions happen in the awkward way one would expect. And after the initial shock of meeting, everyone settles into a seat. Mr. Taylor's eyes wander, wet with emotion, while Mrs. Taylor's pale blue gaze does not leave Matthew. I watch him carefully now too.

The social worker a beat behind noisily takes a stool and pulls out a large file to take her notes. Her expression is grim and she avoids my eyes.

Mrs. Taylor speaks first, very gently. "Do you recognize us, dear?" she asks hopefully.

Mr. Taylor looks away, clenching his hands. He doesn't look like a healthy man. I'd guess at high cholesterol and blood pressure, judging by his ruddy cheeks and reddened nose. But of course, drink could be involved as well, and who could blame him?

Matthew's gaze flickers over the hunched Mr. Taylor before settling back on Mrs. Taylor.

He takes a moment, choosing his words very carefully. "No. No, I don't. But then, I don't recognize anyone really, I'm afraid." He smiles apologetically. "At least not at the moment." His eyes connect with mine. We both know what he just said isn't true: he does recognize someone—he recognizes me. And it suddenly occurs to me what that must mean to him. To recognize someone in a world of strangers. I am the only person he seems to recognize. *But how?*

"But you remember the house, son?" Mr. Taylor raises his head. "Our house. Everything that happened before the, er . . . ?"

The air in the room changes at Mr. Taylor's use of the word "son." The social worker's ears prick up.

Matthew hesitates. There's so much weight in what these people are asking from the situation. I can see Matthew's thoughts whirring. What should he say? Is he Benjamin? If he was to come to that realization, right here, right now—I can't even imagine how terrifying that would be. To know that terrible things might have been done to you but for you to have no memory of those things. Decades lost. Or to have it all rush back in an instant. I realize I shouldn't have let Matthew do this, even though he wanted to; he needs to remember at his own speed. Triggering too much could cause another panic attack. He may be desperate for a past but perhaps Benjamin's past isn't a past worth going back to. Whatever happened to Benjamin Taylor after he vanished couldn't have been good.

Matthew answers with a lightness of touch that makes my heart ache. "Sorry, but I don't remember a house. Any house. If I'm honest with you, I don't remember much of anything before I was found on that beach. I remember what's happened over the last ten days . . . but that's about it, at the moment." His answer is kind but there's a finality to it. How could there not be? Right now he has nothing to give them, there is only future stretching out ahead of him.

The Taylors stare at him, lost, unclear where the conversation should go next. They begin to realize, after all their years of searching, that the prize they were fighting for might have changed so utterly that he may now be just a stranger who doesn't even recognize them.

Mr. Taylor speaks first, breaking the flat silence, trying to infuse it with the magic they thought they would find here. "You look just like him, you know. Our Benj."

"He means you look just how he might have looked," his wife corrects him gently.

"Yes, yes. He was only . . . well, twelve, when he left, you know." Mr. Taylor gives a forced smile before turning to elicit help with the floundering exchange, first from me and then the police social worker. "Doc, what do you think? Sue? Do you think that we might be onto something here . . . ?" He falters, because what can he say? *Is Matthew ours? Is this one finally our Benjamin?*

I look to the social worker, but she remains mute, her expression a dumb show of empathy.

*Excellent. Well, that's helpful. Thanks a bunch, Sue.*

I grasp the untethered conversion. "It's hard to say, Mr. Taylor. All we can do really is wait. There was the chance that Matthew might have recognized you immediately and then we would have known. However . . . I'm not sure that has happened. But memory is a complex system. I think perhaps Matthew just needs time and hopefully things should start to come back to him. And once they do, we should be in a better position to know."

"Of course, of course. We don't want to rush anything." Mr. Taylor is piteously quick to agree.

I notice Matthew's gaze drift away to the window. Jesus. God knows what's going on in his mind. His energy has dwindled, though, that much is clear. He can't keep this up anymore. He doesn't recognize these people, I am still the only person in this room whom he recognizes. This is a dead end. I make a decision.

"I think what would probably be best is if we finished up here for today. We should hear back on a DNA match by later this afternoon, and if it's a fit then we can check back in a couple of weeks and see where Matthew is in terms of recovery by then, if that works for you both?" There's a heavy pause while neither Taylor answers, so I dive back in. "I know it's not the outcome any of us wanted today, but what's important now is Matthew's recovery and giving him the time he needs to adjust."

Mrs. Taylor sits up straighter in her chair. "Yes, yes, Doctor, you're quite right," she says. I can see in her eyes she's already trying to work out what they'll tell everyone outside, everyone back home, the people on TV. Just another false alarm. Twenty-seven years of false alarms.

"Let's go, Jim, come on," she says, sliding her hand into one of his and giving it a little squeeze. He looks into her eyes, lost for a moment until she smiles at him. The bravery, the selflessness, of that smile breaking my heart.

They leave us with promises of more contact to come, at least that will be the official line when they reach the press outside. But I think we all know in our hearts this is the end of Matthew's role in the Taylors' lives. Matthew isn't their son. Watching them walk away hand in hand down the corridor, I find myself hoping they find it in themselves to stop, to stop searching, and finally carve out their own little piece of life in the time remaining.

When I turn back to Matthew he's watching me. He holds my gaze silently for a long while, a calmness settling back between us as the Taylors' footsteps recede. A sad smile breaks across his face and he gives me the tiniest shake of his head. He doesn't know them. He isn't their son. I think of the real Benjamin, out there somewhere. Whether he's a lost forty-year-old man or a twelve-year-old boy in a shallow grave, either way, I hope he's at peace. I follow Matthew's gaze as he watches the couple clear the corner at the end of the corridor.

"It's okay," I tell him. "They'll be fine. You did a really good thing, Matthew. Why don't you head back to the ward and get some rest? You deserve it," I say.

Back in my office I call Peter. I need to find out why the hell this fiasco was ever allowed to happen in the first place. Why a meeting was scheduled before DNA results were confirmed.

"I can only apologize."

Peter can only apologize. And seeing the six missed calls from him on my mobile I'm inclined to believe that he did do everything within his power to stop the Met from wading in without medical consent.

"I wasn't informed of their sudden interest in the case until this afternoon, Emma! If I had been, this would have gone through the appropriate channels instead of the less than ideal scenario we now find ourselves in." This is the most agitated I've ever heard Peter. He pauses to regain composure. "I tried to contact you but I'd imagine you were already in the thick of it there. I'm so sorry, Emma."

"It's fine, Peter, honestly. Matthew was happy to meet them. It wasn't ideal but I think there's no harm done." But then I remember the press still lurking outside. "Is there a line we should be taking with the media? It's not looking like Matthew is related to the

Taylors. I'm guessing the DNA match will come back negative."

"I think it's best to stick to no comment for now, Emma. I'll be liaising with someone at the Met this evening and you can be assured that it will be them and not the hospital taking responsibility for this unfortunate line of inquiry. Let the Met release a statement first." Peter sighs. "As they say, if the job was easy . . ."

I remember my promise to Joe. I'm supposed to resign now. I promised. I dealt with this fresh crisis and now I should stop.

*I should say something to Peter.*

But instead I think of Matthew's look to me in the visitors' room earlier. He didn't recognize the Taylors but he recognized me. I don't know how he knows me but he knows me; who I am, my secrets. Things I've been at pains to forget for so long. I'll never know if I leave now.

And just like that, the moment to say something passes.

"So, how did the fMRI go yesterday?" Peter continues, oblivious. "Anything interesting we should know about?"

I shake off thoughts of leaving and of Joe, and I slip with worrying fluidity back into work mode. "The scan was helpful. I'm still working on the images but it doesn't look like his hippocampus is engaging on anything prior to the day he was found. I'll wait to write it up, but between you and me it's a verifiable fugue."

"Ha. Very interesting. That's . . . well! Good for you! Keep me posted and if you need anything you know where I am."

I don't mention Matthew's reaction to the final fMRI question—*Have you killed?*—I don't mention him knowing my name, I don't mention how strangely close I'm beginning to feel to him, and I certainly don't mention my reasons for staying. Because every one of those admissions would be grounds enough for me to be taken off this case.

That evening Matthew and I work through some memory exercises in his room. Simple card images testing the boundaries between his knowledge and his memory. While he recognizes a picture of the Eiffel Tower, he struggles to remember if he has ever seen it with his own eyes. I explain that triggering is all we can do at this stage. I prescribe an antianxiety medication to counteract any panic induced by our potential triggering and then we call it a day.

Taking the lift down to the lobby, I remember the gauntlet awaiting me outside: the trucks, the microphones, the questions. Dread slowly rises inside me as memories of similar crowds crawl back into my mind. Their bodies pushing, snatching, their graphic, unfeeling questions, the vitriol. Hemmed in by their desperate animal need to know, to know everything: the endless insistent, nasty hows, wheres, whys. The desire to pull apart the gristle of our lives as they rooted around for something elusive, something unknowable: a reason.

The elevator doors open, and my pulse soars as the scale of the crowd outside comes into view. There are so many more vans than earlier, and a more substantial barrier has been erected around the entrance, a press pit behind it. It's dizzying. A blast of red brake lights outside as a car maneuvers in the packed car park.

I brace myself against the elevator handrail as an image flashes through my mind. Blood on my hands.

Fourteen years ago. Blood cracked and dry, a reddish brown across my palms, caught under my fingernails. His blood. I'd find it there for days after.

I shudder. Someone must have alerted the crews outside that I was on my way out of the building, because their cameras are already up, microphones poised and ready. I can already hear their shouted questions. I repeat in my head Peter's instructions to me. *No comment. No comment.* As if in the heat of the moment I might somehow forget my line. The security guards by the sliding doors nod as I head toward them, my heart pounding in my throat, my mouth dry.

Outside, there are the logos of American news networks alongside the British ones now. I suppose everyone loves a happy ending, a reunited family, except, of course, we haven't given them one. We haven't given them anything yet.

One of the security guards steps forward. "Would you like us to escort you to your car, Dr. Lewis?" I don't recognize him but he knows who I am and I'm guessing he knows how far away I'm parked.

"Oh God, yes, thank you. That would be really fantastic. Thank you." I notice the quiver in my voice.

As he leads me through the doors and the squall of questions begins, he opens an umbrella overhead, shielding me from them as well as from the snow. The winter air hits my hot cheeks and cools them as we plow ahead.

Then in the crowd I see a flash of red hair, a face I instantly recognize. It takes me a second to realize that I only know her from a photograph, though. Chris's wife. Zara Poole's red hair is pulled back slickly in a fashionably low bun, her Dictaphone ready in hand. Her expression changes as her gaze finds mine, her smile slipping from her face.

I hadn't realized she was press. We lock eyes only for an instant—there's something disconcerting in the way she's staring. It's not that she recognizes me from school, it's not that, it's something else, and it frightens me.

# 31

# THE MAN

## DAY 11—BURIED

That night Matthew has a dream. A dream so real he cannot clear it from his mind on waking. In the dream he is alone in the ward garden. Everything is so real in this dream, the scent of the plants and the malty earth, the soft rain and the rustle of the trees. He somehow knows his memory has returned, though he does not attempt to access it. He sits quietly, contented, in the garden and closes his eyes. He lets the breeze play across his face but slowly he becomes aware of a sound and his eyes flicker open. The new sound is coming to him from deep inside the landscaped bushes and shrubs of the hospital garden; it is constant, a scraping noise. Scraping, scratching.

*Scratch, scratch, scratch.*

He cannot ignore it. He rises from the stone bench and looks around the garden. There is no one there. He cannot see where the noise is coming from, but it sounds like digging, a creature digging in the mud. The sound makes him shudder.

It seems to be coming from the bushes behind the

stone bench. He looks around to see if anyone has come out to the garden and heard it, but as he looks up at the windows surrounding the garden he notices that there is no one anywhere. It's almost as if the whole hospital were abandoned, with only him remaining. It is just him and the horrible scratching.

He looks back toward the bushes where the sound is coming from. It grows louder, more insistent, like a rat trapped behind a skirting board.

It scares him to think what it may be, back there, what he'll see if he looks. But the noise continues and he knows there is only one way to stop it. He steps toward it, going behind the bench and pushing through the fronds of foliage. He pushes on deeper into the dark branches.

And then he sees him.

A man, kneeling half-hidden, digging in the undergrowth. The man does not look up at Matthew. He just keeps digging, head bowed, scrabbling and clawing with bare hands at the mud. He is burying something, something small. Something important. There is something important buried in the garden. The back of the man's head is dripping with blood. The digging man is so focused on his task he doesn't seem to have noticed his terrible wound. Matthew knows this because the man is him.

Matthew wakes sweating.

The clock in his room reads 4:39. He sits bolt upright in the dark, his heart pounding, listening for the sounds of the hospital around him.

He's not sure if the dream means something or if he should just go back to sleep. Was it a memory, distorted by dreams? Or just a nightmare? Dr. Lewis warned him that the memory exercises they worked on might trigger connections. He recalls the noise in the dream, the noise in the darkness between the plants, insistent, and he squeezes his eyes shut.

Moments later he is out of bed, pulling on his shoes and the puffer jacket Rhoda gave him. He slips from the shadows of his room into the brightly lit corridor, makes his way tentatively past the empty nurses' station and down toward the ward garden. He ducks smoothly into the toilets as an aide passes; he waits a moment and then heads on. The door to the snow-encrusted garden is propped open for night-shift smokers and he slips out easily into the night.

He is certain now that there will be something there. Hidden in the earth. Answers maybe.

When he reaches the stone bench he stops, shivering, the dizzying feeling from his dream returning. He looks up at the sky, clear and starry above, his breath clouding in the air, and he suddenly doubts himself. He thinks of the progress he's making, of Emma, beautiful Emma, of how she wants to help him. Of how she held him, how she's trying to fix him. Perhaps he should go back to bed, curl up in the darkness and the warmth and wait for things to come clear. Every day things seem to be getting clearer. He watches mesmerized as the frost-glittered plant fronds behind the stone bench sway in the night breeze.

*It can't hurt to look behind there, can it?*

He pushes his way into the icy foliage, listening carefully for the sounds of anyone approaching from the ward. Just like in the dream, he finds a small clearing behind the bushes.

Kneeling on the ground, hidden from sight, he starts to move the soft dirt aside, scraping at the mud with his fingers.

Perhaps it was just a dream, he decides, perhaps I

really am going mad after all. He claws deeper and then his nails hit plastic.

Half a foot down, a Ziploc bag in the soil. He stops abruptly, stunned to have actually found something. He looks around, listening, but there is only the distant bleeping of call buzzers, the breeze in the laden branches. He looks down at the small bag, at the glint of metal inside. He doesn't know what it means yet, not exactly, or how it got here, but it seems like the first step toward finding out. Someone put this here for him. He pulls it loose from the crumbly soil and slips it into his jacket.

# 32

## ZARA POOLE

### DAY 11—AHEAD OF THE GAME

Zara Poole is driving along the coastal road between Wells and Holkham at 7 A.M. on a Saturday morning on her way to doorstop Emma Lewis.

The address Zara was given by her contact at the hospital was odd. A house essentially in the middle of nowhere. She expected Dr. Lewis to be closer to the hospital, that would have seemed more logical, but this address doesn't. Not to someone who knows the area. But then, something is off about all of this, as far as Zara is concerned.

Her contact at the hospital, a porter she'd been slipping money to, had been pretty accurate so far. He'd informed her prior to anyone else knowing that a new doctor would be coming, although she hadn't had quite enough time to make any real impact with the knowledge. But the next text she'd received from him three days later had been pure gold. The porter had texted her at 3 A.M. on Thursday, the same night Chris had received that text from Emma. The bright light of Zara's phone had briefly illuminated their dark bedroom, Chris sleeping peacefully beside her. It said:

**He's talking.**
**He's British.**
**No memory.**

A flash of joy cut through the disappointment of Chris's text because finally she had her story. She was the first to get it. Which meant that she had something that other people would want.

She'd quietly slipped out of bed, grabbed some clothes, and headed down to the kitchen. She'd typed up a page of copy, fresh coffee standing by, and then she'd made some calls. Not to the local paper she was currently working for but to contacts she'd been working on for a while. She had new information on Mr. Nobody—she hadn't come up with the name herself, the *Mail* had, but everyone was using it—and she could send through her piece if they were interested in running it. It was source-verified. If needs be she could even give her source's name; she knew she could easily get another one at Princess Margaret's. Who didn't like free money?

She sold the story once and then again and again, and by daybreak, when she was pretty much the sole reporter in the country covering the story, she'd grabbed some toast and headed straight into the storm brewing down at the Princess Margaret Hospital.

By mid-morning a whole new swarm of journalists had descended, eager to find out what Mr. Nobody was finally saying now he could talk. The story was gaining momentum, with newscasters and networks from other countries jostling alongside the crews she was already starting to recognize. Which was fantastic as far as Zara was concerned; there was more than enough to go around, and she was getting article requests from papers and magazines she'd never even heard of, across Europe and now America too. Her preparation had finally paid off.

That was two days ago but it was yesterday that things really kicked off. Zara had simply asked Chris, at breakfast, not for the first time, if there had been any breakthroughs since Mr. Nobody had started talking.

"Apparently, he's not making much sense at the moment. We've been asked by the hospital to defer questioning him again until he starts remembering. His doctor doesn't want to run the risk of setting his recovery back at this stage," Chris had told her.

He hadn't mentioned the text he'd received from Dr. Lewis. He hadn't brought any of that up. Not the list of school staff she'd asked him for either. And he certainly hadn't mentioned asking her out for a drink. So neither had Zara.

But then a call had come through on her iPhone and she'd slipped out into the garden to take it. It was her contact at the hospital; the call was rushed and muffled, clearly made in haste. The Metropolitan Police had just arrived at the hospital. Something big was happening.

Either Chris was keeping more things from her or the Met hadn't told even the local police what was happening. A family was on their way to the hospital to ID Mr. Nobody. The Taylors. The parents of missing Benjamin Taylor.

Because of her, the press were prepped and ready when the Taylors arrived. They'd known the right questions to ask, and as the couple breezed past them without stopping, they got their pictures, they got their "no comments," but most important they got their articles. And then an hour later they got even more.

Mr. Nobody wasn't Benjamin Taylor, the text she received made that very clear. Again, Zara heard it first. The porter had been in the corridor after the meeting, he'd stood back and watched as Mrs. Taylor gave a sad little shake of her head in answer to DC Barker's question. Matthew wasn't their son.

Zara watched Emma leaving the hospital last night. She'd been ready, she'd seen her before, of course, the day she arrived at the hospital when Mike pointed her out as they stood in the coffee shop queue. She'd thought, at the time, she'd looked interesting, smart, and reassuringly out of place. Zara had always felt slightly out of place too; she recognized the look in others.

But last night, with her chestnut hair caught in the wind, cheeks rosy from the camera flashes and the flurry of shouts around her, she'd looked beautiful, Zara had to admit. She hated herself for bringing it down to that but she could understand why Chris might find her attractive—although the idea of it made her stomach lurch with heartbreaking apprehension. The thoughts started spiraling out of her grasp: her Chris with a doctor from London, a beautiful, clever, rich doctor. *Her Chris.* A possessiveness she didn't realize she could muster bristling hard inside her, Zara had just stood and stared, until their eyes had locked. And Emma had looked back at her, haunted, before disappearing into the night. That's when Zara had made her decision.

Zara would find out who Emma was. For the story, of course. She would ask her woman-to-woman: What was going on with the case? Why was she here? And maybe, just maybe, Emma's connection with Chris would make sense. Maybe everything was actually okay.

Zara pulls off the main road and down onto the snow-covered drive of Cuckoo Lodge, wincing at the noise her tires make on the gravel. Obviously it's not meant to be a stealth mission, but the element of surprise does tend to help when someone is opening their front door to a stranger.

There's the chance, of course, that Emma Lewis could just slam the door in her face.

At the end of the drive, Zara pushes her car door closed as quietly as she can and looks up at the house.

She can understand why Emma chose this place. She makes her way through the snow-encrusted picket gate up to the gabled front door and knocks. The sound echoes through the empty house. She waits, then she tries again, harder.

No sound within but echoes. Outside, the sound of the wind through the trees and the occasional burst of birdsong.

She bends now, pushing open the mail slot. "Hello? Dr. Lewis? It's Zara Poole, I was wondering if we could talk?" No reply, just the sound of her own breathing. She hopes she doesn't sound angry or desperate or pathetic, like a crazy girlfriend or a wronged wife looking for an argument, because that's not what she is. That's not why she's here. Chris can do what he likes with his life, she reasons. If he'd rather be with someone else, there's not really anything she can do about that, is there? she asks herself. You can't make people love you, she knows that. And Zara doesn't want to be one of those people, a scorned wife, a victim, the one left behind. So, best not to rail against it, best to take it on the chin, keep her cards close and see how the game plays out.

She's just here for her story, she tells herself. Once she's got the story, she'll go.

Zara straightens and looks up to the darkened windows. No one is in. She turns to look back at the drive. And then she notices. The doctor's little gray car is nowhere to be seen.

She must have already left for the hospital.

Zara pauses. She casts her eyes down the gravel driveway, weighing up her options. She looks back at the empty house.

If she does this, she thinks, she might be able to get away with it. She would definitely be able to hear someone coming down that long gravel drive. She'd certainly have enough time to get out, if she goes in.

She tries the front door handle. It pivots all the way down under her hand but the door does not budge. Locked. She smiles wryly to herself. Of course it's locked. Nobody leaves their front door unlocked, not even in Norfolk. She turns to leave. Then she changes her mind.

She goes around to the back of the house and tugs at the patio door. It won't budge. She doubles back to the side of the house; low to the ground there's a long thin window, a basement window. She crouches to peer in. A dim utility room beyond. She gives the corner of the window a swift tug and nicks a nail. Locked.

She sucks her finger to dampen the smarting and thinks about what to do next. Suddenly concerned, she scans high along the eaves of the house for a security camera. Nothing.

Stepping back from the small window, she thinks of her options. She can just see around the side of the building to her car from here. The drive remains otherwise empty. She makes up her mind and swiftly walks up to the window, cautiously looking both ways before cocking her right foot back and kicking as hard as she can. The smash is loud and satisfying. She braces herself for a burglar alarm but no siren sounds. She nudges out the remaining loose shards with a heeled boot before leaning forward to check the hole.

Inside, the house is quiet and dark. Zara dusts off her trench coat and scans the dark utility room. She doesn't really know what she's looking for, she's never done anything like this before, but she knows she needs to find something and it almost definitely won't be in the utility room.

She heads up the basement stairs, gently opens the door at the top, and steps into the immaculate kitchen. Still no alarm sounds. If she can just find something, anything, to help explain what is going on, why this woman is here, who she is, and how she knows Chris.

Zara takes in the Victorian kitchen, full fruit bowls, fresh flowers in vases, and wonders when the doctor actually has time to do all of this. Perhaps the house is serviced. Because it's perfect. So effortlessly perfect.

She tears her gaze away and wanders on through into the living room populated by deep sofas and expensive rugs. But thankfully, it's messier in here, a soft cashmere throw tossed haphazardly on the sofa, a smudged wineglass on the floor beneath, a tannin stain chalky inside, a dirty plate. So, Dr. Lewis is a human after all.

And then Zara sees it. A glint. The edge of something poking out from under the rich fawn of the throw. The matte silver sheen of it. She reaches down and pulls it out. Emma's laptop.

Zara sits down on the sofa next to it, one hand resting lightly on its smooth brushed-metal lid. If she does this then there's no going back, she thinks. But then, she's already come this far. She's already broken into someone's home. What difference would looking make?

Still she hesitates. She might find something she doesn't like. There could be emails from Chris, more messages. What if looking through her laptop somehow changes everything? She would have to go home to Chris knowing but not being able to say.

No. It's better to look, she decides. Yes, better to know.

She flips the lid and spins the laptop around to face her. It opens to desktop, the tab open on the last page Emma looked at—Chris's Facebook page.

Zara's heart skips a beat, her jaw hardens.

She minimizes the screen and pulls up Emma's iMessages; she scrolls to Chris's name and reads.

Sorry to text so late. Would it be possible to
get a list of past employees at Waltham
House? I can't say why just yet but I
think it might be helpful. Also, might have to
rain check that drink. Snowed under.
Emma x

No problem, totally understand.
I'll get on it & let you know asap &
I just want to say it was great
to see you today Marn. Chris x

It's Emma, Chris! X

Shit, sorry x

Zara stares at the screen, frowning. She reads the messages again, trying to make sense of them. She sits in stillness for a moment and then pulls up Google.

She types “Marn Lewis” and taps search.

Nothing.

She tries “Dr. Marn Lewis” and taps search.

Nothing.

She tries “Marn, Norfolk.”

The search autocorrects to “Marni, Norfolk” and below it pages and pages of search results appear.

Marni Beaufort. The Beaufort family. *Christ*.

Zara catches her breath. *Holy shit*.

A giggle of pure joy bubbles out of her beautiful screen-lit face, because, finally, Zara cannot believe her luck.

# 33

## DR. EMMA LEWIS

### DAY 11—PEOPLE ARE COMING

The call comes at 10:07 that night.

Up until then it had been a comparatively uneventful day of memory exercises and talking through Matthew's positive response to his antianxiety medication. The lack of drama making me feel my decision not to resign yesterday had been the right one. Joe had been less understanding when I tried to explain on the phone. But it would be crazy to leave without knowing how Matthew has come to know so much about me and my father. But of course, I couldn't tell Joe my reasoning in that respect. If he'd wanted me to leave before, he'd have dragged me off himself if he knew my reasons for staying.

I spent the rest of the day at the hospital finishing Matthew's preliminary medical report and fMRI analysis. I emailed it across to Richard Groves at MIT for his opinion. And I sent it on to Peter too. The report included my initial observations as well as all Matthew's scans and test results. Richard's opinion, though obviously not essential, would be extremely useful to me at this stage.

Back at the lodge, I crack open another bottle of wine and heat some pasta. I'm eating when the lodge phone rings, which is a surprise because I wasn't even aware the lodge had a landline. I find it by the window next to the armchair.

"Emma, has anyone contacted you?" It's Peter Chorley. His tone is urgent, brusque.

"About what, Peter?" I ask, momentarily confused by the question. "Is Matthew okay?"

"Yes. This isn't about Matthew, Emma. Has anyone from the press contacted you? In the last few hours?" There's concern for me in his voice; something has happened.

"No. Should they have? Sorry, Peter, what's going on? You're scaring me." I suddenly feel like I've wandered out onto a ledge in my sleep. My vertigo kicking in without a stimulus.

He's silent on the line, I hear him exhale and cover his receiver. A muffled conversation. When he comes back on the line his tone is grim.

"Listen, Emma, I need you to turn your mobile phone off, please. We're sending a police officer around to you now. They'll stay outside your accommodation for the night to—"

"What the hell is going on, Peter!" I erupt, cutting him off mid-flow.

There's another thick silence before he answers.

"They've found out who you are, Emma. The press. We don't know if they know where you're staying, but best to be safe. I have a contact at the press association, he called me five minutes ago. It's going to break online at midnight and it'll be all over tomorrow's national papers." He pauses to let me take this in before continuing. "I'm truly sorry this has happened, Emma. This isn't what anyone wanted."

I stare unseeing out into the darkness through the window.

*This can't be happening.*

"Emma, are you still there?"

*It's going to happen all over again. Just like before.*

I sit down hard into the deep armchair. "Yes," I manage. I need to keep him talking. I don't want him to hang up, I don't want to be left alone with this. "How did they find out?" It seems the next reasonable question. "How could they have found out without breaking the law? Without hacking data?"

"We don't know but we're looking into it. It was a local reporter apparently. That's all I can tell you at the moment."

Zara. It must be Zara. Her face last night outside the hospital. Chris must have told her who I was. That's why she looked at me that way.

"Right. Okay," I hear myself say. "Thanks for letting me know." Then I remember something. "Sorry, Peter—what were you saying about the police? Why are police coming? Am I in any danger here?" The last thing I want is Chris showing up but I'm suddenly perilously aware of how isolated I am out here.

"Um, yes, the police are on their way. They're making arrangements, you should have someone with you within thirty minutes. It's only a precaution, but there are some concerns that the press might have information about your whereabouts. Obviously, the Beaufort case is going to attract a substantial amount of public attention as well. We're just concerned about your safety, and in light of your need to enter the protected-persons program fourteen years ago it would be wise, I think, to be . . . prepared. Better to be over-prepared than under."

*Oh God. This is actually happening.*

I throw my mind back to that autumn fourteen

years ago. The threats, the letters, the hateful words sprayed on the walls of places they put us, people grabbing at us, shoving us, their faces distorted with anger, baying for a kind of justice that we couldn't give them, Joe and Mum and me. I wonder if I hadn't said what I'd said back then if they would have chased us so hard. If I'd have kept my mouth shut, they'd have hated us less. They thought we were lying, that he was still alive somewhere out there, they thought we knew where he was. They wanted the truth even if we weren't entirely sure of it ourselves.

"Emma, did you hear me?"

"Sorry, Peter, what?"

"The police officers, they should be there soon. But in the meantime, it would be best not to answer the door. Not to anybody, until the police arrive. And turn off your mobile. Steer clear of this landline from now on too unless you see it's my number calling, okay? Hopefully, we're still slightly ahead of the game here." He sounds confident but I know what's coming. If I need police protection, this is going to get very ugly. I suddenly feel so incredibly alone. Alone in the woods. Alone in my life. "I'll call you first thing tomorrow morning, if not before," he continues. "Trust me, Emma, it's all going to be fine in the long run."

The line goes dead and I sit in silence, my heart beating loud in my ears. *They're coming for me.*

I pull out my mobile and slide off the power just as Peter told me. Outside the windows, I can make out the flutter of snowflakes falling and beyond that the darkness of the dense forest all around me. I'm a sitting duck in this isolated house.

I head to the front door, deadbolting it. If any doorsteppers get this far, they'll get no farther. I try not to think who else might want to pay me a visit now that the news of who I am is breaking.

I head to the patio doors, tugging hard at the handle until I'm certain it's locked and secure. I pull the heavy tapestry curtains closed across the great expanse of black outside and shiver.

I dash to the kitchen sink and lean over, pulling on the bobbled rope of the blind until the outside world disappears behind it.

I pull the curtains tight in the living room and the hallway, then run up the stairs to check the windows and close the curtains in the two bedrooms. I know that even a tiny gap in the fabric is enough for a long-lens camera and a photographer with enough patience.

When it's all done, and I know everything is secure, I slump down on the top step and catch my breath.

*Is everything locked? What am I forgetting?*

And that's when I hear it. The crunch of a footstep outside on the gravel. *Already?* I hold my breath, listening hard. Shit, the police won't be here for half an hour. It could be a reporter, a photographer, or it could be someone else. We didn't leave fourteen years ago because of the media alone. We left for our own safety. I think of the house phone lying downstairs on the armchair, my iPhone next to it, turned off.

I listen for another footstep. Nothing, just the pop of the fire downstairs.

I stand and start to take the stairs down, wincing at every creak. Outside, a fox shrieks in the distance, and I pause as the plaintive call echoes out through the woods. But no sound of footsteps. Perhaps they have headed around the back. If I can make it into the living room, I can grab my iPhone, and then I can run back upstairs and lock myself in the bedroom. I can call the police from there.

I continue down the stairs, holding my breath. And then I hear the footsteps on the gravel again, two steps this time, someone turning, right by the front door. I freeze. And then the knocking starts. Three heavy pounds on the door.

*Oh, please God, no.*

I stand frozen mid-step and watch as the door handle moves, rattling against the lock. And then I run—I bolt down the stairs, run to the sofa, and dive for my mobile. The screen flashes white. I hear the footsteps outside. Whoever it is, they're on the move. They could easily burst through the thin Victorian windows. I pocket my iPhone, which is still powering on, and grab the house phone as I dart into the kitchen and head for the patio doors. I could make a run for it into the woods behind the house. I could double back on myself through the trees, make a break for the car and head to the hospital, at least there's security there. But I remember my car keys are still on the ledge in the front hall.

*Shit.*

I can't hear the footsteps anymore.

Then, right next to me behind the curtains, a loud *bang* on the patio doors. I shoot away from them, my heart thundering. Someone's right there. And then a man's voice comes, furious and gruff, "I know you're in there, Marni. Open the door!" I retreat farther back into the kitchen until my back comes up hard against the basement door.

*I'll be safe down there.*

Gently I raise the latch and ease the door open, peering down into the darkness below. A chill wells up from the basement. I leave the door ajar enough to shed some light down the stairwell but I leave the lights off. I don't want to attract his attention. Feeling my way down each cold stone step, I creep into the darkness.

At the bottom of the stairs I make a break toward the closet on the far side of the room. But, as I run a brutally sharp stab of pain shoots up through my foot, then another, then another. I fly forward, landing hard, sprawled across the basement floor. Pain thunders through my hands now too as they connect with the sharp objects littering the floor. I try to muffle my reaction but I can't help but cry out at the sheer intensity of it. Raw with wounds, I curl tight into a fetal position—the pain is everywhere. I hold a hand up to the half-light and see the dark wet marks blossom across my palms. Blood. My eyes slowly adjust to the darkness and I see the floor around me is glittering with bright slivers of broken glass caught in the moonlight. I try to crawl to my feet but let out a moan of agony and drop back down. Above me, through the smashed basement window, two booted feet appear, and I'm suddenly blinded.

A flashlight, I think. I squint up into its glare. The man's voice comes again. "What the hell are you doing down there, Marn? Why aren't you answering your sodding phone?" I try to shield my eyes from the glare of the probing flashlight to see the face above me, but as I do he must catch sight of my bleeding hands.

"Jesus Christ, Marn, you're bleeding! Are you okay? Wait—just stay right there, don't move. I'll . . . I'll jump down."

"Chris?" I ask, bewildered.

"Yeah, of course. Who did you think it was? There're basically only two police officers around here." A big tall figure drops down through the broken window into the basement next to me with a grunt. “Oh God. Listen, just don’t move, shit, there’s glass everywhere.”

“What’s going on, Chris? Why the hell did you break my window?”

# 34

# DR. EMMA LEWIS

## DAY 11—WALKING ON BROKEN GLASS

"It was Zara, wasn't it?"

He looks up from my foot, tweezers in hand. "I don't know," he answers thoughtfully. "You mean who broke the window? Or your cover?"

My bleeding feet rest on a towel-covered cushion on his lap as he delicately removes each splinter of glass. Chris had carried me up from the basement and put me on the sofa before he headed off to find a first-aid kit for my wounds.

"Did *you* tell her? Who I was?" I ask.

He looks up at me, his feelings clearly hurt. "What? No, of course not. Why would you think that?" He holds my foot firmly in his hand now and pulls.

"Ah! Jesus, Chris. This hurts so much."

"Don't be such a baby." He smiles, amused. "I can't believe you thought I was coming to get you. That's hilarious. Oh God, not hilarious that you thought someone was coming to get you obviously, but I mean that it might be me—" He fumbles to a stop.

I know what he meant, and to be honest I'm so pleased he's here he could literally say anything right now. I smile. "Well, then maybe you shouldn't be creeping around outside people's houses like a murderer, Chris."

"Yeah, I definitely need to stop doing that." He smiles mutedly before his expression drops slightly. "But someone did ring you to let you know I was coming, right?"

"Yeah, I literally just got off the phone with Pe—with someone." I catch myself. I'm not sure if I should be mentioning Peter at this stage. I know he's in close contact with the police but I don't know if it's above Chris's pay grade. I move on swiftly. "They said someone would be coming. I just didn't know you'd get here so quickly."

But Chris catches my misstep. "Who called you, Marn?" he asks, suddenly serious.

I rub my eyes. I'm so tired. "Please stop calling me Marn, Chris. I haven't been Marn for years. And it's none of your business who called me, okay? That's confidential."

I regret my tone instantly when I see his expression.

"I'm sorry, Emma. I'm sorry about all this, the press finding out. I didn't know Zara would do this. She threw me out this morning, by the way, so . . . I don't know. She thinks we're having some kind of affair." He shakes his head dismissively, as if the thought were beyond absurd. "Anyway, I'm just saying that I'm not sure whoever you're working for really has your best interests at heart. I mean, they could have moved you somewhere safer than this for a start, couldn't they?"

"What do you mean she threw you out?"

"Don't change the subject, Emma."

"What *was* the subject? What? Why I'm staying *here,* in the middle of nowhere? Well, for a start they wanted to keep me away from Holt," I reply indignantly.

The mention of Holt silences him and when I look back he's intent on my foot again. I sigh and fall back into the cushions. "I'm sorry, Chris. I've just got a lot going on in my head right now."

He tugs and another spike of glass pulls painfully free. "Are you scared? About what will happen tomorrow?"

I close my eyes and blow out a soft breath as he pinches another shard out.

"Yes. I am. I'm very scared: for my mother, what she'll wake up to in the morning, for Joe and how he'll have to pull Chloe from her daycare. I'm scared for all of them waking up to reporters on their doorsteps, and it being my fault that their friends won't look at them the same way again, and I'm terrified of the questions, and of the judgment."

"It won't be as bad as before, I don't think. It can't be."

"Chris, have you seen those TV crews outside the hospital? The world is a totally different place than it was fourteen years ago, everything is bigger, faster, meaner. This time it will be everywhere."

"You know, if it makes you feel any better, I didn't read about it, at the time. It seemed wrong to read about your personal life like that. They shouldn't have released some of the things they did. I'm sorry it happened." He wipes both feet with an alcohol wipe and presses on a final dressing. "All done here, Dr. Lewis." He throws me one of his ridiculously handsome smiles, gives my ankles a warm squeeze. His skin on mine.

All the blood in my body rushes up my inner

thighs. *Oh God.* Every natural impulse tells me to pull away from his hands, but his touch feels so good.

My body bypasses my brain. "Would you like a glass of wine, Chris? I know you're on duty but one won't hurt, right?"

He holds my gaze, eyes crinkled around the edges. "No, it wouldn't. And yes, I would."

I pull on the socks he passes me and hobble off on tender Band-Aid-covered feet to the kitchen.

The evening passes in a blur of sensations. The hot flush of wine, his smiling eyes taking in my face, a burst of laughter, his hand resting on my thigh and its electric throb of possibility, and suddenly his warm mouth on mine. The feel of his hands all over me as we kiss, the desperate animal need of it.

Later, I offer him the second bedroom but he says he'll sleep on the sofa, he's supposed to be on duty anyway, and I head upstairs to bed.

I lie there awake, thinking about what happened that night fourteen years ago.

I didn't see my father do it, maybe that's half the problem—or maybe it's the silver lining?

I heard it, though. The crack of it in the night, like thunder, the rip of the double-barreled shotgun as it echoed up the thick carpet of our staircase, along a landing lined with our family pictures, and into my childhood bedroom.

But before the echo of the gunshot there was the helicopter. The sound of it circling in tight loops over the house was what woke me. I'd sat up in bed groggy, blinking into the shadows, as it rumbled over the house, my head throbbing. A headache and nausea from too much sugar and excitement at the fireworks that evening. After a moment Joe trundled into my room too, his silhouette in my doorway. "Helicopter," he'd said croakily as the mechanical roar receded off into the night.

"Yeah," I offered up into the growing quiet. The noise gone as quick as it came.

Joe disappears back to his room and I lie back down with a wave of dizziness and pull my duvet up to my chin. Safe. The sharp scent of spent fireworks in the air.

I think of the bonfire earlier that night, of nice things, of being cold and now being warm. Snapshots of memories. Dad's concentrated face as he lit the sparklers. Mum's smile. The crunch of teeth on burnt caramel. The rush of sugar through my body. Watching the giant pyre as flecks of gold and orange crackled and floated away into the darkness.

Caught half-awake, half-dreaming. A half-dream where I rise from bed, voices in the hallway; I come out onto the landing and see him. My father, pulling on his coat. He's leaving. He sees me standing bleary at the top of the stairs. *Where are you going, Dad?* I ask. *Nowhere, honey. Go back to bed,* he tells me, smiling softly. *But I don't feel well,* I tell him. *It's okay, baby. You'll feel better in the morning,* he reassures me, and he blows me a kiss. And I smile back for Daddy and I go to bed.

I wake up when the helicopter roars overhead again. Louder this time. Lower. I sit bolt upright, a terror crystallizing in my adolescent brain: something is wrong.

Joe scrambles back into my room, skidding over to the bedroom window and disappearing behind the thick silk of the curtains, only his feet visible below.

"What is it, Joe?" I rasp, my throat dry. I really don't feel well.

The rhythmic thud of helicopter blades thumps through the night air. No answer from my brother.

My curiosity piqued, I race into the gap between the curtains, to join him as the big machine hovers overhead a third time. I catch the flash of its floodlight as it sweeps low over our wet roof. Blinding light and sound, the word POLICE emblazoned across its underbelly.

Transfixed, my brother and I watch as it slowly lowers and touches down in our top field, the long grass around it whipping with the downforce of the blades.

We stare out the rain-speckled window as the helicopter doors burst open, and uniformed officers jump out and run toward our house.

And then it comes from downstairs. The noise.

*CRACK*.

A rip of sound. A gunshot, loud and horrifically distinct, cracking through the silent house. My breath catches in my throat and I drop straight to the floor as if somehow I'm the one who's been shot. Terror coursing through me, pure animalistic fear.

Real gunshots aren't like the ones on TV. You feel the sound in your body. It hits you. It's a sound you'd recognize even if you hadn't grown up around it. A sound and a meaning in one. An instant understanding of events.

No further shots, just ringing silence through the house, and the knowledge of what that might mean.

Outside, we hear shouts getting closer to the house. I look across to Joe, crouched next to me on the carpet, his head buried, his pajamas and the floor around him wet with urine, his body quivering.

I make the first move. The animal instinct, to find my dad. I scrabble as fast as I can, low, on all fours across the bedroom floor and onto the thick carpet of the landing. A light on downstairs. Through the banisters I see Mum leaning on the study doorframe, her hand to her mouth. She is staring at something.

The burst of breaking glass from the front of the house, voices shouting.

I don't know why but I run. I run to him, down the stairs, past Mum's outstretched grasping hands, through a doorway I won't ever be able to come back through.

And I find him there in his study. His face and the back of his skull gone. Or rather displaced, pieces of it, of him, stuck in the curtains, hot globules and bone chips on the window's latticework, wet drips and chunks in and on his precious books. His whole life broken open across the upholstery. On his desk four cream envelopes, spattered. Thick watermarked paper—his letters to us inside. One addressed to Marty Fenshaw, Dad's solicitor, one to Joe, one to Mum. And one to me. I don't know why he wrote them. Guilt maybe.

Either way, I wouldn't read mine for another two years.

I stand and stare at what he's done, dizzy, my head pounding and the sound of Mum's gasping breath behind me. The shotgun now propped between two lifeless thighs. His dark blood creeping slow and steady across the oak floorboards toward us.

The room spins around us and I can no longer stop the nausea from rising. I vomit hot sharp bile forward onto the floor.

And suddenly there are police everywhere, swarming into the house, through the front and back. Later I will see the squad cars filling our drive, the riot van, next to Mum's 4x4. They're shouting but we don't hear their words as they pour in, fully armed.

We'd find out later they'd come to seize Dad's hard drive, his papers, before he'd destroyed them;

they'd come to take him in, but he'd beaten them to it. He'd destroyed everything and he was already gone.

We'd find out later that he'd embezzled hundreds of thousands of pounds from charitable funds, that he misappropriated funds meant for survivors of the London bombings. Other people's money. Victims' money. And we'd never find that money.

We'd find out in the emergency room that the headaches and the vomiting we were all experiencing were due to gas poisoning. Dad had disabled the pilot light on the oven, he'd put out the flame and the house had slowly been filling with gas for hours while we slept. The bitter smell of it permeating every room of the house.

They said at the inquest he meant to take us all with him. A last-minute idea, they speculated—otherwise why would he have bothered to write us all notes? Why indeed? After two years of waiting, I found that mine had said only:

*Marni-marn,*

*I love you. I hope one day you'll be able to understand.*

*Your Dad*

He thought we'd be better off dead than without him, that was what he had decided for us. That we were his property to dispose of in any way he liked. We weren't meant to read those letters; he wrote them to our dead bodies. We were all meant to go in our sleep but he ran out of time and shot himself first.

Except I don't think he did. I don't think the man with no face in the study was my father. Which I would later tell the police and social workers. *I saw him put on his coat,* I'd tell them. *I saw him leave the house. He told me to go back to bed. Whoever that person was in the study, they weren't my father, that body wasn't wearing a coat. You never found his coat.*

They'd tell me it was a hallucination from the gas poisoning, they'd tell me they'd done a DNA test on the remains, they'd tell me to stop, but someone believed me. The press believed me. And at first, I was glad at least someone did. But they wanted to know, if he wasn't dead, where had he gone? They demanded to know where he'd gone with all that money. They wanted to track him down and make him pay. And they just wouldn't stop asking. Even after I told the police I believed them, that I must have imagined seeing him. Even after I told everyone I'd made a mistake. They just kept asking and then they got angry and it became dangerous. That's when we had to leave.

I know logically I didn't see him. That logically I couldn't have seen him leave . . . but . . . I did, didn't I?

Shards of memories from that night. Recalled over and over and over. Blood everywhere; I stare at it transfixed. Mum crouched on the floor, her mouth open in a silent scream, spit stringing straight down onto our floorboards. Her eyes searching the approaching faces of police for some kind of answer as to why.

They pull her roughly backward, and like a rag doll she lets herself be carried off, no resistance, something soft and helpless in a sea of uniforms. The world slows right down as they pour into the study around me, finally blocking my view.

As I've said, nobody becomes a psychiatrist by accident.

# 35

# DR. EMMA LEWIS

## DAY 12—REPERCUSSIONS

Officer Graceford arrives at 7 A.M., bringing the stack of newspapers I'd requested through Chris.

Not yet ready to face the TV coverage, I pore over the papers with my bandaged palms as Chris finishes cooking us breakfast. He wouldn't take no for an answer after calling a company to replace the glass in the basement window.

Graceford eyes the apron he's wearing over his uniform and turns back to me briskly. "I'll be covering you at the hospital if you want to go in today," she explains. "If you don't feel up to it, you can stay here in the lodge with Chris until things calm down. It's totally up to you." She smiles understandingly and I want to hug her for her lack of judgment either way.

"I'll have a think about it."

She nods and throws a look back to Chris; his hair is still rumpled from sleep. "I'll be keeping an eye on things at the hospital, Chris. Radio me if anything changes here."

"Will do," he says, trying to remain dignified while holding a spatula.

After Graceford leaves I take a deep breath and flick on the TV. Footage of my face, me walking out of the hospital, furtive, guilty, though of what I do not know. I guess I have a guilty face. The news anchors talk about me, about Dad.

*"The daughter of the late Charles Beaufort, who is estimated to have misappropriated approximately £875,000 from the July seventh victims' charity, as well as other sums from various sources, reemerged yesterday after fourteen years in hiding. Marni Beaufort, now Dr. Emma Lewis, has been working within the NHS under an assumed name."*

Bloody hell. They make it sound like I'm pretending to be a doctor.

*"News sources yesterday uncovered that Marni Beaufort is currently the lead specialist on another case garnering public interest—the mysterious case of Mr. Nobody, the unknown man found wandering on a beach in Norfolk, close to Dr. Lewis's own childhood home. Although currently not under investigation, Marni Beaufort was believed by many during the 2005 inquest into Charles Beaufort's misappropriation of funds and subsequent death to be involved in a cover-up surrounding his suicide. Several sources at the time of the investigation expressed concerns that the body discovered in the Beaufort family home might not have been that of Charles Beaufort and that Charles Beaufort might well still be at large. However, DNA samples analyzed at the scene and during the subsequent police investigation did match with that of Mr. Beaufort."*

I feel Chris's eyes on me. I feel his concern.

I can almost hear his thoughts. Do I think he's still

alive too? That's what he wants to know. That's what everyone wants to know.

Two questions, over and over. Do I think he's still alive? And, where is the money?

I avoid Chris's gaze and focus on the images as they flash up on the screen. Footage from 2005. Shots of sixteen-year-old me cowed by the attention, my terrified expression as alert as a wounded animal's. Shots of the July 7 bombings, interviews with victims about the money he stole.

I flip the channel.

A floppy-haired man in a navy blazer holds forth. *"Yes, that's all very well, Susannah, but what if Charles Beaufort is still alive and out there somewhere, living off all this stolen money he's accrued? I just think with today's technology it's worth looking at the evidence again. What harm could it do? If he's dead, he's dead. All I'm saying is, I think it might be worth the police reopening the case. There were contradictory facts! The daughter saw him leaving the house. That was in her original statement. It was only afterward the story changed. I definitely think it's worth another look."*

The female presenter gives him an incredulous yet indulgent look. *"But come on, Jeremy, didn't he attempt to murder the whole family? Why would any one of them be helping him get away with that? They'd have to be mad."*

*"Actually, not really—if you think about it, it makes perfect sense. The carbon monoxide levels in the house were high but nowhere near fatal yet. It may have been part of the ruse. Get the family in on it. If he'd really wanted to kill them all, he could have increased the flow, and he had a gun, didn't he—"*

*Jesus Christ.*

I flip the channel.

This is going to be worse than last time. Now that I'm over eighteen, all bets are off. I'm fair game.

They think I know where he is. They think I helped him. They think I'm protecting a man who stole from grieving families and tried to kill me and my whole family. But do I think he's alive?

No. *Yes*.

The real truth? I don't know. Because I saw him go. And I know they told me it was a hallucination, I know the DNA test results, I know the evidence. I know and yet . . . the body in the study wasn't wearing his jacket. It didn't *feel* like him. It just didn't. And I don't know where he is, or where the money is, and I don't know the whys of any of it, but—do I think he's alive? Yes. I think of Matthew in his hospital room, and I can't help but wonder if locked away inside him is some kind of answer. After all, he was looking for me.

On the next TV station one of the bombing survivors speaks to the camera: *"Who exactly paid for this woman's medical training? That's what I'd like to know. Isn't it a bit convenient that all that money disappeared and she shows up fourteen years later a doctor? We should be asking where the money for that came from. Why haven't the police followed up on that?"*

Chris, who has come up behind me unnoticed, gently takes the remote from my tight grip and turns off the blaring screen. I realize I haven't blinked for a while, and it feels strange to do so now. He pulls me in close to him and I let him. It feels so good to be held.

"Call your family," he whispers gently. "Let them know you're okay."

I call Joe, it's a brief conversation. His voice is tight and it's blindingly obvious that I should have followed his advice on Friday, although he does me the extraordinary kindness of not bringing that up. He's going straight to Mum's, he tells me. She's seen the news. Apparently, there are already people outside her house. I feel awful. The guilt is almost too much to bear. And even though it feels ridiculous to be giving my brother advice, I feel obligated to give him the same warning Peter gave me. "Don't talk to anyone, Joe, don't answer the phone unless you know who it is first."

I want to call Mum but I can't. The guilt is too sharp. I don't think I'd be able to hold it together. And I definitely don't want her to feel she needs to reassure *me*. God, I don't think I could handle her being brave *for me*. I text her that I love her and I'm sorry and I leave it at that.

At 8 A.M. Peter calls.

"Listen, Emma, we're happy to accept your resignation. If you're not up to continuing, we completely understand. The press attention is fairly unprecedented, and given the circumstances, if you'd rather take some time for yourself, to be with your family . . ."

I've thought a lot about it this morning, about what Peter might say when he rang, why on earth they chose me in the first place, why they'd want such a media liability hanging over their heads, and it occurs to me that I still don't even know who Peter works for. I don't even know that much. It is entirely possible that I'm here to deliberately make people look bad, that that's my whole purpose.

Because how convenient for some if this whole situation were to become a media disaster. Wouldn't that be perfect? Wouldn't a series of monumental blunders before election season be just the sort of thing that might serve certain people very well? A government scandal, an immigration scare, and good old-fashioned healthcare mismanagement all rolled into one. A winning formula for someone.

But none of that is important. What's important to me now is Matthew. Finding out who he is. We're in this together, he and I. I promised him.

"I think I'll stay, actually, Peter," I say. "There's not a lot of point in leaving now anyway, I'm guessing the damage has been done. Today will be the worst of it, I'm sure it'll settle down afterward. And I'm supposed to be here to help Matthew. I'd like something good to come of all this. I'll just keep going, if that still works for everyone?"

Peter hesitates on the line, he obviously wasn't expecting me to say that. But then, what can he do? He can't fire me, I'm sure of that; I'm fairly certain that dismissing someone because they have an inconvenient history is completely illegal—even more so if you knew that history prior to employing them.

"Yes, yes, of course. If you're sure you're happy to continue?" he replies cautiously. "We can do our best to make sure you're protected to a certain degree from the backlash, but there would be only so much we can do. . . ."

"That's fine, Peter. There's security at the hospital for Matthew. Officer Poole is here and Officer Graceford has said she'll shadow me at least for today, and after that . . . well, I'm sure I'll be fine. I'd only be facing the same thing if I was to go back to London."

I follow behind Chris's squad car as we head to the hospital. He leads me in through the back entrance, to keep me away from the growing crowd at the front. I park my little rental car in the service area and head in as Chris watches from his car. I don't know why I haven't been parking there from the beginning, I guess no one thought to tell me, but I'm grateful for it today.

Thankfully, I don't see the extent of the crowd outside the hospital until I'm safely in my office up on the fourth floor. I look down at it through the thin hospital glass, and my stomach flips, the drop below dizzying. The whole thing takes on a surrealist quality from this vantage point, my fear of heights kicking into overdrive as the rush of vertigo makes everything swirl at the edges. Below, the oblivious carnival of media, picketers, and protesters is still awaiting my arrival. I realize I've become politicized. Matthew and I both. We aren't people to them right now, we're symbols. The car park below, littered with protesters from all over the country on pilgrimages with their homemade signs, proves as much. We have been chosen against our will. A man with no memory and a woman with too much. And our fellow villagers, carrying placards instead of pitchforks, have come to drive us out.

They want to know where I've been for the last fourteen years. They want to know where their money is, the money my father stole before he disappeared. That's all they cared about before and I'm guessing it's all they care about now. They think I know where the money is hidden, as if it were pirate treasure only I have the map to find. But I don't have a map. And I don't know where the treasure is buried. That much we all have in common. That and the fact that they don't believe he's dead either.

I think of Matthew in his room on the ward two floors below me.

I let my mind go to a place I haven't let it yet. I know the thought is slippery and dangerous but I indulge it for a moment. A man shows up, out of the blue, who knows my real name, he knows what happened fourteen years ago, and he says he's been looking for me.

*Did my father send Matthew? Could he still be alive, really?*

Could he somehow have sent me Matthew to tell me something? To give me a message? An explanation? Or, perhaps, simply to tell me where that godforsaken money went?

*Don't go down that road, Marn. That way madness lies.*

I look up and watch the snow drifting slowly through the air outside; funny that looking up doesn't make me dizzy, only looking down. The muffled sounds of hospital life and death play out behind me. But how can I know if Matthew has something to do with my father? I can't just ask him. I'm his doctor—more than that, I'm his psychiatrist. I can't introduce my own delusions into his burgeoning memories. No, that really would be crazy. The only thing I can do is wait. I'd need to wait and see if he brings it up. If he gives any indication at all. But until then I need to put it from my mind. I need to forget it. I take a deep shuddering breath and try to clear my head.

Rhoda is on the ward to greet me; she gives me a soft look of concern and then she eyes my bandaged hands.

"Broken window," I say blithely, and hope that's the end of it. Everyone in the hospital must have heard the news by now. Everyone here knows about my past. My family history. God knows what they think. I give her a faint smile and drop the subject.

"Okay. Matthew's made his list," she says brightly, then adds, when I frown, "The list you asked him to make, places he should visit to jog his memory. He seems keen. And perhaps a day away from the hospital might do you both some good?" she suggests carefully.

It's not a bad idea. We'd have a police chaperone, we could slip out the back and do it today. And if there is something Matthew needs to tell me, now might be the best chance.

When I enter Matthew's room he rises from the chair by the window and heads straight over to meet me. To my surprise he pulls me close into a hug. "Are you okay?"

I pull back gently. "Yes, I'm fine. Um, thank you, Matthew." He must have heard the news; he's allowed online now, after all. Everyone in the hospital must be talking about it too.

I step back from him, wary of the growing intimacy. He notices my hands and I shake my head. *Don't ask*. He nods.

I don't think I've ever had this level of connection with a patient before. It's strange. It's not that I don't like it—the problem is that I do, and that is entirely inappropriate.

He clears his throat and turns to grab a folded sheet of notepaper. His list. "This is the best I could come up with, I'm afraid."

I unfold the list, which is short and carefully written.

*Train station?*
*Beach*
*Local harbor?*
*Forest*

"Why the harbor? I get the train station, that was my suggestion. And the beach and forest. You have fractured memories of those places, but why the harbor?"

He shrugs. "I overheard someone saying the police should have checked the harbor for unattended boats. I just thought, maybe I have a boat? Maybe that's how I got here? I don't know, it sounded as plausible as anything else."

I feel myself smile as I fold up the list. The simplicity of his reasoning is disarming. "Yeah, it does. Shall we do this then? Are you ready?"

"As I'll ever be." He moves to the bed and grabs his jacket. "Is it just you and me?" he asks, a subtle brightness in his tone.

It throws me for a second. He wants time alone with me. I feel that slippery thought from earlier skimming across my mind: *Does he have a message for me?* I push the thought away. "Er, no. We'll have a police officer chaperoning us. It's only a precaution, of course—we'll try to avoid the crowd," I say off his frown. "It'll be the three of us. But I don't want you to feel inhibited or on show in any way; they'll only be there to ward off any unwanted attention."

He holds my gaze and gives a quick tight smile. "Great."

I need to get my stuff from the office and let Graceford know what the plan is, so I arrange to have Rhoda escort Matthew down to the service entrance to meet me in fifteen minutes. We'll meet Graceford at the car and head out together.

I run through our destinations in my head as I get the lift upstairs. We can try the harbor in Wells-next-the-Sea first, it's the closest harbor to Holkham Beach, and if that doesn't trigger anything then we can try Brancaster harbor maybe. In terms of his forest, I'm hoping the woodland backing Holkham

Beach will suffice as a starting point. A forest is a forest; it should trigger something.

When I get to my office there is a photocopied sheet on the desk. It's the list of names I asked Chris for the other day. The names of everyone who worked at Waltham during the years I was a student there. He did it. I run my eyes over the names. Some I recognize; others are a mystery. But I don't have time to investigate fully now and I'm not sure how useful the list really is at this stage. Whoever Matthew is, I don't think he worked at Waltham House. I quickly pick up the office phone and press Trevor's extension at the security front desk and ask him to have Officer Graceford meet us outside the service entrance in ten minutes.

I trot down the hospital back stairs as lightly as I can on my still-tender feet, and my mind flashes to Chris. I think of my kiss with him last night, the warm flush of it. Of how it didn't feel awkward being with him this morning, it didn't feel wrong. How Chris took me in his arms. And then I think of Matthew, of that same desperate hungry kiss but with Matthew. Even the thought sends a hot blush straight up the back of my neck.

I don't notice the footsteps on the staircase above me at first. Not until they pick up in pace, tapping out behind me. The tempo changing suddenly to the clatter of an emergency. I pause mid-step and look up through the central stairwell, my vertigo making the perspective swirl and my stomach clench. Several flights above, a male hand, moving quickly, the sleeve of an outdoor jacket. A male nurse heading outside for a sneaky cigarette break? But why so *fast*? Then a voice, aggressive and coarse, echoes loud down the stairwell.

*"Where'd the money go? Eh?"*

Adrenaline crashes through me. He's talking to me. *Oh my God, this can't be happening. No, no, no.* My heart rate kicks up a gear, and I burst into a run, taking two steps down at a time. My bandaged hands cling for dear life to the banister as I spin around to the next flight, his pace relentless behind me. How the hell did he get past security? I pound on as I hear the footsteps behind me speed up, scrabbling and skidding around the stairwell above me.

"That's right. You'd better run, you fucking bitch."

My blood runs cold—he's going to hurt me, I can hear it in his voice. I suddenly realize just how vulnerable I am and momentarily lose my footing on the smooth concrete steps. I manage to grab the handrail again before my ankle twists beneath me and a flash of memory from fourteen years ago blazes through my mind. A fully grown man running at me from across a road, his arm raised, his face contorted, his words loud and filled with hate. And then, out of nowhere, Joe pushing me out of the way. I'd hit the ground hard but Joe had taken the brunt of the man's impact. The anger people had toward us back then, the family who stole their money. All the events like it in the days and weeks that followed, the fear, the hatred, until we finally left our home. Until the police finally had to move us for our own safety. I foolishly thought it couldn't be as bad this time around. But here we are. I guess I was wrong.

I can't let him reach me. There's no Joe here to protect me this time. No police to change my name and relocate me. It's just me, all alone and already wounded. My feet smart as I leap down onto the second-floor landing and swing around on the banister to the next flight, my chaser coming into view a flight above me. Medium build, graying hair, a neat goatee, a flak jacket, but the thing that makes me jolt forward suddenly, barely in control of my own movements, is what I see in his hand.

*He has a gun.*

I open my mouth to scream for help, but like in a nightmare, I can't catch my breath. No noise comes. *Oh God, I am going to die. I'm going to die.* Images of my father's faceless body flash through my mind. A shotgun wound to the head. The blood and bone and skull.

I hear myself whimper as I crash down another flight, praying there is someone at the base of the stairs who can help me.

I hear the gunman's footsteps closing in on me, but I know he'll need to slow before he can raise his weapon steady in his hands and fire. As long as I hear him running I am safe, I tell myself.

Below me the ground-floor doors loom into sight and somehow I manage a shout. My voice echoes loud, reedy and terrified, down the empty stairwell ahead of me, frightening me even more. Behind me he clears the corner as I hit the ground floor hard, scramble to my feet, and burst through the double doors into the service corridor.

Then I see them both at the other end of the hallway, silhouetted in the open doorway, daylight framing them. Rhoda and Matthew. They stare wide-eyed at me, startled, unsure what exactly is happening. Then suddenly Matthew is moving, somehow making sense of the situation. He bursts toward me at a sprint. I want to warn him that the person behind me has a gun, but even as the words reach my lips I hear the doors behind me explode open, the gunman careening through after me. He must see Matthew and Rhoda—I hear him slow. And I whip my head around just in time to see him raise his weapon.

"Get down! NOW!" Matthew shouts, and I do

not think, I dive onto the slippery concrete floor, crashing down hard, the impact vibrating through every bone in my body. Matthew flies past me.

A shot rings out, deafeningly sharp as it echoes through the thin corridor. I roll and see Matthew slam into the gunman. But there is no struggle. In one concise movement Matthew twists the weapon from the man's hands, sliding it away and clear. He spins the gunman around as if they were dancing. A sharp kick to the back of the man's knees forces him to the floor and then Matthew is on him, pressing my attacker's screaming face into the ground.

I rise to all fours and look up the corridor to Rhoda, unsure if the shot fired connected with anyone. She's crouched low to the floor, her mobile phone in her quivering hand, her eyes as aghast as mine must be, but she isn't injured. Somewhere along the corridor, out of sight, there are more shouts. Without thinking, I crawl toward the abandoned gun. And that's when I see it. A white tuft of feathers sprouting from the shoulder of Matthew's down jacket. He's been wounded. The bullet clipped him. I search his face for a reaction but his expression is unreadable as he watches me reach for the gun.

# 36

## DR. EMMA LEWIS

### DAY 12—FIVE'S A CROWD

Outside, with dirty bandaged hands that won't stop shaking, I bum a cigarette off a security guard and carefully light it with his Day-Glo pink lighter.

I start to give Graceford a brief and garbled rundown of events, but she notices the tremors of shock running through my muscles and sends someone to fetch me sugary tea.

I take a greedy pull on the cigarette and let the hot surge of it fill my chest, the engulfing burn and release of it. A little death. God, I've missed that feeling. I know people shouldn't smoke—I've seen a smoker's lung, I know—but everything will kill us in the end, life itself kills us in the end, and like it or lump it, smoking feels good. And right now, it's making me happy.

I'm sheltered here around the back of the building, and although the press are aware of some kind of commotion on this side of the hospital, they can't get to us here, security gates and guards block their way. I don't know how my attacker got through all the security. I think of what could have happened to me if Matthew hadn't been there, if that man had got hold of me, and I shudder. His words as they took him away. *She's done more harm than me. Who paid for her training, eh? How many people have to suffer for her? Ask her that!* I feel shame, thick and inescapable, pulling me under.

Rhoda walks over to join me. She eyes my cigarette, and I manage to hide the tremor in my hand as I lift it back to my lips. Not that I think she would judge me, not after what just happened.

Rhoda didn't rush forward to help, but then she didn't run away either, which is brave. She is a half-hero, if there is such a thing.

"I'm sorry," she says, sipping her hot tea. I take her other hand in mine and give it a little squeeze.

"Not your fault. At all."

I look back past her at Matthew down the corridor, his wound being assessed by Triage. I can't see the extent of it clearly.

"Is he okay?" I ask Rhoda as she follows my gaze.

"It only nicked him. They're popping a few stitches in. He's lucky." She looks back at me with a shaky smile. "But then, we knew that already, didn't we?" I see the uncertainty behind her eyes.

She feels it too. That uneasy relief.

Thank God Matthew had been there. I wouldn't be here if not for him. Perhaps neither of us would be. But how the hell did he do what he just did? I've never seen anything like the speed, the certainty, and the economy of his movements. He must have been trained, though for what, I don't know. Shouldn't someone with that kind of training be missed by someone? Yet here Matthew is in a general hospital deep in the Norfolk coast, in borrowed clothes, desperately clinging to borrowed memories.

Leaving Rhoda to give her statement, I grab some

dressing packs from the triage nurse and head to the doctors' locker room to clean myself up. I change the bandages on my hands in the sink under the mirror. I look gaunt in the reflection, drained of color. I examine my features objectively, hair ruffled, a speck of Matthew's blood on my blouse. *I could have died today,* I try to let the reality of that sink in. I could have been killed by a stranger because of something someone else did fourteen years ago. My pale face blinks back at me in the glass. My haunted face. *Places aren't haunted, Emma, people are.* I try to shake off the thoughts.

I splash my face with warm water to force some color back into it. Outside the locker room Graceford is waiting; she won't leave my side, she says. We head up to my office, and she stands guard outside. I have a moment to myself.

I receive a call from Peter.

He tells me not to leave the hospital. Someone from the MOD is on their way. I guess that *training* we've all noticed has raised some alarms along the chain of command.

I think of the final fMRI question I asked Matthew three days ago: *Have you killed?* I think of how he responded. His expression this morning as I groped for the discarded gun on the hospital floor. We could be onto something now.

Hands still shaky, I google "Princess Margaret Hospital." I need to know who that gunman was. Today's news springs up in the search results. It's ironic that even I need to find out about my attacker from the Internet. The police knew nothing earlier, but the media have done their thing and the facts are rolling in online. The man's name is Simon Lichfield, a fifty-three-year-old with a history of mental illness and some spurious connection to a far-right group. I don't know him. He didn't know me. Nor did he know any of the July 7 victims my father stole from. He just decided I deserved some justice. Maybe he thought I was lying, hiding the money, abetting a criminal, any one of the things he'd heard on TV. So he decided to do the right thing: he made his way here to the hospital armed with a sawed-off shotgun. And he waited for me.

I close my laptop lid and shudder. *What is it about me that makes people think it's okay to kill me?*

People in military uniforms arrive that afternoon. Three of them are shown into my office. Two male officers and a woman in plainclothes. The woman, in her forties, clearly outranking the men. The men take the two seats offered while she remains standing. She introduces herself as Dr. Samuels, looks at my bandaged hands and we do not shake. She briefly explains that they wish to meet Matthew and assess him. She asks if it seemed to me that he displayed any specialist training earlier. I tell her my thoughts as she leans against the tall filing cabinet watchfully. After a moment the older officer speaks.

"And your patient, Matthew, he hasn't mentioned military training or anything like that?" he asks, his gaze gliding over my little gray office.

I slide my list of Waltham House employees deftly under some paperwork, hiding my embarrassing foray into detective work from sight. "No, he hasn't mentioned anything at all about training," I answer. "But I think—well, at this stage it's entirely possible he may not even remember doing any."

The three faces opposite me hide their own particular brands of skepticism as my eyes flit between them. The woman finally clears her throat.

"And it's not possible, to your mind, Dr. Lewis,

that your patient could be exaggerating his symptoms? Exaggerating his memory loss?"

I shake my head. "I'd be happy to show you the fMRIs if you'd like, Dr. Samuels. I'd be interested to know if you've ever encountered a patient who was able to exaggerate the activation of their own hippocampus." It's a cheap shot, and childish, I know, but she's basically just wandered in here and told me I don't know my job. I may very well have almost been shot this morning but I know my fucking job.

I have no real idea who these people are, and they are certainly not attempting to sugarcoat the sense that they're in charge. Since arriving, they have made it very clear it is Matthew they want to talk to, not his doctor.

The younger officer speaks now, his voice patrician and infuriatingly reasonable. "Whilst we understand your point of view, Dr. Lewis, and obviously respect your medical opinion, we do think a conversation with Matthew himself would be in his interest." The older officer nods in silent affirmation. "There is, of course, the possibility that we would want to move him to a more specialized facility if that were to be considered appropriate."

"And who would be assessing the appropriateness of that?" I counter tartly, my eyes flicking back to Dr. Samuels.

"I'm a military psychiatrist, Dr. Lewis, I can assure you that someone with the appropriate training would be assessing that, should it prove necessary," she coos.

"And if it *doesn't* prove necessary?" I ask, matching her tone. "And you've simply interfered with a civilian patient with mental health problems? Then what?"

"Then we would defer to your better judgment.

But I think our involvement at this stage is a risk we should all be willing to take." She moves to the window ledge, looking down at the growing crowd far below. I feel my vertigo lurch, on her behalf, as she continues. "I think we both know it's unlikely that a civilian would have been able to do what your patient did this morning, Dr. Lewis."

She looks back at me, her eyes intent. I look away.

She's right, I know she's right. He definitely knew what he was doing, that is unquestionable. It's incredibly unlikely that a civilian would have been capable of doing what Matthew did.

Yet I hold my ground. I don't know why, but I feel I should protect him. Maybe it's because of the question rolling around in my head: *Why are they only arriving now?* If Matthew is one of theirs, why haven't they come for him sooner?

But then, perhaps that's it, perhaps he isn't one of *theirs* at all? Perhaps he's someone else's? He could be working for a foreign government. Either way, I'm clearly completely out of my depth.

I grudgingly agree to let Dr. Samuels assess Matthew but on the condition I remain present for the assessment. They decline my offer. I cannot be present because sensitive information may be brought up. I realize I am fast losing ground, so I compromise, agreeing to absent myself on the proviso that I *am* present at least until Matthew consents to their interview. Eager to move forward, they agree.

Matthew is already in the consultation room when we arrive. He stands as I enter; I see the bulk of his shoulder bandaged beneath his T-shirt, his left arm in a loose sling. Overkill from the nursing staff but I can't blame them. I haven't seen him since the incident, and the concern for me etched on his face makes my heart leap into my throat.

I watch him grow pale as the two officers enter the room behind me and Dr. Samuels closes the door.

He looks at me questioningly, but he can sense that I am no longer in charge here.

"Hello, Matthew. Is it okay to call you Matthew? I'm Dr. Lily Samuels. We were wondering if we could ask you some questions about what happened today, and about what happened eleven days ago on the ward. Would that be okay?"

"What kind of questions?" he asks.

Dr. Samuels's eyes flick to me before she answers. "Do you have any military training, Matthew?" She pulls out the chair opposite his and sits. "Do you remember going through anything like that?"

Matthew's eyes shoot to me instantly; he's evaluating, trying hard to work out his next move, the *right* thing to say. I pray he doesn't think I've sold him out, but perhaps, in a way, I have.

He looks down a moment before answering, and when he raises his eyes back to Dr. Samuels his expression is impenetrable.

"I think we should discuss this alone," he says, and as if on cue all eyes but his turn in my direction. And I realize I've been asked to leave.

# 37

# DR. EMMA LEWIS

## DAY 12—MILITARY MAN

I pace the nurses' break room and curse myself.

I should have known he was military. I knew it was PTSD. From day one, I just knew. The fMRI results, for God's sake. I think of how stupid I've been, of how easily swayed I've been, thinking he might be something—or someone—from my past. But Matthew is something else entirely. A military asset, AWOL. Possibly a foreign asset or one that's defected. Who knows why they're so interested in him? I realize I might never know. Why would the British military tell an NHS doctor what the hell was going on? I suddenly realize I might not even see Matthew again after this. He might just leave with them after their interview. No goodbyes, nothing, the end. I eye the clock on the wall, and check to see if Graceford is still guarding me outside the break room door. No change.

They've been in there twenty-five minutes. What the hell are they talking about? I pour myself a coffee, adding sugar to steady my shot nerves, and I try not to think about what I've thrown into the fire for this assignment. The fact that I almost died doing this job earlier today. I try not to think of Mum, of Joe and his family. He told me, Joe told me to resign, and I ignored his advice. And in a second it could all be for nothing. A doctor without a patient. A crusader without a cause.

My phone vibrates in my pocket right on cue. I fish it out as I sip the warm dark coffee.

A message from Chris.

**Are you ok?! My god! Just heard what happened.**
**Do you need me to come there?**
**Chris x**

I smile in spite of myself. Chris is worried about me.

There's a soft rap on the door and I look up.

"May I?" Dr. Samuels asks. She doesn't wait for my answer before coming right in and closing the door behind her.

"Firstly, thank you for being so accommodating, Dr. Lewis. I know firsthand how disconcerting this whole process can be. I appreciate it."

"Not a problem." I give her a mock-conciliatory smile. "So, will Matthew be leaving us today?" I try to keep my tone light. Impartial, like a doctor should be.

"No, I don't think he will, Dr. Lewis. Not today. But we'll be keeping in touch, and I may be back over the next few days. Matthew has agreed to undergo a few tests with me at a different facility." She pauses. "But I think he'll be best serviced here for the next few days at least. It's probably best to wait for some of this media interest to quieten before we think about moving him elsewhere."

"Can I ask what he said?" I inquire as she turns away, and for a second, I think perhaps she might leave without answering, but then she turns back. "You know I can't divulge that information, Dr. Lewis. Perhaps you should ask him yourself?"

When I get to Matthew's room Graceford keeps her distance outside. He's ready and waiting for me when I enter, wearing his puffer jacket, the bullet-ripped shoulder now repaired. Tight neat stitches patch over the hole, and I can't help but wonder if he fixed it himself or did Rhoda mend it? I glimpsed her only once since this morning.

"I still want to go out today," Matthew tells me before I can speak. "I don't think we have long left together." He might be right about that. He looks at me patiently, and I realize he's waiting for his answer.

"Er, sorry, what? Go out? What do you mean, go out, Matthew?" It takes me a moment to work out what he's talking about, and then I recall. This morning, before the attack and the terror and gunshots, we'd had a plan. To visit areas that might jog his memory. He can't be serious, can he? "You don't mean our trip?" I ask, incredulous.

He takes a moment before answering calmly. "Yes. Why? Would that be a problem?"

I'm not entirely sure what to say. It's so far from anything I was thinking before. Is that really what he wants after everything that's happened already today? But maybe he has a point: his time here with us—with me—is very fast coming to an end.

"Are you sure this is what you want to do? Today? *Now?*" I ask.

"Yes. I'm sure. *I really think we should go out, Emma.*" There's an intensity to his tone that's impossible to ignore. He wants to get us away from the hospital. There's something he needs to tell me and he wants me to know it. We need to do this and we need to do it now.

Nick Dunning is less than enthused by the idea when I get to his office.

"Well, I certainly don't think it sounds *sensible,* if that's what you're asking." He leans forward on his desk, eyebrows sky high.

"I know, Nick. But I've spoken to Officer Graceford and she's happy to escort us." I gesture to the hallway outside his office where I just left Graceford. "I can call her in if you like. You can ask her yourself." I pray he doesn't take me up on that offer, as, to be honest, Graceford wasn't keen on the plan at all until I explained to her that it was an absolute necessity we do this today. Blessedly, Nick shakes his head; he doesn't need Graceford dragged into this. I plow on. "It's the patient's request to leave the premises, Nick, so, unless we want to section him under the Mental Health Act as a risk to himself and others, and take away his right to leave, Matthew's free to decide." Nick sighs heavily and slouches back into his seat. "Nick, I've done all the tests I can do here. There's only so much clinical work I can do with Matthew, it only takes us so far. He wants to know who he is. We need to get him out in the world, he needs to see things and associate. That's the way we can crack this. I've already got him on drugs to lower stress, which, if it's PTSD causing the dissociative fugue, should be creating the right conditions for his memory to return. But I can't force it. And there's only so much we can do in the hospital. There's only so much therapy and so many memory exercises we can do. If I take him back to the beach, to these places, we might actually trigger something and he might start to remember, Nick. He's ready. He's as good as told me he's ready to remember."

Nick insists I sign a form accepting full responsibility for the patient, releasing the hospital of all culpability—which is not reassuring at all—but I comfort myself with the fact that Groves picked me for this job because of my pioneering methods. And if they're good enough for him, then we should all be fine.

I sign the form in awkward silence and twenty minutes later three of us pull out of the snowy service entrance, Graceford driving, me in the passenger seat, Matthew in the back. We glide onto the main road, away from the press and protesters, and head out toward the open expanse of the Norfolk coast.

Wells Harbour is our first port of call, with its cracked-paint fishing boats in softly faded colors. We slam the car doors and head across the snow-covered boatyard toward the harbormaster's little hut. I watch Matthew's eyes dart over the landscape; he's like a man visiting a foreign country, hungry to take everything in. He's not wearing his sling anymore and a slight stiffness in his shoulder is the only clue to the dressing hidden beneath. I bury my own bandaged hands deep in my pockets as the snow crunches and creaks satisfyingly underfoot. It's so good to be outside. I realize how cooped up I've been recently and draw in the crisp chilly air full of the scent of wood fires and fish and chips. My stomach rumbles and I realize I haven't eaten since breakfast either. I haven't been taking care of myself.

In the harbormaster's office, Graceford asks if anybody new has been mooring here over the last few weeks, but the harbormaster shakes his head. "It's all regulars this time of year. Why do you ask?" he inquires, interest piqued. I suppose we must look like an odd gang. A police officer, a woman with bandaged hands, and a man in an oversize woman's puffer jacket. The harbormaster clearly has no idea who we are and suddenly I want to hug him for being so completely out of the loop. It's almost as if none of today's events really happened. It just goes to show: having your whole life sprayed across the TV isn't the end of the world, not everyone watches TV.

Matthew and I wander around the brittle carcasses of the ships in the dry dock; Graceford hangs back, giving us space, her eyes on the harbor entrance. I know I shouldn't feel so close to him, but the desire to just ask him what he needs to tell me is almost overwhelming. He scans the moorings, the sea beyond, taking his time before finally turning to me.

"I haven't been here before," he says with confidence.

I try to put my analyst head back on. "And it doesn't remind you of anything? None of this throws up any thoughts or feelings? Any images?"

He takes a moment, his collar turned up, the cool wind ruffling his hair. "No."

"That's good, that kind of clarity is good."

I suggest we get some food to take away from the harbor café. The stress and activity of the day have left us all completely famished, so Graceford agrees. We buy three boxes of fish and chips from the otherwise empty café and head back to the police car.

When we get to Holkham Beach, I pull Graceford to one side.

"Do you mind giving us a bit more space on this one?" I ask tentatively.

She frowns and scans the empty beach before answering. "For now. But if anyone turns up I can't risk it." She looks farther along the sands. "I can probably get a pretty good overview of the area from the dune. If you don't wander too far, I'm happy to stay back at that distance for the time being, if that helps. We just don't want a repeat of this morning," she reminds me, her tone concerned.

"No, of course not. Thank you, Beth."

Matthew and I find a patch of dune grass farther off to settle on and we dig into our hot boxes of fish and chips, the wind whipping around us. This must be the closest thing to normal he's done in weeks. I catch him snatching a look back toward Graceford before glancing at me with a puzzled expression.

"What is it?" I ask, a chip halfway to my mouth.

He laughs. "Nothing, just, thank you, for bringing me here." He smiles. "Can I ask you a question, Emma?"

"Of course."

"I was just wondering why you came back here. To Norfolk. I mean, considering everything that happened."

I chew my hot chip and let out a sigh.

"Because of your case," I say honestly. "These types of cases are—" I pause, aware I'm on shaky ground. "I'll be honest, Matthew—cases like yours are incredibly rare. There have only been a handful, really. And I was asked, you know. I wrote a paper, a few years back, about a similar case, and they wanted me on this because of that, I guess."

"You wrote about the Piano Man." He takes a swig of his water bottle.

I look up, surprised at his words. "How do you know that, Matthew? About the Piano Man?"

He looks momentarily thrown, and then his wind-reddened checks flush further with embarrassment. "Er, okay. Shit. I may have looked you up, they let me use the computers at the hospital."

Of course, I forgot we okayed that. He's been looking me up. I bluster, caught off guard by his honesty, "Oh. Okay. Well, yes, so you know about a few cases like yours then. I wrote a few paragraphs on the Piano Man, but mainly I wrote about another case, in America." I feel my cheeks grow hot in the wind as he holds my gaze in his.

"Oh, remind me, I skimmed parts. Another case like mine?" He pops a chip into his mouth, interested.

I nod, the wind whipping my hair out around me. "Yes, I just thought a lot of cases like yours and particularly the case I wrote about had been . . . mismanaged—they could have been handled better. I know, I'm hardly one to talk, given everything that's happened today and the current situation at the hospital, but I mean in terms of diagnosis. Those cases were mishandled. It was bad medical practice." Matthew stops chewing now, he nods me on. I continue with caution; it could be a good sign that Matthew is suddenly so interested in diagnoses. "I believe that in that particular case, the man was misdiagnosed. They said he was malingering but they didn't do an fMRI."

"Malingering?"

"Faking," I clarify.

"Why did they think he was faking, do you think?"

"It's a rare condition. They didn't scan, like we did. Because medicine is a constantly evolving science and sometimes the science is wrong until it's right. They saw no brain damage and refused to believe in a psychogenic explanation." He frowns at the word, so I elaborate. "They couldn't see any actual brain damage, so they assumed there was no real problem. They didn't scan his brain activity. I think his underlying condition was never treated. But you're right. I think I was chosen for this job because of my hard-line stance on the Piano Man. They wanted you diagnosed correctly . . . without all the media attention. I know!" I cry. "The irony of that given our current situation is not at all lost on me, Matthew, trust me."

He smiles. "I *do,* you know," he says, looking out toward the waves. "Trust you."

I feel a warmth blossom inside again and I try to grapple the conversation back around to medical issues. "So, is any of this coming back to you?" I gesture out to the miles of windblown sand crested with grass-topped dunes. The kind of place people remember even if they've never seen it before, a twilight dreamscape, a place between worlds.

He squints out at the vast open space before turning back in the direction of Graceford, a shadow passing over his features. When he looks back at me he sounds disappointed. "No. There's nothing here. Just that first day, just what we already know."

As we walk back to meet Graceford he touches my arm, stopping me. He comes very close so I can hear him whisper over the roar of the wind, his breath warm on my cheek. "Thank you. For coming back here. For trying to help me. I knew you would." I look in his eyes—he's holding something back. He wants to say something but he's not saying it.

"Of course," I say gently, glancing down quickly at his hand, still holding my sleeve. The feel of his fingertips through the fabric. When I look back up he's staring at me; his eyes flick to my lips and I feel my stomach tighten. I look away again, my eyes seeking Graceford in the distance. I take a breath and without thinking I ask the question that's been bubbling away in my head. "Matthew, what did you tell Dr. Samuels?"

He lets go of my arm and smiles, surprised by the question. "Er, I'm not entirely comfortable," he begins hesitantly. "Well, I wasn't comfortable saying it in front of you. . . ."

"Why?"

"Because you won't want to hear it," he answers, his tone suddenly serious. "It's not a good thing."

I feel the hairs on the back of my neck rise. *Oh God*. "What do you mean, it's not a good thing, Matthew?" The tone of our conversation has changed, the air sucked out of it.

He looks away, unsure how to proceed, and steps back, putting some distance between us. "I just—I know how to do certain things. I don't know how I know these things. And I didn't want to say, with you there." He kicks at the sand, silent for a moment. But I can tell there is more coming, so I give him space. "Right, well. When I got hold of that guy this morning—I knew how to kill him, Emma." He's watching for my reaction; I try to keep my face neutral. "I don't mean with the gun. I mean I *knew* how to kill him. With my hands. And—" He breaks off. "And I *really* wanted to do it, you know. I knew what it would feel like and I wanted to do it. Because he hurt you."

"Okay," I say, and for a moment I'm so taken aback I can't think what else to say. He waits for my response and I try to snap back into doctor mode. "It's okay. Whatever you're feeling is okay. Don't block it, just let it come as it comes. We're going to work this out together, Matthew. You are not a bad person. Don't start to think that. Something bad may have happened to you but you are not bad. Okay?"

His hand finds my bandaged one and for a second

the dressings seem to confuse him. "I won't let anyone hurt you again, Marni. You know."

*Marni,* again.

I wonder if the bandages remind him of my burnt fingers. The burnt fingers he seemed to remember that first night we spoke. The same slippery thought from earlier this morning shimmers into focus. And for a second, I'm certain that this man has something to do with that night fourteen years ago. Two thoughts scream through my head: *Is my father still alive? Do you have something to do with him?*

And I'm speaking before I can stop myself. "Matthew, is there something you want to tell me? About why you're here? We might not get this chance again."

He turns quickly to check Graceford's proximity. She's still stationed high on the sand dunes ahead, far from hearing distance, but her gaze finds us as we stare across at her.

Matthew focuses on me, an intensity in his eyes. "Yes. But not yet," he says furtively, and I notice he has taken my bandaged hands lightly in his again. "There's something, but I need more time. Can you wait?"

*This could be it. This really could be it.*

I catch sight of Graceford moving in my peripheral vision, slowly making her way down the dunes toward us. Time really is up.

"Yes," I say swiftly. "I can wait." He squeezes my hands softly, holding me in his gaze, and I feel it through my whole body.

The light is starting to fade by the time we get back to the car, and Graceford suggests we leave the other destinations for another day and return to the hospital. I'm pretty sure we won't get another day, but I agree. I just pray we have the time he needs.

He's silent as we drive back to the hospital, deep in thought. I try not to read too much into his silence. Try not to guess at his thoughts. He clearly wants to tell me something but he was worried about Graceford. He needs to talk to me on my own. *How can I make that happen?* But I catch myself with the thought. Being alone with Matthew might not be such a great idea. I think of the way he looked at me on the beach, his gaze traveling to my lips, and the telltale flip in my stomach. It's common for patients to develop feelings for their doctors. And doctors for their patients. But it's rare for a patient to know so much about their doctor. Rare that anyone could know the things Matthew knows about me. The only other people who know as much about the details of that night are my family and Chris. Matthew feels so close and I shouldn't have allowed that.

I glance at his reflection in the rearview mirror. I'm going to have to make sure I keep our relationship purely clinical, because what he needs from me and the way he makes me feel are starting to scare me.

Thankfully, Graceford accompanies us back up to the ward and waits outside the open door to Matthew's room.

"I think that's enough for today. I'll see you tomorrow, Matthew. Okay?" I keep my tone light but businesslike. There's no time like the present to set boundaries. "We'll do some more memory exercises in the morning, and if we don't hear from Dr. Samuels by the afternoon we can perhaps try another trip then. If you'd find that helpful?"

He ignores my question, starts to unzip his jacket, then pauses. "I know it's not my business, Dr. Lewis, but have you thought about going back?" he says seriously, the quality of his voice matching mine in coolness.

"Back?" I ask, confused. "Back where?"

"Have you thought about going back to your old house?" he explains directly. "Where it happened?"

I feel the blood drain from my face. What is he doing?

His gaze moves past me to the bustling corridor beyond the door, where Graceford waits. Is he worried she can hear?

Perhaps this is what he wanted to tell me on the beach. Is he *telling* me to go back to my old house? Is there something there, at the house?

He reads the confusion on my face and adds carefully, "I'm only suggesting it because it might help you. Sometimes the most terrifying thing is our own imagination. The not knowing. You know? The reality of what happened, whatever it was, will never be as bad as the stories our minds tell us. If you go back, Dr. Lewis, you might see that."

I stare at him. What is he talking about?

*If I go back I might see what exactly?* I can't work out from his tone if this is an instruction or well-meaning small talk.

But he holds my gaze, his voice low as he continues. "I bet as soon as you get through those gates, what happened will seem so much smaller. It'll feel more manageable." I remember what he did for me this morning, how he saved me, how profoundly safe I feel with him.

*Is there something there, at the house, that he wants me to see? Or am I just imagining things again?*

I give him a smile, trying to lighten the weight of the moment and draw a line in the sand. Enough for today. "Thank you, Matthew. But just to be clear," I joke, "we definitely didn't have gates—it wasn't that kind of place."

He hesitates, lost for a second before realizing I'm joking, then a flash of relief bursts across his face.

# 38

## DR. EMMA LEWIS

### DAY 13—TIME TO GO HOME

I get up early the next morning, slip straight into my running clothes, and let myself out quietly into the thick muffling snow. The air's crisp and fresh and I pick up my pace as soon as I've pushed through the low hinged gate at the back of the lodge. I thought about going out the front entrance, but it's too early to make small talk with the officer stationed in the car out there, Sergeant Greene. And I'm pretty sure he'd veto a morning run and I desperately need to clear my head before going back to work today or I'll go mad.

He took over last night from Graceford, and aside from taking him out a coffee before bed, I haven't said two words to him. He's a higher rank than Chris and Graceford and he's certainly less amenable. Chris was waiting with him when Graceford and I got back to the lodge last night. Apparently after that night the local police wouldn't be able to offer twenty-four-hour protection, Chris explained. I guess Chris had told Sergeant Greene this news might be better coming from him. Inside, over tea, Chris explained my options: either I could head back to London and they could liaise with my local force on options going forward or I could leave tomorrow with the protected-persons unit, witness protection, if I felt a continuing threat to my safety.

"Are you joking, Chris?" I'd scoffed. "You seriously think I'm going to change my name again? Run away from this shit again? What about Matthew? I'm his doctor."

Chris tried to be understanding but the facts had an inescapable harshness. "Okay, maybe the protection unit is a little extreme," he admitted. "But you were attacked today. It was an attempt on your life, Emma. And the media are still at the hospital, and trust me, there are a lot of weird people out there. Maybe London is the best option. I don't think staying on this job is a good thing for you or your patient at this stage."

He didn't stay long. I told him as he left that I'd think about it and make a decision soon.

I let my stride stretch out as I creak across the fresh snowfall, my feet and bandaged hands still tender from the basement glass two nights ago. As I find my rhythm my breath deepens, its reassuring huff and the dampened sounds of the forest working to quiet my mind.

*So, do I stay or do I go?*

Up ahead I see a worn path leading off the main track; it's narrow and overgrown but bends back toward the lodge. I should stay close. I turn off and head into the denser wood, branches scratching and pulling, but I keep my pace.

*Stay or go?*

I think again of what happened to me yesterday—the attack, the anger that vile stranger had toward me. He wanted to take my life. He wanted me to die.

I think of the chants and the pickets outside the hospital, and yesterday's headlines. And I wonder in earnest if all of this was really worth it.

I came here for my career but I've stayed for Matthew. To help Matthew, because I'm his doctor and I'm the best and he needed me to stay.

But if I'm honest, that's not my only reason. I'm here because of what he said to me that first night. The way he spoke to me. The things he knew that he couldn't possibly have known. And more than that, the little things about him that seem so familiar to me, his gait, his eyes, the slope of his strong shoulders. No matter how crazy it sounds, the truth is, I'm here because he reminds me of my father. Plain and simple. It's just a feeling. I have put my life and family and career in jeopardy for a feeling. But there is something there, there's something he's not telling me. I think of what he did tell me yesterday. He told me to go back home. I might see something if I go back to that house. Perhaps this is what I've been waiting for.

Ahead the path opens out into a small snow-patched clearing. I slow as I approach, sensing it before I see it. Something about it not quite right.

Something in the undergrowth ahead, a dark huddled mass. I stop abruptly, a shot of pure adrenaline exploding through me.

A man. Someone's here. I'm not alone. I see him crouching close to the ground, the figure, peering out from the tangled branches—as if somehow just bending behind the bush might mask him from my sight.

I flinch back immediately, stumbling away from the figure, a thought flashing through my mind: *Has Simon Lichfield been released?* My sneakers catch on a root and I tumble down, my eyes still glued to the unmoving figure. I freeze, paralyzed in the horror of the moment, but as I look on the figure seems to morph. I catch my breath—it's not my attacker, it's not a man at all, it's an object, some kind of bulky fabric, large and strung incongruously onto the winter undergrowth. The draping of it imitating the bulk of a human figure.

A surge of relief bursts through me and I let out a laugh of pure unadulterated joy. *Thank God. Oh, thank God. I am such a moron.*

I take a moment before scrambling up to my feet. Nothing to be scared of, just good old-fashioned paranoia. Though, I remind myself, someone really did try to kill me yesterday, so maybe this error is less paranoia than due diligence.

Cautiously I approach the mass. Rich burgundy and deep navy, expensive-looking, it has an open zip running jagged along its length. A discarded puffer jacket—like Matthew's. No, it's too large for that. Suddenly I realize what it is.

It's a sleeping bag. Weird.

I wonder how it got here. This is private property, far from the road. The bag couldn't have been flung from a car, dumped as garbage. No, it must have been brought here by someone, then abandoned. I feel the relief drain from my body. Someone has been sleeping out here, just yards from the lodge where I've been staying all alone. I tell myself not to jump to conclusions.

In London it's not unusual to stumble on homeless encampments while running through the woodland parks, but out here, miles from the nearest village, so close to the lodge, the sleeping bag doesn't quite sit right. And it doesn't look like the kind of thing someone down on their luck might own.

I suppress a shudder as I crouch down in front of

the offending object. It looks new, its silky shell and plump downy filling scarcely damaged by the winter elements. It hasn't been here that long, maybe a few nights, maybe as long as I've been here? Perhaps I should run back and alert the police officer.

But I hold off, still thinking it through. After everything that's happened in the last few days, there's a good chance I might be reading too much into this. The bag might just have blown here from a campsite nearby; it wouldn't be unheard of in the strong coastal winds. Or maybe someone was innocently sleeping out here.

I sweep the clearing for other signs of activity, the innocent detritus that campers leave—food scraps, wrappers, ashes, or half-burnt twigs. There's nothing, just the bag.

*Huh.*

I move to the other side of the clearing and look back in the direction of the lodge—I see patio doors, upstairs windows, all clearly visible from here through the gaps in the branches. This is the perfect vantage point for the back of the house. My bedroom window is in plain sight. I imagine it lit up in the darkness of night and fear fizzes through me afresh. Whoever was here wasn't a camper.

They were watching me.

Perhaps they still are—instinctively my eyes flash around me, deep into the dense forest, my breath coming in short gasps. But I see no one, no threat in sight. Whoever was here is gone.

It can't have been Lichfield, my attacker; he'll still be in custody. And he wouldn't have known where I was staying until the news broke yesterday. The only people who knew *Marni Beaufort* was staying here were my family, Peter Chorley, and Chris.

Unless? Unless my father was here? Has he come

back? I sink down into a squat, my breath sucked from me. Could he have been here? I don't stop to think, I rise, head straight to the sleeping bag, and grab it. I pull it to my face, my nose, and I inhale. I don't know why I do it but I do, I try to smell him. I strain for his almost forgotten scent of cologne and cedar and bonfires. But the bag just smells of factory chemicals and damp. Frustrated, I tug it from its tangle of thorns and vigorously shake it out, hoping for what to tumble out I do not know. A message, a note, something. Nothing. Only dead leaves fall from inside.

I stand alone and terrified in the clearing, panting, my breath fogging in the air.

The truth of what happened yesterday hits me once again. I very nearly died. I nearly died yesterday, a man tried to kill me. The bullet that grazed Matthew was meant for me. And it wasn't because of anything I did or didn't do. It was because of what my father did. I almost died yesterday because of him. For the second time in my life.

He is the cause of everything bad that ever happened in my life. He hurt me. He hurt my family. He is the reason we changed our names, he is the reason we left our home, the reason we all tried so hard to start a new life. And I'm still here pining for him. Waiting to find him, to hear it's all not true, desperate to hear that he's alive and well and that he's so, so sorry for what he did.

I toss the sleeping bag away. Whether he was here or whether someone else was here hoping to hurt me, it doesn't matter, the fault is his. I could be at risk for the rest of my life because of him. I feel my anger metastasizing inside me. Only one person is responsible for making me a target. I ball up my hands tight, feeling the wounds ache. Fourteen years of my guilt and wondering what I could have done differently. What *I* could have done differently! Rage flows molten through me, rage at what he did, at what he tried to do to me and Mum and Joe, rage at the media for twisting everything until we were all no longer victims but figures of hate, like him. But most of all, rage because I know with absolute certainty that whether he's alive or not, what my father did won't ever leave me alone, the legacy he's left has touched every part of my life, a legacy I never deserved, and one I can't ever escape from. Or can I? The sound of my own breathing seems to fade out as an idea begins to form.

When I return to Cuckoo Lodge, I head straight around to the front. Sergeant Greene spots me and exits his vehicle.

I explain that I will not be leaving for London today and I will not be requiring the protected-persons unit. I will be finishing my assignment. Sergeant Greene is keen to point out that if I do stay it will be directly against the advice of Norfolk Constabulary—and I tell him that's fine.

"I'll sign whatever you want me to sign but I'm not leaving today."

I watch his car pull out of the long driveway, lock the front door behind me, and head straight to the shower. I peel off my sweat-soaked things and stand for a moment shivering in front of the bathroom's full-length mirror, thick warm steam filling the tiled room around me. I look at myself. I'm older; I'm not sure when that happened to me. Older every year and yet I don't seem to get anywhere. Not like Joe. Not like everyone else.

*Something needs to change.*

I need to move on. Or I'll blink and my life will be over. I need to close the circle. There doesn't seem to be any other way to end this. Matthew told me to go back and he's right. I need to go back. To see what's there, to see if my father is still alive, to face the truth and move on. I need to go back.

My mobile vibrates noisily on the windowsill. I look at the number—it's Peter. I've got a feeling I'm going to be getting a lot of calls now that I've turned down police advice, but that's something I'm more than happy to deal with. I flick my phone onto silent and the problem disappears.

And as if to reward myself for my decision, I let myself slip gently underneath the hot flow of the rainfall shower. *There are no ghosts if you just turn on the lights, and I don't want to be haunted anymore.*

# 39

## DR. EMMA LEWIS

### DAY 13—TURNING ON THE LIGHTS

I'm a mile outside Holt when the knot in my stomach clenches in anticipation; I try to ignore it, concentrating on the road ahead.

I don't have police protection now, not that police protection can insulate you from things that happened years ago. But what if I do need protection from something real, from a threat in the here and now, what if he's there?

I try to shake off the thoughts as small villages roll past the window. Chocolate-box hamlets. Tudor brick, babbling brooks, humpback bridges, and smoking chimney stacks, all that feudal England has to offer. Beautiful and ancient.

The nausea peaks half a mile from Holt. I pull over, swing open my door, and retch onto the side of the road, bile chugging out from deep within me. I try not to think of the gas that he filled our house with, of the sharp bitter smell of it. The smell I'd noticed that night but assumed was the smell of spent fireworks.

I wipe my mouth with a tissue from my bag and

swing back into the car. I give myself a moment and slide back into gear.

Holt finally comes into view as I make my way around a hedgerowed bend. I see the local church spire rising in the distance. Nothing remarkable; it's beautiful, yes, but everything in this part of the world is. Holt's just another picturesque village among many.

I recognize the slight inconsistencies in my memories as I drive through. A postbox is on the other side of the road from how I remember it. As I pass the church, it looks larger, brighter. Little things my memory has altered, as if it's playing a game of telephone, until the reality no longer matches the memory.

I feel the house's presence before I see it. And for a second, I worry it just won't be there. It could have been knocked down years ago, I wouldn't blame anyone either, but as I clear the next corner I see its familiar landmarks: the gentle slope of the drive up toward the garages, the old stable block, the entrance masked on both sides with thick concealing hedges.

I slow the car to a crawl, the lane ahead and behind empty. I don't know if anyone is living there now and the last thing I want to do is drive up to their house and disturb them—there's every chance they'll recognize me from the news. I don't know why I didn't think about this before.

But as I roll toward the turning, I see scaffolding wrapping around the whole upper corner of the house and a large property developer's sign. It's been renovated, perfect. I see the edge of a construction dumpster in the driveway and make my decision instantly. I pull off the road and up onto the slope of the driveway.

I park in front of the stable block. The same peeling green paint, the same sloped concrete and guttering. Not yet renovated. I wonder how much of the rest of the house is still as it was.

I shake off the thought and kill the engine. Silence fills the car.

I look up at the house through the windshield. No builders. It doesn't seem like anyone is working here today, perhaps it's too cold for building work.

I make my way past the rubble-filled dumpster and through the walled arch that leads to the front of the house. I search the corners of the walls for security cameras but then I remember we're not in London. Not every building here has cameras outside it. There's nothing. I won't show up snooping around on any grainy CCTV footage.

I won't be here long. I don't know what I'm looking for exactly, but if there's something or someone here, I'm sure I'll find them.

I make my way toward the little diamond of glass above the front door knocker. I raise my hand to shade my view and peer into the darkness. The same tiles, on the floor. The sight of them takes my breath away for a second. The rich red terra-cotta of them, as if not an hour has passed since we left. I pull away, trembling. I take a breath in and depress the handle. Locked.

I look back inside, past the vestibule, to where the tiles end in a step up and Georgian floorboards take over. The walls are white now. Everything white, fresh and new, light bouncing through a hallway that used to be so dark and cozy. There's nobody there. I tap gently on the glass and wait. The house inside remains still. I can see the edge of the first step on the staircase and no farther.

I pull away and follow the exterior wall of the house around to the living room window. It's so different inside, with state-of-the-art bifold doors that let the garden light pour in, the woodstove long gone and a fireplace with a decorative display of stacked wood in its place. But nobody in sight.

I move around the building again to the dining room window, see a bright clean empty space inside. The kitchen next door is a box-fresh copper-and-slate dream, but my scouring eyes find no answers.

I follow the wall on, then hesitate before the next window. The bare tangled branches of the trellised wisteria are still oddly intact and dusted with snow around the window latticing. I know what this room is. This is his study. An image of him burns through my mind, the way he was before, hunched over his keyboard hard at work, his papers spread around him. Him looking up at me in the doorway and smiling, nearly finished work, nearly done.

Why did he do what he did? The thought comes piercing and strong until I cut it dead. Right now, that's not important, what's important is what's in that room at the moment. I brace myself, for what I don't know. For the face of an old man looking back at me, for the face of the man who let me down as much as another human can—and yet I want to see that face.

I take a strong galvanizing breath and look inside. Eyes stare back at me. I gasp, then realize it's my own reflection in the glass, my eyes looking back at me, and the room beyond takes shape in the dim light. My heart sinks. He's not here.

My eyes search for something, something to wedge my memories into, some kind of clue, but this room is just a room. He is not there. There are no clues, no messages, I've misread this whole situation. He has gone—he died fourteen years ago and now the only place he lives is in my head. He is just a figment of my imagination.

I pull back, emotions so raw and near to the surface I can't tell if I'm going to laugh or cry. I brace myself against the snowy wisteria branches, letting out a jagged breath I didn't even know I was holding. I laugh, tears dribbling down my face. I turned the lights on and there was nothing there. No ghosts. He's not real.

My heart breaks and yet . . . I'm glad.

There are no clues here. Matthew is not a messenger. He has nothing to do with my past, he's just another patient, with problems all his own. I pull myself from the wall, brushing the stray snow from my coat with trembling hands.

And when I look up I see them.

My eyes land directly on them, nestled around the back of the house, as real and as solid and immutable as the building and the trees and the sky. Gates. A brand-new entranceway in from the road, sealed with wrought-iron electric gates.

The ground seems to pull away beneath me like a wave beneath a ship.

# 40

# DR. EMMA LEWIS

## DAY 13—ENEMY AT THE GATES

I try to call the hospital on the way, one hand on the wheel, one on the phone, but the signal is patchy and the automated hospital phone system transfers me from one departmental hold tone to the next.

I try to stay calm, I try to think of a logical explanation as to why and how Matthew could have known about those gates. How could he have known unless he had been there? When had he been there? Had he been there before his accident? Or had he somehow managed to leave the hospital since? Was the sleeping bag I found in the woods this morning his? Has he been leaving the hospital at night? But that's not possible, surely. How could he have left the hospital without anyone noticing. I think of the crowds outside, the security guards, the press. Rhoda. He'd have to be some kind of genius to get past all of that.

But then I remember how he saved me yesterday, the bullet he took for me, the military arriving. And the idea of him sneaking out of his ward doesn't seem quite so crazy.

I scroll through my mobile as I drive; I have three missed calls from Peter, which I really can't deal with right now. I find Nick Dunning's personal number in my contacts and tap. I have no idea what I'll say when he answers, but I need to know if Matthew is still there in the hospital. Because I have a sinking feeling that he isn't.

Nick's mobile goes straight to voicemail, and not knowing exactly how to frame a message, I hang up without leaving one. What would I say? My patient has been to my childhood home somehow. How would I explain that I knew from the start he knew my real name? I scroll to Chris's number, my thumb hovering over it. But again what would I tell him? That I followed my patient's advice instead of his, that I thought everything that was happening here was to do with my father when there's clearly something else going on? No. I toss my phone into my bag and focus on the road ahead.

When I get to the hospital I pull up around the back and head straight to the second floor.

Rhoda and another nurse look up as I run into the ward, trying to assess the situation. Rhoda frowning as I fly past them. An elderly patient reaches out to touch my arm as I slip by the nurses' station, but I pull away with a quick apology and keep moving.

Matthew's bed is empty and made. Everything is as it should be, but no Matthew. I toss my bag onto his bed and run back to the nurses' station.

"Rhoda. Have you seen him anywhere?" I pant.

"Matthew? He was here a minute ago. Probably outside in the sunshine?"

*Outside*. Surely she can't mean out front with the press? Then I remember the hospital garden. I turn so fast my shoes squeak on the floor.

I burst outside into the cold sunlit snow, disturbing a group of relatives sitting with a bundled-up patient.

*Try not to look crazy, Em. Try not to look like you've just lost your only patient, even if you have somehow managed to do just that.*

I scan the garden. It's just me and them. No Matthew. The family group stares at me; no doubt they recognize me from the TV news. I manage to muster what I hope constitutes a reassuring smile and aim it at them while my mind reels.

*Where is he? And who the hell* is *he? It must have been him in the woods watching me, but why? He's had so many chances to hurt me—hell, he even saved my life yesterday. What is he up to?*

And that's when I feel it, behind me, a gentle tug, tug, on the elbow of my jacket. I turn, thoughts still whirring, and look down to see a little old man gently tugging my sleeve. It's the old man who tried to get my attention at the nurses' station a moment ago. Now that I look at him properly it's clear he isn't a patient—no slippers, no wristband, and outdoor civilian clothes.

He peers up at me questioningly, his white hair balding on top, his pink scalp shining through from underneath.

"Excuse me?" he says.

"Yes?"

"Sorry to bother you, Dr. Lewis, I see you're busy." His voice is friendly, with a local lilt. "But could you tell me where I could find Stephen?"

"Stephen?" I repeat, confused.

"Oh, yes. Sorry. Nobody seems to know what I'm talking about today. Must have put me teeth in funny." He chuckles. "Yes, Stephen. Tall chap, dark hair, easy on the eye." He smiles jovially. "I just, well, I saw the local paper yesterday on the bus and, well, I usually get my news from the radio but when I saw the paper I happened to see Stephen looking out at me. Hadn't seen him for a couple of weeks. Thought I'd come say hello." He peers up at me hopefully.

I feel a cold dread rising inside me. *Tall, dark hair, easy on the eye.* A million questions crowd out any single utterance. I gawp at him, dumbfounded, like a complete fucking moron.

"'Cause you're his doctor, aren't you, dear?"

"What is your name, please?" I ask carefully.

"Er. Nigel. Nigel Wilton."

"And who is Stephen to you, Mr. Wilton?" I try to quell the tsunami of panic rising inside me.

"Oh, well, er, I suppose I was a kind of beau of his late mother. Lillian." Nigel blinks at me with a mixture of mild confusion and bashfulness.

"I'm sorry, I'm not sure I'm following you, Mr. Wilton."

"Well, Stephen had been living in London before his mother got ill. Lillian. And then he came back up here when she moved into the care home before she died last year. I met him a few times. Very private, very quiet. He was sorting out her things afterward. Setting everything in order. I think the loss hit him hard. I was quite worried about him. I confess I did try and stop in at the house the last few weeks but I never did see him, and the house was locked up, so I thought he'd gone back to London, and then bam!—I see his face all over the free paper on the bus."

I sink down into the seat by the garden door.

*Matthew is Stephen. Oh shit. Shit, shit, shit.*

The old man bends to cup my hand in his, his kind, wrinkled face worried. "Is everything all right, dear?"

I feel a wave of nausea crest inside me so violently that I have to dip my head between my legs until it passes. I have a vague awareness of Nigel rubbing my shoulder, murmuring something comforting.

Finally, I look up into his eyes. "Mr. Wilton. What is Stephen's surname?"

"Ah, well, that's a tricky one. Now, his mother's surname was Merriman. Lillian Merriman. But when he started doing his acting he changed it, I think . . . to McNabb. Yes. That was it. McNabb, I'm sure of it. He told me why he changed it but I forget. I think he just fancied the sound of it. Got more of a ring to it . . ."

Nigel keeps talking but I'm no longer listening.

*An actor? Oh holy fuck.*

Matthew is an actor. And apparently, not one that anyone in the country recognizes. The story slams together in my mind. A lonely unemployed man tries to take his life after his mother dies. Something went wrong and he was found wandering by the police. He's been lying since the beginning. No, wait, he can't have been lying. I scanned him, I verified a fugue. His memory must have started coming back after the fMRI after that last panic attack. And he kept it to himself. Perhaps that's what he wanted to tell me on the beach? Perhaps he wanted just a little bit longer playing Matthew. I suppose here, with us, he wasn't alone anymore. He just didn't want all this to end. He's been faking.

How could I have been so incredibly wrong about this?

My life pasted across the headlines. My career hanging by a thread. For this? For a malingering *actor*? Did he try to tell me who he really was, was I just not listening?

I rise without a word and stride away from poor Mr. Wilton mid-sentence. Regardless of the whys and the self-blame and everything that will come after, I know with pure clarity that I need to find Matthew, as soon as I can.

When I get back to his empty room, I shut the door securely behind me, drawing the curtain in the door's window. I search his room, tearing it apart, emptying his locker, rifling through his few spare clothes. I strip his bed, pulling pillows from pillowcases and sheets from the mattress. And that's when I find it, nestled underneath the mattress up by the headboard. An iPhone in a dirty plastic Ziploc bag. I rip it out and scroll through its history.

Searches.

*Oh my God.*

Searches on Stephen McNabb. Searches on Stephen Merriman. Notes in the note app titled "Stephen." An address I don't recognize in Norfolk, and directions to it. A note headed "Dr. Emma Lewis." Beneath it a link to the article I wrote on fMRI testing years ago. The times I arrive at the hospital, the times I leave. My old home address. *He was there, he saw those gates.* I think of his face yesterday when I joked about not having gates, and remember how concerned he looked by my joke. He knew he'd made a mistake. He knew he wouldn't have long until I figured it out, if the MOD hadn't worked it out yet already. He knew he'd have to go back to being Stephen and then all of this would stop.

The notes on me say nothing more. Nothing about my past, nothing about the location of Cuckoo Lodge. It couldn't have been him in the woods, how would he have known where to find me?

I pause. And how did he know the things he knew about me, about my past? There are no notes on that. No notes about Rhoda. How would he have known that my house had been filled with gas? I scour the phone's history for some mention of it but there is nothing there. Nothing about Marni, nothing about Rhoda.

How could he possibly know those things about us without looking them up? And last week my identity wasn't something you could exactly google.

I need to find him.

I find the last search in the phone's history. It tells me exactly where he's gone. It's Google Maps, directions from the hospital to a location. But why would he go there? I stare at the screen confused and slowly the truth of what Stephen is doing clicks into place.

*Oh no. No, no, no.*

He knows he's been found out and he's going back to finish what he started. Two weeks ago Stephen Merriman tried to commit suicide and failed and today he's heading back to the same spot. He doesn't want to be Stephen. He doesn't want to go back to that life. I understand his thinking: Once the press get hold of this information, Stephen's life will be plastered across the Internet for all to judge. If his life wasn't hard already, it will be unbearable once his identity breaks. I have to stop him from doing what I think he might be doing. I pocket his phone and run.

I burst out of the security door at the back of the hospital and into the car park, colliding with Rhoda coming the other way. Her hands fly to her chest with surprise but I barely slow to register her before sprinting on toward my rental car. I fish around desperately in my bag for the car keys but I can't seem to find them anywhere. Frantic, I tip the entire contents of the bag out onto the tarmac. "Everything okay?" Rhoda asks, crouching to help me scoop up the contents of my bag. "Graceford was looking for you. She's gone to the garden."

*Shit, Graceford. I don't have time for that right now, the last thing this situation needs is a uniformed police officer.*

"Someone's taken my car keys," I blurt instead. "I left my bag in Matthew's room, and now my keys are gone." I realize I must look insane to her, scrambling around on the ground sifting through my worldly possessions. Two more missed calls from Peter on my mobile. Ugh. "Fuck, I literally just had them," I mutter. Either someone took them, or I must have dropped them or put them down somewhere.

"Did you find Matthew?" She frowns down at me, confused.

I'm not really listening. I'm scanning the car park for something heavy. I remember what the man at the car rental company said. There's a spare key inside the car manual folder in the glove box, passenger side. I see what I'm looking for over by the wall next to the clinical waste bins.

*That'll do.*

I race over to it.

"Because I can't find him anywhere. I looked in the garden, and he's not on the ward or out here. Should we tell security?" Rhoda calls over to me, her tone anxious.

I heft the brick in my bandaged hand as I run back to the car.

This should work. But then, I've never really done this before, so what would I know?

"He's gone," I say, breathlessly pulling up opposite her, the car between us. She eyes the brick. "But I think I know where he'll be." I pull back my arm as Rhoda finally seems to put two and two together.

"Wait!" she shouts as I start swinging the brick forward. "What the hell are you doing with that, you crazy—"

The car window flashes milky on impact, shattering to crumbs. My hand burns white-hot as the sharp crumbles of glass rain over it and I drop the brick. I use my elbow now to push in the crumbled glass that still holds. Once it's clear, I reach through the gap, pop open the glove box door, pull out the manual and unearth the key. My hand is on fire. I flex the fingers and use my other hand to depress the spare door fob. The satisfying clunk of the central locking opening. We're in.

I peer at Rhoda over the roof of the car. "Rhoda, can you drive?" She stares at me openmouthed. If the pain in my hand weren't so bad, I might find her expression quite funny.

"Rhoda! Can you drive?" I say louder, shouting now.

She seems to recover and her focus clicks in. She may not have been her best self in the crisis yesterday, but I almost see her make the decision that she damn well will be today.

"Yes, I can drive," she answers. She yanks open the unlocked driver's door and slides in. I brush the glass crumbs from the passenger seat with the sleeve of my coat as I dive in next to her, slamming the door behind me.

I push the ignition key into her outstretched palm and we lock eyes.

"Where to?" she says turning the engine over and slipping smoothly into first gear.

"The beach. Head out toward Holkham—that's where he'll be. We need to get there fast, Rhoda!" I say. She nods, and once we calmly clear the security barrier she presses her foot on the accelerator and we screech out onto the road.

# 41

## DR. EMMA LEWIS

### DAY 13—BACK WHERE WE STARTED

The car hares down the snowy country lanes, Rhoda's hands tightly gripping the wheel as we bend sharply into the next turn.

I pray that we don't hit a patch of ice.

I've had time to think as we drive. I tried to call Chris, but outside of King's Lynn the phone signal has dropped away and I don't have the benefit of the lodge's Wi-Fi out here. The only way to get help is to find it in person or get somewhere with reception. But we don't have time for that.

Up ahead it comes into view, the lay-by and the path leading directly down to the beach. He'll be there. God, I hope he'll be there. My eyes shoot to Rhoda. "Once you drop me, just *go*!" I shout over the wind buffeting through my broken window. "Just go. Okay? Get to somewhere with phone signal and call Chris Poole."

I scramble into my bag for my wallet, fumble out the crumpled slip of paper with Chris's phone number, and thrust it at her.

"Do you understand, Rhoda? Don't call the police! All right?"

Her eyes flash to me for a second as she shifts down into third gear, and then she quickly snatches the paper. She moistens her lips, eyes back on the road.

"Just Chris!" I tell her again. "Okay? Whatever you do, do not call the police." If Stephen is there to take his own life, the sight of multiple uniformed police officers showing up to potentially arrest him is not going to help me convince him that everything is going to be okay.

I search Rhoda's face. She's weighing my request. She knows that the police might be *exactly* the people she should be calling. But her intuition will be telling her too that the police might cause more harm here than good. Police might escalate this far too quickly.

"Okay," she answers finally, out of time, as we crunch into the lay-by. "No police. Just Chris. Got it! Go! Go!"

I fly out of the car before it stops moving, and I'm running. Pounding across the lay-by's shingle and onto the beach path, sand flying out behind me. My breath rasps high in my throat as I hear the whine of the rental car reversing behind me. She's going to get Chris. To get help.

Because I'm not sure I can stop him by myself.

The trail opens out onto the vast sweep of Holkham Beach, the wind pummeling me as I head up the steep bank of the nearest dune. I need a good vantage point.

I scramble to the top and catch my breath, gasping in air, a cramp spasming deep in my side. I scan the horizon.

A black speck in the distance, hard to see at first;

the tide is out and he's walked out across the wet sand to meet it. If he gets in the water at this temperature, he won't last long before he slips under. That must be his plan, his original plan. I bound down the shifting slope and race across the endless flat of the beach.

A hundred yards from him I slow my pace, breath heaving in and out of me. He's not wearing shoes, he's taken them off; no coat either.

"Matthew?" I yell over the wind.

Either he doesn't hear me or he doesn't want to. I try again, louder, as I jog on toward him, but he doesn't turn. I try something else.

"STEPHEN!"

He stops in his tracks.

I stop now too, twenty yards between us, and watch, panting, as he turns to face me. He holds my gaze, exposed, for a long moment. His eyes full of so much—so much apology, so much vulnerability, so much understanding—and then with a sad smile he shrugs, not carelessly but as a kind of explanation.

Something about it is so touching my heart yawns wide open in my chest. His borrowed clothes, his borrowed life, his cold bare feet and the fact that no one even missed Stephen. Almost two weeks on the front page of every national paper, on the news daily, and only doddery old Nigel Wilton recognized him. Stephen has no one.

But Matthew, Matthew had everyone. It was a no-brainer.

He watches me as I approach him again, and when I'm close enough he opens his mouth to speak.

"It was the gates, wasn't it?" he calls over the howl of the wind.

I nod. "And . . . you had a visitor today."

He frowns, perplexed.

"Nigel. A friend of your mother's?"

His eyebrows shoot up and he lets out a surprised laugh. "Ah, I see."

"Stephen, I'm sorry about what happened to you. About your loss."

He nods mutely, eyes cast across the dunes in the distance. "I never meant for all this, you know, Emma."

"I know you didn't," I say.

Because we never do, do we? Any of us. Sometimes we just start down a road and before we know it things spiral out of control. People get hurt. We get hurt. "Will you come back with me, Stephen? To the hospital?"

He looks past me, back toward the forest, considering his options. "Is it just you here, Emma?"

"Yes. I got someone to drop me. They went back to get help. I wasn't sure what I would find when I got here." I catch a flicker of something behind his eyes and quickly add, "But I can tell them not to come. We can get somewhere with signal, then we can just sort this all out together," I continue. "Just you and I. I promise."

But that's a lie. We both know it. We can't sort this out together. Because now I know who he is. I know and I will have to tell other people and those people will tell other people and then the whole world will know that he lied. So, no, this can't all be sorted out between us.

He knows the game has ended. Unless I decide to try to keep it going.

He studies me for a long moment, weighing his options. "I've been trying to get you on your own for so long now," he says, his eyes warm with feeling. "I wanted you to know. I wanted to tell you, just you—I thought if I could explain everything to you maybe you'd understand—but there were always other people just around the corner. I wanted to be your Matthew so much."

"Come back with me and we can talk, Stephen. I promise you. Just us."

"I don't think so, Emma." He shakes his head. "I think I'll stay here. But thank you. And I'm sorry, you know. Sorry for everything, everything that's happened to you because of me."

For putting my career in danger, my life. He waits for a moment, eyes cast into the distance beyond me as he gives a final nod and turns back toward the sea.

"Stephen, you don't have to do this!" I shout after him.

He turns back suddenly, the floodgates seeming to burst within him, as words pour violently from him, vibrating with emotion.

"I do! All my life, Emma, all my life I've been *invisible*. I thought if I left here, if I went somewhere new, to London, if I started a new life, a new job, things would change. I'd live this amazing life, out there in the world. I'd have these brilliant friends and be part of something bigger, something important. I'd connect. I'd create, tell stories. But it didn't happen that way, it just didn't. It's lonely out there. And people aren't often kind, they're just as broken and as cruel as us. I wasted years, years of my life and on what? Chasing some notion, some dream. And meanwhile the only person I ever really loved died. The only real connection I had." He frowns. "She'd forgotten everything by the time I made it back up here. My mother. I kept putting it off. I knew she was getting worse and I waited too long. She'd forgotten me—she'd forgotten she even had a son! I don't think people can understand how much that hurts. The only real connection you have just evaporating. I could have gone back to London after the funeral, back to my own life, back to my one-bed flat and my shitty part-time job, but why? There's nothing there for me! I could have gone back and hoped for the best, hoped that someday . . . what? That I'd meet somebody? Somebody who really sees me? Who really cares? Who can get past the surface? Do you know how hard that is? The statistical likelihood of that happening? And the lonelier you get, the harder it is to hide it. It festers inside you, like a wound you can't conceal. People sense it, they sense it more the harder you try to hide it. And I'm tired of hiding it. I'm tired of waking up every morning to a future I can't quite see. So, to answer you: Yes, Emma. Yes, I *do* have to do this, because I don't want to go back to the way things were—and I certainly don't want to go back to worse. I would have given anything to be Matthew but I can't be Stephen anymore." His words hang in the air, his chest heaving from the storm of words. His eyes scan the pine forest behind me, lost, because what more can he say, really?

I understand, more than he can ever know. And what he says is true. Things will be worse after this—for both of us. He might face criminal charges—wasting police time, fraud— he might spend the rest of his life in and out of mental health facilities. The press will come down hard on him, for wasting NHS funds, lying to the public, and the most cardinal of sins: tricking them. It will be hard for him to put his life back together, to find the connection he so craves. But then, some people never do. I know I haven't.

I wish there was something I could do to fix this. I was so wrapped up in my own life that I didn't see what was happening right in front of me. I let him down. The guilt is overwhelming.

And as I stand, caught in the amber of the moment, the wind whipping my hair across my eyes, I remember the words we learned at school. We didn't recite the Hippocratic oath during training or swear it but we learned a modern version of its tenets.

- *The health and well-being of my patient will be my first consideration.*
- *I will respect the autonomy and dignity of my patient.*
- *I will respect the secrets that are confided in me, even after the patient has died.*

I watch him turn away from me defeated. I can't let him kill himself. But I don't want to make his life worse. *Do no harm.*

And who has he harmed in all this really? What would be gained by making Matthew be Stephen? *I will respect the secrets that are confided in me.* Perhaps we can let Stephen disappear and Matthew can just take his place.

"MATTHEW!" I call out now loud over the wind. "There's another option!" I shout. "If you'll trust me there is another option." And I say it with such surety I almost convince myself.

# 42

## THE MAN

### DAY 13—BEST LAID PLANS

She explains her plan to me as we walk back toward the car. She hasn't asked yet how I got here, but as we round the path back to the car park the question answers itself.

"It's Rhoda's," I say as she throws me a look, her forehead creased with concern. "She doesn't know I took it," I clarify. "I didn't ask."

I'm not surprised at her concern because her plan is risky. Very risky—but I always knew she'd help me, that she'd be this way: brave, strong. That's why I chose her, because she'd try to help no matter the cost to herself.

I wish in a way I'd found her years ago. Things might have been different.

*They might have been. They might be yet.*

Her plan is simple. I'm going to disappear. Her patient Matthew will disappear. She'll pretend she never found me on the beach today, she'll pretend she never heard the name Stephen McNabb, she'll keep my secret and I can just disappear. All I have to do is promise I won't hurt myself. She wants me to take her to my mother's house. She wants to make sure I have everything I'll need in order to leave—money, documents. She's not sure yet she can trust me not to hurt myself the moment she turns her back. It's reassuring but she couldn't be further from the truth.

I like her. For all her damage there's a clarity to her, a courage. I knew there would be. I knew she'd understand.

I pull Rhoda's car into the drive of the little wood-framed beachfront house. The house that belonged to the late Lillian Merriman.

A compact well-tended garden, lace curtains hanging in the well-proportioned windows, sun-faded paint peeling off the woodwork. Quaint, homey.

I lead Emma up the path and stop at the front door, reaching overhead to lift a key from inside a hanging basket. My elbow brushes against her hair as I do and she moves aside for me, her cheeks flushed. I slide the key into the lock.

Inside it's dim, the curtains drawn, I flick on the lights and a warm glow floods the open-plan space. Bohemian and disheveled. Stacks of magazines, piles of books. Old photographs pinned directly into the wood of the walls. A treasure trove of curios, antique furniture, all slightly faded, slightly broken down.

I watch Emma's face as she drinks it all in. A glimpse into a history, a life. If there's one thing to be said about Lillian, it's that she had great taste. And somehow the ferns and potted plants that litter the room have stayed alive un-watered for weeks. Their fronds still plump and green in the chink of sunlight peeking through the curtained French doors. She pulls their fabric back and winter sunlight floods the room from the beach beyond the glass. She peers out at the waves, the bank of snow-sprinkled dunes.

We're only a twenty-minute walk from where I was found.

"It's beautiful," she remarks, the light from outside throwing her features into relief.

"It is," I agree as she turns back to me.

"Will you miss it?" she asks.

I look around the lived-in room; it's been good to me. "Some of it, I suppose." She's studying my face. Wondering at what thoughts might be buzzing around beneath. I wonder what she sees.

"I suppose I should get my things together, then?" I say, breaking the tension. It's what we agreed. I'll gather enough clothes to last a few days, I'll gather Stephen McNabb's passport, license, wallet, and other information, and then I'll disappear. I'll take Rhoda's car and dump it somewhere along the way. Matthew will simply vanish. And I'll go on to live the rest of my life somewhere else.

It's a nice idea.

She nods and I head through the doorway into the connecting bedroom, leaving her to look around. I know it won't be long until she notices, so I sit down on the edge of the bed and wait. My hands quiver as I look at them. So much rides on what happens next. I look up at the bedroom wall in front of me. Research. Months of work. Months of planning. News clippings, plans, logistics to get Emma here, alone, now. Not that I can remember doing most of it. A small article has fallen to the floor, a clipping about an Afro-Caribbean nurse attacked in a park. I stand and pin it back up next to the photo of Rhoda on the board. Alongside it, old articles on Marni Beaufort. The Charles Beaufort inquiry. Sixteen-year-old Marni in paparazzi pictures, her fingers bandaged on her left hand.

In the beginning, I'd only been looking into Dr.

Emma Lewis—it's her I need—but Dr. Lewis's history only went back so far. But I had resources, I dug deeper, I've gotten good at that over the years. And in Dr. Lewis's past I found Marni Beaufort. With her burnt fingers and her dead dad.

I scan the wall, my wall, so many faces, faces from the hospital, snippets of their lives, little memories stored deep inside my mind. The first time I saw this wall, after the phone brought me here three days ago, I studied it and things started to come together. I realized how I knew half of what I knew. My research, clues I'd left myself. The extent of what I might have done wakening inside me.

I listen to her out there, the soft shuffle of her feet, the *plumph* of her turning over Lillian's old books. I relish these last few moments. It won't take long until she sees the photographs of Stephen on the wall, Stephen and his mother Lillian. Photographs of them gardening, of her visiting him in London, of his smiling face, similar to mine but different. Very different really. But I chose someone believable, it seems. I think I always do. Someone whose passport photo is close enough to me to be plausible. And no one really looks like their passport photo anyway, do they? We all lose a few pounds, we change our hair, we get older.

The room next door has gone silent, she's stopped moving out there. It must be happening. I go over to the doorway and watch her. Her back to me, as she peers at the photographs pinned to the wall, her hand gently resting on one in particular, a faded color photo. Though her back is turned I feel it happen, I feel the realization slowly take her, sinking into every bone in her body, I feel the air in the house around us thicken. I feel her fear as she realizes that the person in the house with her isn't who she thinks it is.

She must feel my eyes on her because she straightens, slowly, and turns, trying so hard to keep calm, to stay in control, to not let the huge waves of panic sweeping through her engulf and drown her. She's already seen what I can do. She saw yesterday in the hospital. She knows there's no use running.

I give her my most reassuring smile. What else can I do? After all, I like her. I want her to feel safe. All of this is for her.

She holds my gaze. Her expression a careful mask. She's calculating her options. I would be too.

I step into the room slowly. I don't want to spook her. She starts to speak but the words catch, she clears her throat and tries again. "You're not Stephen."

"No."

She blinks. "Who are you?"

I think for a second how best to answer.

"I don't know," I say, because that's the truth. If I knew, I wouldn't be here; I wouldn't need her.

She takes a moment to absorb this, then nods. "And what happened to the real Stephen?"

I wonder for a moment if I should lie, if I should keep the terrible truth from her longer. But then I realize she can't help me if I keep lying. "I'm not entirely sure yet," I say, very carefully, "but I'm pretty certain I killed him." I drop the British accent now too, letting myself slip back into my American vowel sounds. Her eyes flare, blazing at me from across the room. She swallows. She's terrified. I can't blame her. So was I when I remembered some of the things I've done.

"I need your help, Emma. Do you think you can

help me?" I say it tenderly, I want her to know she is safe with me, she is protected.

Her eyes flash to the door and back to me.

"I don't want to hurt you, Emma, I promise. I just need your help. I just need you to listen to me, please. I need you to tell me how to fix this. How to fix my mind. Can we just talk?"

She moistens her bottom lip, eyes alive as she studies me intently. She seems to reach a conclusion and her demeanor changes ever so slightly. She seems to settle back into the room. Then nods her head decisively. "Okay. Okay, let's do this. We can do this. Let's talk." She looks around the room, her eyes alighting on the two armchairs that face out to the sea beyond. She gestures over to them. "Shall we?"

# 43

## ZARA AND CHRIS

### DAY 13—TIME OUT

Zara's hair is scraped up tight into a messy bun, loose strands framing her face, as she tries to keep her voice even. "I know it was my idea, Chris, but I want you to come back. Okay?" Chris is perched on the edge of their bed, his eyes fixed on the thick pile carpet they chose together six months ago. "I was angry, Chris. Come on, you're no angel, you lied to me. You didn't tell me you knew her, who she was. I just find a text and I'm supposed to understand why you want to go for a secret drink with another woman? We don't keep secrets."

Chris stays quiet, he hasn't told her what happened the night before last either. The kiss. That long, warm kiss fourteen years in the making. He can't tell Zara how he lights up when he sees Emma, how she lets him look after her, how she makes him feel needed. And how Zara doesn't. How he needs Zara more than she needs him and no matter how long they've been together he still feels closer to Emma.

"Say something, Chris," she prompts, her voice quiet, hopeful.

Chris looks up at her, at his stuff littering the floor of their bedroom, at the honeymoon suitcase open next to him on the bed. "Honey, if I had told you who she was, you would have just written about it. Wouldn't you?" He says it almost tenderly because he reasons, who's he to judge, he promised to love Zara forever and he barely made a year.

"That's not fair, Chris. I might not be an angel, but don't pretend that's the reason you didn't tell me you'd invited her for a drink. Because you were worried I'd write a story about Charles Beaufort. I'm not an idiot. You asked her out for a drink because you wanted to spend time with her. You missed her, right? You liked her, back then, didn't you? Did you guys go out? Did you sleep together back then?"

Chris looks at Zara's un-made-up face—her cheeks are wet, her eyes red, but she's still so beautiful—and he feels a deep ache of guilt. Marni and he didn't go out. He never asked her, he'd been too afraid he'd ruin their relationship, their closeness, that he'd scare her away. So, no, they never slept together. And when Marni left, after her father's death and everything that followed, he thought about her a lot. He wrote her a letter but hadn't known where to send it; he'd asked the school to pass it on but they couldn't. So he'd gotten on with his life, he'd gone to university and fallen in love with the closest girl he could find that reminded him of Marni. Thick brown hair, golden freckles, an infectious laugh. This was before he came back to Brancaster and got together with Zara. Perhaps it had been the way Marni left, the gap she left behind in his life, but he thought about her a lot. Less and less over the years, but every now and then so strong. He didn't think he'd see her again. He wouldn't have made a promise if he'd known she'd come back.

Chris knows he could tell Zara all of that, but why would he hurt her more? What good would it do to explain the reasons? And Zara shouldn't have done what she did. "You're making this about me, Zee. What you did to her was bad. Really bad. It's like you don't think the things you do affect people. You broke into her house. You're so lucky that she hasn't pursued this. Her hands and feet were bleeding, you know. And what you did, about her identity, that was just cruel, really cruel. It put her in direct—"

Chris's iPhone blares to life on the dresser, on the other side of the room, its jaunty tune painfully at odds with the tone of their conversation. Chris makes a move toward it.

Zara's eyes flare. "Don't you dare answer that, Chris. Not right now."

Chris squeezes his eyes shut and lets out a loud sigh. He sits back down on the bed as they wait, wordlessly, for the call to ring out.

After the silence settles, Zara collects her thoughts. "I was angry, Chris. I have apologized. I have said I'm sorry. There's *no way* I could have known what would happen yesterday, you know that. Lichfield was hardly my fault. I couldn't know someone would try to hurt her. You can't blame me for that—"

The phone bursts to life again, insistently.

"Jesus fucking Christ!" Zara whips around, picking it up without checking the number. "WHAT!" A voice on the other end, muffled, and Zara's hand flies up to her forehead. "Sorry! Oh God, sorry. Yes, yes, he is. Who is this? Okay, one second." She holds out the phone to Chris. "It's a nurse from the hospital."

"Who?"

"She didn't say her name."

---

Seconds later Chris bursts from the bedroom and bounds down the stairs, taking two at a time. "And have you called anyone else?" he asks.

Chris frowns at Rhoda's reply, then asks, "Why would she say that?" At the base of the stairs he shrugs on his uniform jacket and rattles his pocket for car keys as he listens to the answer. "Okay! Okay, listen, it doesn't matter, I'm on my way. No, you go back to the hospital if you're on duty, she said just me, right?"

Zara appears at the top of the staircase. *Where are you going?* she mouths, her expression racked with guilt. Chris looks up at her and raises a hand—they'll pick up this conversation later.

His attention is drawn back to the phone. "No, it's okay. Don't worry. I'm on my way to Holkham now," he says, turning away from his wife. "I'll be there as soon as I can."

# 44

## DR. EMMA LEWIS

### DAY 13—TALK THERAPY

We sink down into the two chairs, opposite each other, and I steal a fleeting look to the front door—it's too far, and besides, even if I managed to make it out onto the road, I know he would catch me. I'd feel the weight of him crashing into me from behind and that would be it. No, best not to run.

I rest back into my chair, aware of the bulk of my mobile phone and pager in the depths of my coat pocket. The phone is right there, on silent—I could slip a hand down and get it. But then what? Pull it out and dial? Or just blindly tap at it in my pocket? I vaguely know there's a combination of buttons you're supposed to press to make a secret emergency call, but I have absolutely no idea which ones. Why did I never find that out? I could try my luck anyway but I'd only risk tipping the balance of this situation if he catches my hand moving. I'd only be shortening any precious time I have left. I know I can't outrun him, so I need to outthink him. I need time. I need to work out who he is and what he wants with me.

I watch him settle; he winces slightly as he leans

his shoulder back into the chair, this man who isn't Matthew and isn't Stephen. I ask myself what I actually know about him. I know he knows things about me he couldn't know. He knew my name was Marni as soon as he saw me. And I know he's killed, he's told me as much himself.

In spite of everything that's happened I still can't help but wonder if this does lead back to that night fourteen years ago.

Judging by his demeanor, I don't think he wants to kill me. He's had the opportunity to hurt me already and he hasn't—in fact, he's saved me. A faint glint of hope sparks inside me.

I let my gaze connect unthreateningly with his. I've worked with dangerous people throughout my medical career; the trick is to realize that they are the most vulnerable. They need the most care.

"What is it that you remember?" I ask gently, after some time passes.

He looks away, out the French doors, toward the sea. "Just pieces, really. Only fragments."

I weigh his words, unwilling to be fooled again—there is a chance he's lying. But given the fMRI results only days ago, he should still be only dealing in *fragments,* as he says.

"Tell me about these fragments," I prompt. "Is the memory of the forest one of them?"

He glares back at me, caught off guard. "Yes," he returns, "the forest is one of them."

Slowly his gaze softens and drops from me. "There was a girl," he continues. "In the forest. I was younger, I don't know when this was, what year or where. The memories are only images, sounds, feelings." He pauses, clearly working through the memory as he speaks. "They come in flashes, moments. A young girl with dark hair. The sound of her chasing me, breathing. I feel in the memory that I loved her. I cared for her. I can't remember her name or . . . She's running after me. She was so . . . she wanted to help me. She was so good. An image of her face close to mine . . . she cried when I—I don't remember why I did it—these horrible thoughts—" He breaks off, his eyes glistening in the light from the French doors.

I study this stranger's face, a face I thought I knew, a face I'd come to love in my own way. This man has Matthew's features but someone else's voice, and the things he's saying Matthew would never say.

He swipes away the wetness beneath his eyes with the sleeve of his good arm and looks back at me, searching for a reaction, a judgment, on his partial confession. But I'm used to hearing confessions. I'm used to being a receptacle for awful things, it's part of my job. I keep my face an impartial blank, no reproach, only my willingness to hear more.

"I remember it happening, Emma. I remember my hands around her neck. Her eyes, the life fading, her pupils releasing, impossibly wide, black, endless." He breaks off momentarily, lost in the memory, before snapping back to me. "I remember it happening but I don't remember *me* doing it. Does that make sense? I mean, I wouldn't do that, a thing like that. You have to believe me. I couldn't do a thing like that . . . it makes no sense. These memories I have—they aren't me—I can't have done those things."

His voice sounds reedy and lost. He has no connection to these events, no personal identification with these actions. And for one insane microsecond the idea that, perhaps, these awful memories truly *aren't* Matthew's at all flashes through my mind. The idea that somehow he could be part of the military, that these memories could somehow be someone else's, that he could be part of some kind of program. A neuroscience experiment, a study in memory manipulation, and somehow, Groves could be part of all this.

*Stop it, Em.*

My thoughts stutter to a halt, because, of course, that is not possible. Medically, none of that is possible. I *so* want there to be another explanation to this story, I so want this man to be good, that I'm seriously considering the existence of artificial memory implantation in test subjects. I'd actually rather consider science fiction than believe my patient is a bad person. That's how strong an effect Matthew has on people, consciously or not. That's how much I want him to just be Matthew. An innocent man wronged.

But I know the human brain—what it can and can't do—and memories can't be implanted. Facts can be suggested to subjects, as in the shopping mall experiment, and memories can be embellished or reframed, but they can't be completely fabricated. Not in the way that would be necessary to explain the things Matthew is telling me. Whole life histories can't be manufactured, not by the military, not by anyone. Neuroscience just doesn't work like that; only wishful thinking does. Matthew killed those people, plain and simple.

I try to focus, to distance my understanding of *Matthew* from the person now sitting in front of me.

"Do you think, Matthew, there's a chance that you might have been involved with the military?"

His eyebrows rise at my use of the name Matthew. I realize I haven't said it out loud since the beach. But what else can I call him? He's definitely not Stephen and I have nothing else to go on.

He shakes his head. "No, I wasn't in the army but I might have, um—" He rubs a hand over his tired eyes. "Okay. I think it's . . . Please don't get scared,

Emma, but I think one of the people I've . . . *been* at some point was a soldier. I think I took a soldier's identity." He pauses, eyeing me warily. "I pick people near my age, my build, people who look similar. I think maybe the military people who showed up yesterday thought I was that missing soldier. He will have disappeared. I might have been him for a while."

Matthew took another man's identity. He killed a soldier. He killed Stephen. He picks people and then becomes them, he literally and figuratively *takes their lives*. Images from nature flash through my mind: cuckoos, chameleons, hermit crabs. Existential adaptive behavior.

In a sense, I suppose, I am safe—Matthew can't become me. But then again, that might not stop him from killing me.

How did the military not pick up on any of this in their interview yesterday? But then, perhaps they did, maybe they had their suspicions but needed more time. How didn't I? It occurs to me that this may be the very reason Matthew has chosen now to show himself to me, before things start to slip, before we run out of time together. I can only hope Dr. Samuels picked up on something yesterday, sensed that something was wrong. And someone must have noticed I am missing today. I remember Peter's missed calls and I pray he raises the alarm.

"Do you think the military know who you really are, Matthew?" I ask.

He shakes his head thoughtfully. "No," he says. There's a finality to it that makes my heart sink. "They know I'm not him, the missing soldier, and that seemed to be enough. We just look similar. I think they have nagging doubts, but I'm not what they're looking for. Every now and then, forgetting things has its upside." He smiles ruefully. "I didn't know the answers to any of their questions. I genuinely didn't recognize the soldier's name when they said it. It's strange how quick people are to make up their minds when faced with simple incomprehension. I'd rather not have what I have, but sometimes, it seems, it does take care of me."

He fooled them. Well, not fooled exactly . . . but they certainly didn't find out the truth. The military don't know, the police don't know, and I'm guessing realistically Peter doesn't know. They'll work it out at some point, but will that be soon enough? Right now no one knows what he's capable of, which means no one is coming for me. It's just Matthew and me until this ends however it ends. I try to calm my panicked thoughts. As long as I am his doctor and he is my patient, as long as I keep this symbiotic relationship active, then I am safe.

"You said you'd rather not *have* what you have? What does that mean, Matthew? What do you think you have?" I ask. This is why he needs me and this might be my trump card.

"I don't know but this isn't the first time all of this has happened to me, I know that. The memory loss. A reset in my brain. It's always been like this. I don't think my condition has ever been an exact science, even to me."

"Your condition? The fugue has happened before?" I blurt out in spite of myself.

He nods. "It's happened periodically throughout my life. I never know when. No warning. Sometimes I get years uninterrupted, sometimes only months. I used to have no control over it. One moment I'm living my life and the next I wake up with nothing. I'll come to in an alley, or a park, or a beach somewhere, it doesn't matter where. I'll have nothing, and I'll have been robbed or attacked, or whatever it is that time around, and I'll have no memory of how I got there or what came before. My mind's a blank, then it resets, and slowly, day by day, piece by piece, it comes back. Tiny triggered memories bring things crashing back. A face, a word, a sound, a feeling. And all the things I've learned about myself, jumbled and cryptic. The facts, memories in no order. A mess of information, and I try to piece it together. Where my own memories and the lives of others collide, it becomes confusing. And then, of course, there are some memories that never come back."

"Like what?" I ask, my interest piqued in spite of everything.

"You asked who I am. I don't know. I don't know who I was to begin with. I don't think I ever know, in any cycle of this—I don't think that ever comes back. But I can control the condition to a degree these days. Living like this, it's hard, but over time I've developed coping mechanisms to deal with the resets—to some extent, I have strategies. A few years ago I realized I could bring them on myself. I worked out I could leave myself memory prompts, small things, messages. That's what helps me these days. I found messages this time around. I have to leave a trail between cycles, like breadcrumbs, or it all goes. And I can't have that. I can't start from nothing all over again. I just can't. You can't imagine what that is like. No piece of grit to form yourself around." He holds my gaze with a steely intensity, all his usual warmth gone.

I feel a shiver of dread fizz through me at what he's describing, tinged at its edges with excitement. Because the symptoms he's outlining are a psychiatrist's dream. Somehow, I've accidentally wandered into treating the most fascinating and dangerous patient of my career. Perhaps this is what I wanted? If I was a Jungian analyst, that'd certainly be my takeaway from all this. If I wasn't so completely crippled by fear, I'd pull out my phone and record this.

His symptoms: recurrent fugue, full dissociation from violent behavior, coupled with remorse, shame, fear. It sounds like dissociative personality disorder. Dissociative personality disorder used to be called multiple personality disorder, or MPD. They renamed it in the nineties because there was this common misconception, even in the medical community, that MPD meant a patient had more than one personality. It doesn't mean that, it means that the patient has less than one personality. It is a fragmenting or a splintering of identity. Shards of an independent self.

"When did this start, Matthew?" I ask carefully. "Do you remember how it started?" I encourage him.

"When I was young. A kid. As far back as that. I don't remember my family, if that's where you're going with this. I don't know how it started. My best guess is, I must have lost my family after one of the early resets. You can't go home if you don't remember where home is. So, I lost them. Or perhaps *they* lost *me*." He smiles sadly, and without thinking, I find myself smiling back in sympathy. Because whoever this man is, he has Matthew's face, he has Matthew's smile.

"Either way," he continues, "I don't remember who they were." He shakes his head. "It's strange. You know, I don't think I've ever told another person these things."

He's trying to elicit another personal response from me. He's testing the boundaries of our relationship. I weigh my options carefully before responding. "And how does that make you feel, Matthew?"

He grins at my evasion, aware of my dilemma. Of

our dilemma. The doctor-patient contract is a simple one but so easy to unbalance. He gives a nod of acknowledgment before answering my question. "It makes me feel good, Emma. So, thank you for listening."

Our boundaries successfully reinforced, I shift position in my chair and reorient the conversation. "Do you remember who you were before you woke up on the beach, Matthew?"

"I have flashes of him. I have flashes of being lots of different people, living lots of different lives. I don't know exactly who I was before I was Stephen."

"You weren't actually Stephen, though, were you? You took Stephen's identity."

He sobers at my correction. "Yes."

"And you are certain you killed him? You remember that? There isn't the possibility you just stole his identity?" I say the words as neutrally as I can. I need to be his ally.

He hesitates; the thought seems to be a new one for him. "I can't remember the physical act of killing him, no, but I must have because here I am, being Stephen. And that's how I've always done it in the past."

"How you've *always* done it? How many others have there been, Matthew?"

He studies me, his handsome face open and artless. "Quite a few, Emma," he says simply. "I remember some of them in detail and yet it's like remembering a dream or a nightmare. What I'm doing seems to make sense at the time but it doesn't in the remembering. Do you see? At the time, it seems like the only choice. Like a necessity. Do you understand? To get away or because I needed an identity. If I just stole an identity without killing the person, then I would just be waiting for the day the real person claimed it back. It happened in the early days. I needed an identity to live, to rent a car, to book a flight, to get a job, to live a life. I needed a face, a name. And I didn't have one."

My thoughts go to my phone buried deep in my pocket, so close but so incredibly far. I think of Rhoda sending Chris to a beach I'm no longer on and I want to cry. Matthew has been trying to get me on my own for so long, he's thought of everything. And now I have no way out.

"How did you know my name when we met, Matthew? Why am I here?" I ask, the words coming out almost involuntarily. I notice the slight tremble in my voice.

He hears it too and finally seems to realize that I am terrified to my bones, terrified of the things he has said, terrified of this situation.

"Oh God, Emma. I'm so sorry. Please don't be scared. You must know that I would never hurt you. I promise you. You can't understand how—" He stops and looks down; I notice his hands are trembling too. "You can't possibly understand what you mean to me. You are all I have. All of this is for you. Everything I've done is to find you. To get close to you." His brown eyes, warm once more, dart over my face, searching for understanding.

*All of this is for me?* What does that mean, why did he need to find me? I don't know him. Do I? Or have I just forgotten? I think about who there has been in my life who might try as hard as Matthew to find me. An old patient? Someone from my childhood? I know this can't have anything to do with my father, but I suddenly hear myself blurt out the question before I can stop myself. The question that's been on my mind ever since we met.

"Did someone send you to find me, Matthew?" I

don't care how crazy it sounds, we're well past crazy at this stage.

He looks confused for a moment, so I continue. "How did you know the things you knew about me, Matthew? My burnt fingers. The pilot light. Why did you say sorry for what *you* did that first night we spoke? You pretended to be my father; I don't understand why you would do that. Was it all a trick?" The questions fire from me, questions I've kept stifled at the back of my mind for too long. I hear the bite in my voice but I don't care anymore. "And if it was all a trick, then I'm dying to know to what end!"

He seems taken aback, as if he assumed I knew the answers to these questions already. Though how I could have I do not know. "I see. I'm sorry, Emma, I haven't explained this well. It must be confusing. Let me go back to the beginning. When I woke up on the beach I had a name on my hand. Marn. The 'i' in 'Marni' must have washed away. Not that it mattered. A memory came back to me. I knew I had to find a woman, but I didn't know who. I guessed the name would be important. She wasn't at the hospital and I didn't know how I'd find her, until you arrived. When I finally saw you I knew it was you. I had these feelings"—his gaze shoots straight into me—"these feelings for you, such incredibly strong feelings. I still have them now. I knew that I needed you to understand something, and that there was a chance you might not. But I couldn't remember what it was I was supposed to tell you. I knew that I had done something terrible, I had this guilt, but I didn't know what it was I had done. I saw you that first day. I tried so hard to remember what I needed to say, and you ran to me, and all I could do was call you by your name. When I woke up later, you had gone but I remembered. I remembered who you were, what had happened to you, to Marni, all those years ago. The memories of that night were so fresh in my mind. Your fingers burnt, somehow, on a firework, I think? I don't know. They were bandaged. I remembered your house, full of gas, poison in the air. And a body, blood everywhere. What was done to you. I felt certain that it must have been me who had done those things to you. I couldn't bear that I'd hurt you. I didn't do it to trick you, Emma, I promise, I would never trick you. I thought I did what your father did—but now I see I only remembered the details of that night because I tried so hard to find you. Because I care so much about you." He pauses, unsure if he should say what he was planning to say next. "*I* didn't mean to trick you, but, if I'm honest, I think that's why *he* chose to come here. *He* wanted to use your father as a way in."

"*He?*" I ask, leaning forward quickly in my chair.

"Yes. All of this to get me to you—"

"Who is *he,* Matthew?"

He pauses, a frown crinkling his brow, that then gives way to a look of genuine surprise. "Oh. Oh no. I'm so sorry, Emma. It was, I didn't mean to—there is no one else. It was a turn of phrase. *He, me, Stephen.* Whoever I was before the beach." He watches as the sense of what he's saying sinks in and I lean back defeated. Now it is his turn to ask me a question. "You thought I meant your father, didn't you?" I feel the rush of blood to my face, to my head. Shame. He knows my shame, he knows how stupid I am. Matthew continues but I'm barely listening.

"I'm sorry. I think he wanted you off center, that's why he brought you back here. And it seems like it worked. Easier if he separated you from the people you trust, from your everyday life. Easier for me to get close. But I promise you, Emma, when I said those things in the hospital, I thought they were real, I wasn't trying to trick you. I truly thought I had been the one who hurt you and I was beyond sorry."

I feel exposed, raw and unprotected. How was it so easy to break me down, to strip me back? After all the years of therapy since it happened. After all my training. I try to make sense of the man before me, my persecutor and my savior. "But how did you know those things about me, Matthew? They were private. Who told them to you? There must have been someone else. How did you know things about Rhoda?"

"I didn't know how I knew those things, at the time. About Rhoda, about you. I just saw people's faces in the hospital and memories would come. Information about them. Rhoda in the park, your house, blood on the floorboards, your burnt fingers. Later I remembered I'd left something in the hospital garden, a phone. The phone sent me here, to Lillian's house. I found I knew where to find the key. I found research here. Notes explaining everything." He points back toward the shadows of the bedroom doorway. "There's months' worth of information: On you, your past, your job in London, your life, your flat. On Rhoda and everyone I might have come into contact with at that hospital. Facts on everyone I might need to form some kind of relationship with. So when I first saw Rhoda, I knew what she'd been through, what she needed. And I waited for you to arrive. And then when I came here three nights ago, I realized why I needed you."

He leans forward in his seat excitedly.

"He read your article, Emma. *I read your article*. The one about misdiagnosis. Fugue cases. It was me you wrote about in that paper. You didn't know then that you were, and you didn't recognize me when you finally saw me, but your paper was about my case. I read it, and in it, you believed me. You believed my case, that it was real, that I was telling the truth. Everyone else thought I was lying, faking symptoms, and only you believed me, Dr. Lewis. Granted, you wrote your article years after my case, years after that first incident, but you believed me. You said in the article that you would have treated me, my case, differently. Do you remember? Do you remember saying that? You wrote about the Unknown Young Male case. I was hospitalized in Buffalo, New York. I knew, *we knew,* we had to come and find you. So you could fix us, fix this. I knew you'd be the only one who could."

*Oh my God.*

My mind whirs as I try to process what he's saying. But the Unknown Young Male case was years ago. My eyes flash across his face, his handsome features, his cheeks sprinkled with graying stubble, his tousled hair silvered at its edges. He looks so different from that picture taken two decades ago, older, more muscular, not the skinny young man in that grainy photograph, not like the man I would have imagined he'd grow into. But those eyes. I inhale sharply. I see it now, that same oddly calm gaze, as if he were somehow outside of life looking in. A spectator. It is him. All this time and I had no idea. How could I have missed it?

But there were signs, my God, there were signs. I recall the first instinct I had when Peter showed me Matthew's brain scan, that day in the Wellcome Collection museum, Matthew's pituitary cyst, the thing that really sparked my interest in the case. The symptom that reminded me of other fugue patients I'd seen. But Matthew's cyst wasn't a shared symptom among several fugue patients, it was just his symptom. I had been looking at a scan of the same brain, the same patient twenty years apart.

"That was over twenty years ago," he continues. "I was in my twenties when I first stumbled into that hospital in New York, two black eyes, a shaved head, and no memory of who I was. Richard Groves was my consulting neuropsychiatrist."

*Of course, it was Groves's case.*

"Wait, Matthew," I blurt. "Are you saying Dr. Groves knew who you were? He sent you to me?" My brain scrambles, desperately trying to piece things together. Could Groves really do something like this to me? I can't believe he would knowingly endanger me.

Matthew shakes his head. "No. Groves would have ruined everything. That's the last thing I would have wanted. I needed to make sure Groves wouldn't come. I knew they'd call him first, so I had to wait until I knew he would be too busy to take this case himself. I did my research, I waited until he was right in the heart of something far more high profile. I know the sort of man Dr. Groves is, trust me. That's why I chose to come here, to the coast, instead of London. I knew Groves wouldn't come over here for this. This isn't a big enough draw, not me, not this nowhere hospital. He's at MIT right now, I waited until he was right in the thick of it, his AI research project. I knew he'd call you. You'd be his obvious choice. I made sure you would be. I made sure a few of your colleagues were unavailable. I made sure the job fell to you." He catches my expression, however fleeting I hoped it would be. "They're fine, don't worry," he says. "Well, almost all. Tom Lister—I think he might be—I'm not sure—" He stops short.

*Oh God*. I feel sick. God knows what he did to get me to the top of Groves's list.

He planned all of this. Before he'd even met me, he read me better than I read my own patients.

"You planned all of this?" I ask, incredulous. "And you just trusted the plan would work when you woke up? How could you know you'd remember enough? How could you know you'd forget enough for it to work?"

"As I said, there's not a big margin for error in my life. If I don't plan ahead, I get caught out. I don't have the luxury of absentmindedness. I can carry certain memories from one episode to the next. Physical pain helps memories carry better. I can control the resets now too. A bang to the head is usually enough these days. A mild concussion. I almost control it. Almost. I gave myself a message, in the bathroom mirror of this house, before I smashed one of Lillian's heavy glass ashtrays into the back of my skull. And then I walked out of the house and down to the seashore. I told myself to find you. I told myself it was so very important that I do. I told myself not to fuck it up. When I woke up wet and lost, I had your name written on my hand. A trail of messages led us both here. I left myself a parcel in the garden of the hospital—the phone I'm guessing you found in my room. I knew you'd come and find me. And here we are. I don't want to be this way anymore, Emma. It's getting harder every year. I need your help."

I stare at him, incredulous. "You want me to treat you?"

"Yes," he says simply. "I want you to fix me."

I look into his eyes, see the years of pain, the terrible things he's done but not done, because every awakening seems to be a new birth to him. He must live with the actions of a hundred other selves. Splintered memories from half-remembered situations.

"Can you?" he asks.

I rub my hands over my eyes and desperately try to shake off the fug of stress clouding my brain. "Let me think."

I feel his eyes on me, expectant. I need to get my head straight if I want to come out of this alive. I voice my thoughts as they come. "Okay, so, we know from the fMRI that your memory losses are real. We're already ahead of anyone else in diagnosis terms with that. But the cause? We need the cause." I pause; where to even start with potential causes? I try to relax, to put myself mentally back in Cuckoo Lodge on that warm rug in front of the fire that first night as I brainstormed.

And then I remember—that night the power went off in the lodge—I overloaded the circuit by turning on too many lights. Lesson learned. "Um, okay," I splutter. "When I first saw your CT, Matthew, before I accepted this case, I knew I'd seen scans like yours before. I thought I'd seen other patients with growths on their pituitary glands. But now I'm realizing that those other scans were probably all you. I think that what might be happening when your 'resets' occur is that the pituitary cyst is bursting. Every time you get a knock to the head, or whenever the cyst becomes too large, it's popping. Secreting fluid into surrounding structures, releasing a surge of hormones that are flooding your brain. Overloading your circuits. Those surges could be responsible for the cycles you've described." I watch him take this in, following the logic of my theory to its natural conclusion.

"And we'd need to remove it? This cyst?" he asks finally.

I measure my response. These are hardly clinical conditions. What I have is only a theory, but a cyst might be fixable. "Matthew, I think—I'm not certain—but I think you possibly can be cured. There's an operation we can do. But we'd need a neurosurgeon, you'd have to go back to the hospital with me, we'd have to do tests."

"An operation?"

"Yes. But in the hospital. We'd take it out and, if I'm right, the episodes would stop. The resets. I'm confident they would stop." As confident as a hostage can be about anything.

I watch the light in his eyes burn bright for a moment, then implode as he realizes what the price of this operation will be. He'll need to go back to the hospital. Other people would become involved. This is not the answer he wanted. This is not part of the plan. He would be anesthetized pre-op and then God knows if anyone would even operate on him or if he'd go straight into custody. I'd be long gone when he woke and he'd be left with nothing. All this for nothing. I see him think it through, the careful plan he made for himself falling away beneath him. Curing him means he gets caught. He would lose his freedom. I watch him realize he can't ever escape this situation.

And as if on cue, deep in my coat pocket my hospital pager bursts to life. I jump as the piercing bleeps cut through the silence of the small house. I'd forgotten all about it. Adrenaline suddenly courses through both of us; Matthew's eyes narrow hawklike as I fish the violently vibrating object from my coat and quickly flick it off. I hold his gaze, my breath high in my chest. We both know what that sound means—someone has noticed I'm not where I should be, someone is looking for me. I place the silenced pager gently on the wooden floor between us, a peace offering, a trust exercise. We both look down at its retro bulk sitting there, an undeniable reality between us.

When Matthew finally looks back up at me, I see there's a new brand of sadness in his eyes. That's when I realize we aren't going back to the hospital. He isn't going to have an operation, that isn't going to happen for either of us. He's made his decision. And that is when I run.

I bolt wildly for the door, and for a bright and shining second, I feel certain I'll make it. I feel certain he's letting me escape—after all we've said, after everything that's happened, somehow I've won my freedom. Then his body collides with mine and I slam down hard onto the floor. The breath is torn from me. My body pinned beneath him, he lets me kick and flail for a moment.

"Sorry, Emma," he whispers as he grasps my hair and raises my head. Everything goes black.

# 45

# CHRIS POOLE

## DAY 13—DIRECTIONS

Chris pulls into the lay-by Rhoda left less than thirty minutes ago. The shingle roars as he brakes and bursts from the car. Phone in hand, he bounds out toward the shoreline, eyes desperately searching for two figures.

As he nears the opening out onto the sand he tries Emma's mobile again. Still no signal; he pockets the phone and scans the dunes ahead. He scrambles up a bank, grabbing clumps of snow-crusted grass as leverage to pull himself up the steep slope. He rises panting to the top, hair buffeted in the wind, and searches the glistening sand in all directions.

There's no one on the beach.

"Shit." He fishes out his phone. One bar of signal. He dials Emma's number again. It rings. He waits to hear the soft hum of her voice picking up. Perhaps everything is fine now, perhaps she's okay and she's gone back to the hospital, he thinks. Rhoda told him Matthew had disappeared and they'd come here to find him. Perhaps Emma found him already, perhaps they went back.

Emma's phone diverts to voicemail.

Chris curses. Emma asked for him specifically, Rhoda said. She didn't want the police. Chris frowns, his features to the wind, the roar of it around him. What the hell is going on? She might still be here, they could have walked around the cove. Chris recalls his strange first meeting with Matthew on this beach two weeks ago. Yes, they might have walked farther.

He bounds down the dune, and heads out in the direction of the bend in the shoreline, covering large stretches of sand with each stride.

Then he sees something ahead.

He pulls up short. There are fresh footprints in the sand. Small footprints first. Female. But a long stride. A female, running. He follows the footprints out, running alongside them now, out toward the shoreline. The woman's footprints meet with another set. Larger, male. A man. The prints move in a wide semicircle, a dance, a conversation. This is where she found him.

Chris follows the movements of that meeting. The two seemed to come together and then the male prints lead the female away. The stride is slow; she wasn't chasing, she was following. The male ahead of the female. Her following him. Strange for a doctor to follow a patient. Chris jogs alongside the tracks, looks ahead; the steps seem to lead toward the main car park.

Chris bursts into a run.

He skids to a stop on the edge of the car park. Unlike the windblown beach, the whole car park is still covered in deep snow, and the two sets of footprints are crisp and clearly defined in its unspoiled canvas. Farther out he sees the tire tracks, the speckled brown of gravel visible beneath the compacted snow.

They left in a car—but, Chris slowly realizes,

Emma didn't have her car with her. And that's when he knows for sure that something is very wrong with the picture he's seeing. He races to the tire tracks and slows to study the pattern of footprints around the ghost of the car. What he sees makes his blood run cold. The footprints on the driver's side are male, not female. Chris might have no medical training, but he's pretty certain that patients on psych wards should not be driving their doctors. Something very strange happened on that beach, he's not sure what exactly but he doubts it was a good thing. He pulls out his phone again and dials Emma. The phone goes straight to voicemail.

Chris looks down at the tracks once more, scowling. Where were they going? Should he call Rhoda back at the hospital? he wonders. Or he could call for backup, but he thinks better of that. Emma specifically asked him not to do that. He's got to trust her; after all, she's trusted him. No, he just needs to find her.

He breathes in deep and races to the car park's exit. On the snowy country lane, tracks. The car turned right onto the lane. The hospital is left; they drove right, away from the hospital. And suddenly Chris realizes what he has to do next.

Without pausing, he turns and bolts back the way he came, back to the lay-by where he left his car. Wherever her patient took her, it wasn't back to the hospital.

46

# DR. EMMA LEWIS

## DAY 13—HOME FREE

My eyelids part and daylight breaks through as the blackness lifts. The soft blur of the world sharpens around me. I recognize the window first. Blinking open my lashes, I see its dark wood lattice, the bare tangle of wisteria clinging outside it. We're not at Stephen Merriman's childhood home anymore. We're at mine.

Panic rises inside me and I feel a dark throb pulse through my skull as I dip under again.

When I surface he's standing in front of me, Matthew; he's talking. He's telling me things. Horrible things that have happened. I float in and out of consciousness, from the soft embrace of blackness to reality and back again. He towers over me, his face different somehow. I try to work out what has changed exactly and realize it's that he doesn't care about my opinion anymore. He has stopped trying to be the person he thought he might be, the good person. His voice is freer, skipping along with him as he confesses more, gruesome things I can't un-hear, things he's done and has to remember. I am no longer a purveyor of cures, I am a receptacle for nightmares. He knows there is no way back for him and he wants to tell me all about it. A problem shared. I want the sweet release of unconsciousness to take me again but I have no control over it. Some primal survival instinct is keeping me awake, ready, even though there's nothing I can do.

I know I'm not leaving here. Not if he's telling me this. He's come too far down this road. He talks of names, places, and tells me of the lives of people who never made it home and never got found because of him. He tells me it all with sadness in his eyes but anger in his voice. And I know I won't be allowed to leave here.

I look down at my hands, zip-tied to the arms of a chair. Red welts rise puffy and sore around my wrists. My bandages are long gone. I must have struggled against the ties at some point, though I don't remember doing so. I can see now that the hand I bricked straight through my car window is broken; it lies red and swollen against the armrest.

When I look up, Matthew is leaving the room, saying something I don't catch. I watch his legs disappear into the hallway. He's going to get something. I think about running. I shift my weight forward on the seat but the rush of blood to my head makes me lose balance and I tip forward, crashing down, chair and all, onto the parquet flooring. The side of my head makes a sharp thump of contact and there's darkness again.

It's a strange noise that brings me around. The sound of something being slowly rolled toward me, rising in proximity and volume. Something small rolls across the parquet floor toward my face, then a soft tap on my cheek. Another rolling noise begins, tumbling closer and closer, this time ending with a tap to the end of my nose.

I open my eyes. Matthew is sitting slumped against the wall opposite me, rolling stubby-looking red tubes toward me. Another brushes my lips and I struggle to focus on it. It rolls to a stop inches from my face, red plastic with a coppery metallic end, like a joke shop lipstick but not.

I bolt upright, realizing what they are.

*Shotgun cartridges.*

With a whimper I shuffle back as far as I can while still bound to the toppled chair, my eyes frantically searching the room for the gun.

And then I see it, propped against the door next to a large canvas carryall. The shotgun. *Oh God, oh God. This is real. He's going to kill me.*

I barely have time to turn away before the vomit comes. A retch of pure terror onto the reclaimed flooring, the smell sharp and vile mixed with the fresh-paint scent of the house.

I understand instantly why he's brought me back here. My whole body starts to tremble as the tears come unbidden and silent down my cheeks.

He's going to shoot me in the same room my father shot himself fourteen years ago. I'm going to die here, like this.

I sense Matthew rising opposite me but I refuse to look up at him, so he approaches, squatting down in front of me solicitously. There is something in his hand. A piece of crisp white paper.

"Have a read of this, Emma. Let me know if you're happy with it? I can change the wording if you like but I think I got the handwriting pretty good."

I can't focus on the words dancing in front of me. It's a letter. Some sort of letter. Bizarrely, the handwriting looks just like mine, but I didn't write this. I read the words.

*Please. No.*

It's a suicide note. My suicide note. I didn't write this. I look up at his face hanging over me. He's not just going to shoot me. He's going to make it look like I committed suicide, in the exact same way my father did. That's why he's brought me back here. That's why he didn't just kill me at Lillian Merriman's house. Because when the police find my body here it will tell a very different story. And it's a story I know some people will be more than eager to believe.

Horrified, I think of how the press will twist it, of how everyone will believe I did this to myself. I think of Joe, of my mother, of Chris and everyone at the hospital thinking I chose to die just like my father. I think of the life I haven't even really lived yet. I can't die here, I can't. I pull wildly at my ties and scream, straining every sinew in my body, spittle leaping from my mouth, until, exhausted, I run out of breath. No one can hear us out here.

"Well, I didn't realize my handwriting was as bad as all that." He laughs and pats me on the head jovially. I shrink from his touch and his face falls. He stands back, carefully setting the suicide note down on the floor just out of my reach.

"Listen," he says, his tone serious. "I want you to know, Emma, that this is not how I wanted this to end. This wasn't part of my plan. I don't even know if I thought it would get this far—I can't recall. I don't know how I thought you could fix me. Medication, I don't know, something manageable? But you know I can't go back to that hospital. I appreciate everything you've done for me, I really do, but I'm not going to give myself up for you, I'm not going to prison because of you. Not over here and not back in the States. I hope you can understand that this is the only way to be sure I can disappear again." I start to speak but he stops me with a shake of the head. "I know, I know—*you won't tell a soul. You'll take it to your grave.* Well, that's kind of what I'm banking on with all this. Listen, you're a really good doctor, Emma. You actually care, which is rarer than you'd imagine, but people lie and people change their minds. You'd promise me anything right now, but tomorrow? And I'm not going to hang my chances of freedom on your word when you're tied to a chair. I'm sure you understand my logic. But I will say, I'm truly, truly sorry it's come to this."

He looks at me a moment before turning and moving away. My angle on the floor prevents my gaze from following him. Out of sight I hear him crack the shotgun open, then snap it shut.

*Oh God. Oh God.* "Please. Matthew," I gush, "you don't have to do this. I won't say a word, I *really* promise. You can just go. I'll tell them I couldn't find you. Please." And a thought suddenly comes as if from nowhere, a solution so clear and reasoned it might just save my life. "Matthew! You asked me to fix you. To stop the cycles. But this, this is the moment it all boils down to. If these memories aren't you, if there seems like no way out, if you truly aren't this person, then stop. Just stop, now, and we're halfway there. You can still change this. Don't be this person. You can stop making this happen. But only you can."

He looks down at me, sorrow in his eyes for a moment, and then his expression falters ever so slightly. He takes me in, as if only really seeing me now, on the floor twisted and bound to my tipped-over chair.

He looks down at his weapon thoughtfully before gently lowering it and placing it against the wall.

*Oh God. It worked.*

"I see what you're saying. I understand. Let's get you more comfortable," he says tenderly. "It doesn't look very dignified, down there. You deserve better." He grabs the arms of my chair and hoists it and me up together, in one smooth movement, as if we weighed nothing. But he does not loosen my ties. His eyes avoid mine. And I understand that my words have only made him kinder, they have not saved me. His plan has not changed.

He scans the crime scene again. Me righted, his note before me. My exhausted face, hair plastered to my cheeks with sweat and salty tears. My broken hand, bloating and discolored. My bruised wrists bound to the arms of the collapsible metal chair. My breath is coming high and fast. I wonder how he plans to explain away the contusions on my wrists; perhaps he'll slit them too, or zip-tie them to the gun as if I'd feared missing due to the recoil. Even if it doesn't look like suicide, there are plenty of nutters out there who could have done this to Charles Beaufort's daughter. I met one of them only yesterday.

After he's shot me, he'll cut me free, place the shotgun between my thighs just the way I remember seeing it done years ago. I watch him as he studies me and I see sadness quietly crescendo behind his eyes. I suppose this is our goodbye. The end of his dream. The end of my life.

He squats down before me. "Can I get you anything, before?" he asks gently. "Water, drink, something?"

I snatch a breath, clinging to the suggestion. A lifeline, if only temporary. If he gets water I'll have a few more moments. More time to think.

I nod as calmly as I can.

"Just water?" he asks, attentive.

"Please," I croak, my throat dry and raw from my screams.

"Okay." He rises with energy, momentarily buoyed by his ability to help in some way. He turns away from me with an unnervingly innocent smile and makes his way out of the room.

As soon as he's out of sight I desperately fumble with the ties around my wrists, scraping my skin bloody as I try to force my hand out like a trapped animal. This is all the time I have and I'd better make good use of it. I tug in sharp bursts, squeezing my jaw tight against the excruciating pain to stop myself from screaming out. But it's useless. The ties won't budge.

I start to panic again, struggling madly, wriggling against the binds, and then I hear it, a tiny *plink*. I freeze.

The sound of something small and light hitting the flooring beneath me. I look down between my legs. A Day-Glo pink plastic lighter. The lighter I borrowed from the security guard yesterday to light my cigarette, I'd forgotten all about it. I remember now slipping it into the small inside pocket of my jacket, out of sight and, until now, out of mind. My struggling freeing it from its little hiding place.

If I can just reach it. But it sits right beneath me. I ease myself, gently, down onto my knees and lower my shattered hand toward it, scrambling blindly, unable to see exactly what I'm doing. It must be here somewhere, I saw it. Unless it was a mirage. Wishful thinking gone mad. And with that thought the edge of my baby finger taps straight onto its cheap plastic.

*Yes.*

I try to grab it with my broken fingers but I can't

control the movements. I pull away quickly and shift my weight onto my other knee, dropping my good hand behind me. I stretch as far as I can, I push farther back against the chair. A finger brushes its smooth side. I snatch at it greedily and roll it up into my palm. *Yes*. I angle the lighter back toward my wrist quickly, and roll the flint with my thumb so that it sparks to life. I let the flame burn straight up at the flesh of my wrist and the ties that bind me.

Its heat is not unpleasant at first, until the fabric of my sleeve singes and bursts into flames. White-hot pain tears through me, searing my flesh. I press my lips together to keep from crying out. I feel the plastic of the zip tie softening and melting onto my burning skin until I fear I'm going to scream in pain. The smell of burning fabric and human tissue. I desperately fight the urge to pull away, I stay as still and quiet as possible. And after an eternity, in which I'm certain I can't take it for an instant longer, the melted plastic finally gives. I whip my burning arm straight between my thighs, staunching the flames, the fabric of my trousers sticking to my melted flesh. I can't look at it, the smell is enough. Dizziness overwhelms me. I pray he can't smell it farther into the house. I need to break the second tie before it's too late. I hold the lighter in my burnt hand and set to work on the other tie. The gurgle of running water comes from the kitchen as I work in silence. The second tie begins to melt and I pull the hot jammy plastic until it tugs apart.

I bend instantly and pull at the leg ties. I can't slide the plastic ties off the end of the metal chair legs, as they connect. *Shit*. I quickly hoist my trouser hem up and steady the first ankle tie. I strike the lighter, the hot flint burning into my thumb as I depress the fluid button down. The edges of the flame lick at my ankles but these leg ties are thicker, the plastic won't give as easily. I hold the flame on longer, too long—my flesh screams. I bite back a howl of pain so violent I taste blood; the agony is unbearable. And suddenly the leg tie breaks.

I move to the final tie.

The tap in the kitchen has cut out. I wasn't paying attention. The sound of movement in the kitchen. I try to focus, holding my trembling thumb on the lighter fuel button as the plastic slowly softens in the flame. The sound of footsteps coming this way but the plastic won't give. I'm not going to make it. I need to move. I leap to my feet as I see him turning in to the hallway just as he looks up and sees me.

His eyes widen and I bolt, grabbing the folding chair that's still attached to one ankle, and careen wildly toward the shotgun with every last shred of strength I have. I drop the chair at the last second and with free hands grab the barrel of the gun, fumble it up, and level it straight at him.

He skids to a halt. We both stand stock-still, breathing in time. I cannot believe that worked. I slide my shaking fingers into the trigger guard and try to catch my breath, shallow and high, as I keep the gun leveled at his chest.

"Back up," I order him, my voice croaky. I'm hardly a force to be reckoned with, a barely conscious burnt woman with a chair attached to her leg. But then, I have a loaded double-barreled shotgun, so it doesn't really matter what's attached to my leg, does it?

He backs up.

I shuffle painfully, out of the study and away from him, tugging the metal chair behind me. I keep the gun trained squarely on his torso, the biggest target area, as I go. I edge back along the wall of the hallway toward the front door slowly, my eyes locked with his. His expression is unreadable, just like it was in that hospital corridor yesterday. He takes me in like a house cat watching a robin. Then his gaze flutters, he breaks the look, his eyes flicking down, at something right behind me.

It's a trick, I know it. He's trying to distract me. I'm not falling for that.

I feel it too late, the step down behind me, the little lip down onto the terra-cotta tiles of the entranceway. I forgot.

I lose my balance just long enough for him to rush me.

He hurtles forward but the distance is far enough that I dodge out of his path just at the last moment, breaking my fall on the banister of the staircase. He wrenches the gun free from my hands easily as he passes, but as I lose my footing he catches the edge of my metal chair, tripping and crashing into the front door, his injured shoulder pounding into it hard.

I grab my metal chair and lurch desperately up the staircase, taking two steps at a time. My joints scream at the effort as I reach the landing and slip quickly into the first available doorway, my breath coming in short snatches.

It's my old bedroom. I push my back to the wall and try to catch my breath as I listen. The house beneath me is silent. *What is he doing?*

I look down at the chair, bending to pull at its zip tie, but the now-warped plastic seems even stronger. The lighter is downstairs. I check my pockets, nothing. Desperately I pull off my shoe and try to wriggle my foot out of the tie, but it won't clear my bony ankle. I hear him below, slowly climbing the stairs; his careful speed tells me the gun is raised and ready, in case I bolt out onto the landing. He knows I'm trapped up here.

I look to the window, the only way out. But I can't jump, can I? I think of my vertigo. And then I see the blue edge of a tarp flapping outside. *Oh my God. The scaffolding! Yes!*

I remember seeing it before—the house is being renovated. If I can just get out onto the scaffolding, there might be a way down. I might be okay. I just might.

I move quickly to the window and wiggle the handle as quietly as I can. My heart sinks. It's locked. And then I remember an old trick Dad used to use whenever he lost the window key. I flip both handles of the window up instinctively and pound the middle section where the windows meet. The lock remains engaged but the stress on the gap between the windows forces them to burst open, the lock scraping loudly on itself.

Cold air bursts into the room, cooling my burnt skin. I look out at the scaffolding, my vertigo kicking in instantly. But I have no choice or time. I take a breath and clamber up onto the scaffolding, my free leg first, and then I drag the metal chair up behind me by its zip tie. I grab it and pull it and myself past the window, out of sight. I hear the bedroom door creak open behind me. I stand carefully, now trembling, against the brick of the house, out of sight, the open window next to me. I'm only on the second floor but I feel dizzy just looking at the drop out beyond the wooden planks. I try to control the sound of my breathing. I have to be still, I have to wait. I have to wait for him to get close enough. In the distance, out through the treetops, a flash of light catches my eye, a car coming this way, the police maybe, or Chris? I think of the pager, God knows where it is now. But I know someone is looking for me. For a split second I truly believe it is Chris, coming to save me. Just in time. But as I look more carefully I see the glint of light isn't moving, it's just sunlight reflecting off another building in the distance.

There's a floorboard creak right next to me, just inside the window. My focus snaps back as I see the barrel of the gun slowly emerge through the open window, followed by a hand, and only then a head. He swivels in my direction. And with all my strength I slam the window frame straight back into his face. The glass shatters as it smashes into him. The gun tumbles from his grip out onto the scaffolding as he recoils back into the room.

As the gun skids perilously close to the edge, I scramble for it, my chair clattering along with me. I feel a fresh wave of vertigo wash through me and reflexively jerk back as the gun skitters, then drops off the edge of the scaffolding. I close my eyes and press back hard into the wall. There's a silence before the gun hits the concrete below and fires off loudly into the air. I cower farther back into the wall, hugging the scaffold tight for support.

My eyes flick back to Matthew through the half-broken blood-smeared window. He's doubled over, hand to his face, his nose and lip bleeding; he looks up at me, furious, injured. I know I only have a second's worth of a head start.

I grab the metal chair and scramble away from the window as I hear him start to heave himself out of the window behind me. Ahead I see a ladder at the end of the scaffold, an escape. I plow toward it, white-hot pain exploding through my broken hand as I tightly grip the stupid fucking chair to avoid tripping.

And suddenly it occurs to me, I don't know how

the hell I'm going to get down a ladder carrying the chair. Behind me I hear Matthew's powerful strides and any moment I know I'll feel his arms around me, dragging me down.

I won't make it down that ladder. I'm out of time, scared of heights, *and* I'm attached to a chair. The thought shoots through me: If I can't outrun him, I need to *stop* him. I need to do something or I'm going to die.

I see something propped against the brickwork just ahead of me—it's not ideal but it will do. A stubby two-foot length of scaffold pipe. I feel his presence looming behind me and I dive for it, releasing my chair and reaching out, low, to grab the end of the pole awkwardly. As soon as it's in my grip I spin, throwing all my body weight back toward Matthew. He tries to pull up as I turn unexpectedly. He sees the pipe in my hands and his eyes flare as he careens toward me, but there's not enough time to dodge before the metal pole cracks straight into his knees.

The sound of hollow metal hitting flesh and bone as the pipe smashes his knee joints. He roars in pain, arms flail out for the flat brick wall next to him but there's nothing to get a hold of. And just like that he's toppling toward the open drop. His wild eyes find mine, his arms grasping desperately in the air for a hold. There is nothing to save his fall, nothing except me.

I step back too late. His fingers brush my coat lapel and then seize it, clawlike as he tips toward the void and tugs me with him. I lose my footing and crash down hard on my knees, sliding fast toward the edge as he rolls partway off it, dragging me along with him. I clutch wildly at the rough splintered scaffold planks around me, desperate for purchase, pain shooting from my snagging fingernails. I slide toward the edge, his fist tight around the cloth of my coat hauling me closer. He slips over the edge and I start to fall too, nothing between my upper body and the concrete below. Suddenly I jolt to a stop, pain ripping excruciatingly through my leg. I cry out in agony—the zip tie around my ankle is cutting sharply into the flesh of my leg. We hang there together for a moment, anchored, both of us, by the chair attached to my leg, snagged somewhere along the scaffold platform above. Both of us suspended by the warped plastic zip tie digging deep into the broken skin of my ankle. I catch my breath, gasping in pain, and I look down into his eyes. He clutches my coat, Schrödinger's man. His life still hanging in the balance. My hands fly to his, and I don't think, I push. We're caught for a moment between two states and then I feel his grip loosen, his eyes blaze, and just like that, gravity makes its decision. He slips from me, eyes blank with fear. I squeeze mine shut and hear the wet smack of flesh and bone hitting concrete below.

I hang there taking great gasping breaths. Above me, caught on the scaffold platform, I see the metal chair, my lovely, lovely chair, wedged hard between two scaffold struts, safely suspending me. My vision blurs as hot tears of relief slide from my cheeks down to the snow beneath.

# 47

## DR. EMMA LEWIS

### DAY 13—DO NO HARM

I brace myself against a pole and peer down for the first time, safely back on the scaffolding. Matthew is lying facedown on the snow-covered concrete beneath, one of his arms twisted awkwardly beneath him, the other palm-up on the snow beside him. He didn't have time to break his fall.

Blood pools around him but it's impossible to tell from here if he's still breathing.

A healthy person can survive a fall from up to four stories high if they land the right way. But if they land the wrong way a person can die from just slipping on an icy sidewalk. Reassuring statistics if you're scared of heights.

From up here, it doesn't look like Matthew, or Stephen, or whoever he is, landed in the right way, but the human body is an incredible instrument of survival—he could still be alive down there.

I find a raw edge of scaffold metal and rub the now-stretched plastic tie against it until it finally gives. I push my chair away and struggle to my feet, my muscles quivering. I take the ladder down, rung by rung, salty sweat stinging my eyes. My ankle throbbing like a heartbeat. My wrists weeping, livid with second- and third-degree burns. My broken hand discolored. I must be in shock, because nothing hurts quite as much as it should yet.

When I reach the snowy ground at the bottom of the ladder, I take a large loop around his sprawled body, making a dash for the dropped shotgun. Matthew's body doesn't move. I can't tell if he's breathing yet, I'll need to get closer. I snatch up the shotgun, the back of my bruised skull throbbing as I bend. The gun's cartridges are spent after hitting the ground and I don't have more, but somehow I feel safer having the gun in my hands. If the worse comes to the worst, at least I have another long metal implement as a weapon.

I creep forward. I need to be able to see his eyes. In case they open, in case he attacks again. I prepare myself, imagining the moment when he will leap up and rush me.

As I get closer I freeze. I see the movement of breath on the still pool around him, slow and faint but still there. Blood puddling around his upper chest and face but he's alive.

I look back up to the scaffold behind us. I'd guess it was a fifteen-foot unprotected fall onto concrete. His body position shows he didn't have time to protect his head before he hit. I can't be certain, of course, but I'd imagine his ribs will be completely shattered, his collarbone broken; there will be internal bleeding, organ damage.

I can't see the extent of his head wound as it's hidden against the concrete. Confident I'm safe for the moment, I crouch next to him. His eyes remain closed as I lean in and with extreme caution take a pulse from his free wrist. I watch his eyelids for movement but the papery skin does not stir. The pulse I feel is weak but it's there. It's unlikely he'll be leaping up to do anything at this point, though. I let out a breath. Safe for now.

I set his hand back on the snow gently and look to his pelvis. I'd be amazed if it wasn't fractured. If he stands any hope of surviving this, I'll need to stabilize it. And I need to move him into a recovery position so he doesn't choke on his own blood. I need to get him to ICU as soon as possible. I need an ambulance. I need the police. But I have no phone and I'm trapped in the middle of nowhere. The nearest house is a good twenty-minute walk on legs that are already trembling, and that's if anybody's even home.

But Matthew must have driven us here. I can drive. I check his trouser pockets for keys. Nothing. I stare down at his broken body. What can I do? I choke back a sob. What am I supposed to do?

I take one last look at his body and make a decision. Shotgun in hand, I go around the house to the front door.

In the study I find Matthew's canvas bag, open, as expected, its contents neatly packed: a bunch of zip ties, a box of cartridges, my pager, Stephen's mobile phone, a change of clothes, a serrated knife, and then, in a small Ziploc bag, I find my iPhone. What was he planning to do with it? I wonder. Send some messages and plant it next to my corpse? I root into the bag's side pocket and find Rhoda's car keys. He must have parked by the other entrance, where I parked the rental car before, hidden from the road.

Clumsily I tear open the plastic bag with numb fingers and fish out my phone. I push on the power button and wait. I need to call an ambulance. I can't risk moving him myself, he might not make it. I won't have his death on my conscience. The dark screen brightens and the apple logo appears. I'll call 999, get someone here as soon as possible.

And then I pause. I think of the press swarming, I think of the photos, the headlines, the inquest, my family, and another tenet of the physician's pledge occurs to me:

> **I will attend to my own health, well-being, and abilities in order to provide care of the highest standard.**

*My own health and well-being.* I look down at my burnt and bleeding hands, my breath coming in snagging rasps. I turn my phone off as soon as the home screen appears. I need to sort out my own health and well-being first. I need to look after myself.

I look around the room. I walk over to the handwritten note and pick it up from the floor. I deliberately do not read the dark black swirls of "my" writing before folding it up and slipping it safely into my coat pocket.

I bend and scoop up two fresh red cartridges from the parquet with my one good hand. I crack open the shotgun like Dad used to show me, tip out the spent cartridges, and slide two new ones in. I click the gun back together, grab the canvas bag, and head back outside.

I slump down in front of him, on the cold stone step leading up onto the lawn, and watch him. The winter sun warm on my back, his breathing body sprawled before me, my gun trained on him. And I wait.

He could almost be sleeping, except for the warm wet pool of blood around him. His features, so hard and filled with rage before, have dissolved back into Matthew's pleasingly handsome face. His breath is irregular; he doesn't have long left—he'll die of his massive injuries.

I know I'm in shock, colored specks flutter across my vision. I find my mind wandering and I wonder what his life could have been like if things had been different. Without his condition. I try to imagine the wife he could have had, the kids, the Christmases, the birthdays celebrated with rooms full of friends.

A muscle quakes under his eye, a synapse firing, electrical impulses going awry—God knows what is happening inside his brain right now. I hope his dreams are sweet, I hope he can't remember the awful things he has done.

And just as I think it, his eyes flick open. I gasp.

He blinks, his eyes gradually finding me.

# 48

## THE MAN

A figure slowly comes into focus in front of me, a woman perched on a snowy step.

There is pain, sharp but distant inside me; my cheek is pressed hard against the cold ground. I let my eyes look down to the darkness beneath me, deep red and wet. Blood, perhaps mine. The thought scares me, so I pass over it. I try to move away from the redness but my muscles won't respond. I can't move myself.

*What's happening?*

I search for the figure on the step again, and she sharpens into focus. A young woman, pretty but disheveled, her hair in disarray, a smear of red down her cheek.

Maybe this is a dream, I think, because I can't remember where I am, or how I got here.

She's watching me intently, her eyes wide and wet but alert, and I notice something grasped tightly in her hands, her knuckles whitening around it.

This doesn't feel like a dream. My eyes go back to her face.

*What's going on? What's happened between us?*

She looks terrified, terrified of something, maybe me.

*What have I done?*

I squeeze my eyes shut tight and try to remember.

*Why is she scared of me? Why is she holding a gun?*

I know her, somehow. I take in her features, her faded freckles, her ruddy cheeks, her soft lips. I know her. Yes, she's a good person. I trust her. But who am I? A feeling of dread wells inside me.

*Have I done something?*

I try to ask the figure on the step, the young woman, but the words don't come. I try a second time and they come in a rasped whisper, a voice I don't recognize. "What happened? What's wrong?"

The figure is standing now, trembling. "Stop it!" she shouts, color flooding her face. "Stop it! I know what you're doing, Matthew! Just stop."

Matthew. My name is Matthew. I try desperately to remember her name. If I can just remember her name, then it will all be okay, I know it will, because I know her. We know each other. We're close, I feel it: she trusts me and I trust her. I have such strong feeling toward her, toward—

"—Marn?" her name comes back to me through the void, short and clear.

Her expression wavers. She scrutinizes my face, scowling, appraising me, looking for something. Then she takes a sharp breath and shakes her head in disbelief.

"Marn. I'm sorry if I did . . . I don't know what I did. I'm so, so sorry," I tell her in a voice I don't recognize. "Marn, what's going on? I'm scared."

"Oh my God," she mutters. "Oh my God," she says again. She gently sits back down on the step and lets her head fall softly into her hands, tears running in streaks down her skin as I watch. "What the hell am I meant to—" She's sobbing.

I don't know what to do. I don't know how to help her.

"Marn, I don't know what I did," I say, to comfort her. "You have to tell me . . . what I did."

She looks up slowly.

"Marn, I'm scared," I tell her. "I don't know what's happening. I'm sorry if I did something. I'm so sorry."

She smears the tears from her eyes with the back of her shaky hand.

She seems to make a choice, her energy changing. She wipes her hands on her trousers and smiles at me with forgiveness; I'm flooded with relief.

"Yes, I know you're sorry, Matthew. It's okay now. Everything is okay. It's all going to be fine."

She sets down her gun on the step and slowly makes her way toward me. "Are you in pain, Matthew? Where do you feel it?" she asks softly.

"I can't feel much, Marn. Is that okay?" I peer up into her face and she nods gently.

"Uh-huh. Yes, that's okay. Don't worry about that. Here, let me come around you."

Sitting on the floor behind me, she pulls me up so that my shoulders and head rest against her chest. She slips her arms around me tight and holds me in a hug, safe and warm.

"Don't worry about anything, Matthew. I'm right here," she promises, and slowly, slowly I let myself relax.

# 49

## DR. EMMA LEWIS

### FOUR MONTHS LATER

*I will attend to my own health, well-being, and abilities in order to provide care of the highest standard.*

As new mantras go, it's not a bad one.

I watch her drum her tastefully manicured fingers on her Givenchy midi skirt as warm sunlight streams in through the window behind her, her long dark hair shining in the light, pulled back today in a low sleek ponytail. She taps the stiletto heel of her thousand-pound boots against the thick cream carpet of the consultation room and sighs.

"I don't know," she says finally, her beautiful features puckering into a well-groomed frown. "I don't *know* how that makes me feel, Emma. Should I?"

I shift in my seat, crossing my legs the other way now, rearranging my notepad.

"That's okay, Bahareh." I let the rich sound of her Iranian name roll off my tongue. "Honestly, sometimes it's okay not to know. That's why we're here today, after all." I pause. "Why don't you just tell me what happened at your mother-in-law's this weekend. How did all of that go?" I urge her on.

She stares out of the window for a moment, her wedding rings sparkling in the refracting light as she takes a deep breath, and then she continues to tell me her problems.

People are endlessly fascinating. Bahareh's been coming to see me for six weeks now. Her husband is cheating on her. But that's not the problem as far as she sees it; the problem for her is that she doesn't care about his infidelities—that's what bothers her more than anything else. She'd said that in the stillness of our first session together. "Surely I should care, shouldn't I?"

My private practice opened two months ago on Harley Street. It's small but perfect, a beautifully furnished consultation room in buttery creams and taupe with state-of-the-art tech and an imposing marble lobby. I have twelve regular weekly clients already and my hourly fees are high, so I can pick and choose. And I only work nine to five now.

Of course, none of this would have been possible without the money I received from Peter and the government after Matthew's death. The compensation money I got. Gratitude money. Hush money. Call it what you want.

It was four months ago that Matthew died cradled in my arms.

I look down at my hands resting on the notepad as Bahareh tells me about her nephew's birthday. My right hand and wrist have permanent nerve damage. I've tried to hide the burn marks, the slashes of silvering scar tissue that loop my wrists, with bracelets and the sleeves of my cashmere sweater. I needed minor operations on both hands to remove the fused plastic from my burnt flesh. The joints in my right hand, though reset, ache at night, and when I grip anything too hard these days the pain sears right through me. It always will. A fitting reminder never to hold on to anything too hard in the future, I suppose—people, places, the past.

Bahareh lifts her low ponytail off one shoulder, smooths it onto the other, and pauses. No, she doesn't want to talk about the conversation she had with her mother-in-law before the cake came out.

"It's okay. This is a safe space," I reassure her. "She's not here. This is your time to talk about whatever *you* want. About how *you* feel."

She nods, and her beautiful eyes continue to play across the London rooftops beyond my windows.

I fell asleep holding Matthew that day. Exhaustion, shock, adrenal fatigue. When I woke up, his body lay cold and heavy in my arms. I don't know how long we'd been like that, his thickened blood pooling out around us, framing us against the snow in a circle of blazing red. The light was fading when Peter finally arrived, but the police who arrived with him weren't any I recognized.

Chris was nowhere to be seen. Later I'd find out that he'd been searching for me for hours, along by-roads and lanes; he'd even headed back to Cuckoo Lodge, checked the house. My phone was full of missed calls from him. And missed calls from Peter too.

Peter had been trying to track me down since that morning when I'd first left the hospital in the car with Rhoda. He called and called, my phone still on silent, and when he realized he couldn't get hold of me he'd instructed the hospital to page me immediately. But that page came too late.

Richard Groves had alerted Peter to Matthew's identity that morning. Richard had called Peter highly concerned; he'd finally had a free moment to look at the medical report that I'd emailed him two days before, my report on Matthew. At first, Richard assumed the CT scans I sent him were some kind of joke—that I'd sent him old scans of one of his own previous patients, the Unknown Young Male case. He recognized the placement of the pituitary tumor immediately and checked his old records: the scans were an exact match two decades apart. And that is when he'd realized that I hadn't sent the scans as a joke at all, that I must not be aware, that I had no idea who my patient really was. And, given the unstable nature of the patient Richard knew twenty years previously, he'd called Peter immediately to warn him that I might be at risk.

The police I didn't recognize carefully helped me out from under Matthew's body. With gloved hands they'd bagged my clothes and given me new warm ones, erecting an incident tent around Matthew's lifeless body. A medic in a dark uniform carefully dressed my wounds.

Peter took me back into the house for a "delicate" conversation, warm tea held in my confused and shaky hands. Options were given to me and I made my choice.

Damage limitation was agreed upon.

We decided on a story. Or rather Peter gave me his.

Matthew took his own life. He stole a car belonging to one of the nurses at Princess Margaret's, Rhoda Madiza, he drove that car to the childhood home of his doctor, whom he'd become obsessed with and overly dependent on, and he'd taken his own life. Just a confused man, a desperate man with mental health problems. They could even arrange a typed suicide note. The irony smarts. I ended up doing to him exactly what he planned for me. He jumped from the roof of the house and didn't even try to break his fall.

And my part in all of that story? After realizing Matthew was missing from the hospital, I'd headed to the wrong place to find him. The beach. The place I assumed he'd return to. By the time I'd worked out my mistake and made it to the house, a place I'd mentioned to him only the day before, Matthew was already dead. What could anyone have done? We didn't realize until too late how unhappy he was, but sometimes it's impossible to tell. Tragically, the story goes, Matthew died before we could find out who he was.

I lied. On the record, in my statements to the police, to everyone. Peter led me back outside and I said what Peter told me to say to the officers, in the driveway of my old family home, shivering in the sharp January evening. Damage limitation, Peter called it. I think of the press, of the mistakes I made, and the errors made by Peter, Groves, Rhoda, Nick Dunning, and Dr. Samuels, the military psychiatrist. Matthew slipped through all of our fingers. It's understandable that some people wouldn't want the truth to come out. Who would the truth benefit, anyway? I lied—for Peter, yes, but mainly for myself.

Mr. Nobody's case was investigated, though. Two days after the incident, once I was safely back in London, Peter arrived with plainclothes officers at my flat. They asked questions and Peter told me to tell them everything I had told him. I would not be implicated and any information relating to open cases would be unconnected with the official Matthew story. They wanted to know about Mr. Nobody. So I told them everything Mr. Nobody had told me, about the murders he had committed, about his past, the missing soldier, how I got to the top of Richard Groves's list in the first place. That afternoon the real Stephen Merriman's body was found in his tiny bedsit off Russell Square. He had been dead for over two months, his remains shoved into a suitcase in a closet. The murder was reported in the news but not in connection to Matthew.

Matthew killed the real Stephen before taking his identity and moving to Norfolk. The officers said he may have found Lillian first before choosing to take Stephen's identity. Matthew needed someone that no one would miss but that had a strong connection to Norfolk. Everyone knew Lillian had a son, but he was in London and they'd never really met him. With Lillian in the late stages of dementia, it was easy for Matthew to take Stephen's place in her affections. Matthew had chosen the perfect identity for what he needed. He moved into Lillian's empty house as her son, and while she was away in her care home he started to gather information on me, on all of us; he planned each step out meticulously. Knowing he wouldn't recall hardly anything from before his self-inflicted reset, he laid a careful trail for himself before he set it all in motion. He left addresses for Lillian's house and my old house on a phone that he buried on an evening visit to the hospital just before Lillian passed on the elderly care ward. Later the officers investigating his case would tell me Matthew's phone showed he had been to Cuckoo Lodge, the night Chris was there, the night the news broke about my real identity. Thankfully, I was protected; it was the one night I wasn't there alone. It was only luck that Zara broke her story that evening and I suddenly had police protection; she made me safe without even realizing it. Matthew remembered just enough and needed to get me on my own. He must have collected whatever he needed from Lillian's and headed out to find me. But he couldn't get to me that night, so he had to head back to the hospital. If I didn't know what I know about Matthew, I might wonder at how he got in and out so easily, but if you spend your whole life disappearing you're bound to get good at it. He knew what he needed to do. He lined up the dominoes, stepped back, and tapped them. And all to find me, to get me to fix him somehow.

No one believed Nigel Wilton's suggestion that Matthew was Stephen. A story flared briefly in the *Brancaster Times* and had a sideline in some of the more salacious tabloids but quickly disappeared. It was easy for people to disregard Nigel's version of events as the well-meaning but befuddled ramblings of a sweet old man. And when Stephen's decomposing body was discovered in his London bedsit, Nigel's story was roundly dropped.

Stories have surfaced since about other murders. I am still in contact with Peter and receive the odd fact-checking phone call from the officers I spoke to with him. They found the remains of missing Royal Anglian Regiment soldier Phillip Andrews about three weeks after our chat. He was found in woodland at Thetford Forest Park, twenty miles from the military base he signed out of on leave over a year previously. Another one of Matthew's identities. When I saw his face on the news I couldn't help see the similarities. Of course, that's why he chose him. No wife, no kids, one-bed flat, kept himself to himself. Neither the base nor Andrews's extended family had seen him since he signed out. The situation was bound to raise a few eyebrows at the MOD, an officer returning from Afghanistan and disappearing off the face of the earth, a court-martial-able offense and certainly worth investigating. Whether the MOD thought Andrews had deserted or defected the day they arrived at the hospital I do not know, but when they didn't find Andrews in that consultation room but instead just a man who looked vaguely like him, their work there was done.

And I found out what Matthew did to get me to the top of that list. To ensure that Groves picked me. The investigation has yet to find the missing doctor, Tom Lister; he disappeared after returning home from a backpacking holiday in Sri Lanka last October. Although, looking at Tom's photograph online, I seriously wonder if he made it onto that plane back to Heathrow. Looking at him with Matthew's eyes, he would have been a good match. The last CCTV footage of him leaving Heathrow Airport is grainy, and perhaps it's my imagination, but the tall, dark-haired man caught on film has the same familiar set of shoulders, the same familiar gait, and I can't help wondering if Tom ever actually came back from his trip.

But I kept quiet. It was surprisingly easy to lie, although I hated lying to Joe, to Mum. I've put them through enough over the years, the least I can do is protect them from more fallout.

Thankfully, Mum has been all right since the news about our family broke. Her friends were so supportive when they found out who Mum's husband used to be, they rallied around her, protective and unimpeachable. I can't believe how wrong I got them. They were there for her, her rocks, and they couldn't understand why she'd kept something so big a secret from them.

I understand why she did, though. It's hard to learn to trust again after the person you trusted the most lets you down the most. But if there's one thing she's taught me, it's that it's never too late to learn new things, to put yourself out there, to try again.

After Matthew's death Joe rushed up to Norfolk

to meet me. He stayed over, helped me move back to London the next day, helped me while I healed. Thankfully, I didn't need to go back to the hospital. Chris collected my belongings from Princess Margaret's and brought them to Cuckoo Lodge. I don't know what I would have done without Joe and Chris in the days afterward. They shielded me from the press and worked with Peter to get me home as quickly and painlessly as possible. Joe collected me after my operations, dutifully took care of my food shopping and cooked up healthy meals while I recovered.

Chris visited me in the hospital and afterward, during my recuperation, his towering presence filling my tiny one-bed flat. He's been visiting ever since.

He and Zara filed for divorce last month. Zara was heartbroken when they split, of course, but as one door closes another is jimmied open. Chris tells me she's fine now, she's resilient, she's moving to Manchester to take a job at the *Manchester Evening News*. I wish her the best, no hard feelings my end, we're all just trying to get what we need. I hope she gets hers. I know I should feel bad about coming between them, but if I'm brutally honest, I don't. I've known Chris since we were children. He feels like coming home. It doesn't feel wrong. It's like everything that was good from my past has somehow been kept alive in him. He makes me feel like none of the bad stuff back then happened, or rather that it did happen but it's okay that it did, because I'm still me. Either way, he feels like home to me and I haven't had one of those for a really long time.

Sometimes I fantasize about what would have happened if I had never left Norfolk, if none of it had ever happened and Chris and I had got together straight after university. I like to imagine what our children would be like now, what our house would look like. I've never felt that way about anyone before. It's strange, it's nice. We don't want to rush into anything but Chris has mentioned transferring to London for work. But the more I think about it, the more I think I could move out of the city myself and commute—we'll see.

I didn't say goodbye to Rhoda in person when I left Norfolk, but I sent her a letter thanking her for all her help with Matthew, and for her bravery that day. She wrote back and told me she'd given a reading at Matthew's funeral, a poem she'd read him in the hospital that he'd enjoyed. He would have liked that, I think. The part of him that wasn't broken would have definitely liked that.

I looked back over the Unknown Young Male case a lot in the weeks and months after his death. What a hard and terrifying life to have to live. Every time he forgot, he was accused of faking his symptoms; by his early twenties he was homeless, nameless—without a social security number or a bank account he had no choice, he was forced to live outside society. He moved from hostel to hostel, unable to get a job and heave himself out of his nightmare. The doctors who treated him, Groves included, didn't test him thoroughly, they took no fMRIs, so they never saw the incontrovertible proof that he wasn't faking. That his hippocampus simply wasn't responding the way it should. No one helped him. He had no name and they wouldn't let him have a new one. I can't even imagine how it must have felt for him to be told there was nothing wrong with him when he couldn't even remember his own name. But he didn't crumble, he adapted, he adapted to survive. He morphed into something else, something that, in the end, even he couldn't stand to remember.

He could have had that operation. It might have worked, and after rehabilitation, he would have stood trial. I could have testified to his diminished responsibility on all counts. There is a legal precedent that those who cannot remember committing their crimes cannot be charged with those crimes. But he didn't want that. He knew he would be tried for the crimes he'd committed and, with a condition as rare as his, my expert testimony might not have been enough to get him treatment instead of a life sentence. He may very well have been sentenced for crimes that, in a sense, he hadn't actually done himself. Like being sentenced for a crime you committed in a dream. Either way, he would have been institutionalized for life. I wish I could have helped him.

I hope he died happy. I hope I helped that lost soul trapped inside him just a little bit at the end; I hope he had some small piece of happiness between all that horror.

It's funny, I remember watching Ben Taylor's parents leave the hospital that day, their receding figures walking away down the corridor, hand in hand. I hoped then that they'd find it in themselves to stop looking, to stop searching for the thing they'd lost, and to finally carve out their own little piece of life in the time they had left.

I'm not sorry for what I did. For lying. I'm happy to take the money and walk away. Because there's a limit to how far we should go for others.

I watch Bahareh as she talks, her voice soft and meandering, her plight so clear, so poignant. If she could only see herself through my eyes. But that's my job, isn't it, to shine a light back on her.

I still find it strange how easy it is to see solutions for others but not for yourself. Those years I slogged out sixteen-hour days, no weekends, no holidays, no life—it's hard to recognize compulsion when you're in the thick of it. The compulsion to fill the hole you left, Dad. It's only now I really see it. I've been replaying the same story. I've been replaying you, with every patient, replaying the imagined moment I could have fixed you. Over and over again. Classic PTSD. But I couldn't have fixed you then. And I can't fix you now.

I didn't see you that night at the bottom of the stairs, Dad, you didn't put your coat on and leave; you were just a figment of my addled brain. You're gone.

At the back of my mind, I suppose, I always knew you died, but I was so enamored with the idea you might come back one day and explain it all. Explain it all away. Tell me you didn't do what you did. Or I'd explain it for you, through someone else, through my job; finally I'd work out why you did what you did. Why people do the things they do. Somehow I'd uncover your reasons. But I've been scrambling around for too long now trying to gather together the broken pieces of you, the shattered fragments you left all over our lives. I've been so focused on putting those pieces—and you—back together again that somewhere along the way I came apart at the seams.

But now it's time for me to put myself back together.

Bahareh's warm eyes find mine. "I just don't know why I'm doing any of it anymore. You know?" she coos. "I used to try so hard to please him, to make him love me . . . but now—" She breaks off, lost in thought.

"Now?" I prompt.

"Now I realize. We can't change people, can we?"

"No. No, we can't," I answer. "People have to change themselves."

# Acknowledgments

Thanks go to my fantastic editors at Penguin Random House in the U.S. for all their hard work, faith, and creative support on *Mr. Nobody:* the brilliantly inspiring and supportive Kate Miciak, and the truly wonderful Kara Cesare. And in the UK, at Simon & Schuster, huge thanks to the genius that is Jo Dickinson. It has been such a pleasure to get to work with this world-class team of women.

I'd like to thank my wonderful, clever, and creative agent Camilla Bolton at Darley Anderson. Thank you for answering that first email and everything that followed. You're an absolute diamond!

And thank you to the rest of the fantastic teams at Penguin Random House: Kara Welsh, Sharon Propson, Quinne Rogers, Allison Schuster, Kim Hovey, and Jesse Shuman—and at Simon & Schuster: Jess Barrett, Hayley McMullan, and Anne Perry.

This book would never have come about without a news story that lodged in my head back in 2005. The story of the Kent Piano Man was the jumping-off point for this novel and when I took the idea to my publisher and subsequently looked into the history and research around the fugue cases I was hooked. Dissociative fugue is a truly fascinating/horrifying condition that has the ability to instantly catch the imagination. I encourage anyone who is interested in learning more to search out one of the many fascinating documentaries on fugue sufferers. The moral and philosophical questions this neurological condition raises on the nature of self are endlessly engaging.

Thank you to Dr. Anthony Jack, associate professor of philosophy, psychology, neurology, and neuroscience at Case Western Reserve University, for your medical/neuroscientific eye and technical advice—thanks for making sure Emma knew her stuff.

To Sam Carrack, thanks for letting me pick your brains on the Piano Man case and the media manipulation around it. It was great to meet someone else who was as captivated as I was by the story of an unknown man found fifteen years ago.

Finally, thanks to my wonderful husband, Ross Armstrong, for his week of loneliness in the Caribbean whilst I sat in a hotel room and put the finishing touches to my first draft #deadline #firstworldproblems—Ross, you're a constant source of happiness and inspiration—thanks for being such a lovely and understanding human being.

If you enjoyed *Mr. Nobody,* read on
for a preview of Catherine Steadman's novel

# THE DISAPPEARING ACT

**Have you ever asked yourself what kind of story the story of your life is?**

I always thought mine would be a coming-of-age story. A small-town girl making it in the big city, like Melanie Griffith in *Working Girl* or Dolly Parton in *9 to 5*. Sure, I'd struggle for everything I achieved, but in the end my plucky can-do attitude would ensure I'd triumph over whatever obstacles stood in my way.

Like *Legally Blonde* or *Pretty Woman* or *Pride and Prejudice*, the story of my life would be an uplifting comedy, in turns fun and moving and aspirational. I'd be strong and spirited and a riot to be around. I'd be beautiful and smart and kids would love me.

That's what I thought. But now—looking down at the gun in my hands, feeling the heft of it, its cold reality in my palm—I'm not so sure I got the genre right.

In fact I'm not even sure I'm the main character anymore.

# 1

# THE GOOD WITH THE BAD

## FRIDAY, FEBRUARY 5

Sometimes, no matter how hard you try, you just can't disappear. There's nothing you can do to melt back into the crowd around you no matter how hard you wish you could.

The tube carriage rattles and jolts around us as we clatter along the tracks deep beneath the streets of London. And I feel it again, the familiar tug of the stranger's eyes on me, staring.

I've been in their house. Or at least they think I have, but I don't know them. We're friends already, or we're enemies, but I don't know which. I'm part of some story they love or hate. I'm part of the story of who they are. They've rooted for me, cried with me, we've shared so much, and now I am right here in front of them. Of course they're going to stare. I'm the unreal made real.

On the fringes of my awareness I feel the figure finally break the connection and whisper to the person beside them. I try to focus on my novel, to let my breath deepen and the story wash over me once more.

All those gazes, like robins alighting on me and

fluttering away, wary but interested. I know people always stare at one another on the tube. But these days it's different.

The carriage rattles on shuddering around us.

Since the show started airing, four weeks ago, I'm lucky to get through any journey without some kind of interaction from strangers. A shy smile. A tap on the shoulder. A selfie. A handshake. A late-night drunken gush. Or a hastily scrawled note. And sometimes even, quite confusingly, a scowl.

I don't mean to sound ungrateful; I love my job. I genuinely can't believe how lucky I am. But sometimes it feels like I'm at the wedding of a couple I don't really know. My face aching from meeting so many well-meaning and complicated strangers, while the whole time all I want to do is bob to the bathroom so I can get away and finally relax.

I don't feel threatened by attention, exactly, I know I'm safe.

Although, of course, it's not always safe. I learned that the hard way, a month ago, when the police showed up in my living room after countless calls and emails, finally taking notice when my agent stepped in.

He'd been waiting outside the theater, every night. Not particularly strange or concerning. Just an ordinary man.

I'd leave the stage door tired from work. I'd gone straight from filming on *Eyre* into *A Doll's House* in the West End. At first he just wanted a signed program, and then a chat, and then longer chats that got harder to leave until finally he was following me to the tube station still talking. I had to start leaving with friends. I had to be chaperoned. One day he couldn't stop crying, this stranger in his fifties. He just walked behind me and my friend, silent tears dripping down his slack face. His name was Shaun. I'd tried to sort it out with the police myself but it wasn't until my agent received a package that they took it seriously. He was just a stalker. Not even a stalker really, just a lonely man trying to make friends. I told the police that, of course, but they insisted on following it up, issuing an official warning. I think his wife had died recently.

They wouldn't tell me what was in the package he sent. I jokingly asked if it was a head, and they all laughed, so I guess it can't have been a head. I felt guilty about what happened; the friendlier I had been, the worse it had gotten and the more I strengthened his perceived connection to me. I hope he's doing better now. I wish they'd just told me what was in the package straightaway, though; instead I spent a week imagining the absolute worst. Weird photos. Skin. Teeth. Something his wife had owned. It was just a stuffed toy in the end and a slightly unsettling poem. But it's hard not to think the worst when you're trying not to think the worst.

I know not everyone is strange. But some people are.

At the next stop as I gather my things and disembark, a few eyes follow but when I surface at Green Park and the cold February air hits me, cooling my flaming cheeks, I chalk today's trip up as a success. No incidents this time, no drunken football chants demanding I "Say it! Say it!"

Who knew *Jane Eyre* had a catchphrase?

Who knew Arsenal supporters read Brontë?

And yes, in case you're wondering—much to my shame—reader, I said it.

—

"You're late," my agent, Cynthia, smirks as I plonk down into the restaurant seat opposite her.

"Sorry. Tube," I counter.

She's already ordered us two glasses of champagne. I eye the chilled bubbles in front of me greedily. "Are we celebrating, again?" I half joke as I shrug off my coat, but her silence makes me raise my gaze.

"You could say that. Yes," she says, grinning before pointedly sipping from her champagne flute. "I got a call this morning," she purrs, placing her glass down calmly. "From Louise Northfield at BAFTA. A heads-up if you will . . . Louise and I went to St. Andrews together; we tend to keep each other posted—she loves you by the way. So the word on the street is . . . though they're not announcing the nominees until a month before the ceremony, which is in May, but . . ." She pauses for effect. "You're on the BAFTA list. Nominees. For *Eyre*. Best actress."

For a moment her words don't make sense to me. Then they slowly shuffle into meaning. I feel the blood drain from my face, then my hands, and in its place a rush of serotonin floods in, the like of which I have never felt before, crashing through me.

"Holy shit." I hear the sounds come from me, distant, as I fumble with a shaky hand for my champagne and gulp down a cool, crisp mouthful. The light-headedness only intensifies. Seven years I've worked for this. This is it. This is what I wanted. "Jesus Christ," I mutter.

"That's what I said." Cynthia chuckles, grinning from ear to ear. "Now here's the really good bit. All the other nominees are over fifty, and they've all won before."

I sober quickly, brought up short. "Wait. *Is* that good?"

"Yeah, it is," she says with a laugh. "People love

*discovering* actors, even if they've been knocking around for years. Plus, you've got great credits, pedigree, even though this is your first major leading role. You're academy catnip. A safe bet that seems like a wild card. And everyone will be rooting for you, nobody needs to see one of the 'Ladies in Lavender' win another bloody award."

I let out a nervous laugh and take another swig of my drink. Seven years of auditioning has taught me never to get my hopes up but right now I can't help it; my happiness bubbles up, irrepressible.

Cynthia catches the waiter's eye.

"Could we get a selection of everything? Just, whatever the chef thinks," she says airily, as if that's a thing that people actually say in restaurants. "Nothing too big, just a light lunch." She looks to me questioningly. "Is that okay, hon?" The waiter's gaze follows suit. Both deferring to BAFTA-nominated me.

"Okay, sure, yes, that sounds great," I reply, and the waiter heads off with total confidence in what I'd personally consider to be a very confusing order.

Cynthia leans forward on the table businesslike.

"This is all going to be new for you, and to a certain extent it's new ground for me too. I mean, Charlie Redman won best actor in, what, 2015? But it's different with men, they just show up in a suit. Best actress is trickier. I'll be fielding calls about you as soon as the press release lands in April. So here's my thinking. We've got two months to kill in the meantime. I don't want you tied up filming, I need you free for bigger meetings with this on the horizon. We're going to ride the crest of this. So how do you feel about a little work trip to LA so we can drum up some studio interest? Nom's still unofficial but we can certainly drop some hints."

She clocks my expression and changes tack.

"Sorry, I'm firing a lot at you, aren't I? It's a lot to take in. Here." She raises her champagne flute and clinks mine. "One thing at a time. Congratulations, Mia, you clever, clever thing."

Cynthia has been my agent, advocate, and therapist since I graduated. We've weathered some soaring highs and soul-destroying lows together over the years. In some ways we're unbelievably close and in others we're almost strangers. It's an odd relationship, but then it's an odd industry.

Her energy suddenly changes. "Oh, and I heard about George by the way," she says, her eyes searching mine, alive with curiosity. "That's so exciting for him! He must be over the moon."

I feel the smile slip from my face. I literally have no idea what she's talking about. George? My George?

To my knowledge not much is happening for him. In fact, if anything it's slightly insensitive of Cynthia to bring it up. George hasn't had an acting job for eight months at least and he's an absolute wreck, if I'm honest.

I met George on my first big job—a movie adaptation of *Tess of the d'Urbervilles*—six years ago and we've lived together pretty much from the get-go. We both had tiny parts in *Tess* but our scenes were with the Hollywood star they shipped in to play her and we couldn't believe our luck, and we couldn't believe we found each other. We bought our flat last spring but after that things sort of dried up for George, right around the time they picked up for me. But that never seemed to bother us. Because George isn't competitive like that.

"What do you mean?" I ask.

She looks confused for a second, then frowns. "*Catcher in the Rye.*"

My heart skips a beat—*my God*—I remember the day we taped two scenes in the spare room. That was well over a month ago. George's Holden tape. But nothing came of that. I remember the weird art house direction we took pains to create for the Dutch director we were both desperate to work with, the way the script had changed the ages of the central characters, modernized the story, and transposed it into a university parable set in twenty-first-century New York.

I struggle to get up to speed.

George sent the tape. He got the part. And he didn't tell me.

My mind flashes back through the last month. I think of George sitting quietly in the kitchen reading, leaving the house early to meet friends, rejoining the gym, smiling again after months of depression and . . . *shit*. He didn't tell me he got it. He knew all along and he kept it to himself.

He must have had so many meetings, and chemistry reads, and screen tests since then. He sent the tape before Christmas. Why the hell wouldn't he tell me? How the hell didn't I notice?

I realize I haven't responded to Cynthia yet. "Yes! Sorry. Yes, I know, right! He's a . . . he's a bloody genius."

"I couldn't believe it when I heard. My client Zula's in it too. She's only got a small part but she started rehearsals last week, said she met him yesterday at the cast read-through. Said he looked great. God, he must be so relieved. It was all looking a bit desolate there for a bit, wasn't it?"

"Yeah, no, I know. So great!" The words are coming out of my mouth but all I can think is: *Why? Why didn't he tell me he got the part?*

And then a thought solidifies, and the answer is suddenly very clear, the solution as ludicrously obvious now as it was impossible to imagine seconds ago. "I forget, Cynth, who else is in it again?" I ask as casually as I can. "George told me but I completely . . ."

"Yes, the love interest is—God!—I'm so terrible with names. Naomi Fairn, yes. Chris Fairn's daughter. She's twenty-one, I think, first job since modeling. Seems good, but even if she's not, she'll look amazing in it. Tell George not to worry at all, she'll hold up on camera."

And there we go. I take a slug of champagne and try not to look like my entire life is crumbling.

"Filming starts in, what, a week?" she asks, oblivious to what is happening to me. "I bet they're putting him up somewhere gorgeous in New York, aren't they?" And with that I gently push back from the table, make my excuses, and head to the ladies' room. Somehow managing to keep a smile on my face while I do it.

Locked in a marble-lined bathroom stall, I google: *Catcher in the Rye casting news*. Nothing announced yet. *Yet*. My stomach rolls.

I think of George quietly watching the TV next to me last night, the same as ever. Texting. Now I wonder who.

I google her face.

*Holy shit*.

Things start to fall into place.

I tap on the least glamorous shot Google Images offers me in an attempt to work out what Naomi Fairn actually looks like. It's a makeup-free shot from an impossibly cool magazine. I study the beautiful wrinkle-free planes of her face, and I want to die.

None of those things ever seemed to matter until now.

I read on. Even her parents are cool. Both gorgeous, both actors. Her dad basically was the 1990s. I think of my dad, Trevor, bicycling around the Bedfordshire countryside in an anorak.

With trembling hands, I tap out a message to George, hit send, and unlock the cubicle door. Standing in front of the vast washroom mirror I look at myself, checking my eyes to see if it's possible to tell that my heart is cracking open just by looking.

You can't.

I guess I am a good actress after all. I straighten up my hair, reapply some lipstick, and take in my twenty-eight-year-old reflection. And the face of Jane Eyre stares back at me.

I know what she's thinking, because it's what I'm thinking.

*We're so fucked.*

# 2

# STRANGER AT THE DOOR

## FRIDAY, FEBRUARY 5

I'm home alone, hours later, staring at my text to George.

**Why didn't you tell me about the job? x**

I could have said a million things but I didn't, I said that. And he hasn't replied. So when I hear a knock on the front door—even though he obviously has his own key—I'm convinced it will be him: rain-soaked, sad, and contrite, prepared to explain everything away.

It might sound naive, given the circumstantial evidence, to expect this whole thing to be a purely innocent misunderstanding, crossed wires, but hope has gotten me this far in life. Every *no* I've ever received, in my mind, was almost a yes. And all I've ever really needed was an *almost a yes.*

I turn the latch letting a gust of wind and rain into the warmth of the house. But of course it's not George standing on our doorstep, it's a smiling stranger in a red bomber jacket.

"Hey. Mia, is it?" He's about my age with an easy-going manner and a warm Irish lilt.

"Yeah?"

He looks down at a damp and crumpled piece of paper in his hand. "So, I'm supposed to be collecting George's things."

*"George's things?"*

We both stand there in silence for a moment as I try to make sense of the Irishman's words. When it clicks, fear chases my confusion and then just as suddenly I feel the calming certainty that I must be misunderstanding what's going on here. And yet my grip on the doorframe tightens.

"I'm really sorry, but who are you?" I ask. My voice has a faraway distant sound. Perhaps it has decided it doesn't want to live with me anymore either.

"Sorry, right. I'm Andy." He extends a hand warmly. "I work for, um, Fantastic Movers." He cringes at the company name as I numbly shake his hand.

"Right, okay," I manage, then clear my throat. "I see. And is George coming to—?"

Andy's handsome face creases into an apologetic frown. "I wouldn't have thought so, no."

Two hours later the living room is pockmarked with missing chairs, books, and pictures. Shapes left in the dust that I hadn't even realized was there. The front door is gently pulled to by Andy and once I hear his engine start, I finally release the hot angry tears that have been silently choking me from inside since he entered the house.

George has gone. He's left me and this is how he's done it. After six years of love, or what I thought was love.

No reply to the text I sent him as Andy packed away his things. No answer to: *What the hell is going on?* But then I suppose—actions speak louder than words—it's pretty obvious what's going on.

A thought occurs to me and my thumb hovers over the Instagram search icon on my phone. I know this way madness lies. If I start down this road things will get very painful, very quickly, and yet in a way I want the pain. Pain will fill the room with something at least now that Andy has gone, taking all of George's things with him.

I tap out her name . . .

Her verified account springs up. Her curated, muted-tone online existence exactly as I would have imagined it. Naomi Fairn and her achingly cool life. There's a post from two days ago, a Polaroid photo of a script with her pale hand obscuring the title card, a plain gold band on her middle finger, clear nail polish, and the sleeve of a gray hoodie.

**@Naomifairn:** New job. Can't say yet but this one's special. 🌾

The crop emoji. I always thought that one just represented a generic crop but now on closer inspection I see it is actually supposed to symbolize rye. A fun clue for her intrepid followers. I'm suddenly reminded that she's only twenty-one.

I scroll through her earlier posts looking for him, looking for anything that can explain my now empty house. Something catches my eye. Posted last week.

**@Naomifairn:** Shadows.

January 29th. Hampstead Heath.

A photo of two people's shadows elongated in the winter sun along a path in Hampstead Heath; the tips of her white Converses are in shot and, partially obscured, to their right, the edge of the other person's shoe. My stomach flips; I know that shoe. I pinch and zoom, hunched over and squinting at the phone screen like an octogenarian in my lonely kitchen.

A scuffed navy Adidas. His shoe. I was there the day he bought them. I've gathered them up, abandoned about the house, and put them away for him a thousand times. My heart yawns wide deep inside my chest followed sharply by the acid burn of anger.

*He left me for her. How could he think it was okay to do this to me, like this? After everything we've said and been to each other. Six years. No word. No explanation. Just gone.* The anger inside me twists around itself, a beast ready to scream.

I exit Naomi's account and put my phone up on the kitchen counter. Best to leave it there for now.

I concentrate on my breathing. I try to fight the fresh prickle of tears stinging my eyes. I need to stay calm.

I can't blame Naomi for this. God knows if George even told her about me; she might not even know I exist. I tell myself I can't blame her because I remember being twenty-one, I remember being in love. I need to remember it's him not her. He left; he wasn't taken.

She is twenty-one and George is thirty in November. In the interests of self-preservation, I leave that thought there because that's someone else's problem now.

I let my eyes play across the kitchen, across our things. The ones left behind. Shouldn't we have more to show by now: more than a flat, and a kettle, and a toaster, and a smoothie maker? I know it's not a decision for right now but I wonder if I should sell the flat. I guess it is mine. I put the deposit down and my name is on the mortgage. We're not married after all. I've been covering the full mortgage payment for the last five months anyway. I've been covering most things for quite a while now. In a way, I guess, he hasn't really been here for quite some time. I wonder how on earth I will tell anyone what's happened without dying inside. Without being forced into the role of victim. I am not a victim.

My anger stretches taut again. How could I have been so stupid to love him? To trust him?

I sit up straight, take a breath, and try to refocus. I need to work out what I'm actually going to do.

There was a reframing trick I used to use when I hit a dead end working on *Eyre*. When things threatened to overwhelm me. When I suddenly felt the weight and responsibility of carrying Charlotte Brontë's story. Whenever a scene wasn't working or I was too cold or tired or scared I'd ask myself—what would Jane do? Not what would I do. But what would Jane do if she were here, now.

So I ask myself: *What would Jane do?*

And without a second thought, I know. I've lived with her now for so long.

In the book Jane asks herself: *Who in the world cares for you?* The answer is: *I care for myself.*

I need to care for myself.

She would cut her losses. She would protect herself. Jane would move on. Cauterize the wound to protect from infection. That's what I need to do: control the fallout, change the story he's written me into.

If I were Jane, I'd send a letter, an email. I'd secure another position, far from here. I'd move on and I'd adapt.

I think of my one lifeline, my bright bolt of good news in the darkness. The next few months are going to hurt, but I'm going to be okay. I will not play the role he's cast me in. I will write my own story.

On the counter my phone sits silently. No word from him. Not even an apology. Nothing. I am not even worth a sorry.

Jane would not crack, or cry, or drunk-text. Jane would focus her mind.

I breathe deep and think only of two letters . . .

LA.

And with that thought I pick up my phone and dial Cynthia's number.